Praise for Danuta Kot and *Life Ruins*

'*Life Ruins* has all the elements I love in a novel
– complex characters, an insidious underlying
menace, and haunting landscapes. **This dark
story will suck you in from the first page**'
Stephen Booth, author of *Fall Down Dead*

'A powerful, thought-provoking story,
which perfectly evokes the bleak Yorkshire
landscape . . . **a vital read for any crime fan**'
Kate Rhodes, author of *Ruin Beach*

'Explores real issues, from the perspective
of real, damaged people, and told with a
real warmth and understanding. **Danuta
Kot raises the bar for all crime writers**'
Michael Jecks, author of *Pilgrim's War*

'Powerful and thought provoking . . . I
was hooked from start to finish'
The Bookwormery

'An atmospheric story that will draw
you effortlessly into the pages'
Hooked from Page One

'Engrossing and chilling, [*Life Ruins*] is the perfect
read for a winter's evening where the mind can
roam upon the lives and troubles of others'
Shots Magazine

Also by Danuta Kot

Life Ruins

DANUTA KOT

SOMEONE WHO ISN'T ME

SIMON &
SCHUSTER

London · New York · Sydney · Toronto · New Delhi

First published in Great Britain by Simon & Schuster UK Ltd, 2021

Copyright © Danuta Kot 2021

1 3 5 7 9 10 8 6 4 2

Simon & Schuster UK Ltd
1st Floor
222 Gray's Inn Road
London WC1X 8HB

Simon & Schuster Australia,
Sydney

Simon & Schuster India,
New Delhi

www.simonandschuster.co.uk
www.simonandschuster.com.au
www.simonandschuster.co.in

A CIP catalogue record for this book is available from the British Library

ISBN: 978 1 4711 7597 8
eBook ISBN: 978 1 4711 7596 1

Typeset in the UK by Hewer Text UK Ltd
Printed and bound in Great Britain by CPI
Group (UK) Ltd, Croydon, CR0 4YY

MIX
Paper from
responsible sources
FSC
www.fsc.org   FSC® C020471

To my husband, Ken,
who died on November 25th 2019.

Then,
As sudden silence fell, a kestrel,
An armstretch away, flung against the sun
And flaunted a moment vivid rustglow and
flickering wing
Before a graceful bank, a swoop, a swishing dive
Took it beyond.

From *A Dying*, by Ken Reah

SOMEONE WHO ISN'T ME

Chapter 1

Sunk Island

Andy Yeatson was twenty-four, and he was becoming more and more certain that he was going to die.

Tonight.

He shifted on the back seat of the car as though he was trying to get comfortable and touched the door to feel where the lock was. 'How long is this going to take?' he asked. The girl who was driving didn't respond.

The woman in the front passenger seat half turned her head. 'Don't worry. It isn't far now.' He caught her gaze in the mirror. There was something in her face that sent a chill through him. This woman was dangerous.

How the fuck had he got into this mess? And how was he going to get out of it? He'd been stupid, letting himself get distracted. He hadn't been thinking about his own safety – he'd been worried about Becca. She hadn't been replying to his texts. Maybe she was just

1

pissed off with him, but if he was right, if his boss DS Mark Curwen was right, things were starting to kick-off at the pub where she worked, and some nasty people went in there.

It was a vile night – heavy rain whipped up by one of the storms that battered the town at this time of year. He should have stayed at his desk where he was supposed to be, but the worry kept nagging at him until he'd shoved his chair away, muttered vaguely about checking something out, headed for his car and driven off. He'd decided not to park near the pub – he was supposed to keep out of Becca's way for the next few days and he didn't want anyone spotting him there, but at this time of night, he could just park a couple of streets away, nip in, say hi and make sure she was OK.

He'd been walking along the road thinking about Becca, keeping to the wall for what shelter it gave, when the woman called to him.

'Hey! Andy!' He'd looked round and seen the car on the other side of the road. He knew the woman who was leaning out of the front passenger window, or knew her a bit – the girlfriend of one of his pub contacts. Harmless.

Or so he'd thought.

'You going to the pub? Want a lift?'

He was cold, he was worried, he wasn't thinking. So just like that, he'd got in. The woman was in the front passenger seat, a girl he hadn't seen before was behind the wheel. He'd heard the *clunk* of the central locking, and realised, too late, he was trapped. 'What's happening?' he'd said.

The woman had turned and smiled. 'What you wanted. We're going to meet Stoner.'

Shit, shit and shit again. He'd been in the pub night after night, posing as a buyer, someone after a big deal. He'd been waiting for the meet, and as soon as it was set up, he was supposed to alert his colleagues and get the backup he'd need.

Instead, he was stuck in the car, heading south. No one knew where he was, and there was no one to give him support. He'd made a mistake, and now his mistake could kill him.

Or could it? As far as they were concerned, he was just a small-time dealer who was trying to move into the big time. Maybe they were just going to make him an offer, and all of this was just to be sure there was no one following him.

Or . . . what if they knew he was a cop?

The woman chatted in a desultory manner as they drove down the road that followed the coast south. The girl said nothing, just followed the woman's directions. Andy caught her eye in the mirror once and smiled at her. She went a bit pink and looked away. She was a pretty girl with a mop of fair hair – seemed too nice to be hanging out with this lot.

He had a choice. Go through with the meeting, play dumb. Tell them that he couldn't do a deal like this with no warning. They couldn't just

3

kidnap him off the streets and expect him to come through.

But they knew that, and they'd done it anyway.

He glanced out of the back window, and realised someone was following them. He'd been aware of a motorbike in the road behind them for a while, but instead of passing them and driving on, it stayed about forty metres behind, shadowing them all the way. The rider wasn't concealing himself, just keeping steadily on the same route as they headed further south. The woman must have been aware of it, but she didn't comment.

The girl who was driving asked, 'Why do we need to go all this way?'

'Do I pay you to ask questions?' the woman snapped.

Andy listened with half an ear, looking out for landmarks as they drove down the coast, the bike a constant, on their tail.

The fair-haired girl didn't look like a threat, so it was him against the woman and the unknown biker. Time to change the odds.

They were close to Hornsea. He reached surreptitiously into his pocket for his phone. It would blow the operation out of the water, but he had to send for help.

But the woman was watching him. 'I'll have that,' she said. 'You'll get it back.'

If he pressed the emergency button now, she'd see, and it could take as much as half an hour for his colleagues to locate the phone and get here. They'd still have time to disable the phone, get rid of him, and drive off. Reluctantly, he drew it out of his pocket and handed it over.

The woman looked at it. 'Yours?'

He'd recently changed his screen image to one of Mia at her first birthday party, holding a balloon and grinning. Now he wished he hadn't. 'Yeah.' He wasn't discussing Mia with her, with any of them.

'You're doing this for your kid? Cute.' Her mockery made him angry, but it gave him hope – she was talking as though the deal was on, as though he hadn't been blown. Maybe, just maybe, he was going to get away with this.

She fiddled with the phone for a bit, checking his contacts, his messages – but there was nothing there that could worry her. To his surprise, she handed it back to him. She'd taken the battery out but given it back with the handset, and the tension released a bit more.

Focus, he told himself. *If it's the meeting with Stoner, then just go along with it. Play a bit angry about the way they picked you up. If it's something else, then you get away. You can do this.*

The road stretched ahead between flat, empty fields. He hadn't seen a building for miles. If they kept going this way, they'd end up in the Humber Estuary.

His stomach gave a lurch. He didn't like the thought of the estuary.

The lights caught a road sign as they passed a junction – one narrow lane meeting another narrow lane; Stone Creek Road – and then it was gone.

And now the car was slowing. Andy felt the bump and sway of rough ground. The car lights illuminated a low, red-brick wall. Beyond, still some distance away, he saw the gleam of water.

His fears were confirmed. The estuary. They had arrived.

The car drew to a halt, the bike pulling up behind it. The woman got out. 'Doc,' she said. There was no surprise in her voice. She'd obviously known all along who their shadow was. 'I wasn't expecting you to join us.'

The biker, Doc, grinned at her as he stretched. 'Thought you might need me.'

Andy was caught off guard. This was Doc? Doc was one of the dealers he'd been trying to contact for weeks – and now it turned out he'd known the guy all along. Doc looked relaxed and affable and just for a second, Andy thought it was going to be OK ... But then he caught a glimpse of the woman's face. One look at her hungry, avid expression told him he all he needed to know.

His cover was blown and they'd decided to get rid of him.

He heard the clunk of the central locking system being switched off and reached for the car door to get out. Now he had to bring all his training into play. He pulled himself slowly out of the car, mapping in his head the location of the people around him.

Doc, standing behind him; the woman, moving a bit too eagerly round to his side of the car so he'd be boxed in; the girl still sitting in the driver's seat. And somewhere around, this other guy, this Stoner, might be waiting. He was outnumbered – surprise and speed were the only things that would save him.

Make a plan. Now.

In front of him, dimly lit by the moon, was an inlet. Andy could see small boats pulled up in the mud and make out the name painted on the bows of one: *Joie de Vivre*. It was the perfect place to bring drugs in. Small boats, going in and out of the estuary, never going far afield – who'd even take a second look these days when the coastguard had been cut to nothing?

He'd had no idea this place even existed. This was information he needed to pass on – if he could.

Surprise and speed. Behind him was the bridge they had just crossed. That was the way back to the road, and it was the way they'd expect him to go. Opposite him on the other side of the car, there seemed to be nothing but a deep tangle of undergrowth.

But there was a fingerpost.

That meant there was a path. There had to be.

His few options raced through his mind. Over the bridge and into the water? The tide was coming in. He'd drown in the currents and the lethal mud. That way was closed. The fingerpost? It would be a massive gamble. Any path might be too overgrown to follow. Back along the road? They'd be expecting that and they'd try to stop him, but it looked like his best bet. He'd have to move fast and keep going.

He took a second quick look round. He'd have one chance, and he'd have to get it right.

But there was a man standing on the bridge. Andy's way was blocked. Then the man turned, and as Andy saw his face, relief flooded through him. He knew this guy. He was OK, he was a mate – and then the chill came back. This wasn't a mate at all.

This must be Stoner.

He'd known them all these past few weeks, and he hadn't realised. He'd thought he'd been mixing with the small-timers, the help, and now, because he'd got it so wrong, he was going to die.

Unless he had a plan.

The fingerpost. It was the only way.

Now!

He could feel the adrenaline flooding through him. Time slowed down. Even though there was only the moon to light the scene, everything around him seemed bright and clear as daylight.

He could hear the sound of Doc moving closer behind him, and he braced himself.

Andy's foot shot out as he spun, delivering his kick straight into Doc's knee. Doc dropped to the ground, his mouth gaping. Andy cracked the second kick into his groin and then he was vaulting over the car, sliding over the roof and onto the ground. He dodged the man on the bridge – who moved forward just too late to stop him – and ran, feeling the long grass catching at his feet. He'd been right. His gamble had paid off. There was a path along the top of an embankment where the fingerpost stood.

It was barely a chance, but if he could get far enough away, he could find a house, find somewhere to hide, call in for help.

As he reached the top of the embankment, he glanced back. Doc was struggling to his feet, still doubled over, his hands clutched over his balls. Andy could hear a stream of curses apparently aimed at the other man, who was trying to help Doc up.

The girl was half out of the car, frozen.

There was no sign of the woman.

Andy spun round and forced himself to move faster. He wasn't a sprinter, but if he could put the distance between them, he could keep going. He headed east along the embankment. Try and cut across to the road? No. He could tell from the gleams of water that the land was criss-crossed by drains. It was probably marshy as well. He couldn't risk getting cut off. He was better off higher up.

For the moment.

He couldn't work out which way to go. There were no lights, no buildings, just the dim shadows of flat expanses and the occasional glint of water running in straight lines across the land.

Now he knew where he was. He was in Sunk Island; the marshy area near the mouth of the estuary where only the drains kept the land from flooding. Almost no one lived here. There were just scattered farms and isolated buildings, and vast expanses of emptiness.

If they hadn't seen which way he went, then he might make it.

The path was leading down now, away from the exposed embankment.

His chest was starting to burn. He needed his second wind as he pushed himself forward, listening all the time for the sound of footsteps behind him, or a car engine shadowing him from the road.

Where were they? What the fuck were they doing? He slowed down. There was no sign of pursuit, but they must be after him. They must be somewhere. Where the fuck were they?

The estuary gleamed below him, a barrier he couldn't pass, but he could see something ahead of him. Trees.

Trees, here on the emptiest part of the coast? But trees could hide him. He could climb, get up high where he could see all around, stay safe and make his way back in the morning.

He fumbled in his pockets and pulled out his phone. It took seconds to get the battery in place, but then he had to wait as it powered up. What else did he have with him to help him through the night? Cigarettes, but he couldn't risk smoking. Some gum – that would help to fool the thirst and the hunger.

His phone chimed the start-up signal. *Right. Right.* His fingers were clumsy with urgency as he pressed the keys – call it in, officer down, they'd be here from Hull in twenty minutes, less.

But nothing happened. The signal was gone.

He looked around him. The path stretched away from him in either direction, empty and featureless. Beside him, he could hear the surge of water, the vast and powerful estuary. The trees were the only place to hide.

Then he heard the beat of a bike engine. Cars couldn't cross this ground, but a bike could.

This was it. They were coming. They must know the area well. They knew the path and they just had to get ahead of him.

He spun round and was running, away from the trees, away from the direction of the sound, anywhere.

What was that? A flicker of movement in the darkness close by! He veered away, and something hit him hard. It felt like someone had punched him in the side. He staggered, almost fell, then regained his momentum.

Run.

He was in the open, on a concrete hardstanding, a mesh fence between him and the surging waters of the estuary. A deep culvert at his feet cut the hardstanding in two.

Nowhere to go! He had to keep—

All the strength drained out of his legs. He sank to his knees. There was pain – he'd been aware and not aware of it – was he having a heart attack? He fumbled at his chest, then stared in bewilderment at his hand, stained with a dark, shiny substance . . .

Blood.

He tried to get back to his feet, but his legs wouldn't do what he wanted them to. He was gasping, as if the air he was sucking in wasn't air at all and . . . It was like he was watching from a long way away, and it was OK. He was dancing with Becca, watching the way her hair swung round her face as she moved. Oh, Jesus. Had he got her into trouble as well? He was singing to Mia as he bathed her. *Row, row, row . . . If you see a crocodile, don't forget to scream . . .* and Mia was laughing, laughing . . .

He couldn't find the breath to scream.

He fell forwards, face down on the cracked, dirty ground, and a dark stain spread out around him, running in trickles into the drain as the rain kept on falling.

Chapter 2

The land where the South Holderness plain meets the north Humber foreshore lies in deep isolation; a flat, waterlogged landscape formed over the centuries from the mud of the estuary.

Sunk Island.

Detective Sergeant Mark Curwen left his car by the side of the road and followed the straight line of a drain towards the water that glittered in the early morning light. After the heavy rain, the ground sucked at his feet as if the sea was trying once more to reclaim this land. Ahead, he could see the solitary figure of the constable standing guard over the scene.

He was here to do a job he didn't want to do.

'Where are they?' he asked after flashing his ID at the constable. He took the mandatory white cover-alls and overshoes from the man and pulled them on.

'It's over this way, sir. Near that fence, right by the river – or the sea, I don't know . . .'

'It's called an estuary, Constable.'

The constable was keen to direct Curwen towards the body that lay on a hardstanding by the shoreline. Curwen was in no rush. He knew what he was going to find. A member of his team, DC Andy Yeatson, had gone missing three nights before.

When there was no sign of the young detective constable, Curwen knew what must have happened, knew it was just a matter of time.

And it was. The call had come through an hour ago. The body of a man, found by – what else? – a dog walker. The serious crimes team was already here. He could see the SOCOs going over the flat damp ground, men in wetsuits in the deep ditch of the drain, looking for whatever evidence was left after the heavy rain of the past few days.

Curwen walked along the track to the small group gathered around a tent that had been erected to preserve the scene from the weather. He made himself focus on what he was seeing, on the problems the scene presented. Curwen's role was simple; he was here to identify a body.

The path ended on the cracked, uneven surface of a hardstanding. The drain he'd been following emptied into the estuary via a tidal gate: Spragger Drain sluice. A mesh fence protected the edge, with bright yellow signs warning of the dangers of slipping. Curwen looked down into the water.

One side of the fence was broken and sagging. Water flowed past below him, smooth and dark, the swirls and eddies telling of currents that would quickly overwhelm anyone unfortunate enough to fall in. The drain itself emptied into a deep, stone-walled culvert, crossed by thin beams of wood.

Two men and a woman were waiting for him. One of the men stepped forward, a tall man he vaguely recognised. 'DS Curwen? DCI Hammond. East Yorkshire Serious Crimes.' Ian Hammond. A good officer as far as Curwen knew.

He nodded. 'You want to show me?'

The other man held back the flap of the small tent that was protecting the body. Curwen took a brief look. It was still recognisably Andy, as he'd known it would be. The face had the blankness of death that was often confused with peace. In Curwen's experience, the horror of a death was rarely reflected there. Across the white throat, a dark red wound gaped. Curwen closed his eyes against a sudden, unexpected surge of emotion and turned away.

Hammond said, 'You know him?'

Curwen nodded. 'Yeah. Andy Yeatson. He's a DC with the drugs squad based at Brid.'

'And you've been working with him?'

'He was on my team. We've been chasing down the street dealers in Bridlington.' Curwen looked round, trying to make sense of what he was seeing. Why would you bring someone here to kill them? If you killed them somewhere else, why carry a body so close to the estuary and then dump it on dry land? The drain dropped away beside him, barely protected by some planks of wood. If they'd dumped Andy in the water, the powerful currents would have carried the body miles out. It would probably never have been found.

Hammond responded to Curwen's unspoken question. 'He was in there.' He indicated the deep culvert. 'He was caught in the gate – they must have been in a hurry.' Hammond paused, briefly. 'I'll need to ask you some questions, DS Curwen. What was DC Yeatson working on? What would he be doing here?'

A good question, and one Curwen couldn't answer – or wasn't prepared to, yet. This wasn't where Andy was supposed to be. He was supposed to set up a meeting and alert Curwen to provide backup, not go off on his own. What had happened that he ended up here, miles down the coast? They must have brought him here to kill him, but Curwen couldn't understand why. He pictured the dead face again; the blue lips, the red wound on the livid neck. 'They cut his throat?'

'That's not what killed him.' It was the woman who answered him. She was small with dark hair and a sharp face. He realised she must be the medic come to check the body in situ, pronounce life extinct, before it was taken away.

The body.

It.

'There's a knife wound here.' She touched the side of her chest. 'It will have penetrated the heart – more than enough to kill him. They probably cut his throat to be sure before they dumped the body. I'll be able to tell you more after I've had a closer look.' She turned

16

to Hammond. 'I'll get back. I'll be doing the PM first thing in the morning.' A murdered police officer was always priority.

Hammond nodded. 'I'll be there.' He waited until she was gone, then turned to Curwen. 'I need all the information you can give me, DS Curwen. This is a murder investigation.' He hadn't missed Curwen's lack of response to his original question.

'Of course. What about his phone?'

'We haven't found it. I'll ask you again; what was he doing here last night?'

'I don't know, sir. He was supposed to be in the station in Bridlington.'

'OK. What was . . .?' Hammond stopped as someone called from across the field, one of the SOCOs. The voice was urgent. 'Hang on.' He turned away and hurried across the field.

Curwen had no time to think about his next move; he acted on instinct. Under the guise of looking at something more closely, he slipped his fingers into the inside pocket of Andy's jacket, where he usually kept his phone. Nothing. He tried the other pockets, but the phone wasn't there. *Shit!* No time for anything else.

He hurried across to where Hammond was waiting for him. They walked together over the field to where the coveralled figure was crouched over something on the ground.

It was a dead animal, maybe a cat – the fur was a dull, dark brown. It had been dead for a while, and there was evidence of predation, but there was clear evidence of damage to the head. 'Something hit it,' Hammond said. 'A car? A bike?'

'A boot?' Curwen added.

'Get it preserved.' Hammond's gaze met Curwen's.

Curwen knew what he was thinking – after all the rain, much of the evidence that should have been here would be gone. But some might remain intact on this creature – assuming its death was anything to do with what had happened just a few metres away.

Hammond was distracted by the new find, so Curwen took the opportunity to get out of there, telling the senior officer that he'd be available for an interview back at base.

He had things he needed to do.

Chapter 3

Bridlington

The sky was deep blue, like a summer's day, but with a chill in the air to say that autumn was almost over and winter was fast approaching. The sun cast sharp shadows on the ground and glinted off the metal of the supermarket trolleys stacked in rows by the door. Becca Armitage leaned back against the wall and lit a cigarette, her first since getting out of bed that morning.

Six days a week she worked here, eight thirty until five thirty. Evenings, she worked behind the bar in a town-centre pub, which gave her just about enough to pay the rent, buy food, keep herself going, marking time until . . . what? She didn't really know.

But today, she didn't care. Today – or rather tonight – something good was happening. She turned her face up to the sunshine, and couldn't stop herself from smiling.

'What are you so happy about?' Jade, another of the supermarket assistants, had joined her for a smoke before their lunch break ended. 'Sheryl caught her tits in the till roll?' Becca gave a snort of laughter. Sheryl was one of the other assistants, an older woman who was always complaining about Jade and Becca's work to the manager, Bryan, and always told him if either of them was a couple of minutes late back from their break.

'No. I'm just, you know . . .' She gestured at the sky. 'It's a nice day.'

'It must be something,' Jade persisted. 'It can't be this place. New boyfriend?'

Becca kept her gaze on the parked cars, trying to look cool, but she could feel her face going pink.

Jade laughed. 'You'll learn.' But she said it kindly and Becca found herself laughing too.

A movement caught her eye. Jade looked up and stiffened. A kid was riding a mountain bike across the car park towards the small space where the delivery trucks unloaded and where the staff went if they wanted to smoke. He was speeding towards them, his head down. Becca just had time to take in the gleaming metal, the bright trim before she braced herself. It looked as if he was going to run right into them. But he glanced up at the last minute and saw them. Alarm crossed his face. He pulled the orange handlebars round in a sharp turn, then did a triumphant wheelie before speeding away.

'You get back here,' Jade yelled after him. 'Little shite,' she said as the kid vanished round the corner.

Becca looked at her in surprise. 'Who's that?'

'Our Lewis.' Jade had two kids, a boy of eleven whose dad had never been around and a girl of two. 'He's bunking-off again. I send him off to school every morning, but he never gets there. I've got the social services all over me but what do they expect me to do? Walk him through the gate? I've got to be in work. Little bugger.' But she sounded more defeated than angry.

It sounded like Lewis was trouble, but there was something about the way he'd sailed past them on his board that reminded Becca of crazy motorbike rides up the coast with Jared, her boyfriend from almost a year ago, and the sense of speed and freedom she had felt. Lewis had been playing, having fun, and she could get that. She knew where she'd rather be. 'Do you want to go after him?'

'And get the push? I can't afford to lose this job. I'll get sanctioned.'

Becca didn't know what to say. She didn't have kids – she didn't want them, either. Who would?

'We've got people selling drugs all over the estate,' Jade said, scowling as she nipped her cigarette out. 'Our Lewis is out there with them all the time. And the police? They don't give a shit. Maybe it'd be best if the social does take him. He won't listen to me.' Her phone chimed and she checked it. 'Text from the fucking school. Again. What do they expect me to do?' She sighed. 'We'd better go back.'

Becca put out her own cigarette and followed Jade back into the shop for an afternoon of shelf-stacking and working the tills.

Her shift finished, she stepped out of the hard, fluo-rescent lighting into the tail-end of a late-autumn afternoon. The light was starting to fade, but the sky was still clear, and the air felt mild, even though the breeze off the sea carried a cold bite. She used to think Bridlington was a dump, but she was starting to find things about it she actually liked.

Last winter, things had gone badly wrong. She hadn't meant for any of it to happen; she'd just been trying a help a mate. Not even a mate, really, just someone in trouble. But it meant she'd got on the wrong side of people she should have kept right away from, and she'd nearly ended up in jail, or worse. Some of the people she'd upset might still be around, though she didn't know who they were or where they were. She thought about Jade, angry and upset about her kid, Lewis. The people she'd crossed were just the kind of people who'd sell drugs to kids, no question.

Were they back?

She didn't want to think about it.

Her phone chimed, distracting her. A message on WhatsApp. She looked at it and smiled. Jared. Her first real boyfriend. He'd sent a photo – somewhere with blue skies and high, pointy mountains all around, and he was grinning at the camera. *Cool or what?* The message said. She smiled and texted back *Cool.* Jared had been part of what had happened last year. He was off somewhere doing what he did, leading a kind of random life. Becca could have gone with him when he left, but she had no money. Jared wouldn't have minded supporting her – but she did.

She took care of herself. She didn't take money from anyone, not even her foster-mother, Kay.

What happened last year was over, and what was happening to kids like Jade's Lewis was none of her business.

The summer was long gone and most of the visitors had left, but even now, as winter was approaching, she could see people on the beach; dog walkers, kids digging in the sand, families wandering along the seafront in bright colours. Music from the funfairs and the smells of chips and candy floss floated through the air – the smells of a seaside town.

Last winter, Brid had been a dark place where bad things happened, but maybe this winter, things would be better.

Then she remembered, and found she was smiling again.

Tonight, Andy was back.

Chapter 4

Scarborough

Kay McKinnon pulled on her warm trousers, a wool jersey and a fleece. Despite getting up at five thirty, she was running late. She hated the commute from Scarborough to Hull. At least today would be the last time. Since a fire had more or less destroyed her cottage near Whitby, she'd been camping out in this bland box of a flat. It had been a roof over her head, but she had never felt at home here. Most of her possessions were in storage, and what little she'd brought with her was packed. Tonight, she was moving.

She grabbed her backpack and took thirty seconds to glance at her reflection. She sighed.

Her husband, Matt, used to say she always managed to look stylish. Not these days. What was the point? The deep well of grief inside her stirred and started to rise up. She rode it, let it wash over her and subside. In the early days, in the weeks and months after Matt's death, the sheer magnitude of a pain she had no choice but to endure had the power to drive her to her knees. It was a beast she had learned to control, but not one that was ever diminished.

Matt. He was gone and this was her life now. She had no choice but to get on with it. 'It doesn't mean I've got to like it,' she muttered under her breath, wrapping a scarf round her neck.

Milo watched her resignedly from his bed. He didn't like these early morning starts, when she dropped him off with the dog-sitter on her way into work. She cast a quick eye over the flat, then clipped on Milo's lead. He made a great show of reluctance as he climbed out of his basket, sighing and stretching. 'Come on, Milo,' she said, and grabbed her keys. It was time to go.

As she drove, she mulled over her move. She'd been looking for somewhere closer to Hull, but countrified, somewhere she could go for long walks with Milo, somewhere with birds and the sea . . .

Somewhere Matt would have liked.

A car cut across in front of her and she braked sharply. *Pay attention, Kay!*

It took almost an hour to drive to the outskirts of Hull where she dropped Milo off. Ten minutes later, she pulled up outside the offices of Tania's House, the small charity she worked for that gave support to young drug users in Hull and the small towns up and down the East Yorkshire coast.

The road – as usual – was parked-up, so she stopped on the double yellows – she'd be out again in a few minutes – and went in to collect her files. She was on home visits all day today, which was the kind of work she liked best.

Her boss, Dev Johar, was already at his desk as she arrived. 'Morning Kay. I wanted to discuss those budget changes you asked about, at the meeting this afternoon. Dave and Cath are coming in at—'

'I have home visits all day today,' Kay said, trying to keep the annoyance out of her voice. This was the arrangement – she only worked three days a week, on a varying timetable that was agreed with Dev at the start of the month. She always scheduled her out-of-office appointments on Fridays, and he knew that. Or should know, as it was the system he'd suggested.

'I posted the details of the meeting on Monday, Kay,' he said. 'You should have had plenty of time to rearrange things.'

'I wasn't working on Monday, Dev.' She nodded towards the large sheet on the wall where they all logged their work hours. 'I can't switch appointments around at the last minute.' They drilled into their clients the importance of consistency, of discipline, of keeping up with commitments. The last thing recovering addicts needed was a support worker who didn't follow those rules rigorously herself.

Dev sighed. 'Xanthe always managed to attend meetings. Who are you seeing today?'

'Kyle Clarkson, Ian Taylor and Jassy Greene this morning, Poppy Brooke this afternoon. Jassy's a new client, so I'll need to spend more time with her, and I need to chase Kyle up – he missed his last appointment and he hasn't been keeping up with his probation officer.' Which probably meant Kyle – seventeen, troubled, given to solving the huge problems in his life by self-medication – was back on the drugs again.

'Poppy. You could cancel Poppy and come in for the meeting. She's doing well. She doesn't need this close supervision any more.'

'Actually, I need to talk to you about Poppy.' Nineteen-year-old Poppy *had* been doing well. Kay's predecessor, a young woman called Xanthe Adamos, had found her a part-time job, and Kay had picked up her case with high hopes of getting Poppy back into college to complete the course in beauty therapy she'd dropped out of when drugs took hold of her life.

But in some way that Kay found hard to pin down, Poppy was struggling. She was keeping up with the job, but not much else. Kay had heard just yesterday that Poppy had missed two appointments with her probation officer – something the man had only just got round to telling them.

Dev listened, then shook his head. 'But she's reasonably stable, she's holding down her job. I want you to start the process of moving her on – group support, I think. It's such a shame Xanthe had to leave before Poppy was fully back on track.'

Xanthe had apparently been very cool and down with the kids, and Dev Johar never missed an opportunity to tell Kay how much she was missed. Kay was well on her way to disliking her unknown predecessor, who, for all her skills, had effectively walked out of the job. She'd gone to America to continue her academic studies and left Tania's House in the lurch. It had taken over three months to replace her, and then only with a part-time post. Budget reasons, Johar had told her, which surprised Kay. Tania's House had a turnover of more than £300,000 a year, thanks to some generous donors. But that wasn't the issue now.

'I can't cancel my appointment with Poppy,' she said briskly. 'Let me have a copy of the minutes and I'll respond. I'll talk to you about group therapy for her after I've seen her today.'

Before Dev could extend the discussion – which wasn't going to get them anywhere – she collected her files and made her escape, making it back to the car just as a traffic warden hove into view. She pulled out into the traffic, ignoring a few angry horns as she did so – if you waited for a space, you'd never get out – and drove to her favourite greasy spoon, where she had an egg sandwich and a huge mug of tea to marshal her resources for the day ahead.

But by the time her third appointment was finished, her resources had just about run out. It was almost three. Each appointment had overrun – which was par for the course – and there had been no time for a break or for any lunch. On the other hand, she was feeling optimistic. The delinquent Kyle had admitted to using pills again, but seemed ready to have another go once Kay spelled out the options to him, and the new client, Jassy, seemed well-motivated.

She ate an energy bar as she drove to her last appointment with Poppy. Kay braced herself. Things might look good on paper, but something was wrong. Poppy was starting to slip back, and Kay had to catch her before she slipped too far.

Parking on Poppy's road was always difficult, so Kay parked on the main road and took her stuff out of the back, hoping her car would be too scruffy to interest any passing twoccers. She checked her backpack. All the folders were there – you didn't leave confidential stuff in the car – and what she thought of as her teenage revival kit; cans of coke, cigarettes, sweets – the kind of stuff that had got her through doors in the past, and was always useful for navigating sticky periods in support sessions.

Poppy lived in a shared house in a run-down part of the city. It was an area full of industrial sheds, takeaways, budget food shops, bookies.

A steady stream of traffic flowed past her. The air made her skin smart and there was a chemical taste in her mouth. She was the only pedestrian, walking briskly along the cracked pavement. And yet there were green spaces – a patch of wasteland where a building had been demolished colonised by brambles and dandelions, an old car park, virtually empty, where weeds were forcing their way through the concrete, a buddleia clinging on to a cracked gutter.

She was in the edge lands, spaces where the urban sprawl began to decay, and nature, battered and struggling, began its fight back.

And where people who had lost their way might find a place to survive.

She turned onto the road where Poppy lived. It was a dark street, aligned so it never seemed to get the sun. On one corner there was a vacant, weed-filled space, and on the other side of the road a grey industrial shed. As she walked along the pavement, she passed houses with all the obvious signs of multiple occupancy – uncared-for gardens, overflowing bins, tatty curtains pulled across windows even during the day.

Kay came to the last house. The window was covered with what looked like an old blanket. The gate to the gennel that led to the back of the houses was hanging off its hinges. Looking down the passage, she saw a bike, quite a powerful one, against the wall.

She knocked on the door and waited, her hand poised to knock again. After a few minutes, it opened a crack, and a Poppy's face peered cautiously round it. She was yawning and rubbing her eyes. 'Oh, it's you. What do you want?'

She was like a flower in the middle of a scrapyard, her fair hair hanging in tangled curls round her shoulders, her face pink and white as if she had just woken up.

'It's our appointment,' Kay said.

'Oh. Yeah. Look, I'm a bit . . . I think I've got the flu, you know, so . . .' Poppy made no attempt to open the door further; in fact, she looked ready to close it in Kay's face.

Alcohol flu, pill flu or worse? It didn't look good and Kay wasn't leaving until she found out more. 'I'm sorry to hear that. Let's have a cup of tea.' She smiled and moved towards the door, as if she had no idea Poppy didn't want to let her in. Poppy, after a moment's hesitation, stood back from the door and pulled it open. She was wearing a pair of loose shorts, an over-sized T-shirt with the slogan 'The Sorting Hat Said Broadmoor' on the front, and not much else. Her bare feet were grubby, but they had the pink plumpness of a child's.

There was a sour smell as Kay stepped through the door. The corridor was bare boards with a random carpeting of mail – junk, official-looking envelopes, free newspapers. Kay suppressed the urge to pick it up and sort it. They usually had their meetings upstairs, where Poppy had made herself an attractive bedsit amid the general squalor. Today, however, Poppy led her into the small kitchen at the back of the house and snapped the light on, illuminating a sink full of scummy liquid and a draining board piled high with unwashed cups and plates. Trays and wrapping from past takeaways were strewn across the table, and fall-ing out of the over-full bin. Kay noticed, but didn't comment on, screwed up foil on the table and a spoon scorched black underneath. Her heart sank.

There was a horrible smell, partly like something gone off and partly like an uncared-for public toilet.

Kay tried not to let her reactions show on her face, but Poppy must have seen something because she said, 'Ew. It smells like Greg's been peeing in the sink again.' The look she gave Kay was a challenge.

'I wondered what it was,' Kay said mildly, mentally deleting Greg, whoever he was, from her list of future house guests. What else had gone wrong? Poppy never paid much attention to the rest of the house, but she was always fastidious in her own space, keeping her room and the adjacent bathroom clean and attractive. Kay sat down at the table and Poppy, after a moment's hesitation, sat down too.

'Tea?' Kay asked. Poppy nodded and looked vaguely round. 'Don't worry, I've brought some with me,' Kay added, getting out her flask.

As she poured tea and offered Poppy a handful of the sugar sachets she'd collected from various cafés, there was the sound of footsteps on the stairs. Poppy tensed as the footsteps came along the corridor.

'There you are. I thought I said . . .' The woman who came into the kitchen stopped speaking abruptly as she saw Kay. She was tall and model-slim with long, fair hair. Her face was half-concealed by dark glasses and a scarf draped with precise carelessness around her neck. It was hard to estimate her age. At first glance, Kay put her in her twenties but as she studied the woman's face, she realised she was probably in her forties.

'Who are you?' Her voice had the huskiness of the habitual smoker.

'I'm Poppy's support worker,' Kay said. 'Kay McKinnon. And you're . . .?'

Poppy looked at the two of them, clearing her throat, her hands tearing a tissue into small pieces, and when the other woman didn't speak, she offered, 'This is Leesha.'

The woman spoke to Poppy, not Kay. 'This is what you've got instead of Xanthe?' She lit a cigarette and took a long pull. 'I think I preferred the original.'

It wasn't remotely funny, but Poppy glanced at Kay, then at the woman, and giggled dutifully. Leesha turned slightly to exclude Kay. 'Are they digging them up now or what?' Poppy gave that same nervous giggle. It was the way the playground bully cuts the victim off by enlisting the support of others. Kay could tell that whatever hold this Leesha woman had on Poppy, Poppy wasn't going to go against her. Whatever this woman wanted, Poppy would do it.

Retreat? Come back when the field was clear? It went against her nature, but sometimes it was the best—

Poppy slumped at the table, her face looking paler, shining with the faint sheen of sweat. 'Are you all right?' Kay said, anxious at this sudden change.

'I'm thirsty,' Poppy said. She pushed the cup of tea away. 'This tastes like shit.' The freshness had gone from her face. The debris on the table – the scorched spoon, the tinfoil wraps – coupled with Poppy's sudden collapse told Kay all she needed to know. Poppy had been on opioids when Tania's House had taken her on, her engagement with the charity being one of the conditions placed on her by the court when she was arrested and convicted of possession.

This, to Kay, looked like severe withdrawal. If Poppy was back on hard drugs, she would be back to full-scale addiction very quickly. She was also in breach of her probation, which could have serious consequences. Kay had to stand her ground and fight.

Before Leesha could speak, Kay reached into her backpack again. 'Have some of this.' She produced a bottle of water and a can of coke. Poppy held out her hand, waving the water away and reaching for the soft drink.

She popped it open and gulped it down, then belched. For a moment it looked as though she was going to throw up, but she managed to get herself back under control. Kay nodded at her and turned her obvious attention away from Poppy, while keeping the girl in her peripheral vision as she fished in her bag again and produced a packet of cigarettes. 'Here,' she said. Poppy looked at her. It was like a flash of understanding between them. Kay's gesture said *I know you need something*. And Poppy's said, *More than this*, but she took a cigarette and lit it, drawing on it hard. Her hand shook. She looked at Leesha. 'Did you . . .?'

'I'm going,' Leesha said abruptly. She looked directly at Poppy, who looked back at her, a kind of mute plea in her eyes. Leesha jerked her head and Poppy followed her out of the kitchen.

Kay stood up and moved quietly until she was in a position to see down the corridor. The two women were talking, their heads close together. Kay heard Poppy say, ' ... don't like him ...' and Leesha's response, ' ... doesn't matter. If you want ...' Her masked gaze moved towards the kitchen. Kay stayed where she was. Let this Leesha woman see that Poppy had support.

She went back to her seat at the table when she heard the front door close behind Leesha, then there was the sound of Poppy's feet running up the stairs. She listened as Poppy moved around on the floor above her, then there was silence. After waiting about fifteen minutes, Kay was ready to go upstairs and check, but then she heard movement and Poppy came back down and into the kitchen. There was more colour in her face, but her eyes were unnaturally bright. She'd clearly taken something, but not enough to knock her out. While she was upstairs, she'd changed into a tiny skirt and top, pulled her hair back from her face and fixed it with a clip. It looked pretty – casual but stylish. 'I like the way you've done your hair,' Kay said, stifling all the other things she wanted to say.

Poppy mulled this over, accepting another cigarette from Kay. 'Yeah. I got to go out.'

Kay ran her hand through the shapeless mess her own hair had become. Since a fire that had just about destroyed her cottage near Whitby, she hadn't been bothering with a hairdresser. She'd cut it herself, keeping it cropped brutally short. No wonder that Leesha woman had made fun of her. 'I don't know what to do with mine,' she admitted. 'What do you think?'

Poppy looked surprised, but pleased to be asked. She squinted at Kay over the smoke from her cigarette. 'It needs some product on it. And colour. You could, you know, get it shaped a bit. Feather it round your face. It'd hide the . . . make it look, you know, softer.'

'You think I should keep it short?' she asked, deferring to Poppy's expertise.

'Yeah. Suits you, or it would if it wasn't a mess.'

Fair enough. It *was* a mess. She smiled at Poppy. 'Thanks. Are you still doing hair? Would you do mine for me next time you come to Tania's?'

She thought she saw a flicker of interest on Poppy's face before it smoothed back into cool indifference. 'If you like.' Poppy shrugged. 'Only I'm, you know, too busy to come in. For a bit.'

Push it, or step back? Kay had just seen Poppy being intimidated. She couldn't ignore it. Poppy had to know Kay was on her side. 'Who's Leesha?' she asked.

'Just a mate.' Poppy looked down, rejecting Kay's invitation to talk.

'You need to come to Tania's House,' Kay said gently but firmly. 'You've been missing your appointments with Graham.' Graham was Poppy's probation officer.

'Yeah, well, he's useless.'

Kay rather agreed with that, but this wasn't going to help Poppy. 'But you need to see him. And if you need some more help, we can find that for you.'

'I'm fine,' Poppy said.

'Are you? Listen, Poppy, whatever you say to me, when we're having a support session, is confidential. Whatever you tell me, whatever it is, I can help.'

Poppy's eyes filled with tears suddenly, and she turned away so Kay wouldn't see. 'There's nothing to tell.' Her voice was muffled.

'I can't make you tell me anything,' Kay said carefully. 'And I wouldn't try. Sometimes, if you've got a problem, even talking around it can help. I know you're back on stuff. Is Leesha selling it to you?'

Poppy's laugh was jerked out of her. 'You think you know everything, don't you?'

'No,' Kay said slowly. 'I obviously don't. Come in and talk to me, or let me call you if you'd prefer that. You need help, Poppy. That's what I'm here for.'

Poppy didn't deny it. Her head drooped and she wouldn't meet Kay's gaze. 'It's too late for that. I want you to go,' she said.

It was important now to show Poppy she had control. 'Of course. But you'll come in to Tania's, won't you?'

Poppy looked at her. 'Just to do your hair?'

'Just to do my hair.'

'OK . . .'

Kay left, having obtained Poppy's agreement to come to Tania's House the following Monday. But in the meantime, Kay needed to check her schedule, try and clear a bit of time to give Poppy some additional support. This was more than just a return to drugs – people had relapses, and it wasn't good, but they could find their way back again. Poppy's *It's too late* made Kay think that there was more to this than drugs.

And there was the problem of this woman, Leesha. Was she Poppy's dealer? Dealers had a strong influence over their clients – the clients relied on the dealer for their fixes – but it was a commercial relationship, the dealers relying on the users for their market and their money. What Kay had just seen looked like more than a drugs deal. This Leesha woman was putting pressure on Poppy to do something, and whatever it was, Poppy didn't want to do it.

She had been sycophantic in her interactions with the other woman, and in that exchange by the door, she had sounded scared.

There were dealers who were even more malign than the ones who simply sold the stuff. There were the ones who used the power of supply to make the users, the addicts, do things they wouldn't otherwise do. What kind of pressure was Leesha putting on Poppy?

Kay wasn't going to give up. She needed to get Poppy away from this Leesha woman, and that would involve . . . She thought hard as she walked back to her car. How could she stop Leesha? Get the police onto her? Kay had no proof. Physically remove Poppy from her influence? Residential rehab? Tania's House offered some short-term residentials a bit further north, near Bridlington, but apparently places were like gold, and Kay couldn't see Poppy agreeing to a stay in Bridlington, especially not the way she was at the moment.

As she drove back, she made her decision. She'd fought battles before to win back young people who seemed to be lost beyond hope. She thought about Becca, the foster-daughter she was closest to. She and Matt had been told more than once that Becca was a lost cause, and look at her now.

Not that Becca was in such a good place at the moment.

Kay sighed. That was a different problem for a different time. But she was going to fight for Poppy. She would get Poppy back.

Chapter 5

Bridlington

Becca's flat – or more exactly, her bedsit – was above a shop on one of the main roads out of the centre of Bridlington. The shop was a sell-everything hardware sort of place, and if Becca had wanted mop heads or tin buckets, it would have been handy. As it was, it was just the place she had to get through to reach the stairs to her room.

It was a twenty-five-minute walk from the supermarket, maybe twenty if you walked as fast as Becca did. Walking saved on the bus fare, and anyway, the service was pretty much crap. The weather, that had been so good earlier, was turning. Clouds were gathering. She pulled up her hood and huddled into her waterproof to protect herself from the early evening chill.

When the shop was closed, she had to go in through the back of the building, along a narrow alleyway where people dumped the kinds of stuff you didn't want to look at too closely. Becca had seen needles and used condoms among the dumped rubbish. She always watched where she was putting her feet when she came along here.

She let herself into the backyard, noting again that her landlord, George, the guy who owned the shop, hadn't repaired the lock on the gate yet; it was still held by a loop of string.

Becca unhooked it and stepped through, pulling the gate closed behind her. There were high walls separating the yards along the terrace, and the limited space was crammed with discarded storage boxes, an industrial-sized wheelie bin, some cracked paving slabs and bits and pieces of broken furniture. A metal fire escape ran down the wall from the attic window of Becca's room, ending about three metres off the ground, where a drop-down ladder provided access.

Tucked away under the fire escape and hidden under a tarpaulin was a small motorbike that Kay, Becca's foster-mother, had bought for her at the beginning of the year. Not that Becca could afford to run it, though she hadn't told Kay that.

The yard could have been nice. In the summer, the sun had shone on it all day, and plants had grown up through the cracks in the asphalt, making it look green and garden-y, but right now, it was just a place where all the junk from the shop got dumped.

She let herself in through the back door, checking round as she did so for any sign of the kitten that had appeared just a couple of days ago. She'd often see it pouncing on leaves blown across the ground, and vanishing as soon as it became aware of her watching. It looked very small to be out, and she hoped it had a home somewhere.

There was no sign of it, so it probably did.

Upstairs, she had a quick shower – cold, because the water heater hadn't been on, and anyway, her card was short of credit – then pulled on trousers and a T-shirt, loose, with long sleeves. Carl Lavery, her boss at the pub, could get a bit grabby, so she never gave him anything to grab if she could help it.

She pulled her hair up into a high ponytail. When they were dancing, that time they had gone clubbing, Andy said he liked it. As she looked at her face in the mirror, she saw her cheeks flush. She could remember him watching her that night, here in this flat, when she'd pulled the clip free and her hair had fallen down round her shoulders.

And he was back tonight. She felt a tension inside her that was half painful, half nice as she finished getting ready. A bit of make-up, just to hide the scar that ran down from the side of her nose to her lip, and a brush of eye stuff to make her eyelashes and eyebrows a bit darker, because otherwise they tended to vanish.

She'd first met Andy when he started coming into the pub several weeks earlier, and from the off, he'd treated her like she was a person, not some robot with tits who was there to give him a show while she served drinks.

One evening, before she really knew him, he was at the bar on a busy night, taking time as he decided his order. She'd snapped at him to get a move on and he'd looked at her sadly. 'You don't like me because I'm a Transformer.'

She'd stared back, prepared to take offence. 'What?'

'But I can change.'

He'd said it so deadpan it had taken her a few seconds before she got it, then she laughed because she couldn't believe he would make such a lame joke.

So then it had become a kind of thing that they tried to find the lamest jokes to tell each other: *Snorting Coke* . . . when Becca's drink went up her nose, *Baggers can't be choosers* . . . when she was struggling to get a sack of rubbish out of the door. 'Why doesn't that dosser do a bit of work?' he'd said once, looking across at the barman, Toby, who spent as much time as he could get away with playing on the games machines.

Toby became Dosser after that.

Andy took the piss out of the punters, giving them daft names as well. There was the tall, thin woman who hung out with the bikers, and who always wore a hat tipped forward, shadowing her face, and sometimes sunglasses as well, like she was some kind of celebrity. 'Or gangbanger,' Andy said when Becca commented on the glasses. After that, he started referring to her dismissively as Sal Capone. And there was the fit guy – and didn't he know it? – with long dark hair who looked like some kind of gypsy or pirate or

43

something. Becca once admitted she thought he looked like Johnny Depp. Andy had dismissed this at once. 'Him? You mean Johnny Dip?' That one had made her laugh.

The pirate guy had been Johnny Dip ever since.

But Andy was more than just a punter. As they got to know each other, he admitted he was there for a reason. He worked for an investigation agency specialising in fraud, he'd told her. Carl Lavery, the landlord, was on the fiddle, or they thought he was, and it was Andy's job to collect the evidence.

'Yeah, right,' she'd said. Private detective? He was having her on. Carl, in his old mac, looked more like a private detective than Andy did. Andy called Carl 'Flasher' on account of the mac.

'You're kidding, though? Private detective?' That had made her uneasy. It was a bit like him being a copper, and you couldn't trust coppers. All her life, from her policeman stepfather to the police who wouldn't listen and who had locked her up last year, she'd learned you could never trust them. They might talk nicely, they might pretend they were on your side, but if you fell for it, even for a second, you soon found out how wrong you were.

If you trusted them, then you got what you deserved.

They'd raided the pub a few weeks ago – she hadn't been working, but when she'd heard, it had made her feel sick, the thought that they could come in at any time and turn the place over.

So she didn't like the *detective* thing at all.

'No, it's true.' He'd handed her a card with his name on: *Andrew Yeatson, Financial Enquiries.* 'I'm a real private eye,' he'd added. Then, looking more closely at her face, 'Hey, are you OK?'

'Yeah.' She'd managed a smile. 'Yeah, I'm fine.' It didn't matter, she told herself, if the coppers came here. She wasn't doing anything wrong. *Since when did that make any difference, loser?* a voice jeered in her head.

For a while after that, she'd kept out of his way, but it was like he didn't notice. He'd gone on being friendly, he'd given a couple of the punters a hard time when they'd said things, and before long, they were mates again.

He was nice, easy to talk to, and without really realising it, she'd started helping him – telling him what she knew about the people who came into the bar, telling him if the till roll balanced properly, telling him about deliveries. He was interested in those.

A couple of weeks ago, she told him about that odd time she'd been in the cellar, collecting more crisps, and Carl had come down the stairs, staggering under the weight of two holdalls he was carrying.

When he saw her, he'd dumped them on the floor and she'd edged round him so she could get up the steps quickly if she needed to, but he wasn't planning on being grabby, not this time. 'What are you doing down here, Becca? It's busy. The bar's your job.'

'Yeah, only we were out of—'

'Look, if it isn't behind the bar, we don't have it. You don't come down here without my say-so. Got it?' He'd aimed a pat at her bum as she went back up the steps but she'd been ready for him and moved too fast for him to connect.

Creep.

Later, after closing, he'd sent her down to bring up some soft drinks for the next day. Curious, she'd looked round for the holdalls, but there was no sign of them.

She'd told Andy about it. 'He was really pissed off I was down there.'

'Twat.' That made her feel good, to know he was on her side.

Then she'd told him about the groping, and it had made him really angry. 'You shouldn't have to put up with that sort of shit. Do you want me to . . .?'

She'd shaken her head. She could look after herself, but it was – yeah, it was nice that he was bothered. He'd asked a few questions about the holdalls – not that she'd been able to give him any answers.

'Why do you want to know?' she'd asked.

'Got my boss on my back,' he'd said. And then, to her surprise. 'Do you want to go out, after? There's a new club opened in Hull.'

'Hull?'

He'd grinned. 'You know any cool clubs in Brid?'

She'd smiled back. 'Yeah. OK.'

She hadn't been clubbing since she'd left Leeds, about two years earlier. A long time. And it had been great. They'd danced until three in the morning, and she could have gone on dancing until daylight. He'd driven her back to Brid, driving fast on the empty roads, getting them back to her flat in just over forty minutes. Then he'd kissed her lightly and she'd surprised herself again by saying, 'Do you want to come in?'

He'd smiled that slow smile, and said, 'What do you think? Of course I do.'

She could remember him standing by the gas fire, watching her as she freed her hair from the high pony-tail and shook it loose. He'd caught hold of her hand. 'There's something about you, Becca . . .' He'd been frowning as if he couldn't quite find the words. 'I don't want to make more bad things happen in your life.' His finger had touched the scar on her face. No one talked about that. No one. She'd waited for the famil-iar anger to well up inside her, but it didn't. Instead, she'd just shaken her head.

Once again, he didn't push. 'You'll tell me,' he'd said. 'If we're together, you and me, one day you'll be able to tell me. Right?'

She wasn't sure, but maybe, just maybe she would.

'There are things I need to tell you, too. Not yet. But I will.'

And right then, she'd believed him.

It had been almost morning before he'd left and neither of them had got any sleep. It didn't seem to matter. 'I'll see you at the pub,' he'd said. She'd wandered round the supermarket the next day in a kind of daze, not minding when Bryan shouted at her or Sheryl pursed her mouth up like a cat's bum. Jade had grinned at her knowingly, and Becca had felt her face going red. She wasn't working in the pub that night, Andy knew that, but the night after that . . .

But the next day, he'd called her. 'I've got to go away for a few days – a work thing,' he'd said. 'I'm back a week on Friday.'

'OK,' she'd said, trying not to show that she minded.

'I might not be able to call – it's all work stuff. Look, I'll explain when I get back. Are you OK, Becca? I'm really sorry.' And he'd sounded it. 'Look, don't let Dosser run you ragged, right? And a knee in the balls for Flasher if he gets frisky.'

'Right.'

She was OK that he didn't call, because they'd never called each other – they'd texted, and he kept on doing that. Some of them were the usual jokey texts – *How many Game of Thrones characters does it take to screw in a lightbulb? Only two, but it's a bit crowded* – and some were stuff about the pub; questions about Carl, questions about the punters and – this was something new – were there any more of those bags, could she get to look inside one, could she take some pictures?

But nothing about what had happened between them.

In the end, she'd got a bit mad at him – it was like he'd forgotten who she was. *Piss off about the bags!!!!*

Sorry, he'd texted back. Got my boss on my back. Need all the help I can get ☺ *xxx*

Becca knew about that. She'd never had a boss who didn't give her a hard time, and Andy had talked about his boss before. She wanted to help so she'd looked round the cellar the next time Carl sent her down there, but there wasn't anything that seemed out of place. They could talk about it when he got back.

Tonight.

She was expecting a call, or at least a text. She checked her phone again, but there was nothing.

Why would he text? He'd just come in.

Wouldn't he?

It was almost seven. She headed along the road towards the harbour. The light was just about gone. She was just going past the car wash when she saw Carl Lavery coming out of the café opposite. It called itself an arcade, but it was just a café with a few machines. He was carrying a couple of holdalls, his scruffy mac belted tightly round his middle, his face grim.

Andy was right. He did look like a flasher.

She hung back and watched. He dumped the bags into the boot of his car, a Land Rover, scruffy like him but it must have cost a packet. A kid came out of the café to help him, heaving the holdall up with both hands.

Becca knew him. Jade's Lewis.

He looked across and saw her watching him. His eyes narrowed and he said something to Carl. Becca turned and moved on quickly. The last thing she wanted was a lift from Flasher. She could imagine what being stuck in a car with Carl Lavery would be like.

She hurried off down a side street that cut through to the harbour. The waft of frying drifted from the stalls and cafés, and she realised she was starving. On impulse, she bought a tray of chips she really couldn't afford, covered them liberally with salt and vinegar, and ate them as she walked along.

Why was Jade's Lewis with Carl Lavery? Jade had talked about drug dealers on the estate. Was that what Lavery was doing? Was that why he was so touchy about her being in the cellar that time? But the police had raided the place, and they hadn't found anything.

She'd tell Jade what she'd seen, at work tomorrow.

The pub, the Smokehouse, was just across the road from the harbour. It was a bit early for her to start her shift, but there was just a chance Andy would have arrived early and be in there waiting for her. She crammed the last of the chips into her mouth, and then licked every trace of grease and salt off her fingers.

She wasn't going to think about what she'd seen, not just now. She just wanted to enjoy Andy coming back. She'd think about the rest later.

She was OK. She was more than OK. She was feeling good.

Chapter 6

As Becca walked along the lane to the pub entrance, she saw that Russ, the homeless guy who had started hanging out outside the Smokehouse a few weeks ago, was back. She hadn't seen him for a bit.

There was a sort of alcove by the door that made a good shelter, and that was where Russ sat with a sleeping bag round his shoulders. He always had his dog, Champ, with him. Champ was a big dog with an enormous head who ignored everyone but Russ. If anyone ever tried getting funny with him, Champ would sort them out.

'Hi,' she said as she walked towards him. 'You OK?' She wanted to share her good mood with everyone tonight. Almost everyone.

Russ didn't encourage chat but they'd talked once, briefly, when she came out of the pub for a ciggie. She'd told him she came from Leeds, and he'd laughed and said 'How come you ended up here, then?'

He wasn't a mate or anything, but they got on. More or less.

'Evening,' he said now, after a moment. Champ turned his large head and stared at her coldly, then obviously deciding she wasn't a threat, relaxed again. 'You look like you're having a good day.'

'Yeah. I'm OK. You?'

'I'm all right.' He sounded friendly enough, but she thought he looked sad. Being homeless was hard. She'd lived rough, for a while. It had been lonely and scary and people had bothered her all the time. She'd never slept, not properly, because that was when they got you. You had to learn how to pass, how to look like a normal person with a place to go, how to become invisible. Becca had learned never to trust anyone, especially not people who came round with smiles and offers of help. She had never been so scared in her life as when she had been sleeping rough.

It would be different with Russ. He was big, and you could tell he knew how to look after himself. People wouldn't mess with him.

But she wasn't going to spoil her evening by thinking about that. 'See you,' she said to Russ. She pushed open the pub door and looked round expectantly.

But Andy wasn't there.

OK, it was early. She dumped her coat in the back and went behind the bar to begin her evening's work.

Her good feelings began to fade as the evening drew on. It was getting later, and there was still no sign of Andy. He hadn't texted either. She couldn't stop herself from looking at the door each time someone came in, though not many people did. The pub was quiet

– quieter than she'd ever known it, so there was nothing to distract her, no sign of Johnny Dip or the other bikers, no sign of Sal Capone, the woman who hung out with them.

At first, she'd been pleased the pub was so quiet – it meant that she and Andy could spend some time alone, talking and catching up, only ... time was getting on, and he wasn't here.

She checked her phone again.

Nothing.

Carl came out from the back. She hadn't known he was in. What had he done with the holdalls? Were they in the cellar now? She was suddenly furious at Carl and his holdalls – they were all Andy had been able to talk about when he texted her. 'I'm off out,' he said. 'I'll be back later. Looks like you won't need me until closing.'

'OK.' Carl might be a grabby creep, but at least he trusted her to take care of things. She wasn't sure he'd have left Dosser in charge. *Toby*, she corrected herself. She didn't want to start calling him Dosser to his face – and anyway, Toby was OK. He went out and got the glasses in, which meant she didn't have to squeeze through the crowds on a busy night. He was over by the games machines right now, playing again. Carl left, and she leaned against the bar, trying – and failing – to stop herself checking her phone.

Andy, where was he?

She heard the familiar sound of the pub door swinging open and slamming shut again. This time she was so sure it was going to be Andy that she looked up with a smile, into the face of a total stranger.

Curwen stood opposite the pub, studying the frontage. The name – the Smokehouse – had to be a tacky marketing invention, because the old pub sign, weathered almost to illegibility, said 'The Bell'. Behind the faded yellow banner that promised '–ootball and Hap–y Hour', Curwen could see all the signs of neglect – peeling paint, dirty windows. He wondered why the owner and pub landlord, a local businessman called Carl Lavery, didn't take better care of his property.

Curwen realised someone was coming out and stepped back quickly into the shadows. It was a good job he did, because it was Lavery himself, as if conjured up by Curwen's thoughts. He watched as Lavery stood in the doorway, his bulky figure silhouetted against the light. The last thing Curwen wanted right now was an encounter with the landlord.

It had started a couple of months ago with a simple tip-off from one of Curwen's informants, about drugs coming into Bridlington harbour and being stored in the pub cellar. Drugs teams up and down the coast were trying to pinpoint the source of stuff that was pouring into the area, so this was worth following up.

Curwen was ambitious. His life plan outlined that he'd be DI by now, with DCI in his sights, but his career seemed to have stalled. He needed a big arrest to make his mark, something in his file that said *high-flier, person to watch*.

For the past three months, he'd been working with a small team – Andy Yeatson and a DC called Dinah Mason, recently transferred from uniform – going after the drugs users and dealers in Bridlington, a kind of 'clean the streets' initiative to help the council keep the place attractive for tourists. Their boss, a DCI called Kevin Gallagher, had more or less given Curwen carte blanche, a sign of confidence that wouldn't be missed higher up.

And then one of the street dealers Dinah Mason had arrested made a claim. He'd given Curwen tip-offs in the past and was clearly hoping to cash in another get out of jail free card. He said that two people, people he only knew as Doc and Stoner, were bringing stuff in through the small Bridlington harbour, storing it at the Smokehouse and distributing it from there.

Curwen's big mistake had been to go it alone. He wanted to be the one who carried out the raid and he wanted to be the one who made the arrests. He'd been too eager, too greedy. He'd kept the tip-off to himself, pimped the story, got a warrant and gone in.

He could remember that moment in the pub cellar, when room after room had been searched, coming up with nothing. They were standing there in a small room just off the main cellar, listening to the occasional *glug* from the beer barrels. It was the last place left to search. In the wall, there was a cupboard. The door was locked. 'What do you keep in here?' he'd said to Lavery. He could see wariness enter the other man's eyes.

This was it. They'd found it.

'Not much,' Lavery had shrugged.

'Have you got the key?'

Slowly, reluctantly, Lavery handed it over. One of the search team had unlocked the cupboard door. It'd swung open, revealing rough, slatted shelves. Pushed to the back of one of the shelves was a battered hold-all. The man carrying out the search had used his gloved hands to ease the handles apart and slide the zip back.

A few bags of coins gleamed dully in the dim lights, and there was a mixed bundle of notes – fivers, tenners, twenties – rolled up with an elastic band.

'So what's this?' Curwen had asked.

Lavery had shrugged again. 'Last night's takings. I don't have a safe so I keep it down here until I can get to the bank.'

'You leave it here all day?'

'Quiet night.' Lavery had explained. 'I've got other things to do. No one knows it's down here.' His eyes had narrowed. 'Or they didn't. If I get a break-in, I'll know who to thank.'

Lavery's explanation held up. The flicker of anxiety on his face as they'd opened the cupboard told Curwen there was something to find, but whatever it was, they'd missed it. Even checks by sniffer dogs revealed nothing.

It was a fiasco, and it hurt him, badly. Lavery had put in a complaint, and when Curwen's application for the warrant was looked at closely, the evidence he'd used to support it didn't stand up. He'd been reprimanded, and Gallagher had started closing his team down, leaving Curwen with just Andy to keep an eye on the Bridlington street drugs trade.

It was a bitter pill, and there was worse. He'd been up for promotion. He'd passed the exams, put the time in, applied to the promotions board – and been rejected.

Curwen's informant had turned up a couple of weeks later in Hull, in a squat inhabited by junkies. He was dead, the needle still in his arm.

But Curwen knew Lavery was dirty. He'd known the instant he'd seen that wariness creep into Lavery's eyes.

Curwen owed Lavery big, and he was going to pay him back. Every penny. With interest.

Andy shared his frustration, so when Curwen had suggested Andy keep an unofficial eye on the pub, he was enthusiastic. 'No reason why I shouldn't drink there,' he'd said. 'I'll chat up the bar staff, keep an eye out.'

Andy's brief had been simple: Go in, pose as a buyer looking for a big deal. Find the dealers in the pub, find out when the drugs came in and where they were stored, find Doc and Stoner.

Nothing, he kept reporting back.

Nothing.

Until Curwen almost believed that there was nothing to be found.

And then, just over a week ago, Andy had been approached – no direct contact, no offer, just samples of the drugs that were, presumably, available. He'd been waiting, since then, for the next contact that would lead to a meeting.

Instead, he'd ended up dead.

Curwen stood in the shop doorway, watching as Lavery stopped to say a quick word to a vagrant who was half hidden in an alcove to one side of the pub door. Lavery's stance, and the abrupt jerk of his head, made it easy to translate what was going on. The vagrant was being given his marching orders. Lavery set off along the lane towards the main road.

Curwen knew he'd fucked up. He couldn't tell DCI Hammond, or even his own boss DCI Gallagher, what Andy had been doing – not if he didn't want to spend the rest of his career watching speed cams on the East Yorkshire roads. He needed to know what Andy had found and, once he had the evidence, go after Lavery with everything he'd got. But until he had the evidence, no one could know about this.

First of all, he was going to take advantage of Lavery's absence and get in the pub. Andy had a contact there, a young woman who worked behind the bar.

Becca Armitage, or Becca the Barmaid as Curwen had dubbed her – to himself. Andy had implied she knew something but he wouldn't tell Curwen anything more specific; just that he didn't want to get her into trouble.

That was his choice.

Curwen's was different.

Two birds, one stone. If he could pin the drug dealing on Lavery, and link that to Andy's death, then the black mark of a reprimand on his record would count for nothing – he'd crack the drugs case, and bring Andy's killer to book.

And the killer of the man who'd given him the tip-off. Curwen knew that overdose hadn't been accidental, even though he hadn't been able to convince Gallagher.

Waiting until he was sure Lavery had gone, Curwen crossed the road to the pub entrance. He glanced at the alcove before he went in and was surprised to see the homeless man hadn't moved. He was still sitting there huddled under a blanket, with the mandatory dog beside him. The dog turned its massive head and stared at Curwen. Curwen hesitated, wondering whether to ask the man about Lavery, but right now, he wanted to get into the pub before the landlord returned. He filed the homeless guy away for future consideration.

Time to find out what had gone so wrong. He stepped through the pub door.

Chapter 7

Curwen sat at a table on the far side of the room, ignoring the drink in front of him. He was watching the girl behind the bar; Becca the Barmaid.

She was fiddling with her phone, picking it up and putting it down, cleaning the beer taps, rearranging the glasses, and exchanging the occasional word with the guy who was working with her – a geeky student type who spent more time playing on one of the games machines than he did serving.

Right now, he wanted to locate the two people whose names he had: Stoner, the man Andy was supposed to be contacting the night he vanished, and Doc, whose involvement was less clear. But whatever contact had been made, the information had died with Andy.

He was pretty sure the proof was here. Somewhere. Something that linked this pub to the drugs that were moving up and down the coast. He was still betting on the cellar. These old buildings had a lot of obscure nooks and crannies. Every copper's instinct Curwen had told him it was here. They'd missed it, that was all.

He turned his attention back to Becca the Barmaid. Time to make contact. She might know Doc and Stoner, but the most important thing he wanted from her was information about who Andy hung out with when he was here, and what went in and out of the cellar.

He strolled across towards her, trying to make eye contact before he got there, but she didn't even bother to look up from something she was doing around the cold shelves. She continued to ignore him even when he stood in front of her. Frustrated, he banged a fistful of coins down on the bar, making her jump. *Good.* 'You serving or anything?' he said.

She looked at him blankly. 'What?'

'Got any food on?'

'No.'

He sighed and spoke with exaggerated slowness. 'OK. What have you got? To eat?'

She shrugged. 'Crisps. Nuts.'

'What are those?' He pointed behind her.

'Pork scratchings.' She reached for the card hanging on the wall. He remembered his grandfather telling him that there used to be a picture of a naked woman under the bags, so as they were sold, the punters gradually got the chance to see a nipple. Nothing more than that – which said a lot about the kind of world his granddad had grown up in. But he wasn't spending money on bits of rancid dead pig. There was something about her monosyllabic indifference that got right up his nose.

'Didn't say I wanted any, love. Just asking.'

She rolled her eyes and dropped her arm to lean against the bar, waiting. Had Andy really liked her, this sullen chav? He was tempted to see how long he could keep her here, changing his mind, asking for this, saying no to that ... He wanted to make someone else's day as bad as his, and a bit more.

Then the light caught the faint line of a scar running down from her nose to her upper lip, giving it a slight twist, and he realised where he knew her from. He'd seen her in the custody suite a few months ago. They'd been dragging her out of a cell where she'd spent the last hour screaming and throwing herself at the wall – off her face on something.

A user.

That could be useful ... she was exactly the kind of contact he needed. Maybe this was why Andy had been so wary about making her an official informer. He'd been right to approach with care. 'OK, what flavour crisps have you got?'

The girl sighed and reeled off the list. 'Plain, cheese and onion, salt and vinegar.' He could hear the subtext – *Make your mind up and piss off.*

'No prawn cocktail?'

'No. No dog shit either.'

Comedian. 'OK, salt and vinegar.' She put a bag on the counter. He kept hold of the note in his hand. 'I'm getting a drink as well. What have you got on tap then?' Curwen smiled amiably, a good-natured punter chatting with the barmaid.

'Beer.'

He laughed. Genuinely. He was starting to enjoy her relentless spikiness. What was it Andy had said? *She's nice . . . once you get past the claws*. He realised, as he thought about it, that he didn't know exactly how far past the claws Andy had got. Shit! He should have thought of that. Andy wouldn't have . . . not with her. Or would he? He pushed the thought away. It was something for later. 'Yeah, OK, got that. Tell me about this one.' He pointed at one of the taps – *The Earl*, an IPA. Curwen could talk beer with the best of them.

'It'll make you drunk. So will that one and that one and that one. Right?'

'Sounds OK to me. I'll have a pint. You worked here long?'

'Long enough.' For the first time, her gaze focused on him, as if she was beginning to realise he wasn't just some arse chatting her up. 'Why do you want to know?'

'I'm looking for my mate who comes in here.' He watched her closely as he spoke. 'He's called Andy. He's in here a lot.'

He saw her face flood with colour as her eyes moved towards his quickly, then away. She was definitely listening now, still not meeting his gaze, but she was on the alert as she pulled his drink.

'Andy,' he said. 'Don't tell me you don't know him.'

'OK, I won't.' She pushed the drink across the bar to him.

'He might have got into trouble. With the kind of people you really don't want to get on the wrong side of, if you get me.'

She gave him the same quick glance, but her expression was guarded now. She wasn't giving anything away. 'Yeah, well, I don't know anything about that.'

'Hear me out . . . *Becca.*'

She froze, then turned slowly back. 'What do you want?'

Leaning forward to look as though they were sharing something trivial, part of the flirtation, he put Andy's photo on the bar. 'This guy. Andy. Did you see him in here on Tuesday evening?' Andy was supposed to be keeping away from the pub until after Stoner had been in touch, but Curwen wasn't certain he'd kept to that. He might have nipped in here early doors.

She barely glanced at it, but he could see the flash of recognition in her eyes.

'If he was in here, I need to know who he was with, and what time he left.'

'It was busy. I don't know what people do.'

'Yeah. Busy on Tuesday, quiet tonight. Funny, that. OK. Do you know anyone called Doc? Or Stoner?'

Her chin came up and she met his eye. 'You a copper?'

'Do I look like one?'

She gazed at him for what felt like a long time. 'You smell like one.' She ducked under the hinged flap on the bar and emerged carrying a crate. 'Excuse me.' She pushed past him and let herself into a door just to his left, marked '–ELLAR: STAFF —LY'.

The cellar. Curwen hesitated a moment too long, and the door swung shut. He pushed it cautiously, but it had locked. Shit and shit again.

He'd let his mood get the better of him. He should have stayed the fuck out of it until he could control his temper. Not to worry. If she had form, he could use that to put pressure on her. He'd get what he wanted, eventually.

Then he saw the pub door open, and Carl Lavery appeared, irritably shaking the rain off himself.

Curwen turned away, waited until Lavery had gone behind the bar with a quick bark of 'Toby! Where's Becca?' and vanished into the back, then he headed for the door. Now was not the time to get caught. Anyway, there was a second string to his bow that he could follow up now – the vagrant who'd been sitting outside the pub. That was someone who'd notice things, see what was going on. Andy was – Andy had been – a sucker for a sob story and had probably given the guy money at some time. So the guy would remember him. He might be able to help Curwen, with the right incentives.

But when Curwen got outside the pub, he was too late. The blanket lay in the alcove, but the man – and his dog – had gone.

Angrily, he kicked the blanket out of the shelter and into the damp night.

Chapter 8

As Becca made her escape down the stairs into the cellar, she realised she was shaking. Andy – in trouble? *With the kind of people you really don't want to get on the wrong side of.* She knew what kind of people those were.

Now his texts about the pub began to make sense. He'd got his boss on his back, he'd told her. Or had it been someone else? He'd asked her for help. He'd asked about this cellar, about what was stored there, and she'd just . . . She'd been angry . . .

She hadn't helped him.

And now he wasn't back like he'd said, and a copper was after him. She whipped out her phone to text him, then stopped. She could send him a warning, but she could also . . . She looked round the cellar. What had Andy meant in those texts, things that were stored down here? There wasn't anywhere to store anything, apart from what you'd expect.

But . . . *something in the cellar that shouldn't be here.* What did he mean by that? She looked round. Drinks, boxes of crisps, bottles . . .

The cellar consisted of two rooms. In the first one, barrels were lined up against the wall, hooked up to the pipes and the huge gas bottles that made the beer flow. Carl dealt with all of that, and Becca was glad to leave it to him. Against the back wall, a freezer buzzed. Boxes of soft drinks and mixers were stashed against the back wall. The other drinks were stored in a smaller room, with shelves that ran up the walls stacked with beers, ciders, and a few bottles of spirits. There was a damp, slightly sour smell in there, as if something had gone off and the air hadn't cleared yet.

Against the far wall of the second room was another door, a sort of cupboard, but it was always locked. She couldn't always get down here, anyway. Carl rarely left the cellar key in the till for them. He had done it tonight and she'd just grabbed it and come down here to get out of the way of the copper.

The pig.

The creep.

Asking questions about Andy . . .

Putting the drinks crate on the floor, she went across to the cupboard. The cellar key didn't work in this door. And how did she know that? She'd tried it, out of curiosity. But . . .

The door was slightly out of line. She looked more closely, and saw that the lock hadn't quite caught, like someone had pushed it closed behind them and not checked that it was properly shut. Slowly, she reached out and pulled it open.

Inside was dark. She took out her phone and turned on the flashlight application. The room was a deep, brick-lined space. The floor was flagstones, like the cellar. There were some shelves with old, sagging boxes that were covered with dust and cobwebs. They looked like someone had moved them recently then shoved them back onto the shelves. Was this what Andy meant? She opened the camera and took a couple of shots. In the light of the flash, she saw there was something on the stone floor, bundled into a corner.

A couple of holdalls. She took another picture, then stepped into the cupboard towards them. Andy would want to know what was in them. She grabbed the straps of one and tugged at it. It felt heavy, and the contents made a metallic noise as the holdall moved.

'Becca!'

Her phone almost dropped from her hand. It was Carl, calling from the stairs. 'Becca? What the fuck are you doing down here?'

He hadn't seen her. She could hear his feet on the steps, and pushed the door shut quickly, wincing as the click of the latch seemed to fill the cellar. 'I'm just bringing some stuff up while it's quiet.'

He was in the room now. 'What stuff?'

'Mixers, stuff like that.'

'We don't need it. Leave it. Why are you in here anyway?'

All the soft drinks, all the mixers, were in the other room.

'I might as well bring these crates up,' she said, frantically trying to think. 'If it's busy tomorrow, we'll need the shelves full.'

'I said leave it. What are you doing in here?' he asked again.

What could she say? *Think*! The pig creep copper! Use him! 'There was a copper asking questions, so I just, you know. I didn't want to talk to him. Sorry.' She shrugged

Carl was looking at her. There was something about his face – a kind of cold anger – that gave her a shiver of dread. It reminded her of her stepfather. He always got that expression when He was angry, before He . . . She swallowed the lump that had suddenly grown in her throat.

'What kind of questions?'

'Just, who was in here the other night, that sort of stuff.'

'And what did you tell him?'

He was moving closer. Becca sidestepped around him into the other room. She wanted to get out of there. 'Nothing. I said I'd got to get some stuff and I came down here.'

He was right behind her. 'I'll take that key.'

She handed it to him, and he clipped it onto his belt. 'OK. You did right. You're a good girl, Becca.' He was very close now.

She wasn't going to let him touch her. 'Right.' She turned away and ran up the cellar steps and into the pub, feeling his eyes on her all the way. The pub was still quiet. Toby was leaning against the bar looking bored. Someone else was busy pushing buttons on the games machine; it bleeped and clattered and flashed its lights.

She needed a bit of time on her own. She looked at Toby's fed-up face. 'Do you want to go out and grab a smoke?'

'Yeah, if that's OK. Cheers, Bex.' He ambled off.

She didn't like it when people called her Bex. It reminded her of things she wanted to forget.

She looked round. Carl was still in the cellar and the door was closed. She'd hear him before he saw her. She checked the pictures. They didn't look like they'd be much use, just a couple of scruffy bags on the floor in the corner of the cupboard, but she texted them to Andy anyway.

Maybe it would help. *He might have got into trouble. With the kind of people you really don't want to get on the wrong side of . . .*

He should have said. If this would get him out of it . . .

A few moments later, her phone pinged. She looked at the screen and her heart jumped.

Great, A x

Andy. It was from Andy. He was OK.

Chapter 9

Becca felt confused as she walked along the road towards her flat. The hardware shop was shut, so she had to go along the gennel. The ground felt soft and squishy underfoot. She shone her torch downwards. The light reflected from dark puddles and wet cobbles that were half hidden with mud and trodden-in garbage.

She felt more down than she had for a long time. She didn't know if she was worried about Andy or if she was angry with him. The copper, the pig creep, had said Andy was in trouble, but what did coppers mean by that? She'd been worried about him, and at first, the text he'd sent just made her feel relieved; but the more she thought about it . . . Just, *Great, A x*

No, *Sorry, I couldn't make it.* No, *See you tomorrow,* no *You OK?* Just . . . *Great.*

Maybe she had been wrong about him all along. Maybe she was just a big loser and he was just a creep.

Telling herself she wasn't going to think about him, she unhooked the gate and pushed it open. There was a light above the back door that cast a dim glow across the path, leaving the rest of the yard in deep shadow. She let the gate swing closed behind her.

A movement caught her eye.

Rats?

She looked down and got a glimpse of white and ginger fur vanishing into the corner. It wasn't a rat. It was the kitten. If it was out this late, then it certainly didn't have a home. She didn't know much about cats. This one looked very young – too young to survive out here. She crouched down and reached out to touch it, but it vanished under the huge wheelie bin.

She couldn't leave it. The weather was bad – too wet and cold for a tiny kitten to be out. Years ago, in one of her foster homes, the family had a kitten. There had been something about it – it was so tiny, but it hissed angrily if you came too near and sunk its needle-sharp teeth into you if you touched it. She was only there for a few nights; an emergency placement after being thrown out of her last foster home. Becca hadn't liked the house and she hadn't liked the people, but the kitten had been OK.

She crouched down now, peering under the bin. Rain dripped down her neck and the ground felt squishy underfoot. She held out her hand towards the gleaming eyes, all she could see in the dark, but the kitten backed further under the bin and hissed at her. There was no way she was going to be able to get hold of it.

That didn't mean she couldn't look after it. Tomorrow, she could buy some cat food, but tonight ... She dug in her shopping bag and pulled out the sandwiches she'd picked up cheap from the late-night supermarket.

She spread the empty carrier bag out as far under the bin as she could reach – another hiss told her the kitten was still there – pulled her scarf from round her neck and put it on the bag. Maybe the kitten could make itself a bed. She put the bits of chicken from the sandwich on the bag. It wasn't much, but it was something. Maybe if she fed it regularly, it would start to trust her and she could catch it and take it inside.

She'd love to have a pet – a dog was out of the question, but a cat ... George, her landlord, probably wouldn't like it, but then he didn't have to know. As soon as she got a day off, she could spend some time trying to tame the little animal and get it inside, safe and warm. Making plans made her feel better, took her mind off Andy as she went up the narrow staircase to her room.

Over the months, the bare, comfortless bedsit had started to feel like home. Kay had given her a floor lamp with a red shade. Becca loved it – it was so cool, and its light made the room look warm and welcoming. She'd stuck some travel posters on the wall; she'd bought a piece of red fabric from the market for almost nothing and put it on the bed as a throw. Kay had also given her a rug – another splash of bright red. Jared had thought it was a dump, which was great, thinking of some of the places he'd lived.

Andy had liked it.

But she wasn't going to think about him.

In the right light, the room looked – almost – like one of those makeover rooms on the TV apart from the armchair that came with the flat, pulled up near her small telly. The chair was big, old and battered, but Becca couldn't replace it even if she could afford to. At least it was comfortable.

In the kitchen area, next to the hob, was a shiny new kettle – Kay again – and a bright-red tea caddy that had caught her eye in the market. Next to it, there was a packet of biscuits, the top twisted closed, and the small tabletop fridge that came with the bedsit.

The window rattled and a cold draught blew through the room. It was freezing; the windows didn't fit in their frames, and she didn't have any curtains. She kept looking in the charity shops, but so far, there hadn't been anything. Kay had offered her an old tweedy green pair, but even Kay thought they were real loser curtains.

She lit the monster gas fire that stood against the back wall, not sure how much credit she had left. It would be another day before she had any money to top up her pre-payment card. She had the rent money, but her rule was to put that away as soon as she was paid and not touch it, no matter how broke she was. Getting behind with your rent was the first step towards being out on the streets.

It was late and she should get something to eat. The sandwiches from the late-night supermarket were supposed to be tea tonight and breakfast tomorrow, but the rain had got in while she was feeding the kitten and all that was left was a kind of bready mush with salad and something that smeared grease over her fingers. Biscuits, then. She made herself a cup of tea and flopped in the chair while she ate. She'd had chips earlier. This should be enough.

She could still taste the last of the chips that she'd crammed into her mouth, licking the salt off her fingers as she went into the pub. She'd half expected to see Andy already there and waiting for her.

But he hadn't been. And he had never turned up.

In trouble . . .

Why was his text so . . . so *nothing*, like she was just anyone, not someone special? What kind of trouble could Andy be in? Was it something to do with work? She picked up her phone and looked at his text again: *Great, A x*

On impulse, she texted back *where r u?* and regretted it as soon as she'd pressed send.

She sat there staring at the screen for ten minutes, but nothing came back.

She was too tired to think about it all now. But as she stood in front of the mirror, brushing her hair, Andy came back into her mind. In fact, he'd been there all along. Andy, laughing as they wove their way off the crowded dance space, Andy saying, *Hey, are you OK?* like it really mattered to him, Andy smiling at her as her hair tumbled down round her shoulders. *I don't want to make more bad things happen in your life.*

Was that why he was staying away, because of the trouble and not wanting to bring it near her?

The pig creep copper had frightened her.

It looked like Andy needed her help.

OK, he'd get it.

Chapter 10

Sunk Island

Kay pulled up outside a dilapidated gate and checked the address. This was the place. Haven House, Stone Creek, Sunk Island. It was the first time she'd actually seen the house that would be her home for the next few months, until her cottage sold and she was free to buy a place.

'It hasn't been advertised yet,' her contact at the estate agents had told her. 'I don't know why. The owner passed a couple of months ago.'

Passed. Kay hated the euphemisms for death people employed. They kept telling her that Matt had *passed*, as if he were a kidney stone or something.

But she was fed up with the long commute, the house was available, it ticked the boxes, so she signed up, sight unseen. Now, as she looked at the place she had rashly committed to, she felt a pang of misgiving.

Like a bad blind date, the house didn't look a lot like its picture. The photo on the website had been taken on a good day, against a blue sky and in bright sunlight. Seen in the grey light of a rainy afternoon, the house appeared to be crouched down against the weather, the windows dark and forbidding, water dripping from blocked gutters.

If she'd been asked to describe 'deceased property' she couldn't have done better than this house. It was a square, red-brick construction with tall chimneys. Repairs to the pointing looked long overdue, which probably meant damp. The windows were dark and hung with grubby-looking nets. The front door was heavy timber with iron hinges and locks. In the dull light, the house looked neither welcoming nor reassuring.

Well, she was going to have to live with her impulsive decision. She turned the car in through the gate and parked outside the front door. The gravel crunched under her tyres. The front of the house faced east, so it was already in shadow. A small car was parked to one side of the house, presumably belonging to the agent who had come to hand over the keys.

On the seat beside her, Milo whined. She rubbed his ears. 'You too?' She didn't believe in portents, but his unease made hers all the stronger, even though she knew he was just grumbling because he was fed up of being in the car.

She got out and looked round, ignoring Milo's complaints. There was a hard wind blowing, bringing spatters of rain. She shivered. It felt as if it was coming straight across from the Siberian steppe, cutting through her coat and chilling her bones. Banks of cloud were gathering above her in the vast skies of the east coast. It might still seem like autumn in Scarborough, but here it felt as though winter had already arrived, and spring, she suspected, would be no kinder.

'You must be Mrs McKinnon.' A very young-looking man emerged from the parked car, smiling and holding out his hand. 'I'm Oliver Shaw from the estate agent. I've brought the keys and I'll show you round.' He beamed as though he couldn't think of anything he'd rather do. He looked about sixteen and clearly took his role very seriously.

Kay made herself focus. The drive had been a nightmare of traffic and she'd arrived in no mood to feel positive towards Sunk Island, and in no mood to be cajoled by an over-enthusiastic salesman. She nodded curtly and went round to the passenger side of her car to open the door and let Milo out. He jumped down and shook himself, yawning and wagging his tail hopefully. 'Walk later,' she said and hooked him onto his lead – she wanted to check the security of the garden before she let him off.

'Lovely area, isn't it?' The young man, Oliver Shaw, said, looking a bit nervously at Milo, who was eyeing him with equal suspicion. 'And the house – real character.'

Becca's voice in her head said, *Yeah, right* as Kay let her gaze travel across the house, wondering which character he had in mind. Dracula? Frankenstein's monster? 'What sort of heating system is there?'

'I haven't been inside,' Oliver Shaw admitted, revealing himself as a total rookie. 'The person who's been dealing with this property is off sick, I'm afraid. I know there's a couple of fires, open fires,' he went on in the same tone of voice he would have used to tell her the house came with its own resident Michelin-starred chef. Kay's heart sank. She'd lived with the tyranny of a wood-burning stove at her cottage in Lythe, and if she never saw an open fire again, it would be too soon.

But it wasn't this young man's fault. 'Oh, good,' she managed, hoping her lack of enthusiasm wasn't too obvious. Judging by his face, she hadn't managed that too well. 'Shall we go in?' she said, adding *electric fire* to her mental shopping list.

'Yes. Of course. You do know the house has been standing empty for a while?'

Kay nodded. They'd been clear enough about that. She shouldn't work off her bad mood on this young man, who was only doing his job. She'd just like him to stop being so bloody cheerful about it.

Oliver's estate-agent-ese wobbled slightly as he struggled with the key in the lock. 'Needs oiling. I've got something in my car. Hang on.'

While he was digging around in his boot, Kay took stock of her surroundings. All around her, fields stretched to the horizon in shades of dull green and brown, the land flat as far as she could see. In the distance, through the rain, the estuary caught the afternoon light. Here and there, she could see clumps of trees, and the gleam of water where the drains that kept the land dry ran across to the river. Spragger Drain, Cross Drain – real Viking names, but then, this was Viking territory. They were deep ditches with steep sides, some of them overgrown and hidden. She'd have to be careful of Milo. His insatiable curiosity would surely lead him into one, and she wasn't sure it would be possible to get him out.

'OK.' Oliver had come back and was dripping oil onto the key. This time, it turned. Like a stage magician, he threw open the door and gestured for her to step inside.

The smell of mildew and damp hit her immediately. She'd have to take on the open fires and get the place aired out. She added *fuel* and *kindling* to her list.

'Nice old hallway,' Oliver said. 'Original features.' He slapped the bannister, which wobbled alarmingly. 'Tiles,' he added quickly.

The tiles were nice, Kay had to admit. She smiled encouragingly. And the bannister was an attractive old oak, even if it was falling off. It would look good with all that dark varnish stripped off. If she were planning on . . . Which she wasn't, of course. The last thing she needed was a renovation project.

'Listen,' Kay said, 'I've already taken the house for a short let. It's almost five. I don't want to keep you. All I need is the keys and a quick run through of where everything is, and to make sure it's all working.'

'I can assure you everything's functioning properly. I'll just show you round the basics. It's a beautiful house, though,' he added wistfully.

Kay had to agree. Under what looked like years of neglect, there was a house worth retrieving. It would have been a perfect project for her and Matt in the days when they enjoyed renovating old property. The grief stirred, and she made herself concentrate on what Oliver was saying as she took stock of her new accommodation.

The kitchen was at the back of house and surprised her as Oliver threw open the door. The window was west-facing and the sky was glorious with the colours of the setting sun. Kay squinted round. It looked old fashioned but serviceable – a pot sink, Formica work-tops that were stained but intact. A small fridge. Wall and floor cupboards that seemed sturdy enough. It also looked as though it had been used, and recently. There was a big pan on the hob, a couple of stained mugs in the sink, mud and bits of packaging on the floor, as though something had been opened here. Oliver flushed. 'I'm sorry,' he said. 'The cleaners should have done a better . . . I'll get them to come back and sort this out.'

'No need,' Kay said. She didn't want the hassle of cleaners coming in to put away a couple of bits and pieces and clear up some mess. 'Don't worry about it.'

Upstairs, there were three bedrooms, but one was little more than a box room and was bare. The beds in the other two rooms looked adequate. She'd make the bed up in the east-facing room and get the early morning sun.

'And here,' Oliver said as they came downstairs again, 'is your fuel storage.' He sounded as though he was showing her the jewel in the crown. He threw open a door that led into the space under the stairs. Kay, looking over his shoulder, saw a dark, dusty cubbyhole with some hooks on the wall. She sniffed. Here, there was the faint smell of incontinence she'd been braced for as they went through the house. Oliver saw her expression and his face went a bit pink. 'I think they kept the previous owner's, erm, care equipment in here.'

Milo pushed past him, sniffing the new space eagerly, tracking a smell that had caught his attention to a small door in the back of the cubbyhole. He scratched at it and whined.

Oliver unlocked the door and pushed it open. Milo surged past. 'Milo!' Kay said sharply.

'It's all right,' Oliver said, giving Milo a nervous pat. 'I like dogs.'

Now the door was open, she felt the chill of the outside. 'The main access to the fuel store is from the garden,' Oliver explained. 'It's a storage area in the side of the house. But you can get into it from indoors, from here.'

She was looking into a brick-built space where logs were neatly stacked against one wall and a row of yellow bags – presumably solid fuel – were lined up against the other. There was a door in the opposite wall that must open into the garden. A sheet of hardboard covered the floor and the whole area was swept clean. It was a relief to see fuel available, and a relief to know she wouldn't have to scramble around in the wet and the cold tonight collecting it from an outside store.

She looked into Oliver's face, still bright with the desire to be helpful. 'Thank you so much for coming to meet me. I think I've got it all sorted now. I'm sure I can call you if I need anything.' She'd shepherded him as far as the door before he showed signs of rebellion.

'I still have to . . . I need you to sign for . . .'

'Yes, I know. Help me get my stuff out of the car, yes, that's very kind of you.'

He carried her two big cases and a bag of supplies into the hallway. 'Is there anything you'd like me to take upstairs for you?' He was looking dubiously at the insecure bannister.

'They're fine just there,' she said. 'I need to sort it all out. Thank you,' she added. He really was a nice young man, and she was being a vinegar-faced old cow.

She glanced out of the door at the cloud banks forming above them. 'It looks like it's going to start raining seriously. You should be on your way before it gets too bad.'

She signed the papers to confirm she'd received the keys, that the house was in good order and she intended keeping it so. The challenge of somewhere new was starting to engage her. She wanted to get the place in shape, turn it into her home, even if it was only for a short time.

Chapter 11

As she watched the estate agent's car drive away and closed the gate behind it, Kay luxuriated in the feeling of being in full possession. She'd always enjoyed moving; the adventure of a new house, and a new place to live, new people, new things to do. Not that Sunk Island seemed to offer a lot in the way of neighbours. There was a cottage up by the crossroads, and that was it.

A quick check had shown the garden was secure, so she let Milo off his lead for a run. She was heading back towards the house to start on her unpacking when he gave a sudden bark.

'Excuse me.' The voice seemed to come from out of nowhere.

Kay whipped round. She'd thought she was completely alone, but there was a woman standing in the road outside the gate. As soon as Kay saw her, the woman pushed the gate open proprietorially and came through, her expression hostile. She had one of those faces that looked middle-aged from childhood, not helped by the scarf that partly covered her faded blonde hair and was tied firmly under her chin. There was no car visible on the road, so she must have walked from nearby, from ... Kay looked round. Probably from the cottage along the road? 'Hello?' Kay said. Milo, ever helpful, growled from behind her legs.

'Excuse me, but what are you doing?' The woman's eyes were sharp with suspicion. Who would have thought Sunk Island ran a neighbourhood watch?

'I'm your new neighbour,' Kay said. 'I'm moving in here for a while.'

The woman's face remained suspicious. 'A while?'

'Yes.' Kay held out her hand. 'Kay McKinnon.'

The woman touched it briefly then let it fall. 'Ford. Catherine Ford. I live in the cottage along there. I don't mean to intrude, but we have to be careful. It's very isolated here, and the police never patrol. Just the other night, I went for a walk and I saw a couple of young men in a car, a four by four, just driving round. Strangers. Looking for trouble. They passed me a couple of times. I called the police and I let them see me do it. Not that the police did anything. They never come out here, or not until it's too late.'

'Too late?'

'You didn't hear? They found a body down by the banks of the estuary this morning, near Spragger Drain sluice. No one's told us anything, of course.'

Kay wondered who 'us' were. Sunk Island was barely populated apart from a small number of scattered houses like hers, and a couple of farms. A body down by the estuary. She felt her heart sink, and told herself it didn't have to be anything to do with this place. It didn't have to be anything at all. People fell into the water all the time – and the estuary was treacherous.

Catherine Ford's voice went on, '. . . and someone nearly got killed before that, earlier in the week, a car, speeding, no one from round here. They nearly knocked a woman down. We've had a lot of trouble, you know. Cars at night. Motorbikes. It's getting worse.'

Kay was about to ask what kind of crime there was, out here in the back of beyond, then she realised she was being naive. This wouldn't be petty, opportunistic crime; this would be organised. Farms and old buildings held valuable stuff. There would be old lead piping, lead in the roof flashings, farm equipment in the scattered locations she'd seen on the map, and the only protection would be what people installed themselves.

As if picking up on her thoughts, Catherine Ford looked at Milo. 'Is he a good guard dog?'

'He barks when strangers are around.' Kay hadn't thought about needing a guard dog. Milo would bark, but if he got scared he came to Kay for protection, not vice versa.

'That's better than nothing. You know, this used to be such a lovely house. Hettie – Mrs Laithwaite

– was ill for a long time. She couldn't keep up with it, but she wasn't going to move. She was quite determined.'

'It's not the best house if you're not independent.' Kay found it hard to imagine a sick old woman surviving there, though she could understand the impulse not to leave. Her nightmare was spending her last years in a care home with hoists and commodes and indifferent care workers seeing to her needs. She hoped someone would do her the kindness of chucking her off a high cliff before that happened.

'That said, she did have her family helping – they really looked after her. You don't always get that, these days.'

'That's true,' Kay said non-committally. She wasn't up for a *young people today* conversation.

'The district nurse came, of course, but family's best.'

'Yes,' Kay murmured.

'We thought it was going to be sold. We don't want a holiday let, standing empty half the year.'

'They didn't tell you what their plans were for the house?'

The other woman considered Kay's words as if she was searching for hidden criticism. 'You don't like to ask. Not when someone has . . . passed.'

Kidney stone.

'No,' Kay said neutrally. 'The estate agent told me they plan to sell in the spring. The family.'

'Well, that's more than anyone has told me.' Catherine Ford sounded a bit huffy, and Kay decided it was time to end the conversation. She had a lot to do.

'Well, thanks for—'

'If you need help, any time, here's my number. We have a kind of telephone tree to get people out. Don't rely on your mobile – the signal's poor. And you won't get a decent Wi-Fi connection. You'll be on your own here. At night,' Catherine Ford added.

Kay wondered if the woman was deliberately trying to frighten her. It was a good job she wasn't the nervous type. Did she need to worry? Surely anything worth taking from this house must have gone weeks ago while it was standing empty. She wasn't here permanently. It was nothing to do with her. Despite these self-reassurances, she found herself looking round at the deserted landscape with a shiver. Mentally, she cursed Catherine Ford.

'I'll be fine,' she said briskly, to herself as much as to the other woman. The first drops of the threatened rain were starting to fall and to Kay's relief, Catherine Ford decided to leave her to it. Kay watched her as she vanished through the gate. *You'll be all on your own.* The sun had disappeared and it was almost dark – time to get herself settled in.

Shaking off the unease the conversation had left her with, she called Milo away from where he was burrowing in the soil. His coat was damp and muddy, and she got a whiff of an unpleasant smell – organic, but not quite, rather like the smell of the chemical toilets they used in basic campsites. She sighed. 'What have you found?' He wagged happily, his tongue lolling. She'd have to give him a bath before she let him loose in the house.

First things first. She needed to bring in some wood and kindling to start the fire, but the outside door that led into the storage shed was locked and none of the keys Oliver had given her worked. Someone was taking security seriously, because the door was held with a heavy-duty anchor and hasp, and a secure padlock. It was a good job Oliver had shown her how to access it from the inside, or right now she'd be setting off to Hull to buy fuel and the biggest electric fire her funds would run to.

She shut Milo in the kitchen over his loud protests, then scrambled through the cupboard under the stairs to access the fuel store – she'd phone tomorrow to get that key or the padlock changed. Still, there was plenty of wood. Not as much as she'd first thought – the yellow bags were mostly compost, but there were a couple of bags of fuel and an open bag of what looked like coal. Presumably no one policed the smokeless fuel laws on Sunk Island either, unless Catherine Ford was a fanatic.

Curiosity made her lift up the sheet of hardboard on the floor, and she found a trapdoor underneath it. She tugged at the handle that lay flush against a recess in the timbers, but it wouldn't budge. Well, she wasn't likely to need access.

She took buckets of coal and kindling through to the front room, then she grabbed Milo, carried him upstairs and put him in the bath. While he struggled and splashed, she shampooed and rinsed him, then set him free. He hopped out of the bath and shook his wet coat all over her while she tried to dry him. 'Serves you right for rolling in whatever you rolled in,' she told him.

Kay, sopping wet, had a quick shower herself then put on her old tracksuit, which she tended to wear more and more often these days. She decided she couldn't be bothered to blow-dry her hair. It was so short, what difference would it make? Maybe Poppy could make it look better, when they met. If she turned up. Kay frowned, her concern about Poppy replacing the lingering unease her conversation with Catherine Ford had left.

This wasn't the time to think about that either. It was time to get the fire lit.

Coal was easy to get burning, and it smelled good. Putting her eco-reservations to one side, Kay went back to the fuel store and refilled one bucket with coal, another with wood and kindling. Warming the place up was her first priority, then she'd make up her bed, get something on the stove and settle down for an evening with a good book, a glass of wine and some food.

After a day of travel, work and then sorting out her things, she would sleep well tonight. A horde of boy racers could ride their bikes through her bedroom and she probably wouldn't stir. Despite Catherine Ford's ominous warnings, Kay felt unwarrantedly cheerful as she got to work.

Chapter 12

Bridlington

Curwen lived in one of the old houses overlooking the bay. It was in the converted upper-storey of one of the huge Victorian terraces close to the sea that mostly housed hotels and B & Bs. Property was cheap in Bridlington, even property with a view like this.

The high windows faced east. On summer mornings, he sat there sometimes lingering over a cup of coffee, watching the sun rise over the North Sea. He was sitting there now, a bottle of beer in front of him, oblivious to the lights twinkling out at sea.

He was remembering.

Andy bit into his sandwich, catching a trickle of egg yolk with his finger and licking it clean. It was late, he'd been in the Smokehouse all evening and had texted Curwen, sounding excited, to say he had something useful. Curwen suggested he came to the flat and Andy had arrived with egg and bacon muffins for both of them from the van along the front.

'I needed that,' Andy said. 'I get the munchies by closing time. I can't be in that pub all evening and not drink. I got away with a half tonight.' He patted his belly and said, 'Once this is done, I'm spending a week in the gym.'

Curwen grinned. 'I might join you. OK, what have you got for me?'

'This.' Andy put a couple of small baggies on the table, next to his phone, which he'd dumped there earlier before they stared eating.

Curwen felt his eyebrows shoot up. Slowly, he opened the first one. It contained what looked like a herbal mix. Curwen would have said cannabis, but the rich, resinous smell wasn't there. He sniffed it. Nothing. 'Spice?' he said.

'Yeah.'

'OK.' He started opening the other baggie.

'Careful,' Andy warned. 'That stuff is fucking potent. Too much and you'll go crazy. I mean it.'

He got a whiff of an unpleasant smell like – he struggled for an analogy and came up with stale piss, masked by something sweet and chemical. He gagged. 'Shit. What the fuck is that?'

Andy grinned. 'Shit just about sums it up. This is the new stuff, the stuff we've been having all the trouble with. It's alpha-PVP.' He rattled off the information he had. 'Street names are "bath salts", "cosmic wave". It's like spice, only it starts from a different drug – cathinodes, you know, from khat. It's very close to the flakka they had all the trouble with in the States. It more or less vanished over there – too dangerous even for junkies. It's just too easy to OD, but someone pimped it a bit, and now it's back, it's badder and it's here. I'd rather have spice on our streets than this stuff.'

'Where did you get these?'

'You know I've been putting word out in the pub – my people want access to the big stuff that's coming in, we can move it on faster, make it worth your while, no names no pack-drill and all that shit. So tonight, a kid goes past me on a mountain bike, next thing I know, I've got these packets in my hand and the kid's gone.'

'Any other contact?'

Andy shook his head.

'So who is it?'

'Someone I've been talking to in the pub, but I don't know who. Not for sure. There's a bunch of bikers, probably up for anything. They don't look like big players, but I think they're involved – they probably move the stuff around. They'll know who to pass word on to. The contact name I've got is Stoner – and before you ask, no I don't know him. I just have to wait for them to contact me.' Andy sounded frustrated.

Curwen grunted, but he was pleased. This was the most promising lead they had – they couldn't blow it now. 'Any developments at the pub? What does your informant say? Becca the— Your barmaid.'

'She hasn't seen anything odd going over the bar, or not when she's been there. We talk a lot and she's never mentioned drugs or anything.'

'It won't be happening in the bar itself. If they're storing stuff, it'll be in the cellars. Look, we've talked about this.'

'Yeah, yeah, yeah. I'm not saying Lavery's clean. I'm just saying the pub might be.'

'Get those cellars checked before you write the place off.' Curwen was impatient. If Andy had done his job right with Becca the Barmaid, they'd have that information already. 'What about those bags she saw Lavery carrying? Has she seen any more?'

Andy shook his head. 'I haven't asked her. I'm not getting her into trouble.'

Curwen closed his eyes. *For fuck's sake.* Andy was such a fucking boy scout. 'We need to know what was in them.'

Andy shook his head. 'They weren't down there when she looked later.'

Curwen knew where they would have been. The layout of that cellar was etched into his mind. He could remember the locked door to the cupboard built into the wall, and the sense of anticipation as they opened it with the key Lavery had handed over reluctantly, his face tense. 'There's a cupboard in the cellar. Your barmaid needs to check that.'

Andy frowned. 'I told you. She can't get in there.'

'Lavery's got the key. She could probably get her hands on it. Have you asked her?' It had been a simple mortice lock, a two-lever one. A skeleton key would work. 'You could give her a key that would open—'

But Andy was shaking his head emphatically. 'That's criminal behaviour. I told you. I'm not getting her into trouble over this. She isn't even a registered informant. I'm worried she's already in too deep. Lavery didn't seem too happy that she'd seen him with the bags.'

'Fine. Point taken.' Curwen was pissed off, but now was not the time to alienate Andy. He was a stubborn sod and there was no point in trying to change his mind on this. As Curwen's gaze fell on Andy's phone, still lying on the table where Andy had left it, he began to get an idea. He needed five minutes alone with that phone and . . .

He knew how to get Becca the Barmaid to do what he wanted. And what Andy didn't know wouldn't hurt him.

'OK. They've given you the samples, now we wait until they make contact.'

'You think they will?' Andy said.

'You've put out the right feelers. You can move the stuff on fast and pay top rate – they'll be interested enough to want to know more. And they've given you the samples. They'll be in touch.'

This was where it could get tricky. One whiff of cop and they'd go to ground so deeply Andy and Curwen wouldn't be able to find them again, but Curwen didn't have the backup to protect Andy in the course of an actual meet. What they needed was the contact, details of the meet, then Curwen could take it higher up.

He had to set it up right, to make it his operation, which meant getting everything in place before he reported it in, but not leave it so long that the smugglers realised what Andy was up to and vanished. Or worse. Curwen had his story ready. This lead came from the previous investigation, something he'd followed up in the course of completing his report. He'd dug down a bit, realised it was much bigger than it had looked at first. Curwen would get his big arrest, which would outweigh any reprimand about being overzealous with a warrant, especially if Lavery was pulled into the net.

Curwen *knew* Lavery was involved. What he didn't know for sure was if Lavery was one of the smugglers, or if he was just storing the stuff. Either way, Curwen would be vindicated, and his promotion should be in the bag.

But in the meantime, in case this contact faded away, he needed to get more information about what was stored in the pub cellar. Andy was refusing to involve Becca the Barmaid. But a plan was starting to form in Curwen's mind.

He could ask her. Kind of.

Andy's phone sat there on the table. Curwen wasn't going to get another chance. He picked it up and began turning it over in his hand. 'They'll give you a bit of time to get the stuff tested, then they'll be in touch, set up a meeting. That's when we get the backup and go after them.'

Normal drug deals were simple cash transactions between the dealer and the buyer. Curwen and his team had picked up loads of dealers in Bridlington – rats in a barrel, basically. But Andy and Curwen had been fishing for much bigger prey – the smugglers who were bringing the stuff in.

Curwen was gambling here. He had to call in backup, but not until they'd got enough evidence. A couple of baggies wouldn't cut it, and he couldn't reveal the undercover operation – he and Andy would both be in the shit.

The meet. When the meet was set up. That was the time to get support.

Andy was still chuntering on about Becca the Barmaid.

'Look, about Becca. I'm worried about her. I should get her some protection, get her on the register, get them to pay her for what she's given us.'

'We can't. You know this isn't exactly what we're supposed to be doing. This is off the record until we have something.' Curwen was still on desk duties as the enquiry into the raid wound its slow way onwards, and not keen to be busted down further for after-hours sleuthing.

'Yeah, yeah, I'm cool with that. But I'm not getting her more involved. I want her official as soon as it breaks. She should get something from this.'

'She knows you're a cop?'

Andy looked uncomfortable. 'No. I haven't told her. She really doesn't like us.'

Curwen's plan began to take shape. 'Don't tell her yet. That could put her in danger if it gets out. Wait until they've been in touch again so we know what we're dealing with.'

'OK.'

'We're close, and now we need to play safe. You need to drop out of sight until this is sorted. Stay out of the pub, no contact with your informant, low profile. Nothing that's going to give you away now.'

'What are they going to think if I'm suddenly not around?'

'That you've got what you want and you've no need to go back. They'll get that.'

'Becca's going to wonder what's happened to me.'

'She'll be OK for a few days.' His plan wouldn't work if Becca the Barmaid and Andy were still communicating.

But Andy wasn't backing down on this one. 'No. I need to let her know if I'm not going to be around. I can't just ghost her.'

'OK, OK. Tell you're away for a few days for work.'

'I can text her, right?'

'Best not, and don't call. Remember, if they know you're in contact and anything gets out, she could be in trouble.'

'I suppose. Yeah. I'll let her know I'm going to be away for a few days and then I'll leave it. She's nice, Becca, once you get past the claws. I don't want anything bad to happen to her.'

'It won't,' Curwen reassured him. He held up the

phone. 'How long does the battery last on this? Mine's so fucking complicated I'm lucky to get a day out of it.'

Andy looked surprised. His phone was pretty basic, and Curwen always had the latest piece of gear available. 'Couple of days. It's OK.' He checked his watch. 'I need to get back. I told the babysitter I'd be back by one.'

'I think we're done.'

'I'll be off then. I'll just go for a . . .'

Curwen had been hoping for this. 'Help yourself. Down there on the left.' He held the phone up again. 'Mind if I take a look?'

'Be my guest.'

Curwen held out the phone, and after a moment's hesitation, Andy unlocked it and handed it back, then headed along the corridor. As soon as he was out of the room, Curwen moved quickly. He brought up the home screen, listening for Andy all the time, then he clicked on the store and started downloading the app he wanted, watching in frustration as the slow line moved across the screen.

It had barely downloaded before he heard the cistern flush.

Come on! Come on!

Done.

But now the screen told him the app was installing. He could hear Andy moving around. *Shit* – he was pushing his luck here. Quickly, he went into the contacts list, found Becca's number and ticked the boxes to forward messages. Not to his main phone, but to a pay as you go, an off-the-record burner phone he kept for emergencies. The bathroom door opened and Andy's footsteps came along the corridor. *Shit!* Moving fast, Curwen set the app to delete the messages, and returned to the home screen just as Andy came through the door. 'Thanks, mate,' he said, holding out the phone.

Andy took it and shoved it into his pocket. All Curwen needed now was to download some spoofing software onto his own phone, and he would not only get the texts Becca the Barmaid sent to Andy, he could send texts to her, and make it look as though they came from Andy's number.

What were the chances of Andy spotting the app? Not great – there were too many other apps on the phone. Once this was over, Curwen could manage the same trick and delete everything – or just get rid of the phone altogether.

The raid had been a bad setback, but he was finding his feet again.

Chapter 13

Sunk Island

Kay sat up in bed, suddenly wide awake, trying to work out where she was and what had woken her. Milo was barking. An engine sounded outside, like someone was slowing down, then it picked up and faded into the distance. Milo barked again, a sharp, painful sound. 'Quiet!' Kay said sharply. It was bad enough having the noise of the motorbike – she knew a bike engine when she heard one – without Milo adding to the cacophony.

Then there was another engine – the same one? No, this was the tinny roar of a cheap, souped-up machine, the kind of bike very young men rode around on, the amplified engine noise making them feel strong and invincible. It came closer, then raced along the road outside the gate and faded away into the distance.

The farm thieves? They wouldn't make so much noise, and they wouldn't be on bikes. They'd come quietly and leave quietly. These were just idiots vandalising the silence for the sake of empty roads they could race around. She toyed with the idea of going out to the gate to . . . To do what? Shout abuse at some Hell's Angel wannabe as he roared past on his hairdryer?

Great idea, Kay.

She checked the time, groaning as she saw it was only just after twelve. The hour's sleep she'd had would probably have revived her enough to make further sleep difficult. As she slipped back under the quilt, discarding her now tepid hot-water bottle onto the floor, she thought about how life used to be. In her twenties, she was rarely in bed before one, and after she and Matt married, they often used to sit up into the small hours, appreciating the quiet when they could just be together, catch up with the day, make plans, talk.

Now, she was pretty much done by ten.

Old age tiptoes up behind you, armed with its sock full of wet sand and if you don't watch out, it will get you. Had that happened? People talked about coming to terms with Matt's death, but in truth, the pain could still knock her sideways sometimes. In the aftermath, in the struggle to keep going, had she let herself get old?

She drifted into a fitful sleep where Matt was saying to her, over and over again, 'You have to watch out for it, you know.'

And suddenly she was wide awake again.

It wasn't Milo this time. He was sitting up in his basket, alert, but he hadn't barked.

She pushed herself up, listening, trying to shake the remnants of the dream away. *You have to watch out for it, you know* ... Something in the road? Another bike? Was that what had woken her? But there was nothing, nothing at all.

Then Milo growled, and she thought there was – just on the edge of hearing – a faint sound from downstairs, like the click of a door swinging closed.

Catherine Ford's stories flooded into her mind – cars speeding along dark lanes, people breaking into farms and houses to steal, maybe harm . . .

Milo erupted.

Damn! Hell and blast!

It couldn't be anything. Could it? The house was secure. She'd locked up, there was nothing valuable here, but she wouldn't be able to sleep now until she was sure. Putting on her slippers and wrapping her dressing gown round her, she stood at the open bedroom door. All she could hear was the rain, and . . .

Was it? Could she hear something moving down there in the darkness? She stayed where she was, listening, but she didn't hear it again. Milo pressed against her legs, making a low grumbling sound. 'What is it, boy?' But Milo just pressed closer, the growl steady in his throat.

Part of her wanted to go back to bed, pull the covers over her head and pretend nothing had happened. But another part, the stubborn part, wasn't going to do that. She left the room and moved towards the stairs, looking down into the hallway.

Just shadows.

And silence.

'OK,' she spoke out loud for the comfort of hearing a human voice. 'Tea. Come on, Milo.' If someone had broken in, she was giving them due notice there was someone here so they could discreetly make their exit. Stopping to grab her torch – she didn't trust that ancient fuse box, and anyway, the lights were so dim it would be easy to trip on something hidden in the shadows – she headed down the stairs, making as much noise as she could.

It made her feel like one of her foster kids, one of the girls, who lived in mortal terror of both axe-wielding serial killers and creepy-crawlies. Kay used to be very brisk with all that sort of nonsense, but here she was whistling in the dark to keep her own monsters at bay. The torch was a reassuring weight in her hand. *Get a grip, Kay. There's no one here.* If there was, it would only be a break-in, and the culprit would have scarpered smartly at the sound of Milo's bark.

It was a reasonable precaution to check, though, and she did. The front door was locked, and the downstairs windows were all tightly shut. *Idiot*, she told herself. She'd done all of this before she went to bed. She went down the corridor to the back of the house, using the torch to supplement the dim lighting. Her dressing gown caught on the knob of the door into the cubbyhole under the stairs, which she must have left open. She'd forgotten about that.

Shining her torch into the space, she reached across and tried the door that led to the storage shed. It was locked.

All secure.

As she opened the kitchen door, the moon came out from behind the clouds, filling the room with a pale light. Kay stood at the window, looking out across the flat, bleak landscape where the grasses danced in the rain, their wet sheen glittering in the moonlight, and stunted trees formed strange shapes against the sky. Then the clouds closed in again, leaving her in darkness.

Her hand hesitated over the light switch. If she turned it on, the light would blaze out, saying clearly, 'I'm here.' But wasn't that what she wanted? If people knew the house was inhabited, they'd stay away.

If there was anyone out there.

Which there wasn't.

She was pretty sure now she had been dreaming. Yes, Milo had barked, but it didn't take much to freak Milo out, especially in an unfamiliar place. He'd barked at the motorbikes earlier. That was probably what had woken her up.

She'd always dealt matter-of-factly with teenage night terrors, and now she tried to deal the same way with herself. It was a dream. It was something outside in the road. It had made her uneasy, but it wasn't anything to do with her. She filled the kettle and switched it on, taking a clean mug from the draining board and getting a carton of milk out of the fridge. A cup of tea, then back to bed. She checked her watch again. Three thirty.

Milo was snuffling around, back to his usual self. The kettle clicked off. Kay filled her mug and left the tea to brew for a minute.

Milo let out a sharp, sudden bark.

She jumped, knocking the milk over and flooding the worktop.

Footsteps. Outside. She could hear them clearly, faint but getting louder as they came closer.

Coming straight towards the back door.

Kay froze, her heart hammering. Her gaze locked on the door handle. Could she see it . . . was it moving, or was she . . .?

Milo barked again, a sharp, high-pitched sound.

And the steps moved past the door and faded away.

Kay sank down into her chair, trying to catch her breath. She turned slowly towards the window, knowing what she would see – a face pressed up against the glass.

There was nothing, just the square of illumination from the light, and blackness.

She should open the door, shine the torch into the night and find out who was out there, because no one had the right to be.

But she couldn't.

The rain was beating harder against the window. She tried to pick up the milk container and screw the top back on but her hands were shaking so much she couldn't do it.

Come on.

So someone had been out there. They'd seen the light and they'd gone.

Gradually, the shaking stopped. She grabbed a towel and put it on the worktop to soak up the spilt milk, and picked up her mug. There was just the sound of the rain now, and she was beginning to think she must have been hearing things. Why would anyone be walking round the house in the small hours, in this kind of weather?

The best thing to do would be to go back to bed and ignore all the night-time noises. Old houses were full of weird sounds – she should know that.

Putting her hands on the table, she pushed herself to her feet. She was tired, she'd been asleep and when you were woken up suddenly it was easy to mistake—

Her breath stopped in her throat.

They were back, the footsteps.

Someone had walked right round the house. Looking for what? A way in? And now they were back. She froze, half upright as the faint sound got louder, coming quickly towards the door, closer and closer.

The door. Her eyes were fixed on the handle.

Was the door locked? Had she checked it?

Milo gave an uncertain bark. And then, again, the footsteps went past, faded and vanished.

What, as Becca might say, the actual fuck? Kay stood there wide awake, listening, and sure enough, about ten minutes later, the footsteps approached again.

This time, she was ready. She flung open the door and shone her torch into the night. 'Who are you and . . .'

There was no one there. Water from the gutter was overflowing onto a piece of board that had been dumped outside. Something must be blocking the gutter because the flow of water was slow at first, making a faint pattering sound, then faster and faster, getting louder, and then, as the gutter emptied, slowed, grew fainter and stopped. If you didn't know what was happening, it would be easy enough to mistake the sound for footsteps.

There was no one here.

She leaned against the doorframe, limp with relief. No one was walking around in the darkness. No one was approaching the back door then moving on. There was no one there, and it was time she went back upstairs.

But first, she slipped her feet into her boots, stepped outside into the rain, and pulled the piece of board away. No more phantom footsteps tonight. Her fingers were covered in mud – she hoped it was mud. She sniffed them and smelled that same, sweet chemical smell that Milo had got on his coat earlier.

Horrible. She scrubbed her hands under the tap. It was time to go to bed. The combination of warm tea and the belated humour of the situation eased her tension, and when she was back in the bedroom, she knew she was ready to fall asleep.

111

She asked herself, just as she was dropping off, how it was she'd heard the sound of the overflowing gutter up here in her bedroom. She wouldn't have thought the sound could reach so deep into the house . . . But old houses played odd tricks with sound. It wasn't important. And anyway, there hadn't been any footsteps.

It had been an illusion.

Just an illusion.

And the sound of the door closing? She couldn't have heard that. At all.

Chapter 14

Bridlington

Becca jerked awake, sweating, from a dream. Another one about a locked door and knowing she was trapped in a small space with ... with ... It was all mixed up with a kitten calling from somewhere she couldn't find, even though she looked and looked, while Andy kept saying, *Baggers can't be choosers, Becca, you know that.*

The dream fell out of her head as she sat up, and she was glad to let it go, but it left her feeling anxious and unsettled, like she had urgent things to but couldn't remember what they were.

She fumbled for her phone on the floor beside the bed and squinted at the screen. No messages.

It was seven fifty. OK, time to— *Seven fifty! Shit!* She'd slept through the alarm! She had to be at work by half eight. She fell out of bed and shoved some biscuits in her mouth as she got her work stuff together.

The kitten! She had to feed it and she didn't have any food or any time to get any.

Milk. Kittens could have milk, couldn't they? And she could buy some cat food from work for later.

She gave herself a cursory splash in the shower, slapped on some make-up – just enough to cover the scar. Pulling her clothes on, she gave herself another glance in the mirror – it was OK, the jagged white line didn't really show. The time? What time was it? Five past eight. *Shit!* She'd have to spend money she didn't have on the bus. Bus fare, cat food – suddenly, she was angry. What was the use of working? She was always fucking broke.

She took a carton of milk from the fridge, grabbed a towel, a carrier bag, her bag and her coat and was halfway out of the door before she stopped and went back for something to hold the milk. Her cereal bowl. That would do. She poured some milk into it, then ran downstairs into the yard.

The rain was heavier now.

Working fast, she lifted the tarpaulin that covered her bike and put the carrier bag on the ground. The scarf went on top of that to make a bed in the make-shift shelter. She put the bowl just under the shelter of the tarp and scrambled to her feet.

She'd been concentrating on the kitten to stop herself thinking about Andy, but as she stood up, it all came flooding back – the odd texts, the pig-creep copper, *the kind of people you really don't want to get on the wrong side of . . .*

Everything felt confused, but she had to get to work. Her bus was due in less than a minute. She was out of the gate and running towards the bus stop. Seconds. She had seconds.

She turned into the road and almost ran full tilt into two people who were standing there. Two kids. One was a tall, thin lad she'd never seen before, the other was . . . She took in the small figure and the mountain bike with the orange handlebars.

Jade's kid. Lewis.

What was he doing here? 'Does your mum know where you are?' It was out of her mouth before she had time to question the wisdom of saying anything. Lewis's eyes narrowed, and his mate uncoiled himself from where he'd been leaning against the wall. 'What's it to you, bitch?' Lewis said.

'Don't you call me bitch you . . .'

And her bus shot past her, speeding towards the stop where no one was waiting. Becca spun round, waving at it as she ran, but even though the driver must have seen her, the bus sailed past the stop and vanished. Jeering laughter broke out behind her.

She wanted to smack their stupid faces. 'Your mum is so going to know where you are right now,' she shouted at Lewis.

Fucking bus. Fucking work. Fucking everything. She was left with a fifteen-minute wait or a twenty-minute walk. She wasn't going to wait at the stop, not with those kids hanging round. It made no difference. Either way, she was going to be late.

DANUTA KOT

And she was. It was the first time, but you wouldn't think it from the way Bryan, the manager, carried on. *You're shift starts at . . . If you want to be part of the team . . . I don't expect . . .*

Bryan put Becca in the stockroom as punishment, working on her own, getting the delivery sorted onto the trolleys for putting out on the shelves. Some of the boxes had been standing in the rain and the wet meant that the parcel tape had lost its stick. She went to lift one of them and it collapsed round her, sending tins rolling across the floor. The noise brought Bryan in, shouting at her. 'If any of those tins are damaged, that's coming out of your pay. Jade, you help Becca sort this mess out. And keep an eye on the tills.'

'And shove a broom up your arse and sweep the floor as you go,' Jade muttered, coming in to fill a trolley to take the stuff out onto the shop floor.

Jade was looking tired and drawn. 'Are you OK?' Becca asked.

'Knackered. The little one had me up half the night, and our Lewis, little bugger, didn't go to school yesterday and he didn't come home till gone ten.'

Becca made a sudden decision. Jade might not like hearing it, but Becca had to tell her. What were mates for? 'I saw him, your Lewis. Last night down by the arcade. And this morning, near mine. He was with another lad.' She described the lanky teenager.

'It'll be that Zak – he's an evil git. He goes to the same school. He's older than Lewis, and Lewis thinks

116

the sun shines out of his arse.' Her gaze was suddenly hard. 'Why didn't you say before?'

'I did. Just now. As soon as I saw you.'

Jade's sudden anger faded. 'Yeah, I know. You haven't got kids, more luck you. I'm just . . . I'm telling you, Bex, I don't know what to do with him.'

'I used to wag it all the time,' Becca said. She was going to add, 'And I'm OK,' but that wasn't true, was it? She was trapped here in this dead-end job and she was kidding herself if she really thought she was using her time to make any decisions about her life. She was just . . . a bagger who couldn't be a chooser.

The thought came unbidden: *Where is Andy?*

Jade was trapped too. She had to work to take care of her children: if she worked, she wasn't at home when they needed her. If she left her job and the benefits people decided she hadn't had a good reason, they'd sanction her and she could lose her home. Becca didn't know what to say, and Jade left her alone not long after.

Thinking about Jade made Becca forget her own problems for a while, but by the afternoon, she was back at the bottom of the ladder again. She couldn't stop herself from checking her phone to see if there was another message from Andy, but there was nothing.

She sent him a text anyway: *See you tonight?* and then hated herself for doing it.

After lunch – she only got only fifteen minutes because shitface Bryan made her make up the time she had come in late – she was on shelf stacking. She spent all afternoon kneeling on the floor trying to fill the shelves while people shopped around her. And she was supposed to keep an eye on the tills so she could help out if it got busy.

Her back was hurting, her arms were aching and she was fed up. She stretched briefly then kneeled again in front of the low shelves while shoppers pushed past her, shoving her trolley out of the way, shuffling through the shelf contents disordering what she had just straightened.

She checked her phone for about the tenth time, but there was nothing. Maybe Andy wasn't in trouble at all. Maybe he was just a creep, with his *Great, A x*. And she'd sent a pathetic text about seeing him tonight when he was probably busy telling some other moron about being a private detective and all that shit.

So what if he did come into the pub tonight? She'd show him she wasn't bothered. She'd just be like, 'Hi,' and get on with her job and show him he didn't matter.

She looked at her phone again. Nothing. No messages, and it was only four and her shift didn't finish until six. Two more hours.

Fucking shit. Fucking Andy. Fucking arsehole moron Bryan, fucking waste of space.

The light in the supermarket was flat and dull. It made her eyes feel sore. She stood up again and eased the aching muscles in her back.

And then she saw it. The newspaper stand was in front of her, and the late edition of the local paper, the *Hull Daily Mail*, had just been delivered.

Andy's face looked right at her.

Without even thinking about it, she grabbed the paper off the stand. Andy was smiling in the photo, the way he smiled at her when he came up to the bar, as if she was the only person he really wanted to see.

But the headline . . . SUNK ISLAND BODY IDENTIFIED AS BRIDLINGTON MAN.

It was like someone had kicked her in the stomach.

It couldn't be Andy . . . He wasn't . . . The photo . . .

But it was. It was Andy. Her eyes skimmed the article and fixed on the words *knife attack*. She felt cold and weak, as if her legs wouldn't hold her.

He hadn't been at the pub this week because—

'Becca!' She blinked and came back to the present, suddenly aware of a bell ringing. The paper dropped out of her hands and onto the floor where a passing shopper wheeled her trolley over it. Bryan was shouting across the shop. 'That's the second time I've called you. You're wanted on the tills. And you can pay for that paper. This isn't a lending library.'

She couldn't speak. She just stared at him blankly. *Tills?*

'You're not paid to stand there and read the papers. Didn't you hear the buzzer? You're wanted on Lane 2. *Now*, if you don't mind.'

'Yeah . . . yeah. OK. I'm . . .' But he'd turned his back on her and walked away. She stared after him blankly. But Andy was . . . Didn't he realise that Andy . . . ?

In a daze, she shoved the paper out of the way with her foot and moved towards the front of the shop, dimly aware of people looking at her.

Andy with his daft jokes and texts, Andy, dancing with her, Andy, sitting in his car giving her that smile, *of course I do . . .*

Knife attack. Andy was dead. Someone had killed him. The memories came hard and fast. *Into trouble. With the kind of people . . .*

She went to the till and tried to key in her security number, but her eyes were filling with tears and she couldn't see properly. Her fingers kept fumbling and she entered the numbers wrong. The queue was massive and people started streaming to her from the backs of the other queues which caused more muttering from the waiting shoppers. She mustn't cry. She mustn't let them see her cry.

The people in the queue shifted restlessly.

'Buck your ideas up. You should have been here five minutes ago.' Sheryl, at the next till, was an assistant like Becca, but because she was older, she seemed to think she was in charge. Becca found her anger again. It was better than this horrible, dragging hurt inside her. 'Oh, fuck off,' she muttered.

'What did you say?' Sheryl snapped.

'You heard me.'

'I'm going to report—' Sheryl started.

Becca glared at her and Sheryl shut her mouth, turning away to smile at the woman she was serving. 'Sorry about that,' she said.

The monotony of putting people's shopping through the scanner calmed Becca down. Gradually her hands stopped shaking and slowly the queue diminished. She focused on her job, not letting her thoughts move away from what she was doing.

Don't let them see you cry.

Eventually, she was even able to produce a thin smile when the customer she was serving said, 'Good afternoon.'

She looked up. It was the old man who came to shop once a week. He always bought the same things: a sliced loaf – from the reduced shelf if there was one there – a litre of milk, a small box of economy tea bags, some own-brand cereal, seven tins of cat food, seven small tins of baked beans and seven small tins of rice pudding. He wore a flat cap and an old parka that was about two sizes too big for him. He walked slowly with a stick, stopping frequently to catch his breath.

She put his shopping through the till and helped him to pack it into the small rucksack he always carried. 'How's . . .' she racked her brains, trying to remember his cat's name.

'Muffitt? She's doing nicely, thank you. How about you? Are you all right, love? Only you seem a bit down in the mouth.'

She looked up into his anxious frown and decided he wasn't being nosy; he was concerned about her. 'I'm OK, thanks.' She managed another smile. 'Bit tired, you know?'

'Well, I hope it's because you've been having fun. Young people should have fun. You take care of yourself now.'

She kept her hand on his bag. 'Listen, you know about cats, don't you? What should I feed to a stray kitten, you know, a tiny one?'

'Does it not have its mother?'

'I don't think so. It's, you know, wild.'

'And you can't catch it?'

'Not yet.'

He looked sad. 'Poor little thing. It may not survive, you know that?' Becca nodded. 'Give it kitten food – you can get the little biscuits – and dissolve them in a bit of water.'

'Not milk?'

'Milk might upset its stomach. Keep an eye on it. And try to make sure it has a place to go where it can keep warm and dry.'

'OK,' she said.

He smiled at her. 'It's good there are people like you who care.'

'Becca, you aren't here to talk to your friends. We've still got a queue.' Sheryl's voice cut sharply through their conversation.

The old man turned on her. 'This young lady is looking after me. It's called customer service and if more people thought about it, this would be a better place to shop. You don't listen to her, love, and I hope your kitten makes it,' he added to Becca as he hitched on his pack and made his slow progress to the door.

The exchange got Becca through the rest of the afternoon. Each time she saw Sheryl's scowl, she thought about the old man telling Sheryl off, and it pushed away what she had seen in the paper.

It was as if there were two people in her head. One was still staring at the headline, not believing it, not wanting to believe it. The other was frightened – frightened of the pig, the creep who'd come talking to her about Andy, as if he knew about her, knew about the lame jokes and the chats and more.

And he'd said that Andy might be in trouble . . . *got into trouble. With the kind of people you really don't want to get on the wrong side of, if you get me.*

He'd been right. Andy had been in the worst kind of trouble there was, and Becca had done nothing.

She found she was shivering as she stood outside the shop, grabbing a quick ciggie in her break. The smoke made her stomach feel acid, and a wave of sickness washed over her. She nipped the cigarette out and stowed it back in the packet.

Fumbling in her pocket, she pulled out her phone. She unlocked it and the local news appeared on the screen. She stared at it blankly as the story of Andy's death scrolled past, once, twice, SUNK ISLAND KNIFE ATTACK . . . The third time, she almost tapped it, then stopped. Andy was gone. She didn't want to know any more.

Instead, she scrolled down to Kay's number. But what would be the point of telling Kay about Andy, about the rest of it? What could Kay do? Oh, she'd listen and she'd say things that might make Becca feel better, but she couldn't tell Becca what to do. She wouldn't know.

Anyway, Kay was busy. She was moving and she had a job working with some bunch of losers so Becca shouldn't be bothering her now.

Jade? Jade had her own problems with Lewis.

There was no one to tell.

Andy must have been in trouble, and the pig creep had been looking for him in the pub with his *Do you work every night*, and all that shit.

Would Andy be OK now if she had told the pig creep what she knew? What *did* she know that he wouldn't? They'd know who Andy worked for and what he was doing. But they wouldn't know about the stuff in the cellar.

She took out her phone and went back over her texts. There weren't many – she'd deleted most of them, but she'd kept the ones where he'd asked her out. She read through the exchange again:

Good want to do something later? Go to a club?
Yeah
Wait for you xxx

He'd sent some really nice ones, after. She'd kept those too, and then this one:

Sorry sorry sorry got 2 go away work ☹ *back on Friday miss you xxx*

But after that, it was like he was another person, all the texts were about the bags she'd seen Carl with, and could she get into the cupboard and all that sort of stuff.

She didn't know what she'd wanted him to send, just something that showed she was his girlfriend, something daft, something Andy.

But there'd been nothing. It was like he was saying, 'Get me the information or it's all over.'

And now it was.

Andy was dead and someone had killed him.

Chapter 15

Sunk Island

When the alarm went, Kay could barely peel herself off the pillow. Her eyes were sore, her body felt stiff and achy and all she wanted to do was snuggle down under the covers and go back to sleep.

Milo, sensing her movement, leaped up on the bed and started pushing his nose into her face. The broken night didn't seem to be bothering him.

Grumpily, she got up and went downstairs. What had happened last night? Rain falling from the gutter had made her think there was someone walking round out there. That's what had woken her up.

Except . . .

As she put the kettle on and opened a packet of Weetabix, this comforting explanation became less and less convincing. Yes, there had been rain falling from the gutter, but that was outside the kitchen door, at the back of the house. Something had woken her up in her bedroom, which was at the front of the house.

126

A bike. Or a car. Or . . .

Catherine Ford's voice spoke in her head. *You'll be on your own. At night.*

Yes. OK. But she wasn't some hysterical teenager getting spooked by strange sounds after dark. She was an adult woman and she needed to deal with this like an adult. She poured boiling water over the teabag in her cup and added milk, then set off to take a look round the house.

There was no evidence of a break-in anywhere, though the events were clearer in her head now. She'd heard – no, she'd *thought* she'd heard – the sound of a door closing quietly. That could have been anything – sounds were deceptive at night.

The door under the stairs had been open. She could remember catching her dressing gown on it. But she could remember closing it before she went to bed.

Or could she?

It was closed now. She opened it and tried the door in the wall that led into the fuel store. That was locked tight.

Her waterproof was hanging up by the door. She pulled it on over her dressing gown and slipped her feet into her wellies, which she'd left in the porch. They felt cold and clammy against her bare skin.

As soon as she opened the front door, Milo came racing through and was past her and into the garden, his tail wagging wildly as he explored all the scents laid down overnight.

Kay made her way along the path, looking at the muddy ground. It was a bit churned up, but she couldn't remember how it had been yesterday. She couldn't identify anything that looked like a footprint.

Milo galloped across to her side, shook himself enthusiastically, then streaked away again. Well, at least he was happy. She followed the path round the side of the house, but there was nothing to see. The door to the fuel store was shut tight and padlocked, which reminded her she needed to get hold of that key.

A quick check round the back where the kitchen offshot was located gave her no more information. Despite the rain, the ground was too firm to take any impressions. She looked at the gutter – the remains of a buddleia sprouted up from it. Something else for the estate agent to fix.

There was no help here. No obvious indication of an intruder, but nothing to say there hadn't been one, either. Milo came bounding over again, his tail wagging. Then he stopped, and his nose went to the ground. He was intent.

As Kay watched, he followed the trail he had found to the door of the fuel store, where he scratched at the wood a couple of times, then looked at her impatiently.

'I can't let you in,' she said. 'I don't have a key.'

What was it he'd found? She'd walked up to that door yesterday, but Milo didn't get excited about her smell – she was part of the pack. Oliver had . . . no, he hadn't come round here. He'd shown her the store from the inside of the house.

She called Milo, who came away reluctantly. It could just be foxes or rats or whatever wildlife inhabited Sunk Island, but the trail led to the door and stopped there.

Or had gone through.

She let herself back into the house, Milo snuffling along beside her.

He stiffened immediately upon entering, and she heard the start of a growl in his throat. His hackles were raised. She stood there quietly watching him. He'd picked up a scent just outside the door under the stairs. She opened it, and he pushed past her, his nose glued to the ground, then to the door that led into the fuel store. He scratched it, looked at her, and scratched it again.

She reached over and unlocked it, switching on the overhead light. The tube flickered and kept on flickering.

Milo changed from a sleekly flowing dog to a jerky figure from a cheap stop-motion animation in the strobing light. He clamped his nose to the floor and started sniffing, moving forward, focused and intent. Then he got to the trapdoor, where he stopped and backed off, shaking his head and sneezing.

Kay sniffed the air. That smell of incontinence, of urine-soaked sheets or clothing, still hung in the air.

Milo had picked up the smell again and was following it intently, until he reached the outside door where he whined again and started scratching, wagging his tail, looking back at her eagerly.

Let me through. Let me through.

Kay felt something cold touch her as she thought about last night, in the kitchen, staring at the back door, listening to footsteps coming closer and closer.

If she was reading Milo right, there was a scent of someone he didn't know, coming up to the outside door of the fuel store, coming inside and through the door into the hall. She remembered the sound of a door, closing. The sound that might have woken her.

She went back to the cupboard under the stairs and checked it thoroughly. It was exactly as she remembered it: empty apart from a couple of brooms and a bag on one of the hooks which contained dusters and cleaning rags. There was nothing there and nothing looked disturbed.

Frowning, she went back into the fuel store and looked round there.

That was when she realised something was wrong.

The bags that had lined up against the wall – surely there had been more of them yesterday. She checked – yellow bags with a picture of a blazing fire, bags of fuel. But yesterday, there had been bags of compost as well.

Hadn't there?

If there had been, they'd gone.

Chapter 16

Bridlington

DC Dinah Mason took a seat in the room that was rapidly filling up as the team investigating the murder of DC Andy Yeatson, their colleague, assembled for the first time. She'd been anticipating her involvement in a serious case ever since she'd got her transfer to CID a few months ago now. *Be careful what you wish for.* She hadn't wanted this case. None of them did, not a murder where the victim was one of their own, her colleague, a man she'd liked and respected.

She'd worked with Andy Yeatson immediately after her transfer, as part of a small team led by DS Mark Curwen, getting the drug dealers off Bridlington's streets. She'd liked Andy – he'd helped her and hadn't treated her like the rookie she was. Curwen she wasn't so sure about.

'Good morning, everyone.' A voice interrupted her thoughts, making her jump. It was DCI Hammond, who was the Senior Investigating Officer on the case. Dinah sat upright and grabbed her pen.

The seats were arranged in a horseshoe shape. Hammond took his place at the front of the room. There was a laptop on the desk, and a screen behind him showing an image of Andy as Dinah remembered him; young, bearded, smiling. 'Right. We need to get started.'

Hammond was a tall man, his fair hair going a bit thin on top. His glasses caught the light from time to time, masking his eyes. 'A lot of you knew the deceased, Andy Yeatson, and we all have strong feelings about this case. That's fine, but let's use those feelings to make this investigation as professional as possible. No short cuts, no acting on unsupported hunches, just good, thorough detective work. Right. Let's get started. Here's what we know.'

Slowly, in detail, the story of Andy's death began to unroll. A map replaced Andy's face on the screen, showing the coast, and the vast expanse of the Humber Estuary. A blue line ran straight down the map to a small outcropping by the water. It switched again to satellite view, and now they could all see a small area of land, flat and green with areas of marsh to either side. The blue line had become a narrow trench filled with dull, brown water. A scene of crime officer talked them through it, using a pointer to identify the important locations.

'This area, Sunk Island, is very isolated. There are a few farms and a small number of houses. No pubs, no cafés, no shops, no schools. This drain –' the pointer moved slightly – 'Spragger Drain, empties into the estuary here via a tidal sluice. There's a raised path along the banks, and this bit –' he pointed to a small outcrop – 'is hardstanding. The drain cuts through it, protected by a fence. Spragger Drain sluice. The sluice gate is tidal – the tide comes in, it closes, the tide goes out, it opens. It works by water pressure, no one monitors it and no one lives close by.'

He explained that Andy's body had been dumped in the drain. The post-mortem suggested that Andy had died the night he vanished, but heavy rain had kept walkers and anglers away from the already deserted place, so he wasn't found until yesterday morning. The rain had washed away most of the evidence.

The crime scene photographs appeared on the screen. Dinah felt a frisson round the room, heard a faint murmur. People had been impassive, maybe sad before. Now she saw anger.

She felt it too, a sense of outrage that someone had done this to her colleague – her friend.

The pictures had been taken by the water's edge in a dull, dreary light. The first one showed a hardstanding of cracked concrete where a wire barrier, damaged and hanging loose, protected a deep culvert, and the drop into the estuary itself.

The next photograph was down into the culvert, where something was caught on the rotting timbers. It looked like discarded rags, but a glimmer of white became a face in the next image. This one was hard to look at, because it was clearly Andy, but the eyes were flattened, the features had slipped, just a little, robbing it of its humanity. The mouth gaped, the head lolled back, as if it was no longer fully attached to the body.

The next photograph showed Andy lying on the hardstanding. His face was an unclear white blur, but they could all see the wound where his throat had been cut across. Dinah felt her mouth fill with saliva, and made herself swallow, and swallow again. She could feel pressure in her sinuses and behind her eyes, and started scribbling random notes in her book so she could keep her face concealed.

She wasn't the only one fighting to suppress her emotions.

Hammond was speaking now, his tone austere. 'It's pretty clear he wasn't meant to be found. They put him in the drain and he should have been swept out into the estuary. Some bodies wash up, but not all. We got lucky, though. His clothes got caught on the timbers and kept his head above the water, which is why it wasn't battered to pieces. We got an identification straight away, but this is the only break we've had so far.

'Sir,' one of the DCs spoke up, 'the pathology report says a wound to his chest, but it looks like his neck . . .'

'Yes. The chest wound was fatal. Whoever cut his throat did it post-mortem.'

There was silence round the room. They'd killed Andy, stuck a knife in his chest, then one of them had used the knife again, practically decapitating him. And then they had dumped him in a drain.

Dinah could feel the same determination that was building up in her growing in the room. Andy's death had been brutal. They were going to get the people who had done this.

'Several things we don't know, and we need to know,' Hammond said, taking over. 'Was he killed because he was a copper, or was he killed because he was Andy Yeatson? What was he doing that night? How did he get from Brid, where he was last seen, to Sunk Island? What do we actually know about Andy's movements that night? Karen?'

DI Karen Innes, went to the laptop, and a map of Bridlington appeared on the screen. 'On Tuesday night, Andy Yeatson was on the evening shift. According to DS Mark Curwen, he was supposed to be completing his reports for the drugs operation that had been running through the summer until recently. Instead, he went out at nineteen twenty. At nineteen thirty-five, his car was picked up on CCTV just outside the centre, heading up this road. It was found parked on this side street, about five hours after he had been reported missing.' Dinah knew the street – a nondescript, run-down place with a small amusements centre, a local supermarket and a hand car wash.

'So we don't know where he went after that?' someone asked.

'No. He called his babysitter at . . .' Innes checked her notes. 'Nineteen fifty. He usually called around that time to check everything was OK. He told her he'd be back at the usual time. She thought he was outside when he called – it was quite windy that night, if you remember, and she couldn't hear him properly.'

Dinah wrote *windy* in her notebook, then crossed it out. *Focus*, she told herself.

'Now, this is interesting,' Innes continued. 'She heard someone shout, and Andy said something like, *Oh, hang on*. And then she thought he was talking to someone but she couldn't catch what he was saying because the phone was muffled. Then he came back to her and said, *Got to go. See you later.*'

'How did he sound?'

'Fine, according to her. Like he'd met someone he knew.' Innes zoomed in on the map, showing the side street where Andy had parked. It led back into town, towards the harbour. 'If, as we think, he left his car and started walking, he didn't go back to the main road – he'd have been picked up again on this camera, here. It looks as though he was heading this way.' Her finger traced the route in the other direction, towards the harbour. 'He should have been caught by one of the cameras around the area, but he wasn't. The camera on the main road is the last sighting.

Dinah tried to picture it in her mind. Andy on the phone. Someone calls to him. So – other side of the road? Going past in a car . . . She put her hand up and Innes nodded in her direction. 'Did the babysitter hear a car?' She saw Hammond nod in approval and gave herself a pat on the back before she remembered this was Andy's killer they were looking for.

'She didn't hear one, but it's a possibility. We're going to have to check all the cameras in the area.'

Dinah had a bad feeling that she had just been assigned her role in the investigation, and her heart sank. Checking the cameras was vital work, but tedious and routine.

Hammond spoke again. 'DS Sykes. Dave. The info on Andy's phone might help here.'

Dave Sykes stayed in his seat and addressed the crowded room composedly. He was one of the faces familiar to Dinah, an older man who had worked as a DS for years. Dinah had heard the SIOs liked to have him on their teams because he knew what he was doing, and was thorough and reliable. 'OK. The call DI Innes has just been talking about – Yeatson phoning home to talk to the babysitter – that's the last call we have. The babysitter expected him to call again around twenty-two hundred to say when he'd be back, but he didn't. That was unusual. She said it had never happened before. There's been no other activity on his phone since then. However, we've got a handshake from the tower here as his phone logged in.' He used a laser pointer to indicate a location on the map. 'Hornsea.'

There was a murmur around the room. The signal simply meant the phone was updating its location for the network, but it also confirmed that Andy had left Bridlington and was travelling south via the meandering B-road that linked the coastal villages. 'Have we found his phone?' Hammond asked.

Dave Sykes shook his head. 'The Hornsea signal is the last thing his phone sent. Nothing after that, and a search down by the estuary didn't turn anything up. It probably went in the water.'

'What about his car?' Hammond asked.

'The SOCOs have turned it inside out. There's nothing you wouldn't expect. They're still chasing up one or two things, but from what we can see, Andy left the car, and whatever happened, happened away from it.'

'OK. Let's sum up.' Hammond let his gaze travel round the room. 'Remember, a lot of this is best fit from what we know so far. Don't dismiss anything just because it doesn't agree with this scenario. It looks as though Andy Yeatson left the station – we don't know why, and we need to find out – towards the start of his shift. We have his car caught on CCTV, turning off Station Road and again on the main road here. We know he parked on a side street near the café arcade here, left his car and, as far as we can tell, started walking towards the harbour area. Any questions so far?'

No one said anything. 'He calls the babysitter as expected, he tells her he'll be home as usual, then the call is cut a bit short because he met someone – maybe someone he knew. After that, we lose all trace of him. We need to find out who that was.'

Hammond pressed a key on the laptop, and the image changed once again to the map, scrolling down and down. The roads and villages vanished until all that was left was a flat green emptiness, criss-crossed by straight blue lines. 'That's all we have. It isn't much to go on.' His gaze travelled slowly round the assembled team. 'I'm hoping you can change that over the next twenty-four hours. Right. We'll need a couple of you down on Sunk Island doing interviews. DC Mason – I want you to trace the cars travelling south from Brid. I want details of all the vehicles on that road that goes via Hornsea, and I want to know who went onto Sunk Island that night.'

'Yes, sir.' It was what she'd expected, but still ... Something had occurred to her. 'Sir, I was just thinking ...'

'It's what we pay you to do, Dinah.'

Dinah felt her face go warm, and cursed her tendency to blush easily. 'That pub near the harbour. The Smokehouse. Andy – DC Yeatson – spent a lot of time there on the operation to shut down the dealers. I just ...' She was going to say 'thought' again. '*wondered* if there might be any link.'

They all knew about the abortive raid on the pub. Dinah suspected most of the people in the room had some sympathy for Curwen. They all saw cases where they knew what was going on but couldn't get their hands on the evidence to take things further.

'That's a good thought, Dinah,' Hammond said. It didn't sound patronising, or not *too* patronising, anyway. 'At the moment, we have no evidence to show that he's been near the pub since the raid. His work logs have him round the harbour area, but not in the pub. If he went there, the CCTV will have picked it up. We can't rule it out, but we follow up the leads we've got first. For you, that's finding who went to Sunk Island that night.'

She couldn't argue. It made sense.

The briefing wound up. Dinah headed for her desk to begin the important but dull work of tracking down the cars that had been on the roads that night. She had been learning a lot during her brief time on auto-theft. The activity on the roads was recorded far more than most people realised; CCTV, ANPR cameras, bus cameras, dashcams. What she had to do was identify the car that had taken Andy south, out of all the cars that had been driving round the area that night. It was needles and haystacks territory. She had a lot to do.

'DC Mason!' It was Mark Curwen. He looked as if he hadn't slept, and his normally clean-shaven face was shadowed with stubble.

'Sir?'

'A word. Come with me.'

To Dinah's surprise, he didn't lead the way to the office but to the back entrance that led to the car park, and headed for his car. As he opened the passenger door to let her in, she protested. 'I haven't got time to go anywhere, I'm supposed to be—'

'Checking the cars in Brid the night Andy vanished. I know. I can give you some short cuts, but I need you to listen to me. Sorry about the cloak and dagger stuff,' he said, offering her a cigarette. She shook her head. 'Tell me about the briefing. Are they getting anywhere?'

He and Andy had been friends as well as colleagues. They'd gone to the pub together after work, they'd spent a lot of time discussing the drugs operation in a way that had excluded her. There was no reason not to tell him what was going on. She ran through what Hammond had told them, the paucity of evidence, and the directions the investigation was going.

He grimaced. 'Hammond's not the sharpest tool in the box, if I'm being honest. And he's got bugger all to work with. Listen, Dinah. I'm going to trust you to keep this quiet, for the moment, OK?'

She didn't like this at all. 'If it's to do with the investigation, I can't promise that.'

'There's more to it than you realise. Have they found his phone?'

She shook her head. 'Not yet. Hammond thinks it probably went in the water.'

'But they're still looking?'

'Yes.'

'OK. Listen. I'm pretty sure Andy was following something up, something he wasn't telling me about. I think he may have got hold of a lead to the people bringing the stuff in.'

'What makes you think that?'

'The pub. The Smokehouse. Andy knew as well as I did that there's something dodgy going on in there. I think he had his own private operation on the go. I think he was investigating the pub, and I think he found something.'

'So why didn't he tell you?'

'Straight after that fuck-up of a raid? He's going to come to me and say, *Guess what I've been doing*? He'd need something concrete, and he didn't have it.'

'We should tell Hammond.'

'Don't you see? Andy's carrying out an unofficial investigation into drug dealing, but whatever he found – it's gone. Hammond didn't find anything related to that, did he? You know how Andy was placed. He was a single dad – you know about his wife?'

Dinah nodded. He'd told her once, when they were sitting in the car late one evening towards the end of their shift, eating bacon rolls from the van on the seafront. His wife, Mel, had been diagnosed with cancer during her pregnancy. She'd refused treatment until after their daughter, Mia, was born and had died before Mia was six months old. *Mel and Mia*, Andy had said. He'd smiled. *She liked that.*

'So, times were tough. He had a mortgage, he had childcare to pay for and all the rest of the shit you get when you've got a kid. What's to show he was one of the good guys? Whatever he was doing, you can flip it – Andy was carrying out illegal contacts with drug dealers – he goes to places he shouldn't, meets people we don't know about, ends up getting killed. Live by the sword, die by the sword, you know?'

The idea that Andy could be have been bent silenced Dinah for a few seconds. 'That's . . . You don't think that?' It was more an accusation than a question.

'I *know* he wasn't dodgy. It's a set-up. They get rid of someone who's getting too close, we dismiss him as yet another bent cop. Before I say anything, I want evidence that shows Andy was set-up. If it's anywhere, it will be in that pub, and I can't go in there. Apart from anything else, the landlord knows me. He'd kick me out and put in the kind of complaint that would have me counting cars for the rest of my life.'

Now she knew what he was asking. 'You want me to have a look?'

'I told you. I can't go in there. You're a stranger.'

'How do I explain it if I get caught?' She'd be in trouble, she knew that.

'Go in when you're off duty. You're allowed to drink where you want to.'

As if she'd choose a dive like the Smokehouse. 'But what do I look for? I can't just walk in and start asking questions.'

'Two things. Take a look at the place. If you see anything that we can use to go after Carl Lavery, the bloke who owns it – anything at all – tell me. Second, Andy had a contact in there – the barmaid, Becca Armitage. Try and talk to her.'

'But if she was Andy's informant, then Hammond can follow up.' She didn't want to do this. She really didn't. Something felt off.

'She wasn't, or not officially. She just gave him a few bits and pieces. I think she had a bit of a thing for him.'

Dinah stared out of the car window into the fading light. This story of unofficial investigations had shaken her. What had Andy been thinking of? What had he known that had made him do this? Curwen was hinting it could lead to accusations of corruption. If that was the case, the outcome could be severe. The least of it was a tainting of his reputation, something his family – including Mia as she grew up – would have to live with. His daughter could even lose the pension she'd get for an officer killed in the line of duty, because if Andy had been on the take, then he didn't die in the line of duty. She wrestled with it, then made up her mind. Andy had been one of the good guys, she was sure of that. He'd never have done something that might have harmed Mia.

'OK. I'll take a look, but if I find anything, I'm taking it straight to Hammond.'

'Sure. Just let me know as well. When will you go?'

She might as well get over with. 'Tonight. I'll go in tonight.'

She felt, rather than saw, Curwen relax beside her. 'Thanks, Dinah,' he said. 'And let me know if his phone turns up. There could be something on that.'

Ten minutes later, she was heading back towards her desk with some useful tips from Curwen about making her searches easier, but her mind was focused on what he had just told her about Andy. If he was right, this could add a whole new layer to the investigation – could break it wide open.

She had to tell Hammond, but she'd do what Curwen had asked her first.

Chapter 17

The day at the supermarket had dragged on and on. Becca had moved through it – from till to stockroom to shelves – like a zombie. She couldn't stop herself from thinking, so she forced her mind onto the routine – making lists in her head of things she needed to do, counting the steps from one end of the store to the other.

She wanted to go home. She wanted to fall asleep and not wake up again for a hundred years, like that lame movie about fairy godmothers and shit like that.

Andy. *In trouble, with the kind of people—*

Stop!

Thirty-five steps from one side of the stockroom to the other. Seventy from the stockroom to the till . . .

What kind of people? Why had he been so cold in his texts while he was away?

Five from the first till to the next . . .

She was going crazy. The last thing she wanted to do was go to the pub, because there it would be even worse: the pub was Andy's place, the place where she always saw him and the place where they would text and chat. She didn't want to make nice with the punters, she didn't want to talk to the pig creep copper if he came in again, she didn't want to listen to Toby making excuses so he could go and play on the games machines.

She didn't want to be anywhere.

But that was the thing about being broke. It took all your choices away.

Shitface Bryan kept her late at the shop, pretending the shelves weren't right and the stock was in the wrong places, so she didn't have time to go back and feed the kitten, or to get anything to eat herself. She stopped on the way to buy a tray of chips, but they were pale and flabby, tasting of cheap cooking oil, and after a couple of mouthfuls, they made her feel sick. She was supposed to be behind the bar at seven thirty. She got to the pub with minutes to spare.

Russ was in his place by the door, Champ sitting like a statue beside him. Where did they go when they weren't here? She never saw them around Brid during the day.

She wanted to talk to him, to ask him about Andy. Russ was the only one who knew she and Andy had gone out that time – he'd seen them leaving together that Saturday night. If she closed her eyes, it was like she was back there, both of them laughing about something daft that had happened, Andy holding her hand, lightly.

But that was then. Now was what mattered.

Andy had asked for her help, and she hadn't given it to him. In the end, she'd let him down, so she had to make up for that. Now, even though it was too late, she had to help him.

Russ must see just about everything that went on. 'Hi,' she said as she came towards him. Russ didn't respond, but Champ turned his big head and stared at her. 'Can I stroke him?' she said, reaching her hand out. Russ didn't like people messing with his dog.

He nodded, a quick, single jerk of his chin. It was soothing to run her hand over the huge head, feeling the smooth hair under her fingers. Champ stayed motionless, looking as though he was suffering her touch rather than enjoying it. She wanted to offer him the remains of her chips, but she knew better than to do that. One time, she'd offered him a crisp from a bag she was eating, but he hadn't taken it, not until Russ had said, 'OK,' in a sharp sort of voice. 'I don't like people feeding him,' he'd said to Becca, so she hadn't done it again.

Time was getting on. 'Did you hear . . .' she began, unsure what she was going to say. Russ didn't appear to notice she'd said anything but she had the feeling he was listening. She tried again. 'Did you hear about Andy? You know, Andy who used to come in here?' Her voice was getting more uncertain as Russ didn't respond. 'Only, I read in the paper, today. He got . . .' She couldn't say it. 'You know.'

'Yeah. I heard.' His voice was indifferent. It was hard to go on, but she had to.

147

'I don't get it. I want to know what happened. He was . . . we were like . . . he was a mate.' Why should Russ care about Andy? Or her? Why should he know anything about it?

Russ laughed. She'd never heard him laugh before. 'Is that what you call it?'

She felt her face flush, and lifted her chin. 'Yeah. And I want to know what happened to him.'

'Why would I know, sweetheart?'

'Don't you?' *And don't call me sweetheart!*

His eyes narrowed as studied her. 'You really want to know what I think?'

'I asked you, didn't I?'

'Keep out of it.'

She looked at him in surprise. 'What do you mean?'

He got slowly to his feet. Standing, he towered above her. 'You asked what I think. I'm telling you. Keep out of it. What part of that don't you understand? If you know what's good for you, forget it.'

Before she could reply, he'd chucked his sleeping bag into the alcove and walked away, Champ following closely behind.

Chapter 18

Dinah was true to her word, and after her shift ended at six, she pulled on her coat and walked along Quay Road towards the seafront. There was no point in taking her car – there'd be nowhere to park.

It was one of her favourite parts of Brid – a wide road lined with old red-brick buildings, white stucco, trees and some green spaces. Bridlington was a real traditional old seaside town. Her work sometimes made her forget what an attractive place it could be.

The walk to the narrow side street where the Smokehouse stood only took her twenty minutes. She hesitated outside for a minute, trying to decide what she was going to do.

A homeless man was sitting in the alcove by the door, the inevitable dog – a huge one – sitting stoically beside him. She hesitated, and the dog's head moved towards her, its stare blank and fixed. Neither dog nor man moved as she went past them into the pub, wondering what it was about them that had unnerved her.

As she came through the door, she went straight to the bar. Her first aim was to make contact with the woman Curwen had mentioned, but the only person behind the bar was a tall, skinny guy with 'geek' written all over him. He barely made eye contact as she ordered her drink.

'Corona, please,' she said.

''kay.'

He popped the cap and pushed the bottle across the bar, no lime in the neck, and no offer of a glass, not that she wanted one. 'Nice evening,' she tried, but he'd already turned away to serve another customer. It wasn't a nice evening anyway; it was cold and dank. She'd really let the homeless guy spook her.

She looked round the room. It was large and low-ceilinged. The light was dim, the tables and chairs looked old and battered. The carpet just ahead of her had been repaired with what looked like gaffer tape. There was a bank of three gaming machines against the far wall with a group of people standing round one of them. The table by the machines would give her a good view of the room, and the bar.

She went across and sat down. The pub was middling busy. The group around the machine was quite rowdy. They were watching someone play, shouting advice and laughing as it whirled and jangled and paid out nothing.

A tall man with a tanned face and long, curly hair seemed to be the focus of the group. He leaned across to the player once or twice, offering advice, shaking his head when the gambit failed. He had his hand on the shoulder of a fair-haired woman and as Dinah watched, he gestured towards the back of the pub, and the group started to move away. She noticed he was using a stick and walked with a pronounced limp. His hand on the woman's shoulder seemed more practical than proprietorial.

The player stayed at the machine. His friends continued to shout advice across the pub as they settled themselves round a table, but he ignored them. Then another player had arrived and started using one of the other machines. It was the geeky barman who had served her. Dinah glanced towards the bar and saw that his place had been taken by a woman.

This must be Becca Armitage who, according to Curwen, had a crush on Andy and had given him titbits of information. She looked very young, barely old enough to be working in a pub. In the dim light, Dinah thought she looked a bit uncertain – picking things up, putting them down, going to and fro between the beer taps as if she kept forgetting things.

There was a clanking noise as one of the games machines paid out. The group at the back of the room cheered. The winner raised a fist, pocketed his winnings and ambled back towards his friends. It wasn't the barman who had won, Dinah noted. He gave up on his game and started wandering round the pub collecting glasses and wiping tables in a desultory sort of way.

He picked up the bottle in front of her, checked it and saw it wasn't empty and put it back down.

'Bad luck,' Dinah said.

He looked at her. 'What?'

'I said bad luck. On the machines. You didn't win.'

'Oh. Right. Yeah. That one doesn't pay out. It's just a game.'

'So how do you win?'

'It's an old *Space Invaders* game. You just keep shooting and if you keep your score up, you keep on playing. And you get on the high score list.'

Dinah made a face. 'Does anyone care?' She wasn't into retro.

'Yeah. Loads of people.' He glanced at her, and she could see he was really noticing her for the first time.

She was wearing her standard work gear – smart trousers that weren't too tight, a high-necked, long-sleeved top, dark navy, severe. Her fair hair was cut short and the only touch of frivolity was her bright-red glasses. It was a good way of avoiding the male gaze, but this young man seemed to be assessing her with some interest. Contact with him would make contact with the barmaid easier. 'Retro games are not for me.'

'So what do you like?' The pub was filling up, but he seemed in no hurry to go back to work.

'Fortnite. Far Cry.'

'Yeah? You play online?'

'Sometimes.'

'OK. Hey, why don't you—'

'Toby!' The bellow came from the back of the room. Dinah looked up. A scruffy, overweight man was standing behind the bar. This must be Carl Lavery, the man who'd got Curwen into so much trouble. He jerked his thumb towards the queue that had built up while Becca was working on her own.

Toby rolled his eyes at Dinah, and headed back towards the bar. She got up and studied the games machines as she worked out the best way to get into conversation with Becca, once the pub was less busy. She turned over possible opening gambits in her mind. *Who's the lazy sod you're working with?* And suppose he turned out to be her boyfriend? *You look a bit busy.* And hey, look, you're selling beer. A straight approach? *I think you knew my friend, Andy.*

Her gaze stayed on the screen as she thought. The barman hadn't been joking when he'd said that it was an old one – the graphics were crude and the game-play simple. The screen flickered, showing hordes of attacking aliens, and the high scores of recent players, who apparently included Jonathan Creek, Dag Wentim and Deadpool, scrolled down the screen.

She wasn't doing anything useful here. Time to go and make friends with Becca. Something was nagging at her as she went across to the bar, but she couldn't pull it to the front of her mind. She'd just have to wait. It would come to her.

There was a queue waiting to be served, and Becca, as Dinah had observed earlier, seemed to be struggling. Dinah arrived just in time to hear her say, 'Piss

153

off,' to some grinning drinker who'd clearly said something out of order.

She waited until there was a lull, then she went up to the bar and asked for some crisps, noticing that Toby had vanished again.

'What kind?' The young woman didn't even look at her, just half turned to ask her question.

'Plain.' That was always a safe option. They always had that. 'You could do with some help behind there.'

'Yeah.' Becca slid a packet across the counter, took the money and had the change back in almost one movement. She was with the next customer before Dinah could come up with anything else.

The crisps were cheese and onion.

Dinah stayed and watched as Becca muddled up an order for several different types of beer, and managed a weary smile as the men buying joshed her good-naturedly about her mistakes. She looked tired, and, Dinah noticed as she watched her more carefully, a bit red-eyed.

Someone pushed past her with a brief, ''Scuse.' It was Toby, the barman. He loaded a pile of dirty glasses on the bar. 'Oh, hey, it's you. What Fortnite do you play?

'Battle Royale,' she said.

'Cool. I play Creative. We should get together sometime.'

'Yeah. Maybe.' Talking to him reminded her of the names on the Space Invaders machine. 'Who's Dag Wentim? Is he someone who comes in here?'

'Who wants to know?' He was frowning as he looked at her.

'No one. I've heard it before, that's all. It's unusual.'

He grinned. 'It's not a punter. He's a superhero. That's what they do on that machine – superheroes.'

'So who do you play as?'

His grin widened. 'Play me and I'll tell you.'

'OK. Next time. Your . . .' she wasn't sure what word to use. 'Your colleague doesn't look too good. Is she all right?'

He glanced across at the bar. 'Becca? You heard about the guy they found down the coast, you know, got killed?'

'I heard something,' Dinah said cautiously.

'Yeah, well, he was, you know, seeing her.'

'Seeing her?' Dinah cursed herself for the incredulity in her voice. Curwen hadn't said anything about a relationship.

He gave her an odd look. 'Yeah. Did you know him or something?'

Think. Fast. 'I read that he was married,' she said and shrugged. *No big deal.* She racked her brains for a way to continue the conversation, but he'd ducked under the serving hatch and was back behind the bar.

More people came in through the door. There wasn't going to be a quiet time now before closing. She might as well go. She waved at the barman and got a nod in return. If she came back soon, he'd be her best way in, as long as she hadn't blown it. There was no chance of getting into conversation with Becca tonight, but the evening hadn't been a complete waste of time She'd found out more than she'd expected. If Andy had been seeing this Becca woman, then the whole thing became important for the investigation. Despite Curwen's concerns about Andy, Hammond needed to know.

But first, she'd tell Curwen.

Curwen was in the station's local, drinking with a couple of people off Hammond's team, Dave Sykes and Karen Innes, talking about the investigation into Andy's death. 'Are you getting anywhere?'

Sykes shrugged. 'You know how it is at the start – everything's possible so you look at everything. I dunno, it feels like . . .' He frowned, searching for words.

'The boss is doing all the right things,' Innes said sharply.

'Come on, Kaz,' Sykes said. 'It's like his heart isn't in it. He's just going through the motions. That's what it feels like to me.'

'It's a tough case,' Innes said. 'They were lucky. The forensics from the scene turned up nothing. Same with the post-mortem. We'll get there.'

Curwen wasn't here to talk; he was here to listen. He looked across at Innes. Once, in the aftermath of a messy RTA that had involved scraping a couple of joyriders off the tarmac, they'd spent the night together. It was something they both pretended hadn't happened – there was too much rivalry between them to leave space for anything else. In the recent round of promotions, she'd made it to Inspector. Curwen hadn't, courtesy of Carl Lavery. He knew she wasn't unhappy about his fuck-up. 'You reckon?'

'Of course.' But she looked worried. Being involved in what was likely to become a high-profile case could be very good for her career, but if it went wrong, it could stop her in her tracks.

His phone rang. He checked the screen. It was Dinah. Excusing himself, he moved away from the table to take her call. He listened as she told him what the barman had said about Andy and Becca the Barmaid seeing each other.

Shit! He hadn't wanted her to get hold of that straight away. Given B the B's closed-mouth attitude, he'd thought Dinah didn't have a chance. If his role in Andy's operation came out, he was toast. He tried to sound surprised, and didn't bother arguing when she said she was going to take it to Hammond.

He had nothing to argue with.

Instead, he had to move fast. Hammond would almost certainly get someone to interview Becca tomorrow. But what could Becca actually tell them? He felt himself start to relax. Andy had kept quiet about being police; he'd told her he was a private investigator, which meant he wouldn't have told her about Curwen. Becca the Barmaid didn't have the information to hurt him.

But she knew he'd been in the pub. That wasn't good.

He ignored the voice that was telling him his best plan was to go to Hammond, tell him Andy had been a regular in the Smokehouse, and that Andy had been in there asking about drugs. But then his own part in it would come out, and he could sit back and watch as career climbers like Karen Innes disappeared up the promotions pole while he stayed down here at the bottom.

Fuck that.

He had to do this himself.

He checked the time. It was after ten. B the B would still be at the pub. He couldn't risk going in there again, but he could meet her outside and talk to her. With luck, he could defuse the ticking bomb she represented to his prospects. What Sykes and Innes had told him suggested Andy had been heading for the pub that last night, despite his agreement with Curwen. Maybe, just maybe, she knew more about Andy's last night than she'd said, and might be willing to share it with Curwen.

He might still be able to retrieve something from this mess.

Chapter 19

Cursing the rain, Curwen stood on the corner near the entrance to the Smokehouse, waiting for Becca the Barmaid. It was almost closing time. She would be finishing soon. He'd done his homework before tonight, so he knew she'd been working all day as well as all evening. Come to think of it, the rain might help him. It was a foul night, she'd be tired, a lift home would be tempting. And she'd want to know about Andy.

When he'd talked to her before, they'd clashed. This time, he'd present himself as a friend – one who had come to tell her about Andy. According to Dinah Mason, she already knew, which meant he wouldn't have to deal with any messy emotional stuff, but it would make him look good – the copper who cared enough to tell her about her boyfriend.

He'd been waiting for twenty minutes when a small figure emerged from the doorway, hunched against the rain. The streetlight caught her face. Becca. The collar of her jacket was pulled up around her ears, and she was carrying a plastic bag, but no umbrella.

Curwen was standing in the shadows, more or less invisible. She started walking quickly towards where he was waiting. He didn't want to scare her – not yet, anyway – so he stepped out into the light of the street lamp.

She stopped when she saw him and seemed about to turn back, then came on towards him.

'Evening, Becca,' he greeted her. 'Lousy night.'

She stopped abruptly and faced him. 'What do you want?'

'I've got some bad news about your friend, Andy.' He held out the packet of cigarettes, but she shook her head.

'I heard,' she said abruptly.

'Do you want to know what happened?'

She glared at him. 'Not from you.' He kept his gaze on her face, and her defiance faded. 'Yeah.'

'It's too wet to stand around. I'll give you a lift home. We can talk on the way.'

The rain was running down her face and dripping from her hair. 'You can tell me here. I'm not getting in a car with you.'

He sighed. 'Becca, I get that you don't like me. I get that you don't like the police. I don't know why, and I'm not interested, OK?' Not true. He was very interested, but she didn't need to know that. 'Someone killed Andy. I want to get the person who did that. I think you can help.'

A motorbike went past, curving into the pavement and sending up a wave of water that splashed her legs.

She didn't seem to notice, just stood there looking at him.

'We're getting soaked,' he said. 'Let me give you a lift home. Please.'

She chewed her lip, then nodded grudgingly. 'OK.'

Curwen led the way to the harbour car park. He drove an Audi A8 – more car than he could really afford on his salary, but he couldn't resist it. In a town like Brid, a top of the range car could stand out like a sore thumb and the vandals and thieving gits would be lining up to wreck it or twoc it, so he'd chosen a dark colour, and let it get mud-spattered and look uncared for. But the inside was immaculate and the engine was tuned to the last degree. It drove like a dream.

He opened the passenger door, enjoying the expensive smell of leather, and after a brief hesitation, Becca got in.

'Where to?' He had her address already, but he didn't want her to know that. He drove fast along the brightly lit main road, taking care to avoid the speed cameras, then they left the town centre behind them and were back into dark and empty streets. The wet pavements gleamed in the lamplight.

She didn't say anything and he took his cue from her. They drove in silence until they got nearer their destination and Becca started directing him. 'It's here,' she said, indicating a shop front.

It was closed-up and dark. He knew this was the right place, but it looked empty and unwelcoming.

There was the sound of an engine. A motorbike went past – a brief reflection in the mirror, then it was gone.

'Well?'

This was it. He told himself to tread very carefully. 'Becca, I need your help. I need to find out—'

'I thought you were going to tell me about Andy,' she interrupted. 'I'm not a snitch.'

She'd snitched for Andy. Did he have to get into her pants to do this? 'I didn't say you were. I'll tell you what I want to know, and then you can tell me if you can help. How does that sound?'

She sat back slowly. 'Go on.'

It was hardly a ringing endorsement, but at least she was here.

'I'm going to be straight with you, Becca. No bullshit. First off, have the police been in the pub to ask about Andy?'

She rolled her eyes. 'Yeah. You.'

'Apart from me.'

'No. Not yet.'

'I thought so. Now listen to me. Someone stuck a knife into Andy and left him to bleed to death. Miles away from here, down near the estuary. It was murder and it's being investigated, but I think there's something dodgy going on. The team investigating Andy's murder – and that's not me, I'm not involved – should have been in the pub first off, and they haven't been. I'm trying to find out why.'

'How should I know?' She was still tense and wary. Her eyes looked shiny in the street lights. She sat with her head tilted back to stop the tears from falling – trying not to let him see her cry. Well, he'd wanted to shake her up, and he'd succeeded.

'You don't. But you might know something that will help.'

She sat up straighter, her face still averted. 'What kind of thing do you mean?'

'Is there something dodgy going on at the pub? Anything you've seen, any gossip, anything at all. People talk in front of bar staff. What was Andy after?'

He had to get her talking about the holdalls, about the photographs she'd sent. He wanted to persuade her to get the key off Carl Lavery, go down into the cellar, open that cupboard door and take pictures of whatever else Lavery stored in there, apart from ready cash. He needed that evidence. But if he let her know that he and Andy had talked about it – that Andy was a copper – she'd clam up.

'There's nothing dodgy. It's just a pub.' But her voice lacked conviction. He had a feeling she was keeping quiet in an effort to protect Andy, somehow, even though it was too late. He had to break through that.

'Does the name "Stoner" mean anything to you? Or the name "Doc"?' He was watching her closely to check her reaction. As far as he could tell, there was no glimmer of recognition. She shook her head.

'OK. Thanks. I'd like to say that helps, but it doesn't, not really. Not your fault,' he added quickly, seeing her mouth open to protest. 'You saw what you saw.' He assembled his next words carefully. This was what he was here for. 'You might still be able to do something – about what happened to Andy. I told you I was being straight with you. Andy managed to get himself mixed up with a drugs gang.'

Her reaction was immediate, and hostile. 'He didn't do drugs. '

'No, he wasn't a user. I don't think he meant to get into trouble – but he did. He got on the wrong side of someone – and they stuck a knife in him. Becca, I can't go in there myself asking questions. They know I'm a copper, they won't talk to me.' And Lavery would chuck him out on his arse if he tried. 'But they'll talk to you. Something made them think Andy was on to them. I don't know what it was. If I could find that out, it will point to the people who did it. Do you have any idea?'

He saw her glance at him and then look away. *Come on. Admit what you were doing.*

'I'm not a snitch,' she said again, meaning, he was pretty sure, that she wasn't going to snitch on Andy.

'I know.' He waited, but she didn't say anything else, so he upped the pressure. Maybe a reminder would help. 'I really want to get the people who did this, the people who killed him. Andy left a kid, a little girl. She's got no dad now.'

He didn't expect the reaction he got. She stared at him, her face blank with shock. 'A little girl?'

Curwen opened his mouth to reply, then stopped. *Woah!* Andy hadn't told her about Mia. He could use this. If she got angry with Andy, then maybe she'd stop being so protective.

'Yeah. Mia. Cute little thing. She's not two yet. They thought the world of her.' *Nothing but the truth, Curwen.*

She was still staring at him. 'You mean they were together, Andy and . . .'

'Mel. His wife. Yeah.' He got a moment of sour pleasure from the way her body tensed as she took in the news. That had hit home.

He carried on talking as if he hadn't noticed her reaction. 'I don't know what Andy told you, but I do know there's people out there on these streets, selling to kids, and I want to stop them doing that. You can help me, if you want to. If you don't care, well . . .' He shrugged.

Her face was a white blur in the darkness. 'He . . . He texted me. He was away, but he texted me. Asked me to take photographs of the stuff in the cellar.'

'What kind of stuff?' *The holdalls, you silly bitch. Tell me about the holdalls.*

'Carl, the landlord, you know, put some bag sort of things down there. He got pissed off that I saw them. Andy . . .' He heard her swallow. 'He wanted to know what was in them.'

'Was it just the one time?'

'No. I've been, kind of, watching. I saw his car once on that street that runs down from the main road. He came out of that café, you know? And he was carrying a couple of bags then.'

'And he keeps them in the cellar?'

'I think so. He's always funny about us going down there. There's a sort of cupboard place. It's locked. You're a copper. Why don't you go and look?'

165

Frustration flooded through him. He wanted to get down there and carry out a search but this had to be by the book, or at least look as though it was by the book. 'Because I need evidence and I haven't got it.'

'I just told you,' she objected.

He could just imagine what would happen if he went asking for a warrant because Becca the Barmaid – who clearly had her own experiences with the police, which he must check up on sometime – said she'd seen a landlord put some bags in his cellar. 'That's not enough, Becca. You saw some bags. Nothing wrong there.' He let the silence build up. 'You know, Andy was right about that. You could get those photographs. Of the bags, and what's in them.'

He held his breath while she sat there, very still, very quiet. This was it. This was what he needed. One bit of solid proof about what was kept in that cellar, and he'd be vindicated.

'The cupboard's locked. I don't have the key.'

'But you know where it is. You could get it.'

'Yeah, but . . .' She shook her head.

'I understand that you're scared, but there's no need. I've got your back. Listen, just don't talk to anyone else – there's someone dodgy on the team, and I don't know who it is. Get me those pictures, and I can sort it. It's drugs, Becca. I'm pretty sure it's drugs. Andy—'

But mentioning Andy was a mistake. 'I've told you what I know. Leave me alone!' She pushed open the car door and stepped out into the rain, slamming it behind her. She held her head up as she crossed the road, not looking as she went. A car horn sounded. Then she was gone.

How much time did he have? As soon as Dinah told Hammond that B the B and Andy had been an item, Hammond would send someone in to question her. He was pretty sure now that she wouldn't tell them anything, or not at once. He'd put a stopper on that. If he'd judged her right, his dare – because that's what it had been – would drive her into the cellar, and he'd get his evidence. But he needed her to do that before Hammond got to her.

It was tight, but if it all went to plan, he'd get the photos before Hammond got the information out of her.

The road was empty, the street lamps making pools of light in the darkness. Another motorbike came along the road, sending a spray of water up from the gutter as it passed him and vanished.

Chapter 20

Sunk Island

Kay's day had not gone as planned after her broken night's sleep, and she felt like she was playing catch-up. It looked as though someone had been in the fuel store – but she still wasn't convinced. Compost thieves. The whole idea was so ridiculous, she was beginning to doubt what she'd seen. She *thought* she'd seen bags of compost in there, but she'd been distracted with a hundred other things.

There was no point in calling the police – what could she say? *Some bags of compost that I'm almost sure were there have gone missing, and my dog's behaving as though someone got into the house.*

That would bring them running. Catherine Ford had been very clear about police inaction.

In the end, she decided she'd ask the estate agent to change the locks on the outside door of the fuel store, and in the meantime, she'd buy her own padlock.

Officially, she wasn't working today, but the notes left by her predecessor, Xanthe, were in such a state she'd decided to spend the day getting them sorted out. Cool Xanthe might have been, organised she was not.

Kay spent the morning identifying all the missing areas – visits that had not been properly recorded, rough notes that hadn't been transcribed, contact details that had not been updated. Then she began to write outline action plans for each of her clients so that their support could finally get back into a more structured form.

That brought her to Poppy. When Dev had given Kay her caseload, he'd implied that Poppy was well on the road to a full recovery. That didn't match what Kay had seen.

She turned to Xanthe's notes and started reading, gradually feeling more and more puzzled. What Dev had told her tallied with the information she had here. According to the notes, far from her drug use getting worse, Poppy had been doing well – tapering her use of opioids, coming in regularly for counselling sessions, getting a part-time job and talking about picking up her interrupted college course.

Who was Poppy working for? Kay checked the notes. It was a beauty salon, Carla's. The owner, or manager – it wasn't clear – was a Ms A. Traynor. There was a mobile number and a scribbled note not to call Poppy at the salon during working hours. Kay made a note to check this in more detail later and went back to work.

And then the notes stopped, at least a fortnight before Xanthe left. Kay had already checked the appointments calendar. Poppy had had three appointments in that fortnight. According to the log book, she'd come in as arranged. Xanthe just hadn't written up her notes for these sessions.

Kay knew where the story picked up again, with a strung-out Poppy in a trashed squat in Hull. What she didn't have was the bit in between.

What had Xanthe been doing? She wasn't responsible for the chaos the system had fallen into after she left, but there were about six weeks' worth of records that had just not been properly kept at all, almost as if Xanthe had known she was leaving and had decided not to bother any more.

But according to Dev, Xanthe had more or less walked out, without any warning.

That wasn't her problem. Her problem now was to get her clients back on track.

She was just getting started when the landline rang. 'Kay McKinnon.'

It was Dev. 'Kay. You're not answering your phone.'

'There's no signal here, Dev.' *I did tell you.* 'Use this number if you need me.'

'Yes, well, I wish . . . Never mind. You aren't in the office.'

'You don't say.' *Kay!* Matt-in-her-head cautioned. 'No. I'm not working today.'

'What?'

'I said I'm not working today.' Even this connection was poor.

'Oh. I'm sure the rota says ...' She heard the sound of paper shuffling. 'OK. Well, I've had a call – it should have come to you but as you aren't here ...'

Which I'm not supposed to be. 'This phone call,' she prompted him.

'What?'

'The phone call.'

'The ... Yes. It's worrying. It's Poppy Brooke.'

'What's happened?'

Against the crackling line, she got the gist of it. Poppy had missed yet another appointment with her probation officer – the one she had promised Kay she would attend.

'And he's only just noticed?' Kay asked.

'What?'

'It doesn't matter.' There was no point in telling Dev what he already knew. After savage cuts and part-privatisation, the probation service was struggling. They'd lost too many experienced people, and the people who were working carried caseloads that were far too high. It had turned into a system where ticking the box was more important than doing the actual work. People weren't just falling through the cracks, they were cascading. 'I've got an appointment with her tomorrow.'

'The last thing we want is Poppy taken back to court.'

'I agree. Dev, have you come across a woman called Leesha – possibly a pusher? She's in touch with Poppy. I'm not happy about it.'

'The name doesn't ring any bells. I'll check. Listen, I'd like you to contact Poppy now, please. You are her key worker, Kay.'

By the time she managed to decipher this through the interference on the line, he'd rung off.

The exchange left her in a bad temper. Dev was blaming her for Poppy's delinquency – and OK, she was Poppy's caseworker, but whatever had gone wrong for Poppy, it had happened long before Kay took over her case. It was at times like this when she really missed Matt. Well, she missed him all the time, but he'd always known the right way to soothe her ruffled feathers when she was dealing with the inanities of bureaucracy and jobsworth managers. He would have told her that she wasn't responsible for things that had gone wrong before she took on the job, that Dev was only being an arse because he was insecure himself, that Kay didn't have to worry about her own adequacies as far as the job went, all the things she *knew*, but sometimes didn't quite believe.

'Bum,' she said out loud, and went to make herself a cup of coffee. Milo bounced hopefully towards the door. 'Later,' she said. She sat at the kitchen table, drinking her coffee slowly, letting the silence calm her down.

She picked up the phone and tried Poppy's number, but it only rang a couple of times before the answering service took it. She left a message. 'Poppy? It's Kay. Call me, please. It's important.' Poppy's work? That number was marked clearly with *No calls*. And if Poppy was avoiding her, then calls and messages weren't going to do the trick. Kay needed to get over to the house and talk to Poppy face to face.

Half of her wanted to race out of the house and go in search of Poppy right now, try and talk some sense into her, try and find out what was wrong, but she couldn't work like that. She couldn't set off on a wild goose chase all over Hull on the off chance of finding her delinquent client. She wasn't Poppy's friend; she was her caseworker, and she had an appointment with Poppy the following day.

The sound of rain against the windows roused her from her reverie. She was cold, she was tired and her head was full of fuzz. What was she doing, burying herself in all of this on a day when she wasn't even supposed to be working? Despite the foul weather, she needed to get out.

She made a sudden decision. 'Come on, Milo. We're going for a walk.' The sound of the magic word was enough the send him on a mad race around the down-stairs and it was a few minutes before she managed to catch him and clip him onto the long lead. She pulled on her waterproof, laced up her boots, and they were ready for off.

Outside, the rain had eased a bit and the air smelled fresh and clean. The clouds cast shadows that chased across the ground. The sky was a tapestry of purples and blues and greys. Matt would have loved it here. She stood for a moment, looking out over the landscape. Every minute, every hour, every day took Matt further away from her. Distance was not the problem – distance could be overcome, but there was no way back through time.

And that was what she had to live with. She made herself step briskly as she and Milo set out. The estuary was invisible against the flat landscape, but a ship was moving out there, apparently sailing across the open fields. She stopped and watched it, delighted with the optical illusion.

The estuary. She'd walk that way. Wrapping her scarf more closely round her neck, she set off again. A quick check of the nearest drain showed her that Milo would get muddy if he fell in, but would easily be able to get out again, so she let him off his lead.

He raced around madly, running in little circles, following one trail after another, overwhelmed by a new place and the variety of new smells. She wandered along behind him, her hands in the pockets of her waterproof. The phone call with Dev had been depressing. Did she really want to put herself through that rigamarole of office politics, work in a job that paid her for three days and expected her to be on call for seven? Idly, she played with the idea of retiring, of spending her days walking with Milo, enjoying the changing seasons, living at a slower pace than she had for most of her life, just enjoying the time she had left.

But that was old-woman thinking. She'd tried that,

hadn't she, living in that isolated little cottage outside Whitby, and it had driven her mad. She was loving this walk, but only because it was a treat for her to have some time to herself. If it was always like this, then it wouldn't be the same. Anyway, why was she letting herself be influenced by Dev Johar's attitude? He was wrong, she knew he was wrong, and she'd make him admit he was wrong.

And Poppy . . . ?

Today was not a work day. She'd think about Poppy tomorrow.

Without really planning it, she had been following the line of one of the drains. It ran right down to the shoreline. Letting her curiosity guide her, she followed the grassy path, keeping a wary eye on Milo who was trotting happily beside her. The drain was deeper here and she really didn't fancy fishing him out of it. They crossed what looked like a sluice gate – of course, when the tide was high, the water could run back from the estuary onto the land – and followed the drain down to the shore.

There was something flapping in the wind. As she got closer, she saw yellow and black tape and the words 'Crime Scene'. Much of the tape must have been taken down – this was just a piece left behind – but it brought back to her Catherine Ford's story of a body found down near the water.

This must be Spragger Drain sluice.

But she hadn't talked about a crime, just a death. And Kay had assumed an accident.

The other night came back to her; the sound of a door closing softly, Kay sitting in the kitchen, her eyes fixed on the door as the footsteps came closer . . .

She clipped on Milo's lead and, moving slowly, she walked towards the embankments. There was a hard-standing at the end of the drain, cut by a deep culvert. The tide was out. Below her, the foreshore was strewn with rocks, green and covered with wet seaweed, gleaming in the watery light.

The tracks of birds marked the wet sand, and a single line of footprints showed a walker had gone that way not long before. She looked west and saw that a path ran along the top of the embankment. You couldn't get down to the foreshore from here – it was a steep drop – but further away along the path, it would be possible.

They could walk along here, she and Milo, but not now, not today, so close to the reminders of a death.

The almost monastic silence of Sunk Island seemed suddenly not peaceful, but sinister.

She shook herself. This was the same kind of think-ing that led teenage girls to scream hysterically about ghosts and demons. Hadn't bad things happened at her cottage? Didn't bad things happen everywhere?

It was just that this was such a bleak and lonely place to die.

The clouds were closing in fast. She needed to get back. It took her a moment to get her bearings – the estuary behind her, the house – not visible, but surely over there. Calling to Milo, she set off again across the fields.

She followed the track further inland then turned west. Unexpectedly, in this flat, open landscape, she found herself walking towards a copse of trees. Soon she was in among them – the ground was covered with the dead leaves of last winter and the branches made spider webs against the sky. There were old buildings here – ruins with lichened stone walls, thick and windowless.

She'd heard about this – a gun battery built over a hundred years ago to defend the mouth of the Humber. The trees must have grown up since the last war, as they obscured the view across the estuary.

Milo, his energy spent in his initial mad run, was walking quietly along the path. He wandered among the buildings, his nose to the ground, and she meandered behind him. She'd have to come here another day when she had more time, bring some sandwiches and a flask and explore these buildings properly. She called Milo, who was showing interest in some steps that led downwards into darkness, and turned inland. She looked at the sky. The clouds were gathering and the light was fading.

She didn't want to find herself out here in the dark, away from shelter once the rain started. Time to head back to the house.

Something was blowing across the ground, something yellow. At first, she thought it was more of the crime scene tape, but as she got closer, she saw it was an empty plastic sack, bright yellow with a picture on the front.

She knew what it was before she picked it up.

She had seen one just like it a couple of days before, in the fuel store at her house.

A compost bag.

Chapter 21

Bridlington

Becca's head was pounding as she stuck price labels on tins and pushed them onto the supermarket shelf. Andy was dead.

Bryan's voice broke into her thoughts. 'Becca. Those tins do not go on that shelf. And those are not reduced. What do you think you're doing? You need to buck your ideas up if you want to keep on working here. Get all this stuff off the shelves now and do them again, right?'

She hadn't slept last night, just lain there listening to the rain beating on the window.

Andy . . . the one she shared stupid jokes with, the one who texted her while she was working behind the bar, making her laugh, the one whose face always seemed to light up when he saw her. His slow smile. And the way he had looked at her as her hair tumbled down round her shoulders. He'd talked to her like he cared. *I don't want to make more bad things happen in your life.*

But he had.

He'd been married all the time and he had a kid. A wife and a child he'd never thought to mention. What other lies had he told her? She couldn't bear the thought that he'd been just another lying creep, but what else was she supposed to think?

Baggers can't be choosers.

Last night, after she'd walked out on Curwen, she'd gone inside and sat in the big armchair in her room and struggled not to cry. She kept telling herself Curwen was a pig creep, he should leave her alone, he should . . . But all of that sounded old. If she cried, it wouldn't be because of him, it would be for Andy. And what was there to cry about? She would be crying for the Andy she thought she'd known.

And he had never existed.

And now she couldn't even ask him why he'd lied to her. Maybe he'd split up with his wife. How would Curwen know? Maybe he'd hadn't mentioned his child because . . . because . . .

Who was she trying to kid? He had lied because he was a creep, just like all the rest, and that was the end of it.

At least Curwen had been straight with her. And there was one thing he'd told her that she couldn't get out of her head. The people he was after were pushing drugs to kids.

She knew all about that. She'd seen it, the kids with no one who gave a shit about them, apart from the dealers, and the dealers were just using them. Even kids who had someone to care about them – like Jade's Lewis – could get drawn in. Lewis was starting to hang out with the gangs, Jade had said as much, and Becca had not liked the look of the people she'd seen him with. She'd seen the flashy clothes, the fancy bike. Lewis was in trouble. He was a little shit, but Jade was her mate, and you don't let your mates down.

She could do something. Curwen wanted to know what was in those bags that Carl had stored in the cellar. She didn't have the key, but was Curwen right? Could she get it? Carl usually kept his keys clipped to his belt, but when he was in the back doing the books, or whatever it was he did in there, he left his keys on the table, and sometimes, when he was working in the pub, he left his keys behind the bar. Maybe . . .

When it was her break, she headed straight outside for a cigarette. Jade was there, leaning against the wall, her own cigarette already lit. She smiled a bit wearily when she saw Becca. Becca's face must have shown something of how she was feeling, because Jade asked, 'What's up love? Boyfriend dumped you?'

Becca shook her head. 'No boyfriend.' That was true enough, wasn't it? Andy had never been her boyfriend, not really. He belonged to someone else.

'Well, that's your problem then, isn't it?'

'What is?'

'No boyfriend. You need a good seeing to. That'll make you feel better.'

Becca found herself laughing. That was what she liked about Jade – she had a tough life with no money, two kids, an ex who gave her nothing but hassle and the same shit job that Becca had, but she kept her head up, kept on going.

She couldn't get those pictures for Curwen. There was no way she could get those keys. Curwen had talked about drugs. Andy had talked about dodgy money stuff. Who was it he worked for? She fished out the business card he had given her, but all it gave was his name, Andy Yeatson, and *Financial Enquiries*.

Another worm of doubt started eating away at her. If he'd really been doing what he said, wouldn't the name of the firm he worked for be on his card? Anyone could get a business card printed. If he'd lied about one thing . . .

She took out her phone and looked at the last message, remembering the way it had made her feel relieved at first that Andy hadn't dropped her, and then how it had seemed all wrong. She should get rid of it. She should get rid of all the texts he'd sent, and the card, and just stop thinking about him, just remember he'd been a creep all along and she should have known better.

She really should.

She was about to press the delete key, when a cold realisation washed over her.

The last text had been sent on the night Curwen had first come into the pub, the night she'd sent pictures, the night she had spent the whole evening waiting for Andy to come back. Like he'd promised.

Only he couldn't. The paper, the one she'd read in the supermarket. It said Andy had been attacked on Tuesday night.

When that text was sent, *Great, A x*, Andy had been dead three days.

Chapter 22

It sometimes felt to Dinah that no matter where she was moved to in Humberside Police, her job always reset to traffic. Her first time on a murder team as a DC, and here she was checking CCTV and traffic cameras, trying to find the route Andy took down the coast.

It required real concentration but it was also deadly boring. She had to keep stopping to refocus herself as her mind started drifting away from the task.

At least it had been made easier by the advice Curwen had given her: 'The car you want drove right down into Sunk Island, right? There are only about three turnings off the main road that will take you there. Check those, and you should find the car you want. Then you can backtrack and find it in Brid.'

It was so obvious, she wondered why she hadn't thought of it herself – probably because she didn't think there would be ANPR cameras watching the routes into Sunk Island. It was empty and isolated

– almost no one lived there. Why would anyone bother? But sure enough, Curwen was right. The main routes into Sunk Island were under surveillance.

She'd got the information from the cameras and started working her way through the videos. After a couple of hours, her eyes felt sore and dry, so she stretched to get the kinks out of her back, and took five minutes before she returned to the screen. She fast forwarded, watching closely. Nothing, nothing, nothing . . . *There*. A car. She stopped the tape and took the details then moved on. OK, Nothing, nothing . . .

Her thoughts started drifting to the evening Andy had disappeared. He'd left the police station, driven into the town and parked. He'd been going somewhere, but so far, no one knew where. The pub? It was on his route. Was he on his way to see Becca Armitage? Dinah had to tell Hammond about that.

She'd gone to his office that morning, but he was out all day. The information she had was important, of course it was, but she kept thinking about Curwen's warnings. Maybe she should talk to Curwen first. After all, what had she found out? That the geeky barman thought Becca Armitage and Andy were having a thing. If she told Dave Sykes or someone, the whole team would know at once and speculation about Andy might start. Best take it straight to Hammond tomorrow.

She felt better once that decision had been made and turned back to work.

*   *   *

She'd found Andy's car on an ANPR camera as it left the police station, an image so clear she could see his face. It gave nothing away – he looked serious, focused on his driving.

It was probably the last picture of him alive.

Andy had been on the afternoon shift, which meant he should have come off duty at eleven that night. He'd missed an end-of-shift meeting with Curwen at ten thirty. It was Curwen who had first raised the alarm, calling Andy's babysitter to see if he was at home for any reason, and finding out that Andy hadn't made his usual call around ten to let her know he should be home on time.

A movement on the screen in front of her forced her thoughts to stop wandering.

A car! Damn! Despite everything, she'd let her attention drift. She rewound and watched again from the previous car, forcing herself to concentrate as cars zipped past on the main road, looking for those that slowed and took the turn. The time on the recording was getting close to nine in the evening. It had run now for almost half an hour without any vehicles making the turn-off.

Nothing . . .

There.

Another car.

And a motorcycle. A car slowed, took the turning onto Sunk Island and then speeded up, closely followed by a bike.

She collected the details of the car, but the bike . . .

it had slewed sideways as if it had skidded, so the camera hadn't picked the number plate up. Did it matter? She wasn't looking for a bike. But she captured the image anyway. There'd be enough detail to get make and model information. It should be possible to track the owner down.

OK. Back to the tape. Nothing ... nothing ... nothing ...

Lunchtime came and went. She ate a sandwich at her desk and was just licking the butter off her fingers when Dave Sykes came to check how she was going on. 'Good thinking, Dinah,' he said when he saw what she was doing.

'Mark Curwen suggested it,' she admitted. Dinah liked praise, but only for things she had worked out for herself. 'I didn't think there'd be cameras watching those roads. Why are they even there?'

'Because there's no police presence on Sunk Island, and they've had a bit of trouble recently. A lot of farm thefts – machinery, vehicles, even livestock taken. It's covered by the Hull cops, but by the time anyone gets there, they've long gone. How's it going? Have you found anything?'

'I'm just about done. This is the last camera. I got about twenty vehicles on the other two.'

'Rush hour.' Sykes laughed. 'For Sunk Island, anyway. And this camera?'

'Maybe ten? I'll have to check.'

'Good work. You know if you don't find what we're looking for, you're going to have to widen the search, don't you? There are ways on and off Sunk Island that aren't watched by cameras.'

Dinah nodded. She did know that, and she was dreading it. 'I did this first – if they're here, I should know in time for tomorrow's briefing.'

'Run me through what you're going to do next.'

'I'm going to check them against the databases, get details for everyone who was out and about on those roads.'

'Right. And then?'

'Get the names and addresses, check them against the Vehicle Licensing Authority – look for fake plates.'

'The cameras would have flagged that one up, Dinah.'

Of course, she should have known that. ANPR was there to locate suspicious vehicles, vehicles that were carrying number plates that didn't match the recorded details, wanted people ... 'OK. But maybe check again? And look for known offenders.'

Sykes looked pleased. 'First rule. Don't assume that because it should have been done, it has been done. Always check again. OK, then? What do you expect to find on the databases?'

It reminded her, in a way, of how Andy had helped her – not telling her what to do, but letting her talk him through the procedures she was following, commenting and advising where necessary. 'They'll be Sunk Island residents. There's almost no one round here.' She used her hand to indicate the grey emptiness on the map. 'But there are villages here and here, just off the main road.'

'OK. And you'll eliminate the villagers?'

'No, they'll have to be interviewed. And there might be some visitors. You get walkers and birdwatchers here. There's a campsite and there's caravans over to the east just here.' She put her finger on the map. 'But someone taking that turn-off in the evening, if they don't live there and aren't visiting – I'd want to know what they were doing.'

'OK. Good work, Dinah. I'll tell the DCI what you've been up to.'

He left her to get on with it. Dinah felt pleased. She settled her glasses on her nose and went back to the screen.

A couple of hours later, she'd identified all the cars that went onto or left Sunk Island the night Andy died. One of the cars on her list was probably the car that had taken Andy down to Sunk island.

Find the car, find the killer.

What else should she look at?

She was getting ahead of herself. It was time to check the cars she had against the database of owners and locations. If the database search didn't come up with anything, then she'd have to start again. Let Hammond make that decision.

Fewer than 300 people lived on Sunk Island, and most of them lived in the small villages just off the main road to the north of the area, not in Sunk Island itself. Otherwise, there were a handful of farms and a small number of private dwellings, a camping site to the east, and a small business development down by Stone Creek on the estuary, where a few people kept small one- and two-person boats.

She got to work. A couple of hours later, she had the information she needed. Most of the cars caught by the cameras were registered to people who lived in the small villages just off the main road. There were a couple of 4x4s that were registered to farms. This left her with just six that were registered outside the area. She sent up a quick prayer of thanks that the holiday season was over, or the number would have been far higher.

There were no vehicles that rang alarm bells: no stolen cars, no false plates. Two of the cars were registered to people living on the other side of Hull. Dinah highlighted those names – why would someone who lived close by be driving down to Sunk Island in the evening? One was an overseas registration – she'd have to track that one down – one was registered in Greater Manchester and one was from the south coast.

She checked the time. It was getting on for five o'clock and she'd spent all day in front of the screen. She felt as tired as if she'd been on a ten-mile hike, but not in a good way. The artificial light, the glare of the screen, the hours of sitting had left her with a headache and a feeling of frowstiness. All she wanted to do was go home, order a pizza, have a beer and fall into bed.

That wasn't happening. She'd go for a walk, then drop in to the pub where the team hung out to catch up and get a beer. It was important to keep in touch with the team, to be seen as part of it.

OK, she had a day of solid achievement under her belt. She had a list of locals for the uniformed guys to interview, and a list – a much smaller list – of cars that didn't seem to have a good reason for taking the Sunk Island turn-off. Tomorrow, she'd get in early, put the out-of-town car owners in order of priority, and arrive at the briefing with everything in order.

And tell Hammond about Andy and Becca Armitage.

As she was putting her things together on her desk for tomorrow, she noticed an anomaly. She'd had six cars identified as out of towners, but the system had only given her five names and addresses.

Hang on. Hang on.

She went through everything manually, looking closely at the images again, and she spotted it almost at once.

The car that was registered near Manchester belonged to a woman called Elizabeth Bagnall. According to the cameras, this car had driven away from Sunk Island at around 21.45 the night Andy had died.

She'd missed it because an hour before that, the same car, followed by the motorbike that had its number plate slewed away from the camera, had taken the turn onto Sunk Island.

Why hadn't she thought of that? The car that took Andy south that night would almost certainly have travelled back again. This car was starting to look good. And she had the registration, and the owner's address.

Maybe, just maybe, this was a gotcha!

Chapter 23

Becca arrived behind the bar with her head in a mess. She felt exposed, as if someone was looking over her shoulder, stealing all her secrets. Standing in the back room behind the bar, she checked that last message again. It had come from Andy's phone. The number was there. After a few hesitations, telling herself she was being stupid, *knowing* she was being stupid, she called it.

'*The number you want is unavailable. Please try later.*'

'Becca! Get a move on! We've got a queue!' Carl, shouting at her from the bar. She dumped her coat and came through, locking her bag in the small cupboard beside the chill cabinet. Carl looked at his watch meaningfully – which probably meant the tight git would cut her pay for being five minutes late. That was another of his tricks – cut by half an hour if you weren't there to do the full thirty minutes.

But it was busy, and she was glad it was busy. It was like it used to be before Andy died, the bar lined with punters wanting drinks, the screens crowded, groans and cheers ringing out as teams chased a ball from one end of the pitch to the other. It was like it had come alive again. She was glad, because it gave her no time to think. Everything was back to normal. She could see the familiar faces from other evenings: Johnny Dip and his biker mates, the blonde woman, Sal Capone, with her hat tipped to cast a shadow over her face.

Poser.

They were there, but Andy wasn't. As the evening wore on, she realised nothing was normal and it wasn't going to be ever again, not for her.

It was all changed.

It was like looking at one of those pictures that you couldn't make sense of, where suddenly it was one thing, then if you kept on looking at it, it became something else. She'd thought she'd known Andy. But she hadn't known him at all.

She could still see him standing there against the bar, laughing over some daft joke, easy going, friendly.

'*Why don't skeletons go trick or treating?*'

'*I dunno. Why don't skeletons go trick or treating?*'

'*It's because they have no body to go with.*'

'*Oh, shut up.*'

But it had been more than that. He looked out for her when he came through the door, gave her a quick smile that was for her, not for the people he hung out with – Johnny Dip and his mates, mostly. He'd told her to be careful – not the usual, *Take care*, that people said when what they meant was *I don't care*, but like it really mattered.

He'd seen that things had been hard for her some-times, and she'd thought, at the time, it made him sad. *I don't want to make more bad things happen in your life*, he'd said, like he meant it.

More than anything, she wanted to ask him, *Then why did you do it?*

But she couldn't. And now she'd never know.

'Six fifty,' she said to the punter she was serving. He passed her a tenner and she gave him his change. 'Who's next?'

'Three Newcastle Browns.' It was Johnny Dip himself, who'd been leaning on the bar as he waited, scanning a copy of the local free newspaper someone had left.

She popped the caps on the bottles. 'Three Browns,' she said, pushing them across the bar. 'OK, that's—'

'I gave you a twenty.' It was the person she'd just served, standing there brandishing the handful of change she'd just given him. *Shit*. It was a popular scam, to say you paid with a twenty when you'd only used a fiver or a tenner, and get the extra change. He'd only given her a ten, she was certain.

'Just a minute.' She was waiting for Johnny Dip to count his money out.

'I haven't got a minute. I want my money. Now.'

Becca could feel herself bristling. 'I said. I'll check. In a minute.'

Johnny Dip seemed in no rush to pay for the beer. He was watching the exchange with mild interest, absently rolling up the newspaper he'd been reading. 'You see to this guy,' he said. 'I'll wait.'

She glared at him, not wanting to look as though she was giving in. 'OK.' She banged open the till drawer and checked it. There was a tenner at the top of the pile of notes, the last thing she'd put in there. There was only one twenty, and it was right down at the bottom – no way had he paid with that.

He was trying it on. She looked round the pub for Carl, but there was no sign of him.

'It was a ten,' she said. *And you're a lying shit.*

'I gave you twenty.'

'There's no twenty here.'

He shoved his face forward. 'You calling me a liar?'

Becca shrugged. Then she was pulled smartly against the bar, her stomach hitting the drip tray and making her gasp. The man had reached across and grabbed the front of her shirt. She could feel his fingers against her skin.

Touching her.

No one did that. No one.

Her hand groped under the bar and closed on the sharp knife Carl kept there for cutting fruit. 'Get your hands off me.' She was going to stick it into his arm and she was—

The man released her suddenly, making her stagger back. He was doubled over, clutching his stomach.

His face, what she could see of it, was grey. His lips moved, but all that came out were croaking noises.

The knife dropped from her fingers and clattered onto the floor.

'You know what, mate? You should just piss off.' It was Johnny Dip, who was still leaning against the bar. The man looked at him, looked at Becca, opened his mouth to say something, changed his mind and staggered away still clutching his stomach.

No one else seemed to have noticed anything apart from Toby, who was coming across, looking alarmed. 'Is everything OK?' He spoke to Johnny Dip. 'Was there a—'

'Guy forgot his manners. It's cool.' Johnny Dip closed the thing down and Becca was glad. She didn't want to explain anything, didn't want everyone looking at her. The guy had grabbed her and she hadn't been able to do anything. Johnny Dip had done something to stop him before she could use the knife. She'd wanted, really wanted to stick it right into his arm, rip it open so that . . .

And then the police would come.

Would they even listen?

Not to her.

She was shaking.

'Hey, look, knives get you into trouble. Next time, just hit him with a newspaper. No law against carrying a newspaper.' Johnny Dip was still leaning against the bar, smiling a bit as though he thought it was the best joke, the beer he'd bought still in front of him.

Becca glared at him. She knew she ought to say thanks or something, but . . . he was laughing at her.

'It's the truth. Don't believe me?' He grinned. 'OK, I'll show you.'

He held out the scrunched-up copy of the paper that he had been reading. When she looked at it, she could see it had been rolled up tightly and doubled over, just like it was going to be chucked away or something. But when she touched it, it felt solid, like a piece of wood. Hit someone in the gut with this – well, she'd seen what it could do.

He took it back from her. 'And then you just . . .' He tossed it across the bar, where it landed in the recycling bin. He grinned again, pleased with himself, and picked up one of the bottles. 'Like I said, no law against carrying a newspaper.' He took a drink.

'Hey, Doc. Where's our drinks?' It was Sal Capone. Becca had always thought she was quite young – sort of Johnny Dip's age, and might even be his girlfriend. She seemed to hang out with him and his mates. Only now that Becca could see her more clearly in the light of the bar, she looked quite a bit older, the model-thinness making her look a bit haggard, with lines around her mouth and eyes.

Even so, Becca had to admit she looked cool. There was something about her that made Becca think of a younger Kay. She had an old trench coat slung across her shoulders, a scarf flung with careful casualness round her neck and a black fedora tipped at an angle that shaded her eyes. It was an odd mix but she made it work. Matt used to say that Kay would look good in a feed sack, whatever that was, but it was true, Kay always had that same stylish look.

Or always used to. Not now, so much, when she seemed to live in her old walking gear. The thought made Becca frown and she almost missed what Sal Capone said next.

She'd put her fingers to her lips. 'Oops,' she said to Johnny Dip, for no reason Becca could see. 'Hey, don't we have something on tonight?' She picked up his beer and lifted it to her mouth, ignoring Becca.

Johnny Dip smiled down at her. 'Big time.' He was carefully constructing a roll-up, his attention focused on that.

'You said it. Hey,' she plucked the roll-up from his fingers. 'Join me outside for a while, OK?'

He nodded. 'In a minute.'

Sal Capone looked at Becca for the first time and smiled, just a movement of her mouth. Her eyes were sharp and bright. Andy had been right to name her after a gangster. There was no warmth there.

She was studying Becca closely. 'I know you. Where have I seen you before? What's your name?'

'They call her Becca,' Johnny Dip replied for her, as he completed another roll-up. Becca, who'd been about to speak, closed her mouth, frowning. She could answer for herself.

Sal Capone ignored him. Her eyes wandered across Becca in an assessing way. 'I have a beauty business,' she said, slowly. 'I'm always looking out for models. I think you probably photograph very well. In fact, I know you do. Even with the . . .' She gestured towards her own mouth, indicating the place where the scar made Becca's lip a bit crooked. 'You know, I've seen your picture. On the internet.'

Becca felt her face flush scarlet. A couple of years ago, she'd made a bit of money camming. She'd called herself Bexgirl, and she'd done quite well – until it all went wrong. Sal Capone had to be talking about Bexgirl. 'I'm not interested,' she said.

The other woman raised her eyebrows in exaggerated disbelief. 'Really? Up to you. I pay well, though. Remember that.' She turned away and looked up at Johnny Dip. 'Coming for a smoke? We have things to talk about. I'll wait for you outside.' She headed for the exit, raising her hand in a kind of farewell.

Modelling. Becca was prepared to bet that though Sal Capone might have a beauty business – *might* – when it came down to it the modelling would have more to do with taking your clothes off than putting them on. If she was going to take her clothes off in front of a camera again, she'd go back to camming. Make her own money, not give most of it to someone else.

She looked straight at Johnny Dip, who seemed in no hurry to move. Did he know about the camming as well? Had Andy known? Was that why he'd liked her? Maybe they'd all been perving about her photographs. She'd seen Andy talking to Sal Capone more than once. 'Is she a mate of yours?'

Johnny Dip shrugged.

Becca hesitated. When Curwen first came in, he'd asked her about the people Andy hung out with. They hadn't talked about that last night, so she hadn't said anything. She could tell him about Johnny Dip, but maybe she could get some other names, find out a bit more about what Andy had been doing. 'What do they call her?' she said. The woman had got Becca's name, but she hadn't given her own.

Johnny Dip grinned. 'Lots of things.'

'Wasn't she mates with, you know, that guy who got in trouble . . . ?'

He glanced at her then looked away again. 'You mean the guy who got himself killed? I don't think so.'

'What happened?' She tried to keep her voice casual.

'About what?'

'The guy who got himself killed. I kind of, you know, knew him.'

He shook his head. 'No idea.'

That was what people said when they didn't want to tell you something. Andy had hung out with Johnny Dip, Becca had seen them together. 'But you were mates, right?'

'Listen, love, no one was that guy's mate.' She saw a gleam of amusement in his eyes and felt her face going red. 'Something you maybe need to understand. The guy was all business. A dealer. A wannabe dealer. Sold weed and a few pills. Strictly small-time, strictly pond life. But he had big ideas. He wanted to move up the chain and he pissed someone off big-time.'

'Andy?' Something inside her felt tight with an emotion she couldn't identify, not anger, it was more like sadness. Sadness that this was what Andy had come to. It wasn't true. It couldn't be true. But another voice in her head was jeering, *Yeah, right, he was a lying, druggie creep*. She wasn't thinking about Curwen any more when she asked the next question. She wanted to know, for herself. 'So who? Who did he piss off?'

'Who did who piss off?' Toby was passing a pint to a customer over her head. 'There's a queue, Becca.'

That was rich, coming from him. *Dosser the Tosser*. 'Yeah, yeah. Just a mo.' She turned back to Johnny Dip.

'I don't know, love. And if I did, I wouldn't tell you.' *Which bit of 'leave it alone' don't you understand?*

First Russ, and now Johnny Dip. Warning her off. She shrugged, trying to make it look as though it didn't matter. 'I just wanted to know what happened. To Andy.'

'Well, now you do. Looks like it's getting busy again. Do your job.' He picked up the bottles and turned away, walking with a bit of a limp, leaving Becca feeling stupid and angry.

A dealer. Pond life.

Yeah, well, Johnny Dip was pond life himself.

Curwen had been right. She was too chicken to get the key, and now she didn't even have the names to give him. The late-evening rush had started and she was kept so busy she didn't have time to think about

202

what Johnny Dip had said. She didn't *want* to think about it.

Later, she saw Sal Capone and Johnny Dip standing together by the fruit machines. Their heads were close together and they were talking.

Later still, when they were leaving, a crowd of them, Becca heard Johnny Dip's voice. He sounded angry and impatient. 'It's cool, Alicia. There's no need for any of that.'

'I hope you're . . .'

The rest was drowned in the general pub noise as the door closed behind them.

Chapter 24

Becca was ready to hit someone by the time she left the pub. She wanted to hit the guy who had grabbed her, she wanted to hit Johnny Dip for . . . she wasn't sure what for, but she wanted to hit him anyway. And Toby for being a lazy git who left her to cope with everything. And Carl because he'd made a crack about Becca fighting with the customers when he'd heard about her run-in with the punter and the twenty-pound note. 'Here you go, Becca,' he'd said as he handed her her money in an envelope. He always paid her cash out of the till. 'Your winnings. You'd have an extra fiver if you'd got a knockout.' And he'd laughed again until he started coughing.

Moron.

She was just so tired.

It was starting to rain and there were some odd people around. The guy Johnny Dip had hit with the newspaper might be waiting around, waiting to get her on her own.

At least she knew what to do about Andy. She'd learned her lesson, that was for sure. No more listening to smooth talkers across the bar. It didn't make any difference whether they perved at you, or whether they pretended to be cool and funny, it was all the same.

She shouldn't be sorry he was dead.

She wasn't sorry.

She brushed away angry tears. She wasn't crying because of that; she was crying because she'd got him so wrong.

The rain was getting worse. It dripped in a circle off her umbrella, soaking her legs. As she came round the corner, her bus sailed past her, sending up a spray of water that splashed down her left side. 'Fucking dickhead!' she shouted, not sure if she meant the bus driver or herself. She'd missed it and now she had to walk home – no choice. She wanted to sit down on the wet pavement and scream.

Which would really help, right?

She trudged home through the foul weather, trying not to think about the evening that had just passed, but the more she tried not to think about it, the more it came back. She counted her steps as she walked, trying to push the thoughts away. *One, two, three, four* . . . The man's fingers grabbing her shirt, and she couldn't stop him pulling her forward . . . There was something else, something that had happened that she'd missed . . . She was breathing hard with the effort of keeping the thoughts away, feeling dizzy and spaced out, as if the air she was breathing wasn't reaching her lungs.

She couldn't do anything else. She couldn't get the key. Because she was just a *bagger*, just a nothing who had to work at two crap jobs and still couldn't make enough to keep herself going. Just a loser who couldn't spot a creep when he started perving at her, who ... Her head felt flooded and it was like the thoughts were shouting at her, drowning out anything else. She wanted to scream, *Shut up! Shut up!* to stop them.

She had to stop for a moment, putting her hand against the wall to keep herself upright. She just had to find somewhere she could hide to make it all stop, stop, stop ...

It was OK. The flat was just over the road.

She half ran across and round the corner to the gennel.

She was nearly home.

It was pitch dark. Her feet caught on the uneven ground, making her stumble. Where were the lights? She fumbled for her torch, and through the confusion of the noise in her head, it began to dawn on her that something wasn't right.

She couldn't put her finger on it, but now a cold tension was running down her back, that feeling she needed to be alert, on her guard. She tried to move more quickly, stumbling slightly on the uneven ground.

Somewhere not too far away, a bike revved up suddenly, and then stopped. Something rattled in the darkness behind her.

Becca spun round, but there was no one there.

Someone in one of the other yards, one of the other flats. Nothing to do with her.

She reached the gate and her fingers felt stiff and clumsy as she lifted the chain and pushed it open. Then she realised what was wrong. The outside light wasn't on and the yard was in darkness.

She'd left the light on. She knew she had. Coming back at night, after the shop was shut – she always left the light on.

The gate swung closed behind her, the rattle of the chain making her jump again.

Get a grip! The bulb must have gone, that was all. Or she'd forgotten, or . . .

There was no sign of the kitten in the light of her torch as she made her way across the muddy yard. The wheelie bin stood in a deep puddle, and the shelter – she flashed her torch at it – the rain was getting to that as well. The tarp had blown back and some of the bedding was wet. If more water got in . . . She pulled the tarp back to protect it again. Water dripped off the fire escape and down her neck.

She was wet and she was freezing.

The shelter would do for tonight and she'd put food down before she left for the pub. There were still some biscuits in one of the dishes. The kitten would be fine until morning. She'd feed it and fix the shelter then. Her head was a mess and she was just too tired and too cold to do anything about it now.

The wind gusted. The gate slammed back against the wall and blew shut again.

Becca was at the back door before she realised it, her hands fumbling in her bag for her key. She got the door open, then shut and locked it, her heart hammering. She ran up the stairs to the landing and pressed the light switch. To her relief, the fluorescent tube flickered into life.

Why had she thought it wouldn't?

She let herself into her flat and turned on the floor lamp, the one with the red shade that Kay had given her. It always made her feel good, having that light, seeing the way it made her room look warm and welcoming and, just a bit, like the places on the makeover shows on the TV.

But tonight, the magic didn't work. Tonight, it was just a light in a tatty bedsit.

She slumped down in the armchair, not bothering to take her coat off or light the fire. She couldn't find the energy to do anything more than just curl up here and let the thoughts take her. What was the point in resisting them? They were true, weren't they?

The creep punter's fingers curling into the fabric of her shirt, *touching* her, her stepfather's footsteps on the stairs as she hid under the sheets, too chicken, too chicken to fight Him, too chicken to help Curwen, she was just what her mother used to call her, a waste of time, a waste of space.

And Andy, watching her as her hair tumbled down

round her shoulders, but his face was sad. *I don't want to make more bad things happen in your life . . .*

But you did! She wanted to scream at him. *You did!*

And Matt was smiling at her. They were sitting on the floor of the room Becca had just wrecked, and he was helping her to keep the thoughts away. *Don't hate yourself. Don't waste your anger, Becca. Use it.*

But Matt was dead. She missed him so much she almost couldn't bear it. And Kay. She missed Kay, too. Why hadn't she been to see her in her new house and tell her about what was happening? Kay was busy, but she'd want to know.

She really, really needed to talk to Kay.

Her hand fumbled with her phone, but it was too late at night. She couldn't call Kay now and wake her up. Tomorrow, she promised herself.

Just thinking about Matt and Kay was making the thoughts slow down, making the noise in her head quieter. Now she could think properly, and start to make sense of what had happened tonight.

She wanted to help, wanted to find out what had happened to Andy, but what she'd told Curwen was right. There was no way she could get those keys off Carl. She wasn't being chicken; it was just a fact.

If she could, would she have done what he wanted?

She kind of thought she would. Slowly, she uncurled from the chair, pulled off her wet coat and lit the gas fire, then she made a cup of tea and opened some beans and sat in front of the fire eating them out of the tin.

And then she remembered the main thing she'd found out that night: the message that said it came from Andy's phone, but couldn't have done.

Because Andy had been dead.

And now she thought about it, what about the other messages? All the ones about getting in the cellar and taking pictures, the ones that hadn't sounded like Andy, because . . .

She closed her eyes and breathed steadily. Don't let the thoughts come back. Just . . . *don't*.

The rain was even heavier now, hammering on the window. A gust of wind made the dormer rattle and a waft of chilly air blew across the room. The gas fire flickered. She pulled the throw off the bed and wrapped it round her shoulders, but she was still cold.

She thought about the kitten – tiny and bedraggled – hiding in its carboard shelter. In this weather, the puddles would get bigger and bigger and seep under the tarp. The water would soak through the carboard and turn it into a soggy ruin. The bedding she'd put in there would get wet and before too long, the kitten would be soaked, then its fur wouldn't keep it warm, and then . . . Even though she was inside, with food in her and a hot drink, sitting in front of a fire, she was cold. The kitten only had its fur and the shelter of a cardboard box.

And she hadn't even tried to feed it because she was cold and tired and sorry for herself, and she'd let herself get scared by broken lights and banging gates. Who was the pond life here? She couldn't leave it outside in this. She had to get down there and either make sure it was in proper shelter or catch it.

Somehow.

Concentrating hard on the kitten to stop the thoughts coming back, she grabbed the milk carton and a handful of cat biscuits, then pulled on her still-wet coat and slipped her small torch into the pocket. And a towel – she might need it to throw over the kitten if it came out.

Leaving the light on in her room and in the corridor, she headed down the stairs. There was no light on the stairway – George seemed to think the light from the upstairs corridor would be enough.

The small storeroom at the bottom of the stairs was pitch black. The torchlight illuminated the stacks of boxes and the bits of junk piled up in the old sink. She could hear water cascading down from the gutter and when she opened the back door, it was like looking through a waterfall.

Pulling up her hood for some protection, she stepped through the sheet of water. The ground was a sea of mud and puddles. She should have come out sooner. She followed the narrow path of light made by her torch to the fire escape and felt her stomach clench as she saw that something had pulled the tarp away again from the makeshift shelter. The box was a sodden mess on the ground, the bedding scattered. What had happened? The wind? A fox? There was no sign of the kitten.

She checked the wheelie bin, its other hiding place. The huge bin was standing in a puddle that had filled the gap underneath it. If the kitten had been hiding under there, it would have drowned.

Whatever had happened to the shelter, once it was gone, the kitten would have moved to the wheelie bin to hide. And then the water would have risen, and the kitten would have been trapped. Was it under there right now? And she'd just gone in and left it.

This was her fault. *Useless, waste of time, just . . .*

Shut up! she told herself. *Not now!*

The faint, narrow beam from her torch lit up small patches of the yard that suddenly seemed like a vast space with too many hiding places: the bottom of the fire escape, the tarp, gaps left in the wall by loose bricks, boxes stacked up for recycling collapsing in the rain.

There was nowhere to start.

Light gleamed back from the puddles on the ground. There was something lying in one and for a moment, her stomach dropped, then she saw it was just an empty plastic bottle. She picked it up so she wouldn't stumble over it – '*Premium Paraffin Fuel*', the label said.

What?

There'd been no plastic bottle when she came through before.

The beam of her torch moved slowly across the ground – the puddle rising up under the wheelie bin, the bottom of the wall, the narrow gap under the gate, the space under the rotting metal of the fire escape, the ruined shelter, the tarp, boots . . .

Boots. They hadn't been there before.

She froze.

There was someone here. Someone had been here doing something with paraffin. Someone . . .

She swung the torch back to the shadows under the fire escape, lighting up the space, but now there was nothing there, just the wet bricks of the wall, a plastic bag stuffed with what looked like rags and cardboard someone had dumped, the sound of the rain, falling, falling . . .

Hands grabbed her from behind, pinning her arms to her side, and before she had a chance to struggle, she was shoved forward, hard, as something hooked round her ankle.

Her face smacked into the side of the wheelie bin, then she was on the ground, feeling the gravel and the mud on her bare hands. Something came down on the back of her neck, pressing her face into the wet dirt.

Mud filled her mouth and nose.

She was drowning.

She lay there, too dazed to struggle. A voice above her, low and hoarse, whispered, 'Snitch bitch.'

Then a light blazed suddenly, flames, a burning rag held above her head. She could smell the paraffin and the person standing above her laughed.

She struggled onto her knees, and something smashed into her ribs, making her fall and roll over again. He was standing over her, straddling her. She could see long, thin legs and above that, the rest of the figure was just a shape in the darkness. In the dim

213

light from the upstairs window, a hand came into view, a hand holding a rag or something. She gagged as she breathed in the smell of paraffin.

The click of a lighter.

She curled up with her arms over her face at the flash of heat as the rag was lit, then it was gone and she heard the *whuff!* of something igniting.

Something splashed over her face. Shit! *Shit!* He was pouring paraffin in her face, he was going to set her alight. Panic got her onto all fours and then she was dragging herself to her feet despite the stabbing pain in her ribs and pounding in her face where it had hit the bin.

Not the fire! *Not the fire!*

She heard laughter again and then the sound of feet moving away. The gate swung open. She turned, grabbing the wall for support and saw a figure, tall and thin, silhouetted in the light from the alleyway, then the gate swung shut leaving her in the darkness with the flicker of flames and the smell of paraffin in the air.

A bitter flavour filled her mouth and she spat and spat.

Chapter 25

Becca struggled to keep herself upright. Her face throbbed, her neck felt bruised and her ribs sent a stabbing pain through her side each time she took a breath.

She needed to . . . she needed to . . .

She lifted her arms to her face. She'd thought she was covered in paraffin, but she wasn't. What had happened? She caught the whiff of a foul smell. She didn't know what he'd poured over her, but it made her gag, and then she was throwing up, welcoming the heavy rain as it ran down her face and soaked through her clothes, washing her clean.

The paraffin bottle had been empty. He'd already used it.

On what?

A flickering light was illuminating the yard. The plastic bag under the fire escape, where it was protected from the rain, was burning. What had he been trying to do? Set fire to the building? The plastic bag was stuffed full of something – rags, cloths, she couldn't tell. Even in her panic, she could see that it presented no threat.

She was missing something. She knew she was. Something inside her was shouting urgently to do something, *do* something!

In the light from the flames, she saw her torch, which she'd dropped when she fell, lying on the ground. She picked it up and shook it, and it came on.

The rain had soaked right through to her skin now. She was shaking partly from the shock and partly from the cold. She had to get inside, get warm, clean herself up. Then she could decide what to do.

Using the wall as support, she stumbled across to the flames. Best put them out, though what had been the point of setting the fire in the first place? A small bottle of paraffin, the rain, a fire on the wet ground in the yard – why?

Snitch bitch. A warning? This is what we'll do if . . .

And then she realised. She knew what she'd missed.

The kitten.

She was on her knees at once, pulling the burning rubbish out of the bag, ignoring the pain in her hands where the melting plastic stuck as she grabbed at it, burning fabric, rags soaked in fuel.

And wrapped up tightly in the middle was a small, furry bundle.

They'd been trying to burn the kitten.

She pushed the smouldering cloths away and shook the hot ashes off her hands. She had the kitten now but it was lying wrong, as if its legs were in the wrong place.

Oh shit, what had they done to it?

But its mouth opened and it made a faint call.

It was alive.

Becca staggered to her feet, keeping her hands steady. Holding the kitten in one hand, she shone the torch on it, forcing herself to look.

She felt a rush of relief as she saw what the problem was. It looked all wrong because it was tangled up with something – someone had tied it up – her fingers struggled to sort out the tangle – some kind of tape. But it was alive, and as far as she could tell, it wasn't damaged by the fire. She needed to get it into the warm.

She tucked it under her coat and hurried back up the stairs, ignoring the pain in her hands, the dull ache from where her face had hit the wheelie bin, the sharp pain in her ribs where he had kicked her.

She dumped her coat and shoes on the floor outside the flat, then took the kitten in. The overhead light was just a fluorescent tube, but it gave her what she needed, a bright, white light. She put the kitten down on the rug and looked at it. It lay there quietly, not struggling any more, and that alarmed her.

Someone had wrapped sticky tape round its legs and its neck. The roll of tape was still there – whatever was going on, Becca's arrival had stopped it.

She got her scissors out and, working carefully, slit the tape so it began to tear. The kitten squeaked a couple of times as she pulled the tape off. 'Sorry. I'm sorry,' Becca said.

It was probably good that it squeaked, right?

Its fur was soaked and bedraggled. For a horrible moment, she thought her attacker must have poured paraffin over it – how did you get paraffin out of a cat's coat? – but there was no smell of the oil, just a frizzled patch where the burning rag had been lying against it. Becca picked up the scissors, and cut that chunk of fur off. The skin underneath seemed fine, pink and healthy, not burned.

She put the little animal on a folded towel in the armchair which was, Becca knew from experience, the warmest place in the flat, then she heated up some milk and soaked the cat biscuits in it until they dissolved. She offered the mush to the kitten, who licked it off her finger, then struggled to its feet to crouch over the dish Becca put in front of it.

She felt a flood of relief. It was eating. It was OK.

And it was making an odd sound. She listened anxiously. It was a strange, rusty sort of sound. Then she realised. It was purring. All the tension she'd been holding inside her relaxed.

She'd done it.

The kitten had survived. It was going to be OK.

And now for her. Just about every bit of her hurt and her hands were really sore. She could see where the ground had torn her leggings, and the skin was grazed, blood showing through the dirt. In the mirror, she could see a bruise forming high on her cheek where it had hit the bin. There was a cut on her lip and the side of her face was scraped.

But more than that, she felt dirty, soiled. She needed to get under the shower and let the water wash her and wash her until she felt clean.

Snitch bitch.

Someone had come here to warn her off. But whoever it was can't have planned to attack her. There was no way he would have expected her to come down again, so late, into the rain and darkness. She felt a cold disgust as she realised someone must have been watching her, and for longer than today. They must have seen her with the kitten, and they'd planned to leave a warning on the doorstep for her to find tomorrow morning – the kitten, burned.

She didn't want to think about it, but it wouldn't leave her mind – the flames and how it had been trussed up so it couldn't escape. There was a really sick person out there, someone who knew where she lived, someone who'd seen her talking to Curwen.

Snitch bitch.

Dead right she was. She'd let herself be scared into silence once in her life, but never again. Never. And no one hurt the things she cared about. They'd hurt the kitten. They'd planned to hurt it worse.

The red mist that was rising in her head smothered the thoughts. All that was left was anger. And a sudden understanding of what Matt had meant when he'd told her not to waste her anger, but to use it. She wanted to smash broken glass into the face of whoever it was who hurt her kitten. But she wasn't going to do that.

As she swallowed the last of her paracetamol, she made her decision. It didn't matter that getting the cellar keys would be difficult – she'd do it. She'd find a way to get in there and then she was going to get some proper photographs and give them to Curwen.

Andy might have been a creep, but she was going to find out who had sent that text message – who had sent all of them because she knew now it wasn't him. Someone had been watching them, someone knew what was going on, and they'd used it, used *her* to hurt Andy. She'd find out who it was, who had killed him, who had left his little girl without a dad. He'd lied to her, but that didn't matter, not right now. What mattered was that now he was dead.

She'd get the answers, and then she'd make them sorry.

Chapter 26

Dinah had wasted no time the night before when she'd spotted the car leaving Sunk Island. It was long after her shift finished, but she couldn't leave it. She'd called Dave Sykes.

'Good work. I'll let the boss know. Get onto the Manchester people and get them round there. Find that car, find out who's been driving it and where it's been. OK?'

But after that, it had been frustration. By the time she made contact with the Greater Manchester force it was after midnight, and now, the next morning, she still hadn't heard anything.

The briefing was about to start – she couldn't go in there with her job unfinished. She called the Manchester number again, but the man she'd talked to the night before was off duty, and it took several frustrating minutes to find someone who even knew what she was talking about.

'It's a car that's involved in a murder enquiry,' she kept saying. 'A police officer was killed.'

Eventually, she found herself talking to someone who knew about it. 'It isn't your car,' the man said briskly.

'But it was there,' Dinah insisted. 'I saw it.'

'Not this one. I'll send the report through.'

She couldn't wait. Someone offered to bring the report through to the briefing, and she ran down the corridor, arriving just as Hammond was about to start speaking. He waited, pointedly, she thought, until she found a vacant chair.

She sank into her seat, still trying to make sense of what she'd heard from Manchester.

The findings from other parts of the investigation were proving depressingly thin. There was no trace of Andy's phone – it was almost certainly in the estuary and irretrievable. His car had been taken apart and every bit of it checked, but the search had come up with nothing, or nothing useful. 'There was a chemical trace,' Dave Sykes said. 'Alpha PVP – that drug we've been having trouble with, the one that sends the kids crazy. At some point, Andy must have had some in his car.'

Dinah remembered what Curwen had said, about Andy being on some kind of mission, and how it could be misinterpreted. But Hammond had to be told. And he had to know about Becca at the pub.

As if he'd read her thoughts, Hammond turned to her. 'Dinah, how are you getting on with the car searches? DS Sykes said you'd identified a car that might be of interest.'

'I'm waiting for a report on that one, sir.' She explained the focus of her searches and got an approving nod from Hammond. 'Show us on the map, please.'

Dinah found herself standing at the front of the room. She regretted her hasty dressing that morning – trousers and a sweatshirt, rather than her smart trouser suit. Looking professional was important. She called up the map on the laptop and showed them the turn-offs and the different routes that might take a car into the heart of Sunk Island. 'We don't know where he was killed,' she said, 'but it's reasonable to assume they came down close to the water.'

Her pointer followed the banks of the estuary. 'Andy was found here – that's the Spragger Drain sluice. There's no road, but there are tracks. The closest you can get to the estuary by car is here, Old Hall Road. It actually crosses Spragger Drain. After that, it's rough tracks. You'd need an off-roader or a bike.'

'We talked to the people at the farm the day after we found him,' Innes said. 'They say no one went past that night, and that's probably right. They've got cameras on their gates after all the thefts, and the dogs are out.'

'You can bring a car down here to Stone Creek,' Dinah went on. 'It's about three and a half kilometres from there to the sluice. So what I'm saying is that these roads here, here and here are the best way in to get down to Old Hall Road, or to Stone Creek. I looked at the other roads as well, but these were the ones I went to first.

'This car is the one I think we need to focus on.' She showed them the images, the red Fiesta turning onto Sunk Island road, followed by the bike that had slewed round.

'A bike,' someone said, linking it to what she'd said previously. 'Have you got any more information on that?'

'Not yet. But what I did find . . .' She showed them the picture of the red Fiesta leaving Sunk island by a different road. 'It turned west, towards Hull, but the owner lives near Manchester.'

Hammond was sitting forward, his gaze intent. 'You've been on to Greater Manchester?'

'Yes sir. I'm just waiting for their report. I was talking to them just before the briefing. They say this can't be our car.'

As if on cue, the door of the briefing room opened, and a woman came in with a sheet of paper. 'Report for DC Mason,' she said.

Hammond took it and read it in silence. 'It looks as though they're right. This car belongs to an Elizabeth Bagnall, who lives in Stockport. She's in her eighties and is a chronic invalid.'

'So someone else is using the car,' Dinah said.

'No.' Hammond gave her back the report. 'They checked it and it's in no condition to be driven. Mrs Bagnall has a live-in carer who says the car hasn't left the drive for weeks. The Stockport people were able to confirm that.'

Dinah brought up the image on the screen again – a red Ford Fiesta with the correct number plate leaving

Sunk Island and turning left along the main road. 'I checked with the DVLA,' she said. 'It's taxed and it's got its MOT. Why pay that? Why keep the car if no one is using it?'

'Cloned plates,' Hammond said. 'Cloned from a car identical to the one they're using, so the ANPR won't spot it.'

Dinah felt deflated. Her big lead, and all the time, the car was sitting in a garage in Greater Manchester. But as Hammond picked the topic up, she began to feel better. 'Whoever cloned those plates might have known the original car wouldn't be out and about. There could be a connection. Let's get details of the owner's family, friends, any other contacts who'd have that information. Let's get ANPR sightings of that number over the past month and see what the car's been up to. If they thought they had a safe number, they might have been using it for a while.' And it was when people got careless that they made mistakes, and mistakes was what got them caught. He looked at Dinah. 'Good work, DC Mason,' he said.

So her big break was a big break after all. Now was the time to get in with her next bit of information. 'There's something else,' she said. 'I went into the Smokehouse the other evening, just . . . I mean, I got talking to the barman and he said—'

Hammond held up his hand. 'Later, DC Mason. Right. You all know what you've got to do. How did the drug get into the car? Karen, check though his record of recent arrests, see who he picked up and what they were carrying. We need to find that car with the cloned plates, and we need to keep checking for any sign of his phone. Karen, bring me up to date later, will you?'

The team began to move on. Dinah hesitated, not sure whether she should go back to her desk, but Hammond indicated she should wait.

Once the team had dispersed, he looked at her. 'My office,' he said. Once they were in there, he closed to door and sat down at the desk, leaving her standing. 'DC Mason, tell me why you decided to go to the Smokehouse. You do remember what I told you at the first briefing?'

Curwen's casual, *You're allowed to drink where you want to* suddenly seemed very thin.

'You said there was no evidence of a link, but I thought it wouldn't hurt to—'

'DC Mason. There are issues around that pub that you may not know about. It's part of a serious complaint issued against this force. If there was any evidence linking Yeatson's death to the place, we'd go after it. But there isn't. Now, I'll tell you this once, and I expect you to listen. This is a team. You want to look into something? You ask DS Sykes or you ask me. You don't go off on your own. If you can't follow that rule, then maybe you need to rethink your position. You were transferred – when?'

'Just a few months ago, sir.'

'Right, and the role carries responsibilities. I don't

want to be worrying about how you deal with those when I write your performance review.'

'Sir, I—'

'Did you get that, DC Mason?'

'Yes, sir.'

'Right. Now get on with those car checks. We need to know where that Fiesta went.'

'Yes, sir, but . . .' He was about to interrupt her again, so she said quickly, 'Andy was seeing someone in the pub. I think. The barmaid.'

'DC Mason, how many times do I have to say this? That is not part of your job. I don't want the team distracted from important work by this kind of speculation. Your job is to find that car, and find out who knows the Bagnall woman's car is off the road. Now you've got that bit of gossip off your chest, do you feel ready to do that?'

He wasn't just ignoring it. He was trying to shut her up, and trying to stop her from talking about what she'd found out to the others. She opened her mouth to protest, caught his eye and closed it again.

'Yes, sir,' she said.

Chapter 27

Curwen sat at his desk, looking at his phone impatiently. He was trying to think of his next move. He hadn't given up on Becca the Barmaid. He'd issued a challenge, and she looked like the type who would respond to that. He hated to admit it to himself, but there was something about her he liked.

What else had he got? He went over everything she'd told him. There wasn't much, except she'd seen Lavery with the holdalls more than once since that first time, and – hang on, hang on – she'd seen him with them coming out of ... He sat very still as he tried to recall that conversation in his car. She'd said: *I saw his car once on that street down from the main road. He came out of that café, you know? And he was carrying a couple of bags then.*

That street that runs down from ... He came out of that café ... Something was ringing bells.

He went onto Google Maps and looked on street view.

There was the café B the B had mentioned – which called itself an arcade. There was a hand car wash over the road. It was where Andy had parked that night, where he left his car, just before he vanished.

Coincidence?

Maybe.

Maybe not.

So who owned that café? A quick check in a local business directory told him it was owned by a company called Docklands Holdings. He went onto the web to check it out.

Docklands Holdings had a registered office address in Bridlington, and its director was Carl Lavery.

Connections. This whole case hung on connections; he was sure of that.

Lavery owned a café with arcade machines. They'd take money or tokens every day and they'd be emptied every night if the café stood empty. Was this what Lavery was bringing back to the pub, holdalls of cash from the arcade machines?

Now Curwen was getting a bad feeling, a truly bad feeling.

Could he have been so wrong? For the first time, he felt the whole structure of the case he was building up against Lavery start to crumble. Maybe he was just what he seemed to be: a local small businessman who was probably involved in a fair bit of minor dodgy stuff, but nothing that would help Curwen.

Because he couldn't think of anything else to do, he went on with his checks. Lavery's business interests were wider than Curwen expected, and the investigation started to draw him in. Lavery also owned the car wash and garage on the same street as the café, and several holiday lets. He couldn't access more than the basic financial information on the company – where it banked, the names of the directors.

Or in this case, director. Carl Lavery was the sole director of Docklands Holdings, and the company banked with the Bridlington Building Society, a small, local mutual that didn't look like the place a serious lawbreaker would keep his money.

On the other hand, car washes and cafés were notorious locations for drug deals and this, at least, gave him reason to keep on hoping.

Had he got the right man but the wrong business?

What had Becca the Barmaid said about the pub cellar?

He got out his phone, the burner he kept for unofficial stuff. This was the one that had received the messages he'd forwarded from Andy's phone. He hadn't looked at it since Andy's body was found.

He scrolled down to the messages marked from Andy, and almost dropped his phone.

There was a new one. One he hadn't seen.

The date was . . .

Shit! How had he missed it? Becca the Barmaid had sent a photograph from the cellar – the fucking cupboard! And there they were, the bags, except the silly cow hadn't got a picture of what was inside them. And these didn't contain petty cash or the previous night's takings. They were bulging.

The image had been sent three days after Andy died, the night he'd been in the pub talking to her.

And the phone – fuck it! – had sent the automatic response, 'Great', that he'd programmed in. But Andy was dead. His phone was presumably at the bottom of the estuary. How had it forwarded the message?

Slowly, Curwen managed to calm his wilder speculations. If he just stopped to think, it was easy enough to work out. Andy's phone hadn't been disposed of, and it was still active, or it had been. The battery would be dead by now. Andy must have dropped it . . .

Curwen thought fast, running scenarios through his head. They were all assuming Andy had been taken, killed and dumped, but if he'd dropped his phone, he might have got away, might have been running. The location of the phone could give the investigation important information about where he had been killed. Dinah had already told him that they didn't know the exact location, or not for sure.

So why hadn't the phone registered on the searches? He knew from Dinah they hadn't found it, but they should have been able to. He had the information right here – the phone had been active after Andy's death.

It must be because the signal was intermittent. Sunk Island was notorious for its poor connections. There was no location for the phone when the search was made because it hadn't been able to connect, but later, for a fatal few seconds, it had.

A high wind moving the trees around, making the tower sway – that could have given a brief connection that had picked up and transmitted the message. And

231

that meant that somewhere in the records there would be a signal that might help them find the phone.

If they found Andy's phone, they'd find the app, and they'd see that messages had been forwarded. The number wouldn't link to him, but the phone records would give them a location – not pinpoint it, but give a location within a few hundred square yards. And he'd made contact with that phone at Bridlington police station, and also at his flat.

If they found the phone, he could be in trouble.

He'd fucked up. No promotion, a black mark on his record and the other high-fliers would take off around him, leaving him behind. He'd end up on a team run by Karen Innes, having to defer to her decisions, call her 'ma'am.' Well, fuck that. That wasn't going to happen.

Could he locate the phone himself? No, stirring up the phone company for their records would surely come to Hammond's attention. Best sit tight on that one.

He needed to get that information about Lavery's company. If he could link Lavery to the drugs, just about everything would be forgiven.

Right. Who owed him a favour?

He picked up his phone and keyed in a number, cursing as he got the messaging service. 'Dom? It's Mark Curwen here. I need some information, urgently.' He outlined what he knew, and hung up, praying that his mate, Dom Maskall, a forensic accountant, would be around and would check his messages fast. Maskall owed Curwen some favours, including the time Curwen had managed to get a charge of ABH against him – when he'd thumped the man who was screwing his wife – dropped by 'losing' a piece of key evidence.

Now, if he needed financial information on the quiet, Maskall was the person he went to. Right now, he wanted all the information Maskall could get for him on Lavery's company, Docklands Holdings.

He had to get the thing finished, get evidence that would allow him to bypass whoever was protecting Lavery.

He had to clear up this mess. There was still time.

'Sir?'

His heart raced as he spun round. Dinah Mason was behind him, her neat blonde hair shining under the strip lighting, red glasses slipping down her nose. She looked angry and agitated.

'What's the problem, Mason?'

'I spoke to the DCI, sir, about the woman in the pub, about Becca Armitage and Andy. He went ballistic. He said it was a side issue and that if he couldn't rely on me to do my job, then I was off the team, and I wasn't to distract people with this by talking about it.'

As Curwen listened to her story, he got more and more confused. He'd wanted to keep Hammond away from Becca the Barmaid because her involvement with Andy would have to be investigated, which could be bad news for him. But now Hammond knew Becca and Andy had been seeing each other, and hadn't just ignored it. He'd dismissed it – and kept it away from the team.

What the fuck?

'I'll look into it,' he said. Mason had no option but to accept that and get back to work, leaving Curwen to try and work out what the fuck was going on.

Another possibility was starting to form in his mind. Maybe Lavery had kept out of trouble because he had better protection than Curwen could ever have realised. Lavery wasn't just a small-time landlord of a run-down seaside pub. He was a businessman, and Curwen suspected he'd only just started uncovering the extent of Lavery's interests.

Was one of those interests a senior police officer?

If so, it wasn't just Curwen's career that was fucked. He was in danger of ending up like Andy almost had, at the bottom of the estuary.

Rule one: if someone is out to fuck you over, the only thing to do is to fuck them over first.

He had to get Lavery, and fast.

Chapter 28

Bridlington

Becca's night was an endless replay of dreams about things chasing her, hands grabbing her, her stepfather's footsteps on the stairs, her mother's voice calling her a liar, and periods of wakefulness that were almost welcome, when the pain in her shoulder and her neck dragged her out of her nightmares. She must have fallen into a deeper sleep at some point because when she opened her eyes again it was daylight and for a moment, everything was peaceful – until she tried to move her neck and pain brought the memory of last night flooding back.

She was so stiff it was hard to move, and there was no more paracetamol. The drug had barely helped anyway. She remembered Jared with his collection of opiates that, right now, much as she hated pills and pill-heads, would have been welcome.

Remembering him made her feel so alone she could hardly bear it. She got out her phone and scrolled through the photographs, stopping at one of her and Jared standing by his bike on the cliffs at Kettleness. She missed him, but they couldn't sort their lives out together, so they had to do it apart.

She hoped he was doing better than she was.

The kitten was scratching and scraping around. She could hear the click of tiny claws as it pattered across the floor. What was she going to do with it? She could ask George if she could have a kitten, but what if he said no? Best keep it and say nothing. For the moment.

Slowly, she pulled herself out of bed, and moving carefully, went and got some more kitten food and milk. The kitten was back on the armchair, but the mess on her scarf that she'd left on the floor showed what it had been scratching and why it had got down in the night. She picked the scarf up and shoved it into a plastic bag – it was beyond cleaning. It could go in the bin.

She needed to buy stuff – cat litter, something to put the litter in, more food, more milk. It was all money and she just didn't have enough. She extended a hand towards the little animal. It had been so timid before, but now it stayed put as she stroked its cheek and heard the buzz of a purr.

She felt a glow of triumph. It liked her.

She'd always managed on her own, so she'd do it now, somehow.

Hoping it would be OK without a litter tray for a bit longer, she fed it, then went and stood under the shower until the hot water ran out, scrubbing the dirt off herself and washing her hair. Reluctantly, she looked in the mirror.

Her face was bruised and her lip was swollen where it was split. Her knees were grazed, and there were bruises all over her body. She could tell people she'd fallen, but what would that make them think? That she'd been drunk, that's what they'd think.

It was her half day at the supermarket today and she thought about pulling a sickie. She *was* sick. It was hard to move, she was hurting so much, and her ribs were still painful where the shit, the dickface, had kicked her. Why not give herself a day off to recover?

Because she needed the money.

And although part of her wanted to give up, to stay away from the pub, show them she'd got the message, that she'd understood, that anger – the anger Matt talked about – came back. Why should she? They'd hurt Andy – and he was a creep and she didn't care, she *didn't* – but his kid, that wasn't right, and they'd hurt her kitten, and they'd hurt her. What had she done to them?

Nothing.

She was going to the pub tonight, she was going to ask questions and she'd find a way to get into that cupboard and take those pictures. She'd show them they hadn't managed to scare her away.

But right now, she had other things to think about. It was already after seven and she had to be at the supermarket by eight. She pulled her clothes on and looked at her bruises in the mirror. Make-up wasn't going to help – she'd just have to face them down.

The kitten. Milk in one dish, biscuits in another. She limped downstairs to the junk room at the bottom of the stairs and grabbed one of the boxes. It would do for a tray. She went back upstairs with it, each movement making her wince, and filled it with torn up loo paper – that would do for the moment.

OK. Coat, bag, phone, purse . . .

Her purse.

She usually left it on the small table after she got out her card for the meter, but it wasn't there.

She hadn't used the card last night.

She scrabbled in her bag, then tipped the contents out over the bed. It wasn't until she'd gone through everything three times, and tipped the bag up and shaken it, that she was prepared to admit it.

Her purse was gone.

That was her card for the meter with at least five quid on it, her bank card and . . . *shit*. The envelope with her money from the pub.

She went cold as the implications struck her. That was all her money. What was she going to do? Her head was aching, her face hurt. Everything hurt, and now she had no money. She wanted to sit down on the bed and cry.

And that's really going to help.

She lifted her chin. They wanted to stop her. Well, she wasn't going to stop. She was going to keep right on doing . . . She wasn't even sure what it was she had been doing, but she was going to keep on doing it anyway.

Now, she needed to get to work. Losing her job wasn't going to help. She could see if Bryan would give her any overtime. And she could tell Carl what had happened. He might pay her again. *Yeah, right.* That was going to happen, wasn't it?

He might be prepared to sub her. At a price.

But she had to have money, right now. Feeling as though she was taking the first step towards a sheer drop, she took a ten-pound note out of the rent and headed downstairs, back towards the yard, looking carefully across the ground as she went in case her purse was there.

It wasn't, but she could see the evidence of a scuffle, the empty paraffin bottle still lying on the ground, the burned pile of rags. She didn't even know who it was who'd attacked her. Johnny Dip? Carl? Did he know about the pictures? Was it Carl sending her fake text messages from Andy? But why would he? He didn't want her snooping around in the cellar.

And now she had to admit she was scared. She might not know who had attacked her, but she knew they were still out there. It felt unsafe to step out of the flat. Even the road would have felt dangerous, but she had to go out the back way and through the gennel – the shop didn't open until nine.

Feeling horribly exposed, like someone was going to jump her at any moment, she pushed open the gate and looked round, her phone clutched in her hand. The gennel was empty and when she got to the end, she saw the road was quiet – a few people walking along, and . . . Her feet slowed. There was a bunch of kids standing on the corner, crowded round someone she couldn't see. The group shifted as she approached and she saw the lad in the centre of the group, who'd been hidden before.

It was Lewis, Jade's Lewis.

No bike today.

She took in the designer gear and the cool trainers that she knew Jade couldn't possibly have afforded, but the clothes were scuffed and stained, his lip was bleeding, his face looked pinched and he looked scared – petrified. He might be a little shit, but he was still just a kid, her mate's kid, and he looked like he was in deep trouble. Hadn't she been there herself? He was what? Eleven, twelve? About the same age she'd been when everything finally fell to pieces.

On impulse, she stopped. 'Lewis?' she said.

One of the lads, the tall, lanky one she'd seen with Lewis before, looked round. His hand was in his pocket, gripping something. 'Fuck off, bitch.' Slowly, the others began to move towards her.

Her mouth felt dry. She stepped back, out of arms reach, and held up her phone. 'Do you want the coppers here?' she said.

240

'Yeah, like . . .' The tall, lanky lad was sneering, but while the attention of the group was directed towards her, Lewis ducked, turned and ran. A bus was heading down the opposite side of the road, pulling into the stop. He was across the road, almost under the bus wheels and scrambling onto it before the others could react. 'Let him go,' the lanky guy said. His eyes, cold and empty, met hers. 'You're dead, bitch.'

They turned and sauntered away.

Becca's legs felt shaky. She ought to do some-thing, but she didn't know what. Lewis was safe, for now. The others were gone and she had no idea who they were. She hesitated, then saw that her bus was just pulling into the stop. She couldn't lose half a day's pay. It was hard to run. She stumbled towards the bus, waving, and by some kind of miracle, the driver waited for her. 'Morning, love,' he said cheerfully as she eased herself up onto the platform. He waited until she was in her seat before he pulled away, a small kindness that made her eyes sting.

Were those lads intending to hurt Lewis, or were they just giving him a warning? She could still see the flat menace in the eyes of the lanky kid. *You're dead!* She knew what he had in his pocket.

Was it just a threat? Did he know something about last night?

Snitch bitch. She could still see the silhouette of the man who had attacked her, against the dim light of

241

the gennel. Was it him, the tall, lanky lad? The voice was wrong, and she thought the person she'd seen silhouetted against the light wasn't as tall, but she couldn't be certain. It was all swirling round in her head in a confusing jumble – Lewis, the knife, the attack, the text message – and she could feel, deep down inside her, the thoughts starting again: *useless, waste of space, loser, loser, baggers can't be choosers, Becca* . . .

She closed her eyes and let them wash over her. Like a rowdy crowd in a shopping mall, they flowed past, pushing and shoving, and then they were gone and she could breathe again.

There were other things to worry about, and she made herself focus on those. Where was she going to find ten pounds to replace the money she'd taken out of the rent? How was she going to manage when she'd lost a week's cash? There was just the remains of the tenner and it would be – she did the sums rapidly in her head – it would be nine days before she got paid again.

There'd be no money for heat, for food, for the kitten.

She couldn't take any more out of the rent money. George had been OK recently, but he wouldn't be if she went into arrears. He'd made that clear when she moved in. You paid up or you were out. She put her face in her hands, then realised people were looking at her, and sat up again.

But she didn't know what she was going to do.

When she got to the supermarket – on time, thanks to the bus driver – Bryan took one look at her face. 'You can't go on the tills like that,' he said.

'It's nothing. I . . .' She didn't know what to say, and ended up with 'I fell over', which was probably the worst thing she could have said.

'I don't want to know about that,' he said. 'Well, you'd better work in the stockroom this morning. It's not convenient. I've got two people off today.'

'I'm sorry.' She'd sworn she wouldn't apologise but she needed his help. 'Listen, are you short-handed this afternoon? I could stay on.' She could manage without her half day. Work here till five-thirty, then go on to the pub. She could do that.

'I need people on the tills and the shop floor. You can't—'

'I can cover it with some make-up,' Becca said, hearing the eagerness in her voice. 'I could, you know, keep the shelves stacked and stuff. People wouldn't notice.'

'Absolutely not. We can't have our staff out in the shop looking as if they've been brawling. I'm not happy with your attitude to the customers anyway. I've been told you even swear in front of them.'

Sheryl. The cow. 'I don't,' she said quickly. 'That's not true. But this afternoon, I'm sure I could . . .' She heard the pleading note in her voice and hated herself for it.

'No. Absolutely not,' he said again.

So that was that. It was like being caught in a trap and she couldn't see any way out of it. All morning she shifted boxes – wet from the rain so she had to watch out for the tape giving way – loaded trolleys for shelving, checked inventories on the system, trying to ignore the stiffness and the pain. Her mind was going over and over the problem. How could she get some more money? At least it stopped her thinking about anything else.

You're dead.

She caught up with Jade when she came in later in the morning, and told her quickly about what she'd seen. 'He looked really scared, Jade.'

Jade shook her head wearily. 'I don't know what to do. We had the police round yesterday for him. Little sod. He pretends he's so tough but he just about wet himself. I think he dobbed some people in, and now they're after him.'

'Won't they – you know, the police – give him some protection?'

'Them? Don't make me laugh. I said, I told them, you can take him. Put him in one of them units. He won't listen to me.'

'Really?'

'He's going to get himself hurt,' Jade said. 'Maybe they can keep him out of trouble.' Her words were angry, but her eyes looked haunted as she stubbed her cigarette out. 'Are you OK?' she asked, as if she'd only just noticed the bruises on Becca's face.

'Yeah, I'm fine,' Becca reassured her, and Jade just nodded without making any further comment.

By midday, her ribs were on fire and every bruise seemed to hurt twice as much. All she wanted to do was go home, curl up on the bed and sleep, but she had to walk past the bus stop, even though her bus was waiting there as people climbed on board. She was broke. A small box of own-brand cat biscuits had cost her almost two quid, leaving her with three pounds to last her until she was paid again. OK, she could – just – feed herself and the kitten for the next few days. Her rent was due at the end of the week and she was ten pounds short. It might as well be five hundred for all the chance she had of getting it. And there was no point in asking Bryan for an advance. He'd enjoy saying 'No.'

The walk home took an age, she had to move so carefully with the stabbing pain in her ribs. She didn't want George to see her bruised face so she went past the shop, heading for the entrance to the gennel. As she reached it, she saw two of the lads from earlier hanging around, their hoods pulled up, their shoulders hunched. The lanky one wasn't there. These were younger. *They're just kids*, she reassured herself, but when they saw her, their eyes turned towards her like guns.

You're dead!

She stopped.

The voice came from behind her and she spun round, half expecting to feel the punch that would be a knife in her ribs.

'Becca? It is Becca. Isn't it?'

A car had pulled up beside her and the driver, a woman, had wound the window down. Becca stared at her, taking in the short fair hair and the bright red glasses. 'Who . . .?'

The kids melted away and were gone.

Chapter 29

Dinah watched as the lads who'd been hanging around vanished into the surrounding streets. She didn't know them, but she recognised the style; the designer hoodies, the air of swaggering menace. Kids who hung around with gangs, kids who'd been drawn into the apparently easy pickings available from the street drugs trade.

The fair-haired young woman who'd been about to talk to them spun round in response to Dinah's call. Dinah had recognised her – Becca Armitage, Andy's girlfriend. Dinah was shocked as she saw Becca's face. She'd been hurt – someone had hit her, if Dinah knew anything about it. There was a bruise running down towards her jaw, her lip was swollen and she reacted to sudden movement as if she was in pain.

The pieces began to slot together: Andy had a girlfriend at the pub, and the girlfriend had some connection with the kids the dealers were using. Was there a motive here for Andy's death?

Who had hurt this girl, and why?

Dinah knew she shouldn't be here, but she also knew Hammond was wrong. It was possible – probable – that Becca Armitage knew something, something that might help find Andy's killers. She'd been his girlfriend, so she'd want to help, right?

Dinah wasn't disobeying an order; she hadn't gone near the pub. She'd seen this woman, Becca Armitage, being threatened – maybe – by some of the kids who hung around with the gangs. She wouldn't be doing her duty if she didn't follow it up.

If Becca Armitage didn't know anything, then there was no need to say anything to Hammond. If she did . . . *Wait and see*, Dinah counselled herself.

She put on her best friendly smile as she got out of the car. 'That looks nasty. What happened?' As soon as she spoke, she knew it was a mistake to ask the question.

'What's it to do with you?' Becca was instantly suspicious.

'I'm Dinah Mason. You work at the Smokehouse, don't you?'

There was a long hesitation before Becca said, 'Why?'

Dinah took out her ID. 'I'm investigating the murder of—'

Becca turned away. 'I've already talked to someone.'

Curwen. He'd said he'd been into the pub. She knew from her months of working with him that

248

Curwen had a real talent for getting up people's noses, and it looked like he'd managed to ruffle Becca Armitage's feathers. 'I know, but I've got a few more questions to ask. You live above the shop, don't you? Could I come in? Or we can sit in the car.'

Becca looked round, along the street where the kids had vanished. Dinah understood at once. She didn't want to be seen talking to Dinah. 'We can meet somewhere else, but I really need to talk to you.'

Becca chewed her lip and winced as she caught a painful bit. 'You might as well come in.' She pulled her hood up to hide her damaged face and led the way through the shop door, which was propped open with a stack of zinc pails. A familiar smell of polish, wood and household chemicals told Dinah this was an old-fashioned hardware shop, like the one that used to be down the road from her nan's. A large man sitting behind the till glanced up as they came in. 'Afternoon, Becca.'

Becca mumbled a response, keeping her face turned away. 'Good afternoon,' Dinah said, probably overdoing the chirpiness judging by the look of deep suspicion the man gave them as they walked through to the back of the shop.

'Only I'm not meant to come through this way,' Becca said over her shoulder.

'You use the alley?' Dinah asked. 'It's a bit . . .' She didn't complete the sentence. She wasn't here to criticise. 'He didn't seem to mind,' she said as she followed Becca up the narrow, dark stairway.

'George is OK.' Becca was fumbling with her key. Dinah followed her into a small bedsit room.

She could see at once that Becca had made the best of poor material. The room was painted white, which could have been bleak and cold, but it was warmed by splashes of bright red – a rug on the floor, a throw, a red lampshade. The same colour was picked up by a red tea caddy next to the kettle. Posters on the wall showed patterns of light – fireworks against the night sky, some kind of festival illuminated by flames and flares, a lake reflecting a forest. A mirror opposite the window helped to light the room up and create a sense of space. Dinah could recognise taste when she saw it, and Becca Armitage certainly had it, to judge by this room. 'You've made it nice,' she said.

An expression that was almost a smile flickered across Becca's face before it settled into suspicious impassivity again. Something skittered out from under the bed, making Dinah jump, and vanished under the big armchair which had been covered by a warm-looking textured throw. 'You've got a kitten,' she said. She loved cats.

'Yeah. What do you want? I've only got a few minutes.'

'Yes. Of course. I wanted to ask you some questions about Andy Yeatson.'

Becca's chin lifted. 'Why should I know anything?'

'They told me at the pub you were his girlfriend. It must have been a shock when you heard about what happened to him.'

Becca shrugged and turned away. She picked up some clothes that were piled up on a chair and started folding them. Dinah suppressed a moment of anger. This display of indifference was just a front, she was pretty sure. Becca Armitage didn't trust her. Well, Dinah was prepared to take her time. 'We're having trouble getting information about what Andy was doing that last night. I thought you might be able to help. Did you see him?'

'I haven't seen him for weeks,' Becca said. 'Nearly a month now. I don't know anything.'

'You haven't?' That was unexpected. 'Why was that? Did you break up?'

'He had to go away. For work.'

This was something new. 'Did he say where?'

Becca shook her head. 'Just away. For work. He texted—' She stopped speaking abruptly.

'He texted you?'

But Becca just shook her head. 'No. He didn't.'

There was something off here. Dinah spoke carefully, feeling her way. 'He went away for work?' Andy must have been playing some kind of game. He hadn't gone anywhere, Dinah knew that, but she couldn't imagine Andy stringing a young woman like this along.

'I said so, didn't I?'

'Yes, you did. Did he tell you what his work was?'

251

'Yeah. He was an investigator.'

That was a strange was to put it. 'An investigator?'

'He was like, you know, a private investigator. You're supposed to be finding out who killed him, and you don't even know . . .' Her eyes narrowed. 'That wasn't true, was it?'

Dinah wanted to defend Andy, but she wasn't going to lie. 'He *was* an investigator, but not a private one. He was a detective with the local police.'

Becca went very still, then busied herself with the clothes again, unfolding the ones she'd already folded and shaking them out. She dropped the shirt she was holding onto the floor and turned back to face Dinah. Dinah looked at her, taking in the bruised face and noticing, for the first time, red marks on Becca's hands that looked like burns. Something bad had happened here, and recently. 'If you're in any kind of trouble, if people are giving you a hard time, I can help.'

'I'm OK.'

The barriers went back up. Becca Armitage's defensiveness aroused Dinah's curiosity – why was she so suspicious? 'Listen, Becca. Andy didn't tell you the truth about what he was doing. I don't know why. He shouldn't have lied to you. But he was a good man. He didn't deserve to die. And he's left a child – a little girl. She's already lost her mum. Now her dad's dead too. I want to get the people who did this.'

'Yeah, well, I . . .' Becca Armitage's voice died away

and she was staring at Dinah. 'What do you mean, lost her mum?'

'He didn't tell you? Andy's wife died. Shortly after the baby was born.'

Becca just stood there, staring at Dinah. She looked very pale and the bruise stood out, dark and ugly on her face. 'His wife . . . died?'

'Nearly two years ago.'

'And he was a copper?'

'Yes. I worked with him.'

Becca turned away and started packing stuff into a bag. 'You need to go. I've got things to do.' Her voice was muffled.

Dinah waited, but Becca didn't say any more. She put her card down on the table. 'Think about what I said. If Andy hid anything from you, he was probably trying to keep you safe. If you think of anything that might help, get in touch. And if anyone . . . you know. You've got my number if you need it.' Dinah waited a moment, but Becca didn't say anything and didn't turn to look at her.

Dinah was thinking hard as she went down the stairs, hearing the flat door close decisively behind her. Things were happening here, things the investigation team needed to know about. She had no idea why Hammond was dragging his feet, but she was going to bring it up at the next briefing, and she was going to have all the facts that were available to back up what she was saying. Then let him ignore it and try to throw her off the investigation.

She left the building via the back door into the yard, rather than go through the shop. She wanted to check a few things out.

The yard was small and enclosed. The high wall, with the narrow alleyway behind it, meant that it was isolated. A lot could happen here with no one knowing. Her gaze moved round, noting an empty plastic bottle, and the remains of burned rags and paper. She remembered the red burn marks on Becca's hands.

Using her pencil, she picked up the plastic bottle and read the label. *Premium Paraffin Fuel*. She slipped it into an evidence bag. Her lips tightening, she collected the burned rags, even though the rain would have washed away most of what was on them, and slipped them into an evidence bag too.

She looked round the yard. A large wheelie bin occupied a lot of the space. There was something under the fire escape under a tarpaulin. She lifted it to check. A bike. A Yamaha. Small engine, but it could probably move. She dug around a bit more, but there was nothing else. She wanted to get back to the station and talk to Curwen, but there was no time. DCI Hammond had told her to get across to Stockport and check out the lead she'd found to the car. That would take the rest of the day.

She just didn't have enough information. She knew that Andy had been into the Smokehouse as part of an investigation – it had to be, otherwise why all the cock and bull stuff about being a private investigator?

Becca Armitage, his girlfriend, had been attacked and hurt.

She didn't know who had hurt Becca, or why. She didn't know specifically what Andy had been investigating at the pub.

Becca Armitage wasn't talking, and Dinah couldn't be sure what her involvement was.

But she was going to find out.

Chapter 30

It was afternoon before Curwen heard back from Dom Maskall. His accountant friend had really come through for him.

As Curwen listened, he began to realise just how much of a mistake he'd made with Carl Lavery. The raid on the pub had been a botch from the start. If he'd done his homework, he could have got Lavery without putting Andy at risk at all.

But that was water under the bridge.

'Docklands Holdings,' Maskall said. 'On the surface, there's nothing dodgy going on. Money comes in, money goes out. Most of it's done with cash, so the records might be a bit off; the businesses are a bit more profitable than I would have expected, but there's nothing there that would make anyone want to look more closely.'

'But?'

Maskall laughed. 'Exactly. *But*. Your man obviously knows what he's doing. Now there is something from the accounts three years ago. Docklands

Holdings sold a couple of properties in Bridlington and one in Hull. They got five hundred thousand overall – made a small profit on each one on paper, but once you took running costs into account, they made a loss, so there was no tax liability. Now this is where it gets interesting. Did you know your man is a philanthropist?'

'Lavery?' If there was one thing about Maskall that drove Curwen mad, it was the way he dangled information, teasing, wanting a reaction.

'I mean he gave three hundred thousand of that money to a charity.'

Curwen's jaw dropped. That was crazy. He would have been less surprised if Lavery had been caught sacrificing seaside donkeys to the rain gods. 'That makes no sense at all.'

'Believe me, it makes a lot of sense once you start looking. I haven't managed to get a close look at the charity yet, but you can be sure that when it spends that money, some of it will be coming back to your man.'

Curwen still didn't get it. 'He gives away three hundred grand and gets some of it back? Why not just keep the money? It's accounted for, you said so.'

'That's how it looked. Now listen. The charity banks with the Bridlington Building Society – it's just a small organisation, local, you know? They did the checks and their Money Laundering Reporting Officer put in a report saying the money coming from Lavery via Docklands Holdings was legit, which it was. *Except* the MLRO missed one important point. The company that bought the properties is called . . . hang on, hang on . . .' There was the sound of a keyboard tapping. 'There you go. CaLa. It's called CaLa.'

'Carla? You mean like a girl's name?'

'No. CaLa.' Maskall spelled the name out. 'It's based in Hull, but like your Brid business, it does holiday lets, car washes, things like that – businesses with a high cash turnover and a clientele that is hard to track. They have a "massage" parlour as well. You know?'

Curwen could hear the inverted commas round the word. He knew all too well what Maskall meant. 'So what did the MLRO miss?'

'The owner of CaLa is your man, Carl Lavery. No one checked the money that came from CaLa.'

So if the money from CaLa was dodgy, Lavery had cleaned it up by selling some property to himself. 'OK, he made the cash legit, so why give it away?'

'Because it isn't a one-time operation. He can't keep on selling stuff to himself – he'll get caught. But once a charity has a record of regular donations from a checked and legitimate source, how hard is anyone going to look? What you need to see is a breakdown of the charity's outgoings. Somewhere on there, hiding behind a big wall, you'll find Carl Lavery.'

'So Lavery keeps donating and no one checks after the first time?'

'Not if they've squared off the MLRO. Cash? Girls? There'll be something. He's got a report that shows the first donation was fine. After that, he can do soft reports that won't turn up anything, but if anyone starts asking questions, all the paperwork is in place. He's in the clear, just looks as though he's not very good at his job.'

'How do I get to see the charity's books?'

'You don't, without a warrant. Can you get one?'

Curwen thought about it. Did he have enough? He just wasn't sure. Maskall wouldn't go public with this – the information was strictly between him and Curwen, and as it wasn't a legitimate search, Curwen couldn't use it himself. 'I'll need more, from a source I can show my boss.'

'OK. I'll tell you what. I know the firm that does the accounts. I'll give them a ring, ask a few questions, see what I can come up with.'

'When?'

'I'll do it today and get back to you.'

'Don't let them know you're onto them.'

'Don't worry – I'll say I've got a potential donor wants to know. There'll be something there you can use.'

So it wasn't the drugs. It was the money from the drugs. Money that came in as cash, untraceable money, but money that had to be cleaned up and accounted for.

It was as simple as that. Curwen didn't need Becca the Barmaid. He didn't need the pub. He just needed to start tracking the money until he had enough evidence for a warrant. 'What's the charity?'

'It's based in Hull. It's a drugs charity. Tania's House.'

Maskall rang off.

Chapter 31

Hull

Kay got into the office early on Monday. Her case files – after a couple of days of hard work – were now up to date. She wanted time to get on top of things before her clients started arriving. That afternoon, Poppy should be there for her appointment and Kay was hoping to find out more about what had gone so wrong.

She also had things to sort out about the house. It was simpler to call from here. The phone signal was just too unreliable from Sunk Island. After her walk yesterday, she'd almost called the police to tell them about the possible break-in and the empty compost bag blowing around the field. It was only the bad signal that had stopped her. But after thinking about it, she wasn't sure. What could she say? The empty compost bag was a common enough brand. She couldn't say for sure if it was the same as the bags she had – maybe – seen in the store.

And anyway, the whole idea of people breaking in and stealing a few bags of compost was just – farcical. She knew there were thieves targeting Sunk Island, there were break-ins and – if Catherine Ford was to be believed – the police weren't chasing it up, or not with any enthusiasm, so how much attention would they pay to her story?

The best thing she could do now was make sure the house was secure and forget it.

She was just calling the estate agent when Dev Johar walked into the office. 'Can I speak to Oliver Shaw, please?' she said, trying to ignore Dev.

'What is it concerning?'

'The rental property on Stone Creek.'

Dev was making signals at her. She held up one finger and mouthed 'Won't be long', as someone picked up at the other end.

'Mrs McKinnon?'

'Oliver Shaw? I wanted to—'

'This isn't Oliver Shaw, Mrs McKinnon. I'm David Sheldon, and I'm looking after the Stone Creek property. I was off sick the week you took it over. I'm sorry I wasn't here to respond to your query. It all went through very quickly and I'm—'

'I needed somewhere fast. Don't worry about it. Two things – the key for the outside storage shed is missing and I'm not happy about the security. Can you get a new lock fitted? I can organise that myself if you prefer. And is there a possibility of extending my rental after the three months is up?' Despite the compost thieves, despite Catherine Ford's dire warnings, the house still ticked all her boxes. There was no way she'd get her cottage sold and a new place bought in the eleven weeks she had left on the lease. She'd much rather stay there than move again.

'I'm sorry, Mrs McKinnon. I need to explain. We made an error. This property wasn't supposed to be on the rental market at all. There's no question of the lease being extended.'

'I have a contr—' Kay began, but David Sheldon continued smoothly,

'Of course, it's our error. We've talked to the owner and he's prepared to let you stay, but you will have to leave the property on the agreed date.'

Kay wanted to ask more questions, but Dev was looking impatient. She'd have to leave it for now. 'And the new lock?'

'There shouldn't be any issues with that door. We put the padlock and hasp on ourselves. No one else has a key. You don't need access from the outside, do you?'

'I will if I have a fuel delivery,' Kay said.

'I'll see what I can do.'

Kay translated that as *I'm not going to do anything about it unless you start hassling me seriously.* The news about her rental had rather taken her breath away. What was the company doing with the property if it wasn't supposed to be on the rental market? Selling it, presumably. But it wasn't up for sale either.

That was weird. She wondered if she could get hold of the owner's contact details and talk to whoever it was directly. Someone had got their wires crossed somewhere.

'Kay?' Dev's voice was annoyed.

She'd have to think about this later. She put the phone down and smiled at him. 'Good morning, Dev. Did you want me for something?'

She could see him trying to decide whether to comment on her phone call. She wasn't due to start work officially for another ten minutes, but she was damned if she was going to point that out. She wasn't the office junior; she was an adult and a professional and Dev was going to treat her like one. She gave him a raised-eyebrow smile. *Can I help you?*

When he realised she wasn't going to tell him about the phone call, he said, 'What are you doing about Poppy? Her probation officer is planning to report her as failing to keep up contact.'

Which would be bad news for Poppy. Kay needed to put a stopper on that. 'She has an appointment today. If she doesn't come in, I'm going to chase her up. I need to talk to the probation officer myself. Is he aware of the staffing problems we've been having here?'

'He's been kept fully informed,' Dev said stiffly. Kay bet inwardly that he didn't know how delinquent Xanthe had been. The fact the Poppy had been left more or less without support for weeks should help to keep the probation officer at bay, but Dev was right about one thing. This was urgent. The last thing Poppy needed right now was to be back in court, possibly facing a custodial sentence.

'I'll talk to him after I've seen Poppy.' *If she comes in.* 'I have Xanthe's notes up to date now.'

'I think I should talk to him,' Dev said.

'Of course. And so should I. He needs all the information we have.' She kept her gaze on Dev's face, daring him to tell her she wasn't to speak to the probation service.

He broke eye contact first, turning away and heading into his office, pushing the door shut behind him.

Kay sighed. She didn't want to spend all her time here at loggerheads with her boss, but if she let him start walking all over her, taking over areas that were her responsibility, she might as well give up now.

She'd spent a couple of hours the evening before going over Poppy's notes. She had to be prepared today – this might be the last chance she had to make Poppy trust her. Something had gone horribly wrong in Poppy's life, and Kay wanted to know what had happened. She was starting to get the picture, but had found nothing that would account for the anxiety – almost fear – she had seen on Poppy's face.

She worked through her morning appointments, and Poppy's appointment time drew near, then passed. Kay waited, and she waited, but there was no sign of her. She tried Poppy's number a couple of times, but it just said the phone wasn't available – no chance to leave a message even.

Her client after Poppy turned up and Kay went through her session with him, then the client after that, a young woman who seemed to be getting her life back on track.

Like Poppy had been doing.

It wasn't until late afternoon that Kay was prepared to admit that Poppy wasn't coming, and she wasn't going to get in touch.

Then her phone rang. She grabbed it and checked the screen.

It wasn't Poppy – it was Becca.

'Becca love. Is everything OK?'

'Why wouldn't it be? Can't I just phone you without anything being wrong?'

So that's a no. Becca's instant defensiveness told Kay at once that something was up. 'Of course you can. Don't be daft. So, how are you?'

'I told you. I'm fine.' There was silence, and Kay waited. Her heart sank a bit. Becca obviously had something she wanted to talk about, but wasn't sure where to start. 'I need some money,' Becca said abruptly.

Becca hated asking for money, and would routinely reject any offers Kay made to help her out. 'Of course,' Kay said again. What had happened to push Becca to the point where she had to ask? Kay needed to tread carefully here. Becca was perfectly capable of taking offence at any questions. 'How much do you need?'

There was a long silence, then Becca said reluctantly, 'I dunno. Maybe fifty?'

'When do you get paid again? I'm only asking because I don't want to leave you short,' Kay added quickly.

'You won't. Look, forget it, I'll be fine—'

'No, it's no problem, I'll transfer it to your account later today. So, how's it going?' Kay changed the subject quickly before Becca could get into her stride.

'Yeah. OK.'

'Why don't you come and visit – or better still, why don't I come and see you?' Becca didn't have transport apart from the bike, and getting to Sunk Island on public transport was impossible.

'Yeah, OK.' Becca seemed distracted, and Kay's worries began to grow.

'Let's fix a date, now.'

'Yeah ... I just ... Look, you know the police ...' Becca began.

'What about them?'

'Well, you know, if they think you know something ...'

The alarm bells were starting to go off. Becca and the police formed a toxic mix. She had never been charged with a crime, but she'd come to police attention more than once, and years ago, before she'd come to Kay and Matt, she had spent time in a juvenile detention centre. She had been suspected of setting fire to the house where her mother and stepfather lived. The case had been dropped for lack of evidence, but the police at the time thought Becca had done it. Kay had never believed it. 'Something about a crime? Something the police should know?'

Becca immediately went on the defensive. 'What do you mean, something they should know?'

'OK. Sorry. Go on.'

'If there was something . . . someone had been telling you lies, you know, about what they were doing? And you don't know what's true anymore and what isn't?'

'I can't say, Becca. I don't know enough. Who's been telling lies?' She was completely at sea now. Someone had been stringing Becca along by the sounds of it – and Becca valued truth, at least from people she trusted, more than anything. Maybe she would remember she trusted Kay and would tell her more. 'Who was telling lies?'

'I don't know!' Becca's frustration burst out. 'I need to find something out, I need to tell *someone*, only I don't know which one to . . .' She broke off.

'To believe?' Kay couldn't pussy-foot around. This sounded too serious. 'You could tell me. If I knew what was happening, I could give you some advice.'

'No. Look, forget it. I'm just being, you know, para-thingy, like Matt used to say.'

'Paranoid? Matt never said you were paranoid. He said you had good reasons to be suspicious of people. Wouldn't it help to talk about it?'

'No. It's OK. I've decided what I'm going to do.' Before Kay could respond, Becca said abruptly, 'What do you do with cats? Kittens.'

'Kittens?' Kay blinked, wrong-footed by the change of topic.

'Yeah. There's this kitten, and I don't know, I mean, what it eats and that kind of stuff. You know.'

'Hang on. What about this—'

'I told you. I've decided.'

'So what are you going to do?'

'Nothing,' Becca said. 'I'm not going to do anything. I don't want to talk about it.'

She was seconds away from hanging up. Kay said quickly, 'OK. I didn't know you were planning on getting a kitten. How old is it?'

'I didn't,' Becca said indignantly, picking up Kay's unspoken comments. 'It was just living in the yard, and someone . . . well, it needed a home so I've got it in the flat.'

It was probably feral. *Like Becca.* 'That's a start. Keep it warm and feed it. There's cat charities – do you want me to look some up for you?'

'Listen, you couldn't look after it, could you? For a while.'

'I'd love to,' Kay said. She liked cats. 'But there's Milo.' Kay was pretty sure Milo would enjoy a kitten too, but not in a good way. 'It wouldn't be safe.'

There was something wrong, Kay knew it, and she needed to get Becca to talk. The kitten was a way in – like Poppy and the haircut, though so far that hadn't worked. 'Why don't I come up to visit at the weekend? Then I can see the kitten. How does that sound?'

'Yeah. Maybe. I'm working.'

'All weekend?'

'Not . . . I might . . . Let's go out. I'll meet you in town and we can go out.'

Now the alarm bells were ringing loudly. Becca's evasiveness confirmed her suspicion that something bad was going on, something Becca knew she wouldn't like. Something presumably tied up with this police thing she had been asking about. Should she challenge Becca now? No, better wait until they could meet face to face and Becca couldn't hang up on her. 'OK,' she agreed. 'We can go shopping for your kitten, how does that sound?'

Becca sniffed round this suspiciously, looking for catches and hidden hooks. Kay waited patiently until Becca said, 'Yeah. OK.'

'Right. Let's make it Sunday. Are you working that evening?'

'How do you think I pay for stuff?' The sharp, touchy response told Kay exactly how on edge Becca was.

'Becca. I'm not criticising, I just need to know. If you're working in the evening, I'll try and get there early, OK?'

'I might not be. I don't know.'

'It doesn't matter. I'll still get there early. Hang on – let me give you my new address, so you have it if you need it. Got a pen?' She waited for confirmation, glad that Becca was repeating it as she spoke, because that meant she was writing it down.

'Sunk Island . . .?' Becca's voice trailed off.

'Are you OK?'

'Yeah. I just . . . I don't think I can make Sunday. I'll call you, right?'

This was bad. Becca had done an about turn and was backing off. Kay had no idea what was going on, but something was very wrong. She had to maintain the contact, remind Becca that they trusted each other. 'We could just have a cup of coffee,' she suggested, trying to keep the frustration out of her voice. *Let me help you, Becca!* 'Maybe go for a walk along the front?'

'I forgot. I'm doing something.'

There was something Kay had to say while she had the chance. 'Listen, before you go. This thing you told me about . . .' Kay had been thinking about it. 'Don't talk to the police until you've had some proper advice. I can find someone.'

Becca's 'It's nothing,' didn't sound in the least convincing to Kay.

'Or give me the details, and I can do it.'

'No.' That was instant. 'I said I knew what I was going to do, right? Stop going on about it.'

'Give me a call and let me know what happens,' Kay said, making it clear she wasn't going to drop it.

Becca hung up on another *Yeah, yeah.* Kay sat at her desk staring into space.

It sounded horribly as though Becca was in trouble again. Kay didn't like her sudden switch about their meeting – why had she changed her mind? And this story about the police, someone telling lies . . . Had someone drawn Becca into something criminal? If so, she needed legal advice, and she needed it now.

Kay got out the address list of advisers that Tania's House used. Could she talk to one of these people? But Becca wasn't a Tania's House client, and no legal adviser would talk to Kay in detail if she insisted on keeping the case anonymous. Anyway, she didn't know enough.

She still had a few contacts in the child services department. Someone might be prepared to talk to her off the record. The trouble was, Becca was an adult now, and Kay had no idea of the nature of the trouble Becca might be in.

She had to get Becca to talk to her. The important thing was that Becca didn't do anything impulsive, and that was a bit like saying a tennis ball shouldn't bounce. One way or another, she was going to visit Becca, and soon.

With a sigh, she picked up the phone and called Poppy's probation officer.

Chapter 32

Bridlington

Becca put her phone down. She'd been wrong to try and involve Kay. Whoever was coming after her – and she still didn't know who it was – was dangerous. She wasn't going to put Kay in danger too. She'd done that before, and Kay had almost died.

She looked at the piece of paper she'd scrawled Kay's new address on. Sunk Island, where Andy had died. She picked up her phone to enter the information, then stopped. Someone had texted her using Andy's phone after Andy had died. They might be able to read anything she put on her phone. Until she knew for sure if her phone had been hacked, she wasn't putting anything on there that she didn't want anyone else to know. She stuck the bit of paper on the wall so she wouldn't lose it.

After everything she'd heard, what did she really think about Andy? She, herself, without all the stories other people had been pushing at her? And the answers were clear: he wasn't the kind of man to play around if he had a wife. He wasn't the kind of man to get involved in drugs. That was how she'd seen him when she knew him. Everything else came from other people, after he'd died. Her and Andy – it had felt like something good, and it had been.

That was what mattered.

There was a sharp sting in her leg. She jumped and looked down. The kitten was climbing up her, digging its little needle claws in. It landed on her lap, looked at her with wild eyes, shot over the back of the chair and across the room, then it was back, trying to climb her leg again.

It was playing, and she found herself laughing at it.

It was good, having a kitten. She'd never had a pet before. It needed a name. She touched its fur, which was a kind of mix of colours, and reminded her of Kay when she was cooking, all the jars of yellow and red and brown, cinna-whatsit and things like that.

Spice. That would be a good name. Spice just fitted, somehow.

She'd told Kay she wasn't going to do anything about all the stuff that had been happening, but that was just to keep her off her back. She knew exactly what she was going to do. She was going to do what Curwen had asked: go to the pub, find a way to get her hands on those keys, go into that cellar, open the cupboard and get photos of those bags, and what was inside them.

And a plan was forming in her mind. She started work at the pub in just over half an hour, so tonight, she'd try it out.

She filled Spice's dishes with water and the last of the cat biscuits – she'd have to remember to hit the late-night supermarket on the way back – and let herself out of the flat, locking the door behind her.

There was a small group of kids hanging around on the corner. It was the same ones she'd seen before, except there was no sign of Lewis. After this morning, was he too scared to come out? If he'd talked to the police, and they knew it, he should be scared. She remembered Jade's unhappy face. Lewis was in trouble.

She didn't want the kids seeing her leave, didn't want them to know the flat was empty. She went back along the gennel so she would come out at the other end. In the darkness, her feet stumbled on the uneven surface, but she didn't dare use her torch in case anyone was watching. She kept looking over her shoulder. The lights from the other houses illuminated patches of ground and made odd shadows on the walls, one stretching in front, one moving up behind her as though someone was following her, making her look round nervously, but there was no one there.

Half of her wanted to turn back, forget about the pub, spend the evening hiding in her flat, but if she wanted to get whoever was after her off her back, then she had to do this. She had to go into the pub and get the information Curwen wanted, the information Andy had been after.

She moved forward, and collided with someone who stepped out of the shadows into her path. A hand grabbed her arm and she jerked it away, twisting, trying to free herself, until the voice penetrated her panic. 'Listen. You got to listen. Please!'

She already knew who it was as she pulled him into a patch of dim light. Lewis. Her bag had fallen onto the ground in the struggle and he handed it back to her like a peace offering. She pulled it onto her shoulder. 'What are you doing?'

'I got to hide. They're going to get me. Please!'

She looked into his face. It was smeared with dirt. His lip was swollen and she remembered the other lads had hit him . But it wouldn't just be hitting, would it? They all carried knives. What had Jade said? *I think he dobbed some people in, and now they're after him.*

'What are you doing here? Why aren't you at home?'

'I have to tell them! I never told them coppers nothing!'

Just a kid, trying to get himself out of trouble and just getting deeper and deeper into it. And now she had to decide what to do to help him.

'Listen, can you get home?'

'They're waiting for me.'

'At home?'

He shook his head. 'Out there.'

'OK.' She chewed her lip. She didn't have Jade's number to call her. Call the police? Lewis wouldn't stick around for that. She had to find a way to get him home. 'Right. Listen. If you go along the gennel that way . . .' She pointed him in the direction away from the main road, the direction she'd been heading. 'You'll come out in a side street. The bus into town stops on the corner. You'll see it – there's one due in ten minutes. I'll wait with you until we see the bus, then I'll walk along the road to where they're waiting. They'll be looking at me. They won't see you get on the bus. OK? Then you can go home.'

Lewis wiped his nose on his sleeve. 'Got no dosh.'

'Got no . . .? Never mind.' Becca dug in her pocket and found her last couple of pound coins. 'Here. Take these. Ask your mum to pay me back tomorrow, right?'

'Right.' Something like a smile twitched on his mouth for a second.

They walked to the end of the gennel and stood in the shadows. Soon, she saw the lights of the bus in the distance along the road. 'OK, give me a minute, then get to the stop. They can't see you from here.'

She stepped out onto the main road and walked as fast as she could manage towards the shop, and the corner where she could see the group of kids, waiting. Was she being crazy? Were they here for Lewis, or were they here for her?

Snitch bitch. The crazy thing was, she didn't know anything to snitch about, but they must think she did.

Closer now, and the kids saw her, recognised her and focused in her direction. She lifted her chin and walked straight towards them, as if she hadn't seen them, as if they meant nothing, and she saw them hesitate.

Then she heard the sound of the bus. The noise of its engine briefly drowned out any other sounds, then it was past her. She didn't dare look at it to see if Lewis was on it, but she looked back along the road, and there was no one waiting at the stop, so he must be. Lewis would be safe, for now.

The road was clear. She crossed over, and the kids didn't try to follow her. Even so, she kept up the brisk pace, trying to ignore the stabbing pain in her side and the way her neck ached. She wasn't sure how she was going to get through the evening, but she had to get to the pub, get those pictures from the cellar, send them to Curwen. She had to do it for Andy.

Had she done enough for Lewis? Reluctantly, she pulled out her phone. Curwen or Dinah Mason? In the end, she decided on Dinah Mason, but she wasn't answering. Becca left a message – she told Dinah what had happened and asked her to make sure Lewis had got home safely. There wasn't much else she could do.

Now she had to think about staying safe herself.

Drugs. Dealers. Users. It was a world you stayed right out of if you had any sense. All she'd done was ask Johnny Dip about Andy. It didn't sound like much, but she felt uneasy inside, as if she had done something she knew was stupid or dangerous, but she didn't know what it was she had done. She just knew that after that, bad things had started happening.

That thought came again, that Johnny Dip had said something important, something she should have noticed at the time, but whatever it was, it still wouldn't come back. It wasn't Johnny Dip who'd attacked her. The figure she'd seen at the gate hadn't looked like him. Not tall enough, and too thin.

As she walked along the road, she replayed her talk with him in her head to distract her from the pain in her side and in her neck, but there was nothing that seemed important, just all the bullshit about Andy. He hadn't threatened her, he'd warned her off: *If I did, I wouldn't tell you.*

And now she *was* planning to do something that she knew was dangerous, the first chance she got, tonight, if she could. She was going back in the cellar, and she was going to take those pictures and send them to Curwen. Get the keys, go down into the cellar, open the cupboard door, open the bags, take the pictures and go. It would take her five minutes, that's all.

It would help if she had someone to watch her back, but there was only her. She'd just have to get on with it.

Chapter 33

Sunk Island

Kay was just putting a pizza in the oven when the landline rang. She was looking forward to sitting down and eating. Fed up with convenience food and ready meals, she'd made the pizza from scratch, making her own dough, preparing a selection of fresh vegetables, a tomato sauce she made with a *sofrito* and tinned tomatoes, the whole thing topped with some buffalo mozzarella she'd found in a shop in Hedon. The fragrance of basil and garlic was filling the kitchen, and her glass of wine was already poured out and waiting.

As she picked up the phone, half expecting it to be Becca, she checked the time. No way was that pizza going to overcook.

It was Dev Johar. Her eyebrows went up. 'Dev. How can I help you?'

'Kay. I'm sorry to call you at home, but I thought you should know. There's been an issue with Poppy.'

Kay's heart sank, but it was no surprise. She'd been expecting this since Poppy failed to turn up for their appointment. 'What's happened?'

'She got picked up earlier. She was carrying some stuff. It isn't enough for a dealing charge, but it's close, and because she's on probation, it's serious.'

Serious meant that a custodial sentence had to be on the cards, especially as Poppy hadn't been fulfilling the conditions of her probation. If Poppy ended up in prison, it could be the end for her. Even a few weeks in jail could confirm Poppy as a lifetime addict. And it would be short lifetime at that. 'How can I help?'

'Poppy's been released on conditional bail. Apparently, she left the police station around midday with someone from the salon where she works.'

'I should have been told at once,' Kay said. This was the second time she'd heard news about Poppy at second or third hand.

'I've only just heard myself,' Dev said. 'One of the PCSOs I know called me.'

Why had it come from a Police Community Support Officer? Why hadn't Poppy's probation officer called Tania's House? Kay could guess. Because he was undertrained and carrying a caseload that was far too big. But the news wasn't all bad. Not entirely. Kay tried to find something to be optimistic about in the fact that Poppy was still holding down her job, and had an employer who thought enough about her to support her through this setback – and she'd left the police station with a responsible adult.

'Where is she now?'

'That's what we don't know. She isn't answering her phone. I can't get any of them at the house. The trouble is, I'm in still in York. Can you get over there, see if you can find out what's going on?'

Kay was already getting her stuff together. 'Yes. Of course. I'll try the house first.' Where else might Poppy hang out? She was running possible locations through her head as she packed her bag, the phone cradled against her shoulder. 'If she's ignoring your calls, she obviously doesn't want to talk to us. I'll try, but I'm not optimistic.'

'OK. I'm heading back now, but it'll be a while before I'm there. You can call me – I've got hands-free. Kay, I have a bad feeling about this.'

So did Kay. 'I'll set straight off.' She put the phone down and allowed herself a moment to slump wearily. She'd been looking forward to a quiet evening – she had a book she'd been saving, a glass of wine, her pizza. Racing out in search of a troubled teenager was the last thing she wanted to do, but that was what she'd signed up for.

But before she went, she was going to try the number of the salon where Poppy worked. It was well out of hours, but there might be someone there. Poppy's employer was obviously someone Poppy felt she could trust, so it was worth a try.

Poppy had a part-time job at Carla's Place, a beauty parlour based in Hull. According to Xanthe's notes, the owner had been aware of Poppy's problems, happy for her to do some work there and get some experience towards a return to college, or a full-time job somewhere else.

And when she'd been bringing Poppy's file up to date, she hadn't really looked at the job – just noted that Poppy was still working there, and been impressed by what Xanthe had managed to negotiate for her. It wasn't that late. Could Poppy be at work?

She checked the location on Google Maps.

According to the map, the salon was located not too far from the city centre, but in an area of industrial sheds and overgrown parking spaces. There was an open drain running through the middle of the space, surrounded by what looked like waterlogged wasteland – an industrial Sunk Island in the middle of the city.

It was an odd place to have a beauty salon, but Hull was undergoing urban renewal on the back of the funding City of Culture had brought in. The area could be on the way up, and might be a good spot for a trendy new place to be located. What she needed to do was find out if Poppy was there, or if anyone knew where she had gone.

According to the local business pages, the salon was still open. There was a link to a website, which Kay clicked on. The landing page had the name of the salon emblazoned across it in fancy pink lettering, with the words *for a memorable experience* written in smaller letters underneath. The image was the face of a beautiful young woman who was pouting at the camera – presumably demonstrating what Carla's Place could do for its clients.

Kay had imagined the salon as somewhere cool, trendy and minimalist, but the website made it look as retro as you could get.

She clicked on the menu. Under the claim: *Carla's Place offers a first-class service at very reasonable prices*, there were buttons to click for booking, for information about prices, news and events, a gallery and a *contact us* link.

Kay hesitated. She needed to check if Poppy was there but she didn't want to go through the main switchboard, where she would have to identify herself in some way. That could alienate Poppy even more.

Most salons these days operated on a contract basis. The therapists and the stylists paid for the space, the equipment and the reception staff, but were effectively self-employed. Just another aspect of the gig economy.

Maybe she could try and contact one of the stylists . . . Had Poppy given her any names? Kay racked her brains, but she couldn't remember Poppy mentioning anything like that. OK, she could check the people who worked there, see if any of them rang a bell.

There wasn't a list of stylists or beauticians, so she clicked on the gallery link to see what she could find.

And now a list of names appeared: Krissie, Layla, Jazmyn . . .

Kay's feeling of unease had been growing. With some trepidation, she clicked on the first name, Krissie.

A thumbnail appeared showing a woman standing with her back to the camera. Her hair hung down her back. She was wearing a camisole and a thong. *Krissie is in her mid-twenties, with long dark hair. She is a size 10 with a 34e bust.*

Underneath were reviews from recipients of Krissie's services. Kay's gaze skimmed the top line of the first one, then she stopped reading. She went back to the gallery and scrolled down the list of names: Layla, Jazmine, Dolores, Kitty, Maggie, Nadia, Polly, Michelle, Clara ...

How naive had she been? How naive had they all been?

Slowly and reluctantly, she clicked on *Polly*.

Polly is in her late teens with long blonde hair. She is a dress size 8 with a 32c bust.

Could Polly be Poppy? The description matched. Would Poppy be careless enough to use a name so close to her own? Would she even care? Kay couldn't help remembering Becca and the time she had worked as a cam-girl on a sex-chat website, making short, soft-porn videos. It had all been over by the time Kay knew about it, but Becca was still dealing with the damage it had done to her life.

Becca, at least, had had no physical contact with her clients.

Carla's Place was a massage parlour that sold sex by the quarter hour.

And someone from Tania's House had sent Poppy there to work.

She'd been there for months, from before Xanthe left to now, and Kay had been stupid enough to take the information given to her at face value – OK, Poppy had been evasive in their encounters, and Kay had been working hard to gain her trust. They'd focused on Poppy's drug use and her return to counselling and support, but even so, Kay should have been on top of this at once.

She'd read the notes, priding herself on her professionalism and feeling smugly superior to Dev Johar, totally missing the fact that Poppy's key worker had found her a job in a brothel.

This was Kay's responsibility. With the bitter taste of failure in her mouth, she understood she'd left Poppy to wander into a dark, dark world with no support at all.

There was no excuse. Carla's Place didn't even pretend to be a beauty parlour, and the kinds of services it offered were barely veiled – a sliding scale of rates from forty pounds for fifteen minutes to a hundred for an hour. Any doubts were dispelled by the images in which young women – their faces concealed – were pictured half-naked in suggestive poses.

And Poppy had left the police station in the charge of someone who worked there.

Kay was in a quandary as she collected her stuff together. She needed help, but she didn't know who to ask. Xanthe had known. She must have known. What about Dev?

Dev had sounded truly concerned about what was happening to Poppy, and he'd sent Kay out to look for her. Faced with a crisis, he'd dropped his jobsworth fussiness and shown professionalism – or was his unusual concern because he knew what was going on and was trying to distance himself?

She couldn't be sure, but she couldn't alert Dev – yet – to what she was doing.

She needed to find Poppy first. She needed to deal with this. Now.

Chapter 34

Bridlington

The pub was quiet when Becca got there, and for once, Toby arrived the same time she did. She'd got so used to him being late that she'd almost forgotten what time he was supposed to start. She could see him checking out the bruises on her face. 'I tripped,' she said quickly.

He grinned. 'Good night, was it?'

I was here all evening, you moron. When did I have time to get drunk? But she didn't say it. What was the point? 'Where's Carl?' she asked, trying to sound casual.

'He's in the back. He said to call if it got busy.'

This was what she had hoped for, but her stomach clenched with nervousness. When he was in the pub, Carl kept his keys attached to his belt, but she'd seen him a couple of times when he was working in the back – sorting out the paperwork, he always used to say – with the keys on the table beside him.

Her plan – if you could call it a plan – depended on this. It might be possible – just – to get hold of the keys while they weren't attached to him, but he might catch her, and she honestly didn't know how he would react.

She didn't want to find out.

If she was going to do it, she needed to do it soon. Her mouth felt dry and she could feel her heart pounding. For once, frustratingly, Toby stayed behind the bar instead of wandering off to the games machines. He leaned against the beer taps. 'I'm moving on,' he said. 'This place is dead.'

'Yeah.' She didn't want to engage him in chat. She wanted him to get bored and drift out into the pub.

'So what's the news about your mate?' he said.

'My mate?'

'The guy that got – you know.'

You know. Killed. Murdered. That's why Toby was hanging around. He wanted all the gossip. And she could give him some, if she chose to. Instead, she shrugged. 'No news.' But there was something she wanted to know that he might be able to tell her. She wanted to know who was spreading the stories about Andy being a dealer. Was it Johnny Dip? Or had Johnny Dip got it from someone else? 'Everyone keeps saying he was involved in drugs, but I never saw that. That guy, Johnny Dip. He said—'

'Who?'

Moron. Toby wouldn't know who Johnny Dip was. 'You know, the pirate guy. The biker. Doc.'

'Doc? Who . . .? Oh. Yeah. What about him?'

'He seemed to think Andy was dealing.'

Toby was frowning. 'I dunno. I'll tell you something, though. I heard—'

'Anybody serving here?' There was a punter at the bar. Toby went over and the man began a long, rambling order with pints and halves. He seemed to have come in with a load of mates.

Now or never. 'I just need to check on something with Carl, OK?' Her voice sounded odd in her ears, though Toby didn't seem to notice. He just nodded acknowledgement, looking distracted as he juggled the different glasses.

Making herself breathe slowly, Becca pushed open the door that led into the back of the pub. There was a small, rather scruffy kitchen where lunchtime food was done. Through the next door was the room Carl called the office, a big room that would have made a comfortable sitting room, but everywhere was piled up with papers, empty boxes and other junk. There was a big wooden table in the middle of the space where Carl was working, and a large, saggy armchair.

Becca stood in the doorway, her legs feeling shaky.

She didn't have to do this. She could just . . . leave it. Andy was dead, she couldn't change anything. She *should* leave it, leave the pub, leave the supermarket, leave her flat. Move on.

Loser! Waste of space! Pathetic . . .

'Carl?' Her voice came out sounding high, and Carl looked round in surprise.

'Becca! Did you want something?' He didn't look pleased.

She steadied her breathing and stepped into the room 'Um. Yeah. I . . .' The keys were beside him, on the table. A small bunch, a couple of big keys, a car key, and the ones she wanted. Two yales.

'Look, Becca, can't it wait? I'm busy.'

She made herself smile. 'Yeah. Sorry. I'm, I wanted, I'm a bit short this month and I wondered if . . .'

He'd seen her face now and swivelled round in his chair. 'What happened to you? Been fighting with the punters again?' He laughed, and she could see how his belly shook under his shirt. His face looked red.

Heart attack on legs, Kay would have said.

She wanted to glare at him, but forced herself to laugh as well. 'Yeah. No, I just, you know, tripped on the stairs. Only I . . .' She was at the table now and the keys were there, right in front of her.

'You want a sub?' Carl was looking at her now, his gaze running up and down her. She knew what Carl was like, so she never dressed up for the pub – no tight tops, kept herself covered. He'd never paid her much of that kind of attention, apart from getting grabby in the cellar that time.

It was getting harder to smile. 'Yeah, just a few quid, you know, to see me over . . .'

'You could do with buying yourself some stuff,' he said. 'Show your tits off a bit. The punters like it.'

For a horrible moment, she was back at her mother's house, hearing His footsteps on the stairs, hiding under the covers, knowing it wouldn't do any good, but . . .

'Yeah. I could.' She flinched as his hand touched her waist and ran down over her bum and the tops of her legs.

'You're a pretty girl, Becca. I could give you a raise. If you want.'

'Yeah. Maybe.' *Take your fucking hands off me, you . . .* Now. Do it now.

Her hand jerked out and knocked the bunch of keys onto the floor. 'Sorry! I'm sorry!' she heard herself babbling.

'It doesn't . . .'

This bit hadn't been part of the plan, Carl perving on her, but use it. *Use* it!

She was down on her hands and knees reaching for the keys that lay under the table. He'd be looking at her bum, she knew he would be, as she reached under the table, unclipped the two Yale keys and crawled back out. 'Sorry,' she said again, scrambling to her feet. She dumped the keys next to his papers, knowing he wouldn't look.

He pushed his chair away from the table a bit and patted his lap. 'Tell you what, why don't you stay here for a bit? Show me what you can do for your raise? It's quiet, there's no need for you to go right back out there.'

'No. It's getting busy. Toby'll come through! I could . . . later. After we close!'

He looked put out. Becca felt her hands clench into fists, then – and the relief flooded through her – there was a tap on the door and Toby stuck his head round. 'There you are,' he said to Becca. 'We've got a queue.'

'I'm just coming.' She looked at Carl and forced herself to smile again. 'Later,' she said.

Back behind the bar, her legs were still shaking. This was her last night at the pub, she knew that. She served drinks, getting the queue down, and suddenly it was quiet again.

'I'll just be back in a minute.' She lifted the hatch and went through, leaving Toby behind the bar before he could protest.

She had to move fast, but everything hurt, slowing her down. She unlocked the cellar door and hobbled down the steps into the dim basement. Bottles gleamed from the shelves but she ignored them and went to the other room, to the cupboard in the wall.

She looked back up the steps. Nothing, and the door had shut behind her. OK.

She unlocked the cupboard door.

They were there, the holdalls, stuffed into a corner. She pulled one out a short way and tugged at the zip. It was jammed, and the more she pulled, the worse it seemed to stick. She felt sweat break out down her back, and forced herself to be calm.

The zip moved a short way. Pulling the fabric tight to keep it straight, she managed to open it a bit more, enough to get her phone inside.

OK.

She fumbled in her pockets and got out her phone, opening the camera. The flash would do it. Squeezing her phone through the gap, she took the picture, seeing the flash light up the inside of the bag. *Right!* She took several more shots to be on the safe side, pulled the phone out and shoved the bag back into the corner of the cupboard.

Then she heard the heavy tread of footsteps above her.

Carl. She was under the back room where he was working. It sounded as though he was coming towards the bar.

Quick! She took pictures of the holdall and packages from as many angles as she could, one after the other, no time to check, then she stuffed the phone back into her pocket.

She pushed the cupboard door shut, then went back up the steps, her stiffness making her clumsy, making her stumble and almost fall as she caught her shin on the stone riser. The pain made her eyes water. Then she was at the door. No time to mess around. She opened it a crack, slipped round and let it swing slowly shut behind her.

Carl came through the door into the bar area as she stood there, breathing fast.

She heard the slow whisper of the hinge above the door that stopped it slamming. The click as the door closed seemed to echo like a gunshot.

'You OK, Becca?' Carl was looking at her, frowning.

'I'm fine,' she managed. 'Just . . .' She hoped he'd think her breathlessness was because of what had happened earlier, and breathed more deeply to make her tits stand out. He noticed that and grinned appreciatively.

She felt dirty. 'I'll just get on.'

He looked straight at her. 'I'll be seeing you later. Toby, go and bring those crates in from the back.'

She ducked behind the bar. She had to talk to Toby. He'd started to say something, *I'll tell you something, though. I heard . . .* but a punter had interrupted him. Carl kept his eyes on her as he wandered over to the games machines and checked the screens. It was like having a fly crawl over her.

'Toby, what were you going to say, you know, before you served that guy?'

'When?'

'You know, about people saying he was dealing.'

'Oh. Yeah. No, it was just that—'

'Crates.' Carl was right by the bar, looking at Toby. 'OK? Now, not next week.'

Toby gave her an eye roll. 'Tell you later,' he said and vanished in the direction of the yard.

Keeping right away from Carl, who had come behind the bar and was checking the shelves, she served drinks and busied herself cleaning the bar and polishing the beer taps. She got the impression that Carl knew exactly how she felt, and was enjoying it, that he'd like making her do things for the extra money even more if he knew she was hating it.

She had to get the keys back to him. Her original plan had been to go into the back again and drop the cellar keys on the floor, as if they'd come off the bunch when they fell off the table. Now, she wasn't going anywhere near that room. She couldn't rely on Toby to interrupt them another time.

And the photos. She had to send them, even though her phone might be bugged. Curwen? She'd promised to help him, but he'd lied to her about Andy. Did that make a difference? What else could she do with the pictures? Dinah Mason? Dinah didn't know all that stuff about the cellar. Curwen did. And Dinah seemed too . . . too nice.

Curwen was a shit. Sometimes, that was what you needed.

And he knew there was something going on here. It had to be him. He might be a creep, but he wanted to get the people who'd killed Andy. That was good enough for her.

She found his number, and pressed send. OK, the photos were gone. Then she dropped the keys on the floor behind the bar, near where Carl had been standing. It was the best she could do.

She didn't have any more time to think about it as a wave of people came through the pub door. There was a match on. It was going to be busy tonight.

She worked fast, wondering what was keeping Toby. He should be back behind the bar now – it was all she could do to keep up with the growing crowd.

'Sorry,' she kept saying as she served the waiting punters to a chorus of, 'Getting over here any time?', 'Decided you work here after all?' but it was all good-natured enough. She got their drinks, smiled thinly at the banter. She needed to know what Toby had been about to say. She'd remind him when he came back from wherever he was hiding.

But he didn't. It got busier, and she had to work all-out to keep up with the orders. Where the fuck was Toby? She took a breather in a brief quiet period, looking out into the pub to see where he'd got to. There was no sign of him.

Carl came behind the bar looking put out. 'What's going on? Are you on your own?'

'Toby's out collecting glasses.'

'He spends too much time— What the fuck are these doing here?'

She heard the chink as his foot kicked the keys against one of the chiller cabinets.

'What?' She kept her face turned away, looking at the guy she was serving.

Carl didn't answer. She glanced round and saw that he was looking at the keys in his hand, then he turned without saying anything, and headed towards the cellar door, leaving her to deal with a crowd of impatient punters.

She'd had enough. It was hot, she was scared and she was beyond tired. She just wanted to get out.

The latest punter was moaning because she'd got his order wrong. She put the glasses down on the bar, said, 'Hang on,' and walked out of the bar and into the kitchen. She grabbed her coat and, not waiting to put it on, she pushed the back door open and went out into the yard. This was where Toby was supposed to be collecting the crates, a job that should have taken him ten minutes. There was no sign of him.

She had a bad feeling about Toby, a really bad feeling. She kept thinking about the attack at her flat, the smell of paraffin, the voice hissing *Snitch bitch!* at her as she lay on the ground.

What could she do? Call Curwen? Would he even help? He wanted the pictures – but she was pretty sure that he didn't give a fuck about what happened to her once he'd got them.

But he cared about who had hurt Andy.

Dinah Mason might help. She'd tell Dinah about Toby and maybe she'd . . . But she needed to get out of here. Before Carl noticed she'd gone.

The pictures were on her screen. She looked at them as she walked quickly back towards her flat along the dark streets. At first, she couldn't make sense of them – the bags seemed stuffed full of paper or something. Had she done it all for that, been groped by Carl, walked out of her job, maybe got Toby in serious shit, and the stuff she wanted to photograph was all wrapped up in paper so no one could tell what it was?

But then one picture came on the screen, and this one was clearer.

The bags were stuffed full of money. Folded bank notes, and she could see the glint of coins.

Not drugs. Money. What was going on?

There was nothing from Curwen, no message, nothing.

She was almost home now, and caution made her slow her steps. It was dark but she could see the reassuring glimmer of the outside light from her yard. Even so, she couldn't stop herself from looking back and checking each shadow before she passed it.

There was no sign of the kids who'd been hanging round earlier.

Nothing's wrong, she kept telling herself. *No one saw you go into the cellar.* She was fishing in her bag for her keys as she walked, but she couldn't find them. They should be clipped onto the little ring inside her bag, but they weren't there.

Her feet slowed. She remembered Lewis grabbing her, and her bag falling to the ground. Had he taken her keys? Was the whole thing some kind of trick to get . . .

She froze.

It was like before.

The yard gate was swinging open.

She'd closed it. She had definitely closed it.

Someone had been here.

She edged carefully into the yard, braced herself and shone her torch round the space.

Nothing.

Just the bulk of the wheelie bin, the space under the fire escape empty apart from a pile of wet, half-burned rubbish, the tarp concealing her bike.

There was no one here.

But someone had been here. Someone had opened the gate. She knew she'd closed it.

And as she approached the back door, she saw that, too, was open. She could see it in her head; Lewis, coming through the yard with her keys, leading the group of kids, his price to stay safe.

Except whoever had gone in there hadn't used her keys. The lock was splintered where someone had kicked the door in.

Her stomach clenched. She couldn't go in. They might be waiting for her up there. Call the police? Would they even come? A break in at a scruffy bedsit. Yeah, right.

Curwen. She'd helped him. He might come out if she . . .

Spice! She'd left Spice up there alone.

She was running up the stairs before she'd even had time to think about it. Her stomach was knotted in terror. What was she going to find? What had they done?

Her torch showed stains on the treads, marks of mud and she didn't know what. And there was a smell, like . . .

Please! She didn't know who she was talking to, she was just . . . *Please!*

She reached the landing and snapped on the light.

The door to her room was wide open, the lock smashed.

Whoever had done this, they'd gone. There was no one there.

Inside was chaos.

Everything was scattered across the floor – her clothes, her bedding, her plates and cutlery. Someone had emptied the remains of what was in her cupboard across it all – red sauce, brown sauce, what was left of the milk. The lamp – her lamp with the red shade – was pulled over and the shade was crushed and broken as if someone had stamped on it. The blind was pulled off the window and torn to pieces. The contents of the waste bin were strewn about the room, and – now she knew what the smell was – there was shit smeared across the walls.

Her legs gave way and she sat down hard on the floor.

Where was Spice? She pushed herself to her feet and made herself pick up the soiled bedding and stuff scattered on the floor, and the chair – all the stuffing was coming out. It was slashed across, and so was the mattress and her quilt.

Everything.

She checked everywhere, under the chair, under the bed, in the corners and cupboards and other hiding places, blinking the tears away as she got more and more frantic.

She knew what she was looking for, she knew what she would find; a small furry body that showed she should never have tried to help the kitten, that trying to help just meant that someone had killed it, and it would have been better if she'd never touched it, if she'd just left it alone, because didn't she know by now? Anything she tried to care about just got trashed. Look what had happened to Kay. Look what happened to Andy. Look what almost happened to Jared.

Waste of space! Loser! Pathetic . . .

But there was no sign of Spice. Whatever they'd done to the kitten, they hadn't left the evidence behind.

She huddled into her coat. The room was freezing and it stank. Listlessly, she began to gather up the stuff from on the floor into a big pile. Black bags – she needed black bags, shove it all in and chuck it. She didn't want it any more. Any of it.

She didn't want to stay here.

She didn't want to be anywhere.

There were stains on her hands. Holding them away from her, feeling the sickness in her throat, she crossed the corridor to the bathroom. As she turned on the taps, she heard a squeak.

There was movement, and Spice emerged from a hole in the skirting behind the toilet, yawning and stretching.

Once again, Becca's legs felt shaky. She scrubbed her hands clean, soaping them again and again, not able to see what she was doing because this time she was really crying, then sank down with her back to the door, and gently picked up the small cat. It gave a mew of protest and chewed at her finger as she sat there with it held under her chin, stroking the soft fur.

How had Spice got in here? She'd left the kitten shut in the room.

Lewis.

Maybe he hadn't brought the other kids here. Maybe he'd taken her keys so he could hide out in her flat. Maybe that made more sense to him than going home to a place where the gang knew they could find him.

And in that case – had he seen them coming and hidden Spice, knowing what the gang would do to the kitten if they found her? Who had he seen, though? Who had done this to her flat? And where was Lewis now?

And Toby. What had happened to Toby? Someone must have heard that he was about to tell her something, and had stopped him. Who? Carl had been in the back – no, he'd been there the second time, when she'd asked Toby to tell her and he'd sent Toby outside on some job or other.

When the bar was busy.

Carl.

Andy was gone and now something had happened to Toby, because of what she'd done.

And there was worse. A cold feeling was growing inside her.

Scribbled on a piece of paper on the wall above the sink – Kay's new address. Only she hadn't written *Kay*. She'd written *Mum*.

Whoever they were, they knew Sunk Island because they'd killed Andy down there. And now, they knew her mother lived there.

She pulled out her phone and dialled Kay's number. There was no point in being secret now.

The phone rang and rang. Becca told herself Kay wasn't answering because it was late, she wasn't answering because she was asleep, she wasn't . . .

She sent a text: *Call me now!!!* And stood there, frozen, in the middle of the trashed room.

She had to do something.

And now, her mind on high alert with panic, she realised what it was she was trying to remember. Days ago, when Curwen first came into the pub, he'd asked her. He'd given her two names: Stoner, and Doc . . . It wasn't something Johnny Dip had said – it was Sal Capone , the woman he'd called Alicia. She'd come over. *Hey, Doc. Where's our drinks?* And then she'd looked at Becca and said, *Oops.*

Because she wasn't supposed to call him Doc.

And Toby. She'd called Johnny Dip 'Doc', and Toby seemed to know who she meant. Then he'd vanished. Johnny Dip was one of them. She'd asked him about Andy and he must have sent them round to scare her off. This time, he must mean business. And he knew where Kay lived.

She had to get out of there, fast.

Chapter 35

Curwen was packing up at the end of his shift when Sykes came back into the office. 'Any news?' he asked. He wanted to keep an eye on Hammond's investigation – it wasn't just a case of covering his own back. Something was off.

'Not really.'

His phone rang. It was after midnight – who was calling at this time? He checked the number. Becca the Barmaid. Not so long ago, this would have been a major triumph, but now it had the feel of yesterday's news. 'Curwen. What's up?'

Becca was talking fast, stumbling over her words, talking about spice, about a kid called Lewis, about K, about Sunk Island. He pointed to his phone, rolling his eyes at Sykes, and moved away.

'Hang on, I'm not getting this. Start at the beginning. You came back to your place – what time? Where had you been?'

'The pub. I've been working. I took some more photos. In the cellar. I think they know. I sent them to you.'

He checked. 'Got them.' A week ago, this would have been a big deal, but he already knew what the bags contained, and by themselves, they didn't count for much.

'Listen, you've got to do something. I think they've got my mate's kid, Lewis. Your lot talked to him a couple of days ago. And Kay, my mum, my foster-mum . . .'

He listened as it all came out. He didn't have time for this. It was irrelevant now. Dom Maskall had come through. As he had predicted, Docklands Holdings were, on paper, supplying a range of services to Tania's House, things that would be hard to audit. According to these figures, Lavery made the donation, and got a bit less than half of his money back – but this time, it was clean money. Curwen was pretty sure he hadn't uncovered the half of Lavery's business interests. This looked like the tip of a massive money-laundering iceberg – and he'd found it.

The financial crime team had taken what he told them very seriously, and there was talk about warrants. This time, Lavery wasn't getting away with it.

And OK, Becca's photos showed that there was money – a lot, this time – hidden in the pub. Let Lavery get away with the *last night's takings* excuse this time.

'Leave it with me,' he said. 'I'll send someone round.' Becca the Barmaid had let a kid from one of the drugs gangs get hold of her keys, so she shouldn't be too surprised to come back and find her place trashed. He'd pass it on to the duty team – they'd take a report coming from him seriously, even on a busy night. The best thing she could do was wait for the patrol car then go and spend the night with a friend.

He was about to pick up the phone on his desk to make the call, when it rang. It was his contact from the financial crimes section. 'Someone's tipped them off,' the man said. 'We're going in tonight. You coming?'

Curwen had been waiting for this moment for weeks. Of course he was.

Becca stood in the bedsit, shivering in the cold from the broken window. 'I'll send someone round,' Curwen had said. But he hadn't seemed bothered.

They could be back any minute. How would he know she was safe?

He'd got what he wanted and now he didn't care.

Well, she could deal with that. Being on her own was what she did. But Kay – she had to get help for Kay and she no longer had any faith in Curwen. She dug in her pocket and pulled out the card the other detective had given her.

Dinah Mason.

One pig-creep, another pig-creep. Did it matter? But Dinah Mason had told her the truth about Andy.

She'd been stupid to think she could trust Curwen, but maybe, just maybe, Dinah Mason was OK. She had to take the risk. For Kay.

This time she was able to be clear. She cut through Dinah's confused questions, and told her what had happened. 'They've trashed everything. And they've got my mum's address. She lives on Sunk Island and she's not answering her phone.'

Dinah got it at once. 'Right. Listen. I'm sending a patrol car to you. Get out of the flat. Keep out of sight until the car gets there. It'll be marked. And I'll get someone down to your mum's at Sunk island, and I'll get them looking for the kid. Don't worry. I'm on it.'

Becca opened her sent texts and forwarded the photos to Dinah, but there was no time to add an explanation. She had to go.

Chapter 36

Sunk Island

Kay pulled on her coat and double-checked her bag for keys, thermos, energy bars and her teenage survival kit. The fragrance of the pizza still hung in the air, but now it was an unappetising, cooling lump on the table.

She laced up her boots. Milo, who usually leaped to his feet when he saw her getting ready to go out, was snoozing in his basket. He opened one eye, but didn't move. Kay had wondered about taking him with her – but the back streets of Hull at night? That wasn't a safe environment for a dog. He'd be fine here. She went to the door.

The rain was coming down in vertical rods. Kay hesitated, pulling her hood up over her head. She heard the sound of a bike revving up.

It was nearby, but there was nothing in the road.

Just darkness.

She locked the door behind her and stepped out into the night.

Her torch threw pale circles on the gravel of the path as she headed round the side of the house to where she'd left her car. The wind caught her and she stopped, trying to keep herself upright as it screamed round her, whipping the hood off her head and lifting the skirts of the raincoat. She shivered as the rain splashed against her legs.

Something blew across the path, something familiar. She grabbed at it, feeling the rain soak through her gloves.

A yellow compost bag.

The light from her torch barely seemed to touch the darkness as she turned it towards the door of the fuel store.

There was nothing there, or nothing she could see; just the door, firmly closed in the wall, the hasp padlocked shut.

But she was suddenly on major alert, everything in her urging her to move fast, to get away and out of the enclosing darkness and onto the road. Her fingers fumbled as she unlocked the car and slipped behind the wheel, aware of the water dripping from her boots and from her coat.

She pulled the door closed and turned on the engine, using the car lights to illuminate the garden.

Just dripping shrubs, the door to the fuel store, and beyond that, deep shadow. There was nothing there.

And the yellow bag? It could have come from anywhere. She had to go. Poppy needed her.

* * *

Half an hour later, Kay was driving through the night-time streets of Hull, her speed well above what it should be. The rain had eased off, but her headlights still reflected in shards of brightness from the wet roads. If Poppy wasn't at home, where should she start to look? March into a massage parlour and start demanding access to one of their girls? The idea was so ludicrous, it made her smile, but it might come to that. This was deadly serious.

No point in worrying about it until she'd checked to see if Poppy was at home. The fact she wasn't answering her phone didn't mean much. Would Poppy be in bits, or defiant? Would she be high on whatever it was she was taking at the moment? Kay was through the centre now and heading towards the backstreet where Poppy lived. The street lights were lit, but towards the end of the road, one of them was out and the approach to Poppy's house was in deep shadow. A car – a red Ford Fiesta – was parked outside.

As Kay pulled up, the front door opened and some-one came out – a tall, slim figure wearing a hat with the brim tilted forward over her eyes.

Leesha.

Now Kay knew who Poppy's employer was.

As she watched, Leesha closed the door behind her with what looked, to Kay, like stealth. Kay thought she would stay in the car until Leesha had left, then changed her mind. The woman would have informa-tion about Poppy, and Kay needed that.

She got out of the car as Leesha came onto the road. 'Is Poppy in there?' she asked, not bothering with any of the social stuff. She had been sure this woman was Poppy's dealer, now it looked as though she was her pimp as well. Kay wasn't going to pretend.

'It's the new, not-so-improved Xanthe,' Leesha said. She didn't seem surprised to see Kay – in fact, she looked almost as if she was expecting her.

'Is Poppy in there?' Kay repeated.

'Why do you want to know?'

'That's none of your business.'

'Poppy's fine.' The other woman studied her, her eyes shadowed by the brim of her hat. 'I don't think she wants to see you. She's gone right off Tania's House for some reason.'

'Then she can tell me that herself,' Kay said.

Close up, Leesha was looking rough. From a distance, she was the picture of elegant cool, but her face looked drawn and her lips looked thin and dry. It made Kay wonder if Leesha was a user herself.

'That's up to her.' Leesha dug in her bag, looking for something. She seemed in no rush to go.

'Yes. So I need to see her,' Kay said.

'Good luck with that. Do you really think she'll let you in?'

'Has she taken something?'

'Don't look at me. What Poppy does in her own time is her business. Something you might like to remember.' She was holding a packet of cigarettes and shook one into her hand, putting it between her lips and flicking her lighter.

'Until she breaks the law. My concern right now is Poppy, if you'll let me past.'

'Oh, I'm not stopping you. Nosy old bitch, aren't you?'

Kay moved round her and went to the door. It was locked. She tried the bell, which, of course, didn't work, then knocked, waited and knocked again, all the time aware of Leesha standing there watching her, enjoying her dilemma.

'Do you have a key?' Kay asked her.

Leesha smiled. 'Maybe I do, but Poppy hasn't given me permission to hand it over.'

Kay knocked again, louder. Poppy could be ignoring her, but she could be ill. If Leesha had been with her, then she'd almost certainly have taken something. The silence behind the door was ominous. 'She could be ill, seriously ill. Just let me in, and go.'

'Kids. They do stupid things,' Leesha said, drawing on her cigarette. She blew a perfect smoke ring.

Kay began rattling the door handle, but the door was firmly locked. The windows? Could she justify breaking in? There was a malice in Leesha that alarmed her more than she was prepared to show. Leesha would enjoy watching Kay start to get flustered, to panic, to start acting rashly.

OK. Think. You've dealt with difficult people most of your life. 'If Poppy's taken something, and it's harmed her, the person who supplied it can be charged,' she said. She pulled her phone out of her pocket. 'I'm calling the police.'

'That's going to help Poppy *so* much, isn't it? After she's been arrested and all that.' But Leesha sounded wary now.

'Only if she's carrying. If she's taken something,' Kay said, keeping her rising concern hidden under an equitable tone, 'which, of course, you might have supplied, then she needs help. And you, as the supplier, are responsible for the outcome.' She held the other woman's gaze.

Leesha chewed her thin lip. Kay thought she could see a mark there, as if the skin was torn. 'I'm not sticking around to watch poor little Poppy being arrested again. I told her you and Dev wouldn't like it.' Her voice was a sing-song parody of a child telling tales. 'Do you know what Poppy said? She said "Fuck Dev." Do you think she does? I could tell the police she said that, only maybe I misheard. Maybe she said, "I fuck Dev." I'm pretty sure that was it. Now I think back.'

Bluff and counter bluff? 'Are you sure your car is clean? If you've been supplying drugs, it won't be. Give me the key, or I'm calling the police. Now.'

'Poor old Dev. End of his career, don't you think?' The jeering note in Leesha's voice stirred Kay's anger.

'You want to talk to the police about sexual exploitation? Fine. And selling Poppy illegal substances, shall we talk to them about that as well?' Kay lifted her phone and took a picture of Leesha. The image caught the car in the background, the number plate clearly visible. Kay held it up to show the other woman. 'I can prove you were here.'

She didn't expect such a strong reaction, but Leesha snapped, 'You bitch!' and tried to slap the phone out of her hand. Kay shoved it firmly into her back pocket and stood her ground.

'Give me the key, and go, and I'll delete the picture.'

Leesha stepped forward, reaching for Kay's phone. She might be thin, but she looked as though she had a wiry strength. Her lips were drawn back into something resembling a snarl. Kay had the door behind her – nowhere to retreat. She hadn't thought this through. She hadn't thought Leesha would attack her, not out here, in public.

Except the empty street wasn't public at all.

And then a phone rang. Leesha swore, grabbed her phone out of her bag and glanced at the screen. She looked at Kay. 'Do it then.'

Kay had taken the opportunity to slide away from the door and had space behind her to get away. Watching Leesha closely, she got out her phone and opened her picture album. 'You give me the key first.'

Leesha threw a key down onto the pavement. While she was distracted, Kay uploaded the image to WhatsApp and sent it to herself. Then she turned the phone so Leesha could see it, and, crouching down to pick up the key, she pressed 'delete'.

Leesha was already getting into her car. The engine started and Kay had to jump out of the way as Leesha drove straight at her before pulling away. As the sound of the engine faded, Kay realised she was shaking. It must have been something urgent that had made Leesha leave so abruptly – she'd been lucky.

Forcing herself to breathe more steadily, Kay turned the key and pushed the door open.

It was the smell that hit her first; foul, organic, fishy and sweet. It was like the incontinence smell in her house at Sunk Island, like the smell Milo had got on his fur.

'Poppy?' she called. 'It's Kay. From Tania's House. I'm here to help.'

Nothing.

The bulb in the hallway wasn't working. Kay moved carefully through to the kitchen, feeling the rubbish under her feet. She turned on the kitchen light and left the door open to get some illumination into the hall. The kitchen was more or less as she remembered it. The smell was worse in here, and the floor was sticky as if something had been spilt.

No sign of Poppy.

Slowly, reluctantly, she made her way upstairs. There were two bedrooms, and each one was a wreck. Kay would have thought they'd been burgled if she hadn't already seen the chaos Poppy and her house-mates lived in.

Kay checked each room, but again, there was no sign of Poppy.

Where was she?

She made her way downstairs and was about to call Dev to let him know what she was doing, when she heard a scuffling noise.

It came from a cupboard she hadn't noticed before, under the stairs.

She pulled it open, and at first, all she could see was a pile of junk – coats, shoes, old boxes, rubbish – just stuffed into the space. Some of the jumble slid off the top of the pile, landing at her feet. As she watched, it heaved and a hand reached out and tried to pull the coats in closer.

Poppy was there in the darkness of the cupboard, huddled under the stairs, buried under the junk.

Kay touched the reaching hand. 'It's OK, Poppy. I'm here. You're safe.'

The pile exploded. Poppy leaped up, her eyes staring, her mouth wide in a soundless scream, her hands reaching for Kay's throat. Kay went down under the sheer force of Poppy's momentum, feeling Poppy's hands like iron bands round her neck, far stronger than her fragile appearance would have suggested. She was making sounds now, a kind of 'Ah, ah,' with each exhalation, then she screamed and fell over sideways, curling up on the floor. She was saying something now, words that Kay could barely decipher, they were so garbled. 'I didn't know,' Poppy seemed to be saying. 'I didn't know.'

'You didn't know what? Poppy, it's all right. You're safe now.' Kay could barely get the words out, her throat hurt so much. She was still on the ground where Poppy had thrown her, struggling to get up.

Poppy was writhing on the floor, then she crawled away in an odd crouch, and scrabbled at the cupboard door which had swung closed. Her breathing was rapid and shallow. Kay struggled to her feet, grabbed her phone and pressed the emergency button.

Ambulance and police. She had no idea what Poppy had taken, but it looked really bad. The girl was overheating, the sweat pouring off her, and her agitated movements were only going to make things worse. Already, it was affecting her breathing and probably her heart.

The damage to Kay's throat made it hard to speak. 'Ambulance,' she said. They'd bring police support once they heard what Kay had to say. As she gave her story, having to repeat it a frustrating number of times as her voice gave out, she watched Poppy cowering in the corner formed by the staircase and the wall, trying to pull the scattered coats over her. If Poppy attacked again, Kay didn't have anything left to fight her off. She'd heard about the extraordinary strength some of the new synthetics gave to users. Poppy was drawing on resources she didn't have, and Kay's resources were starting to run out.

Kay was still speaking rapidly into the phone, explaining Poppy's symptoms, when there was a terrible scream. Poppy staggered to her feet, pushed Kay hard against the wall and ran into the kitchen. She froze for a moment, looking round wildly, then threw herself at the back door, which shattered in an explosion of glass.

Chapter 37

Bridlington

Moving fast, Becca shoved her purse and her keys into her bag, and her phone into her pocket. She left Spice in the bathroom where she should be safe. There was nothing else she could do. She slipped her coat on, saw the stains on it from where she had dropped it on the floor, and pulled it off again, then she was heading out of the flat, pulling the door closed behind her.

DC Mason was right. They should have been waiting to get her. Why hadn't they been?

Her feet clattered on the stairs as she ran down. The back door was still swinging open.

The yard was empty in the dim glow of the outside light. No torch. She'd forgotten it. Was someone waiting there, in the deep shadow under the fire escape? She edged past, half crouching, her keys clutched in her hand, the ends protruding between her fingers. *Touch me and I'll hurt you! Touch me and I'll hurt you!*

Like dark nights when she was a kid, when He . . .

Don't think about that. That was then. Think about now!

The yard gate was closed. She remembered she'd pulled it shut when she came through earlier.

She stood at the gate, breathing hard, waiting for the hand on her shoulder, the arm locking round her neck.

Snitch bitch.

Move!

OK, out of the gate and into the pitch black of the gennel. Her feet stumbled on the uneven surface. She wanted to run, but she had to move carefully, not fall, just . . . She felt her way along, her hands touching the damp, crumbling brick of the walls, her feet slipping in the mud, until her groping hand found . . . nothing.

She was at the side street that led to the road. Now the faint glow of the streetlights lit her way.

Her breath came more easily. It was going to be OK. She was going to make it.

Don't lose it. They could be out there in the street, they could be coming along the road now.

She edged her way along, then she crouched down, using a low wall beside one of the shops to conceal herself as she looked along the main road.

Nothing.

Where was the car, the fucking car Dinah Mason had promised?

She looked the other way. No car there, either.

But a motorbike was coming towards her, barely visible as it was showing no lights. It was moving slowly and the engine was throttled down low so it was almost silent. The figure of the rider was just a dark shape against the light of the street lamps.

Becca froze, watching the moving bike as it came closer .

The light of the streetlamp shone briefly on the face, on the bare head and the long, untidy hair.

Johnny Dip. Doc.

He was here. He'd warned her off and she hadn't listened and now he was here.

She sank lower behind the wall, and moved backwards into the darkness of the gennel where the shadows would conceal her. There was no sign of the car Dinah had promised, and she didn't have time to wait. You couldn't trust the coppers; you should *never* trust the coppers.

But she knew what she was going to do. If Dinah couldn't be trusted with the car for Becca, then she couldn't be trusted about Kay. Becca was going to have to deal with that.

She didn't have her coat, but she'd picked up her bag and she had her phone and her keys. She had no choice but to use her phone. She sent a quick text: *Coming to you. On my way!* as she moved quickly back along the gennel, stumbling as the uneven ground caught her feet, and then she was back at the yard gate.

Her fingers fumbled with the sneck as she looked over her shoulder.

Where was Johnny Dip? How close was he?

The gate opened and she was back in the yard, her breath coming too fast, her heart beating so hard she thought everyone must be able to hear it.

The bike.

She dug in her bag for the bike keys, her fingers fumbling with panic. Tissues, her house keys – she flung them all onto the ground – then her hand closed over them. She dragged the tarp off the bike and using all her strength, pushed it away from the wall.

Hurry!

Johnny Dip could be coming along the gennel right now.

She swung her leg over the bike and held her breath as she put the key into the ignition. It had to work. It had to.

There was a click as the engine switched on.

She waited, listening.

Nothing.

There was nothing.

She turned off the steering lock, put the bike into neutral, listening all the time.

Where was he?

In her mind, she could see him waiting outside the yard gate, smiling, ready to grab her as she came through.

She couldn't ride it across the yard – she'd have to wheel it. In their last couple of months together, Jared had shown her how to do this. Dismounting, she kept the weight of the bike supported against her hip, and leaned into the handlebars. It was heavy, but she got it moving.

A plan. She had to have a plan.

OK. Get it to the gate, then . . . The gennel ran along the back of the block of shops and joined a side street at either end. Johnny Dip must have reached the first side street now. He could even be in the gennel. But he wouldn't have his bike. He wouldn't ride it along the gennel, he'd just park it in the road.

Did they know about her bike? They must do. One of them had been here in the yard.

Snitch bitch.

She pushed the bike to the yard gate and stopped again to listen.

Silence.

But that meant nothing. He might be out there, waiting for her. He could be anywhere.

Panic took her now. She had to go.

Now.

She needed a fast start. OK. Jared had shown her this as well. She pushed the gate open, swung her leg over the bike, gave it full choke and set off, leaning away from the turn as she came out of the gate into the muddy alleyway. The sound of the engine seemed to fill the night as if she'd shouted, 'Here I am!' at the top of her voice. She took a left out of the gennel, up the side street away from the main road, and opened the throttle.

No one came after her.

Once she'd put some distance between her and the flat, she stopped, looking round all the time, then she turned towards the town centre, taking the Hull road.

In the distance, she thought she heard the sound of a siren.

The car Dinah had sent? Too late. She was off.

She was going to find Kay.

Chapter 38

Hull

Kay sat in the waiting room. The medics had been treating Poppy for what seemed like forever, but she still had no news. She could tell – even before the speed with which Poppy's gasping, spasming form had been rushed into resuscitation – that it was touch and go. Poppy's face had been a mask of blood when they strapped her onto the trolley, and two policemen were needed to subdue her despite her injuries from the broken glass. Against Kay's expectations, they'd been oddly gentle with the frantic girl, calling her 'love', and making light of whatever demons she thought were after her.

Kay gave the paramedics as much information as she could, which wasn't enough. She had no idea what Poppy had taken. She also gave the police Leesha's name as far as she knew it, and the photograph of Leesha's car. She called Dev – who listened without much comment – then drove to the hospital herself.

She'd sat with Poppy for a while, wiping her face with a damp cloth. Poppy looked at her once and her lips moved. 'What is it?' Kay leaned in to hear.

'I didn't know,' Poppy whispered. But then her body spasmed into what looked like a fit, and Kay was hurried out, back into the waiting room. She wasn't family and she wasn't going to waste their time by arguing. At some point, Dev arrived, and took down the details Kay had to give him. As she told him about Carla's Place, his face went grey. 'I'll get on to the police. We haven't done what we should for Poppy.' His gaze met hers. 'I mean, *I* haven't. Are you all right to stay?'

Kay nodded. She felt bad about leaving Milo, but he had food and water. He'd be OK for now. Dev left, promising to come back later. 'Don't worry,' she said. 'I can manage on my own if necessary.'

It was after two in the morning. She got herself a cup of coffee and a Kit Kat from the vending machine. The coffee was thin and tasteless, but at least it was hot. She was just finishing the Kit Kat, having abandoned the coffee halfway through, when a woman in a white coat came down the corridor towards her. 'You're with the girl who came in with the overdose?'

'Poppy,' Kay said.

'Are you family?'

'No.' Kay explained her role as a support worker.

'Are you in touch with her family? Can you help us contact them?'

'As far as I know she's been out of touch with them for over a year. She's from Barnsley, originally.'

'We really need to make contact.'

That sounded bad. 'I'll contact a colleague, see if we've got that information. Or they might have it at the college. How is she?'

The woman sighed. 'I'll tell you what I can. She's very poorly, I'm afraid. We don't know exactly what she's taken. We've got blood samples but by the time we get the results, the stuff will be out of her system. The panic made her body temperature shoot up – it was forty when she came in. We've managed to reverse that, but we're looking at possible organ damage. And some of these synthetics lodge in the brain. She could be looking at serious neurological impairment. At this stage, we just don't know.' She gave Kay a severe look. 'These are not recreational drugs.'

The woman was tired and needed someone to take her frustration out on, Kay could see that. 'I know,' she murmured. 'I thought I was getting through to Poppy, but she had a setback.'

'Let's hope it isn't a permanent one,' the woman said with the same severity. She was treating Kay like a fellow professional, albeit one who had failed in her duty. And that was fair enough, because Kay had.

You can't save them all. Matt's mantra when things went wrong. It was true. Kay wasn't responsible for Poppy's addictions, and she wasn't responsible for what Poppy had taken tonight, but she wasn't sure she'd done enough. If she'd tried harder to maintain contact, maybe, just maybe, Poppy would have called her after her arrest, rather than Leesha. 'Can I see her?'

The medic shook her head. 'She's asleep. We're observing her for now and then we'll do some more assessments later this morning.' She smiled, suddenly looking more human. 'She'd have died if you hadn't got help for her. Try not to worry. She's young, she's healthy enough. She might make a full recovery. I'm not writing her off, not yet.'

But too many people were all too willing to do that, Kay thought as she headed towards the hospital exit. Write off young drug users like Poppy, and write off troubled young women like Becca.

When she came out of A & E into the main waiting room, to her surprise, she saw Dev leaning against the wall reading a book. 'We've got the police at the office,' he said, sounding tired.

'For Poppy?' Kay asked. 'Tonight?'

'No. They've taken the computers and all the financial records and . . .' He shook his head. 'There's something big going on and no one's telling me anything. I can't . . .' He spread his hands in confusion, then seemed to shake the subject off. 'No doubt someone will tell me something soon. There's a lot going on we don't know about. Poppy's our concern now. How are you?'

For the first time, Kay found herself warming to him. 'I'm fine.' She told him what she knew about

Poppy's condition. 'They're worried about her. They're trying to contact her parents.'

Dev made a face. 'I hope that'll help, but last time Poppy saw them, they blamed her drug use on her choice of career. Apparently, embryonic lawyers and doctors never use drugs, but you can't expect anything else from trainee hairdressers and make-up artists. And this other stuff ... this ... Carla's Place ... Poppy's going to struggle, coming back from that. I feel responsible. I really took my eye off the ball with Xanthe.'

It was true. Kay did him the courtesy of not trying to justify what he'd done – or failed to do. 'I can help her,' she said. 'It's nothing I haven't seen before.' Escape route number one for troubled teenage girls – and some boys – was the arms of a pimp.

Dev nodded. 'You know, Poppy loved her course, and she was doing well, but her parents were always putting it down. She spent her entire first year getting brilliant grades and feeling as though she was wasting her time.'

The burdens of parental expectation. All these people wanted was the best for their children, and yet they seemed blind to it when it came along. Come to think of it, wasn't she always trying to get Becca to do something more rewarding? But Becca wasn't like Poppy. Becca wasn't studying something she loved, she was working in dead-end jobs she hated. 'Do you have children?' she asked Dev.

'No. You?'

'Just my foster children.'

'Yes. I'd heard you did a lot of fostering.' He shoved his book into the pocket of his raincoat. 'There's no point in hanging around. They won't let us see Poppy now. I'll drive you back to your car. It's late. I can drive you home if you want.'

'Thanks, but to my car is fine.'

'There's not much of the night left. I've got a spare room if you want to stay over in Hull.'

The prospect of falling into a bed close by was very attractive. She was exhausted. But Kay valued her privacy more than anything these days, and staying over at the home of someone she barely knew didn't appeal. Anyway, there was Milo. She'd left him for far too long. 'That's very kind of you, but I really need to get back.'

She switched on her phone, and it immediately pinged, then pinged again. She checked. There were two messages.

From Becca.

Call me now!!! was the first one. It had been sent shortly after midnight.

What had been going on?

For Becca to text so late, and so urgently, it had to be serious. And then – it was getting worse *Coming to you. On my way!* That had been half an hour later. Becca had no transport, so how ...? Even Becca wouldn't set out to walk.

Her bike? She could be heading south to Sunk Island on a bike that had been standing unused under a tarpaulin for weeks and probably hadn't had any maintenance in all that time. The last text was almost two hours ago – if she'd found her way, she'd be there by now, but there was no further message.

Kay pressed the key to call, but Becca's phone went straight to voicemail.

Oh God. What had happened?

Dev was watching her. 'Something wrong? Can I help?'

'Not right now, thank you, but I'd appreciate that lift to my car. I really need to get back.'

As she followed Dev to the car park, she tried Becca's number, once, twice, three times, but each time she got the same response.

Becca's phone was switched off, or she was somewhere with no signal.

On her own, at Kay's house, on Sunk Island.

And now Kay remembered leaving the house, the yellow sack blowing across the ground in the darkness, and close by, the sound of a motorbike.

Chapter 39

Bridlington

Dinah had been chasing up the Stockport connection, the car belonging to the elderly Elizabeth Bagnall. She'd expected Hammond to liaise with the Greater Manchester force and get one of their people to interview the old woman. Instead, he had sent Dinah.

So she'd found herself in the cosy hallway of Elizabeth Bagnall's house, stuck with the horrible feeling important things were happening, and she was in the wrong place, as if she was stuck in one of those dreams where your way back was blocked no matter what you did.

By the time she'd crawled round the outskirts of first Leeds then Manchester, then checked in with her Greater Manchester Police contact, it was well into the evening before she'd arrived at the Stockport house. Elizabeth Bagnall was too ill to talk to her, already in bed in fact, but the woman living with her, Janet Sandison, who was either a long-term friend or a partner – Dinah wasn't sure of her status – had been very chatty.

Dinah had explained what she wanted, and that she had a warrant, if necessary, to check the car, but the companion waived the formalities. 'Fancy doing that. Using the number of an old woman's car. Liz might have got into trouble.' But she confirmed that as far as she knew, the car hadn't left the drive for weeks. Dinah went to check it. Would the Sandison woman notice if the car vanished overnight? Probably, but Dinah had learned early from Curwen never to take anything for granted. Janet Sandison had given her the keys. 'I don't drive myself,' she'd said.

Dinah had slipped behind the wheel of the old Fiesta. When she'd tried the ignition, nothing had happened. OK, the battery was probably flat, as it hadn't been driven for so long – but she would have expected a flicker of life. She'd opened the bonnet and had a quick look. It wasn't hard to find the problem. The engine relay had been removed.

'Did you know this had been done?' she'd asked Janet. There didn't seem any good reason why the car should have been immobilised unless someone wanted to make sure it stayed put.

Sandison had looked anxious. 'I did it,' she'd said. 'I hope it was the right thing. I was told it would protect it. I didn't want it getting stolen, sitting on the drive like that.'

Janet Sandison didn't sound as if she had the technical know-how. There was something odd here.

Watch out for odd things. It was something else Curwen had told her.

'Why didn't Miss Bagnall just sell the car?' she'd asked. 'It's taxed and its MOT certificate is up to date, but . . .' It sounded as though Miss Bagnall had been unable to drive for some time, and wasn't likely to start again – so why pay good money for an unused car?

'The family don't like to think she wasn't going to, you know . . .' The companion had shaken her head.

'The family?'

'Yes. Well, it's just her niece now. Her sister died a couple of years ago, but her niece keeps in touch, keeps an eye on things. It was her told me how to make sure the car was safe. She was worried about joy riders, and people like that.'

'She told you to disable the car?'

'No. Well, she told me what to do so it couldn't be driven.'

Dinah had tried to keep the excitement from her voice. She wanted the details of this niece, this woman who was so keen to make sure this car stayed off the road. Miss Sandison had been a bit reluctant at first, but after thinking about it, she'd said, 'She deals with most of Liz's finances. It was Liz's sister first, but after she died, her niece took over. It was all signed and sealed before I came on the scene. Liz talked about changing it but she never got round to it. You know how it is.'

Dinah didn't. Her own finances were mostly non-existent, but what possessions she did have, she watched with care. 'Her niece has power of attorney? Can you give me her contact details? It would be much simpler if I just talk to her.'

'Yes, I suppose so.' Janet Sandison had led her back to the house and rummaged in a drawer as Dinah waited. 'Here.' She'd taken out a business card and handed it to Dinah.

Alicia Traynor, Director, CaLa Enterprises, Hull.

There was a phone number and a post code. 'Thanks,' Dinah had said. She'd wanted to ask some more questions, but the relative lateness of the hour had caught up with Janet. Dinah had decided further questions could wait for now. It was late and she had to drive back to Brid. She was behind the wheel, fastening her seat belt when her phone rang. She checked the screen, but she didn't recognise the number. She answered with a feeling of trepidation.

It was Becca with a story of a break-in and vandalism. As Dinah listened, she could feel herself going cold. 'Right. Listen. I'm sending a patrol car to you.' She gave Becca more instructions, trying to make sure she'd covered all the bases. 'Don't worry,' she said. 'I'm on it.'

After Becca hung up, Dinah dithered for a minute. She had to chase up the Alicia Traynor connection, and make sure someone would question Janet Sandison and find how much more – if anything – she knew. But there was a raw urgency to Becca's call she couldn't ignore. Her first instinct was to contact Hammond, but she was no longer confident she could trust him to help Becca. In the end, she called Dave Sykes. 'I've got information about the car,' she told him, and explained quickly what had happened to it, and gave him the details for Alicia Traynor. 'There's something else.' She ran through what she knew about Becca Armitage and about the break-in at Becca's flat. 'I think the kid conned her to get the key off her and then they went in and trashed the place.'

'Looking for something?'

'I think so. Andy Yeatson was seeing her, so maybe that's got something to do with it.'

'Yeatson was seeing her? Why didn't we know about this? Why didn't you tell—?'

She cut through his questions. 'I did. I told the boss this morning. Listen, I think they could still be after her, and—'

'I want to hear what she's got to say. You reckon she's part of the drugs scene?'

Dinah outlined what she'd seen at the flat, and the evidence that Becca had been attacked. She could feel Dave Sykes' disapproval radiating down the phone and wanted to defend herself, but needed to get help for Becca first.

'I've sent someone round,' Dave said. 'And a car to pick her up. We need to talk to this Armitage woman. Now. Right, get yourself back here – we need to get all this in detail.'

Dinah's head was spinning as she tried to work out how much trouble she could be in. She needed to prioritise – the whole thing was out of her hands now, but Becca could still be in danger. Dinah needed to let her know what was happening. She called her as she ran along the road to where she had left her car, but there was no reply. The phone rang and rang. Frustrated, she sent a text. *Are you ok? Get back to me.*

As she slipped behind the wheel, she tried to sort things out in her head. It would take her over two hours to get back – by that time, whatever was going to happen to Becca would have happened. What would Hammond say? What would he do? And Becca – Dinah had been quick to dismiss her as a user, a kind of low-life, and had been surprised at Andy's choice. She could remember Becca's prickliness, her apparent lack of concern about what had happened to him, but as the conversation came back to her, she began to wonder . . .

That odd exchange when she'd talked about Mia, about Andy's baby, an orphan now, and all the colour had left Becca Armitage's face. What was it she'd said? *His wife died?*

And then she'd turned her back and started sorting through a pile of clothes as if she didn't give a shit . . . or as if she didn't want Dinah to see the emotion on her face. Dinah understood that. She'd schooled herself not to show her own feelings, especially not at work. She could remember turning away and involving herself in some random task when something upset her so no one would see the tears in her eyes.

She was leaving Stockport now. She needed to get back as fast as possible, but she pulled in at the side of the road just before it joined the Woodhead Pass across the Pennines and checked her phone – there was no response to her text. On the off chance, she tried Becca's number again.

This time it was answered, but not by Becca. It was someone who was cagey until she identified herself. She was talking to one of the PCs Dave Sykes had sent to the flat. Becca wasn't there. Her phone had been found in the mud in the backyard of her building.

Of Becca herself, there was no sign.

Chapter 40

Curwen had got his way, and things had moved faster than he had believed possible. Despite his low-key approach, Dom Maskall's questions to the Tania's House accountants had rung alarm bells. They'd contacted the police. Search teams had gone into the Tania's House offices in Hull at once and taken the books apart. Less than an hour ago, they'd arrested Carl Lavery and were in the process of searching as many of his business premises as they could find. Curwen had no idea why things had happened so quickly, but he wasn't looking a gift horse in the mouth.

'It looks like you were right and there is a drugs link,' the man leading the search told him. Though Curwen had no close friends among his colleagues, he was generally liked and respected – he was seen as a good copper. Everyone knew about the fiasco of the first Smokehouse raid, and most of them had been sympathetic. 'We've found large amounts of cash stored at the pub and in a couple of the holiday lets.

He'll say it's all legitimate – he gets paid in cash – but there's too much. No way he can explain it all away. The money comes in from the drugs, he cleans it up, everyone's happy.'

For Curwen, it was a result. It wasn't what he'd been looking for, but it would do nicely, thank you. Money laundering. Was Lavery the banker for the gang? Or did he just take a cut for converting hot money into usable money? Money launderers were prepared to lose forty to fifty per cent of the value of the dirty money in order to clean it, but that still left them with plenty.

This could get him his promotion.

Finally, he had time to think about Becca the Barmaid's phone call. He'd promised to deal with it, but he'd shelved that when he got the call about the raids on Carl Lavery's premises. Whatever had been going on with her was probably finished by now. He had planned on going home – God knows, he'd earned it, but he needed to deal with this first.

He was mulling over what to do when he saw Karen Innes coming through the office towards him. She didn't look happy. 'Curwen.'

'Yeah?'

'I wouldn't look so pleased with myself if I were you. Do you have any idea how much trouble you're in?'

Curwen managed – just – not to let the surprise show on his face. Trouble? He'd just uncovered evidence of a major money-laundering ring!

Oh shit. Had they found Andy's phone?

'Don't know what you're talking about, Innes,' he said, managing to keep his voice casual. He suspected she wasn't fooled.

'Looks like you don't need me to tell you.' She nodded over his shoulder, and Curwen saw his boss, DCI Kevin Gallagher, heading towards him. He scowled at Curwen. 'My office,' he said abruptly. Innes, he couldn't help noticing, looked pleased.

Keeping his face carefully blank, Curwen followed Gallagher through the office door. His mind was working fast. They'd know about Andy in the pub – Dinah Mason wouldn't have kept that to herself – but they wouldn't know that Curwen had sent him there. Andy's phone? That could only raise a suspicion. Enough to put a blight on his future progress? Maybe, but it would be impossible to prove. There was nothing there that would lead to an instant bollocking, so what was all this about? 'Sir?' he said as Gallagher threw himself into his chair, leaving Curwen standing.

'Curwen, what the fuck have you been doing? Weren't you told to keep away from the Smokehouse?'

'I did, sir.'

'Right. So why were you looking into Carl Lavery's finances? '

Curwen hesitated. If he wanted the credit for the money-laundering bust, he'd have to put his hand up to the investigation. He made his mind up. 'Sir, I always thought that pub was dodgy. I didn't go back

– I screwed up the first time, but this is something else.'

'And why did you screw up? You listened to some little scrote who spun you a line.'

Curwen felt the hot anger of humiliation again. No one had spun him a line – he didn't fall for things like that. 'It was more than that, sir. It was a solid tip-off.'

'Which was wrong.'

Curwen couldn't answer that.

'So why did you go back? Why did you disobey explicit—'

'I didn't go near the place.' No point in mentioning his first contact with Becca the Barmaid. That *had* been a mistake. 'When I was writing my report, I saw something in the finances that looked off. I checked it out, and the next thing I know is the fraud people are going in mob-handed.'

'Curwen, did it never cross your mind that if you picked something up from a low-grade informer, people whose job it was to get that information had picked it up as well? Louder, clearer and in more detail than you? Officers from the National Crime Agency have been following a lead for weeks, Curwen! Weeks! Drug importers, Curwen. They were on the track of the importers. Thanks to you, they had to go in before they were ready, before Lavery had time to get rid of the evidence.'

'And Andy Yeatson?' Curwen had not expected this.

Gallagher shook his head impatiently. 'We already know who killed Yeatson. Hammond could have made an arrest a couple of days ago, but if he had done, he'd have blown one of the biggest drug ops we've had for a long time. He agreed to wait, gather evidence and hold his fire.'

Curwen was silenced. *Shit!* A covert operation, under his fucking nose, and he'd missed it. And he'd sent Andy into the pub right into the middle of it. Had they spotted Andy? Was that why ...? Suddenly, his coup didn't seem like such a big deal. He was starting to feel sick. Had the undercover guys let Andy be led to his death and kept their mouths shut so their investigation wouldn't be compromised?

'Curwen?'

He still had to cover his back. 'With respect, sir, what I found had nothing to do with drugs. Or the pub. I found some dodgy accounting and followed it up.'

'And that triggered the gang. They've been carrying out a massive dump up and down the coast, getting rid of the stuff. We've had to go in sooner than we wanted, before we were ready. Which part of *stay out of the fucking pub* didn't you understand?'

If he'd known. If he'd fucking known ... If Andy had known ... 'I did stay out of the pub, sir. I can't act on information I don't have.'

Gallagher's face darkened. 'You obey orders, Detective Sergeant. That's what they're for. Now keep out of the fucking way. You've done enough damage already. Go home, Curwen. I'll see you here in the morning. Nine o'clock. I don't want to see your face again until then. Get out.' Curwen left the office, resisting the temptation to slam the door behind him.

He had no intention of going home. Things were happening and he needed to be here.

The NCA. *Jesus.* And he'd had no idea. He was thinking fast as he went to his desk. If those shits had stood by and let Andy be killed . . .

He forced himself back to the practicalities. Gallagher said he was in deep shit. Well, Gallagher could go fuck himself. His first thought was that he'd blown it. But he was beginning to realise that he might be OK. He'd followed up a legitimate query. And this time, he'd covered himself every step of the way. Hadn't he? His dealings with Becca the Barmaid? He doubted she would say anything, but if she did, he could work round it. His financial queries? Perfectly legitimate response to evidence. The texts that the app had forwarded from Andy's phone? Those would be trickier to explain. He'd better get rid of those. In fact, it was time to get rid of that phone altogether.

Andy's phone. If they ever found it, lying some-where in the vast expanses of Sunk Island, and if it was identified, then it could tell a story that he really didn't want to come out. He'd better make some plans to cover his back.

He told himself that overall, he was ahead. He'd been instrumental in uncovering a money-laundering racket. And if that investigation blew a big drugs' bust? Nothing to do with him.

He should have been feeling good. Instead, he felt sick, as if he'd swallowed something rotten. He was tempted to change his mind and go home after all, but first off, he needed to find out what had happened to Becca the Barmaid. He owed Andy that.

Twenty minutes later, tiredness forgotten, he pulled out of the car park and headed south.

Chapter 41

Sunk Island

Becca was freezing. She'd forgotten how cold it could be on a bike and she didn't even have her coat – it was still on the floor where she'd dropped it. Her jumper was warm enough, but not for riding along dark roads in the night. As soon as she put some distance between herself and the flat, she stopped and checked the storage box on the back.

There was no helmet but there was a padded jacket and a pair of gloves. Kay had given them to her with the bike.

She dug in her bag for her phone. She needed to check the map again, though it looked pretty straight-forward – get on the Hornsea road and just keep heading south.

Her phone wasn't there.

She checked her pockets, remembering her frantic dig through her bag for her keys, just letting stuff fall onto the ground. Had she dropped her phone as well?

She must have done. It wasn't here. She'd lost it, and she couldn't go back.

Shit. *Shit!*

She didn't know the way. She couldn't get to Kay, couldn't warn her, couldn't . . .

Stop.

So she didn't have her phone. But she'd looked at the route to Sunk Island, and she had Kay's address. All she needed was to be sure of her direction.

Jared had taught her about finding your way. He'd taught her to find north using the stars, but she didn't even need to do that. She just needed to keep the sea on her left – and the signposts would tell her where the sea was when she came to a junction. If she was on the right road out of Brid, soon she'd join the A1033. A left turn from there would take her into Sunk Island. After that, she had to head south until she got to a crossroads. According to the map she'd seen it was just empty – hardly any roads, just . . . nowhere.

There didn't seem to be too many houses. It shouldn't be too hard to find the one that was Kay's.

OK. She could do this.

The road ahead was empty. She opened up the throttle and headed south.

Forty-five minutes later, despite the gloves, her hands were numb and she was freezing again. She was travelling blind and she had no idea if she was heading the right way or not. She'd followed signs where she remembered names and kept the coast on her left.

She was on a main road now. If she'd got this right,

it would be the one she wanted, the one where she could turn off into Sunk Island. If it was wrong ... then she was lost. There was a junction ahead, a left turn. This one? There was no signpost.

Her lights picked out the road name.

Sunk Island Road.

This was it. She was almost past the turn. She swerved and hauled the bike round, the tyres giving a horrible squeal. The bike, briefly out of control, skidded from one side to another, and then she was upright again and heading on into the night. A horn blared as a car raced past on the main road, and then she was in the countryside on a narrow road that ran into emptiness and silence.

This place was just nothing, just the middle of nowhere. It couldn't be far now. Who'd choose to live here?

Kay would.

And she knew she was telling herself all these things to try and get rid of the fear that was growing inside her. She wasn't scared any more that Johnny Dip was after her – he'd have caught up with her fast if he'd seen her go. But she was scared about what was happening, scared that she might be bringing trouble down on Kay, scared about what might have already happened to Kay, about being lost in the night in this place where the land seemed to go on forever.

The place where Andy had died.

The road was getting narrower and after the village, there weren't any houses. When she shone her headlights to either side, it was just field after field after field. Maybe it went on forever. Maybe she'd just keep on driving, on and on, and she'd never find a house, never find Kay, never find her way back.

She was so tired it was hard to think. Her headlights wandered across the road and she realised she must have fallen asleep for a second. And suddenly a crossroads came straight out of the darkness at her. She jammed on her brakes, feeling the wheels skid before she got control again.

Jared's voice spoke in her head. *Fuck's sake, Becca.*

All right, all right. She almost said it out loud. She stopped the bike and climbed off, stretching and easing her tight muscles. She could do this. She could keep going. She used to go dancing all night in Leeds when she was a student. She'd driven with Andy right down to Hull and they'd danced until the small hours. And she'd got up for work in the morning feeling great.

She could do this.

She'd made it here, kept herself on the right route all along. This was Stone Creek Road, and there was a house, right here at the crossroads. Her spirits lifted. How many houses were there in Sunk Island? There was a good chance this would be Kay's. And there was a light on. Someone was in.

But it wasn't Kay. The car outside wasn't Kay's and no dog barked when she opened the garden gate and approached the front door.

OK, back on the bike. You can do this.

In her headlights, the road was just a stretch of

tarmac that vanished into darkness. There were no houses, nothing. She was back in the nightmare.

Another crossroads.

Still nothing.

What kind of place had Kay moved to?

She was near the end of Stone Creek Road and hadn't found Kay's house. Defeat closed over her. Maybe it went on after the crossroads. Wearily, she climbed back on the bike and drove on, following the long curve of the empty road, and then there was another house ahead on her right.

She felt herself relax. This had to be Kay's.

Had to be.

She pulled up. The car outside was a battered Land Rover, but that didn't mean anything. Kay might have a visitor. Her car might be hidden round the side of the house. Becca walked up the short path, but there was no sign of another car. No dog barked.

She stood there, not wanting to accept it, but she had to. This wasn't the right house.

She straddled the bike again and sat there for a few minutes, letting the disappointment fade, then drove slowly along and before too long, she saw a hedge, a wall, and then dimly shadowed against the sky, a roof with tall chimneys.

This one probably wasn't Kay's either. Kay probably didn't live anywhere near here – Becca must have misread the address and she'd just have to deal with it, because that's what you did when things went wrong. You dealt with it.

She pulled up outside the gate. It was standing wide open, but there was no sign of a car. Becca climbed slowly off the bike. If this wasn't Kay's then she'd gone so wrong she'd have to . . . She didn't know what.

Slowly, she went in through the gate. She kept telling herself this couldn't be Kay's because she couldn't face the disappointment, not again. No car. Her heart sank.

As she approached the window, there was a sudden explosion of barking, and she saw Milo jumping up, his furious barking changing into excited whines as he recognised her.

Relief flooded through her. This was Kay's house and, OK, no car meant Kay wasn't here, but if she'd left Milo, she wouldn't be away for long. She checked her watch. It was after two, but Kay would have to be back soon.

'It's OK, Milo,' she said as Milo's whining reached a higher pitch. Could she manage to get in? She set off round the house, looking for a back door.

And there was a car. It was pulled up in the shadows by the side of the house, near a door like a cupboard in the wall, which was open.

'Kay?' It came out as a whisper.

'Who's started that fucking dog off again. We'll have half of the—'

The voice came from behind her. She turned, sharply.

A tall, broad figure stood there, his hair in wild curls – she couldn't make out his face, but she knew who it was.

Johnny Dip.

But he was in Bridlington. She'd seen him at the flat.

And now, like her, he was here. He had a fast bike – of course he'd got here before her.

He was looking at her. 'What the . . .?'

'Right, that's the lot,' came another voice. 'We need to get moving. That dog's going to wake the neighbourhood.'

'Go in there and shut it up. Cut its throat or something.' A third voice; a woman. Two people were hanging back in the shadows, watching Johnny Dip.

For a moment, Becca froze, then she spun round and ran the only way she could, round the house, towards the back.

She was stumbling across rough ground in pitch darkness, and she could hear Milo barking, but nothing else. Oh, God, where was she? She couldn't run, it was too dark, she was going to fall – where was she, where could she go, where was Kay?

A torch shone directly in her face, blinding her. Someone's arms went round her from behind, a hand clamping over her mouth and lifting her clear of the ground. 'Are you going to keep quiet?' She knew that voice. It was Johnny Dip.

She sank her teeth into his palm, and he cursed and dropped her. 'You just couldn't keep out of it, could you?' he said, rubbing his hand. There was an odd expression on his face that looked almost like regret, and it frightened her more than threats. He didn't want to do what he was planning to do, but he was going to do it anyway.

Someone was coming towards her through the darkness, silhouetted against the paler light of the sky. A feeling of cold washed over her. She recognised that figure – it was the one she'd seen standing by the gate as she lifted her head from the ground, the night she'd been attacked.

Snitch bitch.

The torchlight caught a gleam of fair hair and she realised who it was.

The woman from the pub. Alicia. The one Andy had called Sal Capone, treating her like some kind of joke.

Only she wasn't a joke.

This was the person who'd tried to burn a kitten alive, who'd kicked Becca in the ribs and laughed. Her legs started to shake. She was frightened – really frightened.

She swung away, trying to run, but Johnny Dip grabbed her arms again as she struggled wildly. There were more of them, and they were bigger and stronger. She didn't stand a chance.

They'd got her, like they'd got Andy.

Chapter 42

Becca was going to be sick. She tried to move, clear her mouth and nose to breathe fresh air, but she couldn't.

Her hands were fastened behind her and she was lying face down on some kind of carpet that felt gritty against her skin. There was a sour smell and she felt herself start to retch. She couldn't be sick. She couldn't open her mouth because they'd taped it shut. She could barely breathe. If she threw up, she'd suffocate, choked by her own puke.

They'd argued for a bit about what to do with her. They'd taken her into the house, letting themselves in with a key. The woman had taped her arms behind her and wrapped tape round her ankles, pulling it viciously tight. From behind some door or barrier, Milo barked hysterically.

'Get rid of the fucking dog,' Alicia said. 'I'll do it if you won't.'

'Leave it.' Johnny Dip wasn't saying much, but the others seemed to be listening to him. 'And we leave her. By the time anyone finds her, we're gone. Get that tape off her mouth. She'll suffocate.'

'Doc, you moron, she's seen us.' Alicia threw herself into an armchair, rolling her eyes in exasperation. 'I've sorted the other one – let's get this one out of the way.'

'Who's the moron here? How many times do I have to fucking tell you? If you'd left that "other one" alone, we'd be in the clear. Just keep her out of the way for a few hours, and we'll be gone. You harm her, and they'll keep on coming.'

'You really believe that? You really think they'll leave us alone?' Alicia stood up and came across to where they'd dumped Becca.

'No. They won't. But they don't have the money to keep after us – unless you make it another murder enquiry. I know how this works. Isn't that what you pay me for? Just lock her in the shed and go.'

'We need more time. If it hadn't all blown up tonight – thanks to *her* . . .' Becca braced herself, but the kick against her bruised ribs forced a scream out past the gag.

'Lay off. We've got the time we need if we stop arsing around here. Now, shut her in and let's get moving.'

'OK, OK. You're no fun.' Alicia's long fair hair shimmered in the light from the dim bulb. 'You'd better make it up to me later. Right. I'll see to it.'

She came across now and pushed Becca roughly onto her back. 'You're lucky you aren't getting another scar to match the first.' She ripped the tape off Becca's mouth and Becca felt the skin tear.

Johnny Dip stood up. 'I'll put the stuff in the van and get up there ahead of you. I'll make sure it's secure.'

Alicia looked across at him. 'I'd better deal with the car first.'

'Cool. Where are you going to take it?'

'I'll leave it at Stone Creek. They won't find it until tomorrow.'

'Doesn't matter if they do.'

'So you say.'

Johnny Dip left the room, and Becca felt as though some protection was gone. She'd been struggling against the tape, working her wrists up and down, but now she lay quietly, trying not to draw Alicia's attention to her. She heard the sound of feet moving towards the door. Milo exploded with wild barks again. *Be quiet, Milo. Be quiet.* Then the door opened and shut. Soon, Becca heard the sound of an engine and saw the shadow of something moving across the window.

Johnny Dip was gone.

'Right,' Alicia said. She came over to Becca with the tape in her hands. Becca tried to roll out of the way, and drew her legs up. She could still kick, try and keep the woman away from her.

'If you kick,' Alicia said, 'I'll hog-tie you.' Without warning, she dropped onto her knees on Becca's chest, knocking all the air out of her lungs. As Becca struggled to get her breath, Alicia pulled her head round, and wound more tape round her face, covering her mouth. 'Yeah, right, Doc, we leave her to shout the place down. Clever, that.'

Becca, looking into Alicia's eyes, thought they were older and colder than anything she'd ever seen.

It was hard to breathe. She heard the ripping sound of the tape again, and a strip was pressed across her eyes. She forced herself to lie still – panicking was the worst thing she could do. She'd learned that the hard way when they restrained her in the detention centre.

There were more footsteps, and someone else came into the room. A man's voice said, 'They've gone. What are we going to do?'

'What Doc said. Get rid of the evidence.'

The man sighed. 'OK. Shall we get her into the cupboard?' There was something familiar ... Becca couldn't place it.

'I said, evidence. I said, get rid. We can't leave either of them here. They've both seen us. Doc's lost it – he's too soft. It's dangerous. He's got to go too.'

'Yeah? And who's going to see to that?'

'You need to watch your mouth.'

'OK, OK.' The other voice sounded apologetic; a bit scared. Becca understood she wasn't the only one who was frightened of Alicia.

'The others know what to do. We don't need to worry about Doc, we just need to get rid of this lot.'

'Might have been better if you'd left the kid behind.'

'To talk to the cops? Are you crazy? They'd have been waiting for us when we got here.'

'Yeah, but ... OK, OK. You're the boss.'

'Right. Just keep remembering that.'

'Fine. But what if Doc's right? We get rid of the stuff, they can't prove anything. We're clear.'

'Don't you get it? This isn't the end. Don't listen to Doc. We get out of the way, we lie low, then we come back.'

The kid? Who were they talking about? Becca tried to struggle to her knees, forgetting that she was blind-folded by the tape, she couldn't see. A lump of cold fear began to grow inside her. Johnny Dip hadn't said anything about a kid. He'd just told Alicia they should leave Becca in the house and dump the car.

'So we don't leave anything. Come on, help me put her in the car. We've messed around for long enough. Do you want to go to jail, pretty boy like you? You won't be out again for thirty years.'

'Shut up.'

'Here. We'd better ...' Becca felt something soft land on top of her, then Alicia rolled her over quickly and something wrapped round her, covering her head. A blanket. They were hiding her in a blanket. In case anyone was watching? Who would be watching here?

She could hear footsteps as the man came across the room towards her. Becca tried to roll away, tried to draw her feet up to kick, but the pain and her struggle for breath had taken away all her strength.

'Where is he?'

'In my car – it's just down the road. We can pick him up.'

'OK.'

They grabbed her arms and legs and lifted her. She felt the chill of the night air as they carried her outside. The pressure on her arms made it hard to breathe, and her bladder was contracting with fear. She had to fight it or she would wet herself.

She wasn't letting them see that; see how scared she was.

And she was scared. It was hard not to panic, not to scream, not to start crying – and if she cried, her nose would fill up and she wouldn't be able to breathe. She'd suffocate, die, just because she didn't have the guts to ... The anger saved her. It didn't take the fear away, but the rage surging through her was like new energy.

She was going to survive this. She wasn't going to let them do this to her. She twisted her body and kicked her legs forward, hard, feeling the man stagger. He swore and dumped her on the ground.

Now! Free herself from the blanket, get to her feet, try and—

Her legs were taped and she fell. Her arms were held behind her so she couldn't protect herself and she landed hard, knocking the breath out of her body.

'I warned you,' Alicia's voice said. A hand gripped her hair. The blow across her face made her ears ring. They forced her to her feet. Becca, bruised, blind and dizzy, could barely keep her balance and the two of them half lifted, half dragged her across the rough ground. 'Put her in,' Alicia was panting a bit with the effort.

She felt them lift her into the boot, then the lid closed, trapping her.

Chapter 43

The drive through the narrow, unlit roads of Sunk Island was tricky at the best of times. When you were so tired you were falling asleep at the wheel, it was downright dangerous. As Kay turned right onto Stone Creek Road, she wound her window down to see if the cold air would keep her alert. At least the chances of meeting another car were small.

At the very moment she thought that, lights appeared on the road ahead of her, coming her way.

Fast. The idiot was driving far too fast! Her addled brain dithered, but reflex had her winding the wheel hard to the left and she was slamming on the brakes, scraping along the hedge as the car – some kind of off-road vehicle – shot past, its horn dopplering into the distance, leaving silence behind.

Kay gripped the steering wheel, her heart hammering. She remembered what Catherine Ford had said: *A couple of young thugs in a car, a four by four, just driving round.* Were they poachers or thieves or road-hog vandals, or . . .

The shock and her anger had done what the cold air had failed to do. She was wide awake, and alert. Slowly, she turned on the engine – the car had stalled in its mad skid into the hedge – and carefully pulled away. There was no sign of any lights, but her window was still wound down and she thought she could hear, somewhere in the distance, the sound of a bike engine.

What kind of things went on here at night?

Becca should have arrived at the house by now and even have found her way in. And if she hadn't? She'd surely wait. She'd hear Milo barking and know that Kay wouldn't be away too long, except she had been. Poor Milo had been on his own for hours, longer than she'd ever left him before.

Even so, Becca must be waiting. It wasn't sinister that she hadn't called when she found that Kay was out. Phone reception on Sunk Island was poor, and she probably hadn't been able to get a signal.

Kay was driving faster now. The road was straight and the land was flat and open. The moonlight cast a faint illumination across the fields and caught the gleam of the drains. After the intrusion of the speeding car, the night was silent and still.

She told herself again that it would be OK. She'd either find a sleeping Becca in the house, or a pissed-off Becca waiting in the front porch, but it would be all right.

And Poppy?

She couldn't do anything about that now. Poppy was in the best hands. Becca was on her own and needed her. The road curved to the right, the final route marker before she was back. She was round the corner – and saw chaos ahead.

Police cars were parked in the road, their lights flashing. There were people in her garden, small groups talking, making urgent gestures. A cold hand seemed to close round her stomach.

Becca.

Slowly, she drew up at the side of the road and got out. The police. Oh God, what had happened? In the background she could hear Milo's barks, high-pitched and frantic.

She recognised Becca's bike, parked in the road. She'd made it. But there was no sign of her.

'What's happening?' Someone grabbed her arm. It was Catherine Ford looking scared and excited, a coat pulled over some pyjamas, boots on her feet.

'I don't know. What did you see?'

'Nothing. It was just a few minutes ago. All this noise. And then lights. It's trouble, I knew there was trouble.'

Kay didn't have time to talk. She had to find Becca. Shaking off Catherine Ford's hand, she headed for the gate, where a uniformed constable was standing. 'What's happening? Has someone been hurt? My daughter . . .' She was starting to lose it. She breathed deeply and began again. 'I live here. Has someone been hurt? My daughter was here. I need to know where she is.'

'And you are . . .?'

'Kay McKinnon. I moved in a few days ago.' As her fingers fumbled in her bag for some ID, she wanted to bang her fist on something, start shouting, demand they tell her what had happened to Becca, tell her what was going on, but she had dealt with the police enough times in the course of her work, and knew how to act. Be calm, be clear, be factual. Insist on your rights, maintain your authority. She was Becca's family – or the nearest thing Becca had to family.

Keeping up the facade of calm, she produced her driving licence and waited as the man studied it with what seemed like forensic attention to detail. 'I can't let you go in the house, Mrs McKinnon, not yet. Is that your dog? You can collect him.'

'Has anyone been hurt? Becca was supposed to meet me here. My daughter. I'm worried about her.'

'I'll get someone to talk to you.'

Her heart plummeted. Something had happened to Becca and now they were getting someone to break the news. 'Come on. It's a simple question. Has some-one been hurt?'

'Did you say you're Becca's mother?'

Kay whipped round. A woman had come up behind her as she was talking to the uniformed constable. 'I can deal with this,' the woman said.

The young constable looked relieved.

Kay looked at the woman. She was wearing a dark trouser suit, her fair hair was cut short, and in the intermittent light from the police cars, Kay could see the frames of her glasses were bright red. 'Her foster-mother, yes.'

'And your name is . . .'

'Kay McKinnon. Yours?'

'I'm DC Dinah Mason. Have you heard from Becca?'

'Yes. She came here – or she texted me to say she was on her way, and now I arrive to find all of this. That's her bike over there. What's going on?'

'You'd better come with me.' Dinah Mason guided her through the gate, away from the cordon and the small group of onlookers. The garden was even more crowded as more cars arrived. People seemed to be wandering randomly round the garden. She noticed a group of people around the fuel shed. The door was wide open, and a quick glance showed that they were working on the trap door.

Becca? Could Becca be . . .? 'Please,' she said to Dinah Mason. 'Tell me what's happened to Becca.' She heard Milo's distressed bark again. 'My dog,' she said.

Dinah Mason called across towards the house, and someone emerged with Milo on a lead. He yipped frantically when he saw her, and as she took the lead, he danced excitedly round her feet, then lifted his leg for what seemed like about ten minutes. Not for the first time, she wished he could speak, and tell her what he'd seen tonight.

'First of all, Ms McKinnon, I need you to tell me where you've been this evening.'

Kay met her gaze. She could do battle, or she could cooperate. She had no legal status with Becca and this woman could send her away and tell her nothing. 'I'm worried about my foster-daughter, Becca Armitage. She texted me earlier – after midnight – to say she was coming to see me and was on her way. I know she got here – her bike's parked in the road. I need to know where she is now.'

The detective's face shut down into professional blankness. Oh, God. Had they got Becca locked up again? Did Kay need to prioritise getting Becca some legal help?

'We need to know the same thing,' DC Mason said. 'We didn't know she had a connection with Sunk Island until this evening. We found the texts to you on her phone. She dropped it near her flat.'

That explained why Becca hadn't contacted her. Briefly, Kay felt relief, then came back to the realisation that though Becca had made it here, she was missing. 'Then why are you here?'

'Mrs McKinnon, I can't say—'

'Is Becca in trouble? With the police?' Kay asked bluntly. 'Has she been arrested?'

Dinah Mason shook her head. 'I wish she had been, then at least we'd know she was safe. We don't know where she is. If she came here, she isn't here now.'

'Tell me what happened,' Kay said. 'I might— I know Becca very well. If there's anything that might help her . . .'

She listened with growing alarm as DC Mason told her about Becca's involvement with some investigation going on at the pub where she worked, the attack on her flat. 'We searched it,' Dinah Mason told her. 'Someone had trashed the place, but we found illegal drugs. More than just for personal use. We already have some evidence of Becca's links with the local drugs gangs – she has connections with the kids they use.'

Kay felt a red-hot surge of rage. She wanted to bang tables, barge through doors in search of the people who were doing it again, blaming Becca when she was in danger, missing on Sunk Island in the dark, in the middle of the night. She had to make this woman listen. To find Becca, she had to get this woman on her side. 'Listen to me. Becca is missing. She was here when whatever happened, happened. She does not do drugs. You have to stop thinking about that and concentrate on finding her, or . . .' She could hear her voice rising and forced herself to calm down. 'I am telling you now. Becca is in danger.'

DC Mason nodded, and with the same, infuriating calm, said, 'This is why I need you to answer some questions, Ms McKinnon. Can you tell me where you were this evening?' she asked again.

Kay opened her mouth to tell DC Mason she wasn't answering anything until she knew about Becca, then changed her mind. Maybe, just maybe, Kay knew something that would be useful. DC Mason's face changed as soon as she mentioned Tania's House. Did this mean they were now on the same side? Or were they now implacably opposed?

'You work for Tania's House?'

'Yes.'

'OK. And you've been staying here, at this house, since . . .?'

'Less than a week. Listen! Becca—'

'Ms McKinnon, we are looking for Becca. I need this information to help find her. Do you know anything about the previous owner?'

Kay stepped hard on her frustration and fear. She didn't know if this Mason woman was sincere, or if she was just collecting evidence to use against Becca, but there was nothing she could usefully do apart from cooperate. She explained about Hettie Laithwaite, and looked across towards the gate, to where Catherine Ford was still observing. 'That woman there is a neighbour,' she said. 'She knows more about it than I do, but as far as I know, Mrs Laithwaite was infirm for the last few months of her life and was cared for by her family.'

'Her family? Where are they now?'

'I don't know.' Kay frowned, trying to remember. 'The neighbour said they visited. A lot. They were in and out all the time.' She looked at the other woman, realising. 'It wasn't family, was it?'

Mason shook her head. 'I'm only just getting up to speed on this myself, Mrs McKinnon, but whoever came to visit the old lady, I don't think it was her family.'

Cars in the night. Strange people in the area. A dead man found near the estuary.

It was all coming together in a picture she really didn't want to see.

And Becca was missing.

Chapter 44

Becca struggled and thrashed around, banging herself against the hard, enclosed walls. She couldn't straighten up. She couldn't sit up, she couldn't breathe . . .

Stop. She had to stop. She swallowed hard, acid burning in her throat. Breathe. In through her nose. Out. In. She wanted to open her mouth wide and take great gulps of air and each time she tried she couldn't and the panic threatened to take her over again.

Remember.

In the dark.

Her stepfather was coming up the stairs and she wanted to run away, hide in the cupboard, hide under the bed . . . But He liked that. He enjoyed the chase. The only escape was into herself. Right down inside her head, far away, *No Becca here! No Becca here!*

She repeated the words to herself over and over and gradually her breathing slowed and her heart stopped trying to hammer its way out of her chest. It was OK. It was OK. She'd be here for a while, but as long as she didn't panic, as long as she just . . .

The man had gone. She was alone with Alicia. If it came to a fight, Becca would win. She'd have to.

With your arms and legs tied?

They were going to dump the car. That's what Alicia had said. They'd dump the car and leave her. So why was her heart still thumping in fear, why was she still on the edge of losing it?

She heard the engine start, and the car bumped along an uneven surface then turned left. Becca forced herself to think about ways of escaping, anything to stop the panic from flooding through her again.

She worked her hands against each other, trying to tear the tape, but it just seemed to fold into ridges that dug into her wrists. The effort was making it hard to breathe. She had to take it steady.

She'd get out of here. She could do it.

The car was slowing down. They must be at the place the woman was planning to dump it. Then Becca could get herself free, get back to Kay's house, make sure they'd gone, break in and call the police. Call Kay, call Curwen. Call Dinah. And get the shits who—

'All OK?' Becca froze. It was the man's voice from before, the one that had sounded oddly familiar.

'Have you got him?' The voices were muffled, but it wasn't hard to make out what they were saying.

'Yeah. Here you go. Get in.' The car rocked, as if someone had landed heavily on the back seat. Then she froze as she heard a voice she knew. 'You let me out of here. You don't get to—'

She knew that voice. Lewis! They'd got Lewis.

There was the sound of a slap, then Alicia spoke. 'Any more of that, and I'll give you something to complain about.' She didn't sound angry, just cold, and – Becca's stomach lurched – a bit excited, as if she wanted Lewis to go on making a noise so she could do whatever she was threatening to do to him.

The man spoke. 'Why are you making a fuss, Lewis? It's like we told you when we found you at the flat – we're just getting you out of the way before the cops come. Nothing to worry about.'

'You going to . . . to dump the snitch?' Lewis's voice wobbled as he spoke. He was trying to sound tough, show them he was one of them, but he just sounded like a scared kid. They'd found him at her flat – so he wasn't meant to be there. He must have been too scared to get the bus. He'd snatched her key and gone and hidden in maybe the worst place he could have chosen. But he'd hidden Spice from them. He'd done that.

Alicia laughed. 'Yeah, Lewis, we're going to dump the snitch.'

'Then can I go home?'

'Yeah. When we're done, you'll go home.'

What was happening? Now the fear was growing. She knew now they wouldn't leave her in the car until daylight – she'd be found too soon. What did Lewis know that she didn't? *Dump the snitch . . .*

Her breathing quickened and she felt her heart start to race.

There was something bad, something very bad on the way.

She strained her ears, listening. She heard the car door open, and felt the vehicle rock slightly as someone – presumably the man – got in. 'Right. All sorted. Are you sure about this? Doc went crazy when you got rid of that cop shit.'

Cop shit? Andy? *Listen*. She struggled to hear what they were saying. The words were half drowned-out by the noise of the engine.

'I told you – Doc's out of it. He's gone.'

'They're going . . . get rid?'

'Yeah. It's sorted. We'll . . . this lot and go up there to meet them.'

'So . . . what now?'

'What do you think? I'm . . . our other problem. We take the car . . . the track to the end of the drain – the tide's in. We can dump it in the estuary, pick the other car up and we're away.'

'. . . really enjoy your work, don't you?'

And Becca heard that giggle she'd heard before – once in the pub, and once in the yard, not the laugh of someone who'd just heard a joke, or someone who was having a good time, but of someone who enjoyed the kinds of things no one should enjoy – like Andy bleeding to death on the ground or the screams of something burning.

We can dump it in the estuary, pick the other car up and we're away.

Then she understood what they meant, and panic gripped her. She felt the warm flood as her bladder let go. She was struggling – not with any plan, just fighting, fighting, until she could barely breathe, her heart hammering out of her chest. She had to be free but she was buried in darkness, she was trapped, and she had to get out, get away.

They were going to leave her locked in the boot, and they were going to dump the car in the estuary. It would float for a few long minutes then it would sink as it filled up. The water would creep into the trunk as she tried to keep her face above the surface but slowly, slowly it would fill, covering her mouth, her nose, and she would struggle and struggle and then ...

She screamed and screamed and screamed, but her mouth was sealed.

Chapter 45

Dinah left Kay McKinnon with hollow promises that they were looking for Becca. As far as she could see, it was turning into a complete fiasco. She didn't know what was going on, just that Hammond looked furious, someone had jumped the gun on something and triggered this massive response. Were they concerned about Becca? She didn't know. All she knew was that Becca Armitage had come down the coast to Sunk Island but there was no sign of her, and the search teams were taking the house apart.

She knew that Andy Yeatson had been involved in something to do with the pub, some kind of unofficial crusade that had made him present himself as a private investigator to Becca Armitage – or so Becca claimed. It puzzled her that Andy had been prepared to put Becca in harm's way. It wasn't just gossip about the punters she'd been passing on. She'd been taking photos down in the pub cellar – she'd sent some to Dinah, and if drugs – or anything like that – were involved, then that was dangerous. It was well out of order for Andy to ask her to do that.

And out of character. Andy Yeatson was a good cop. And because he was a good cop, he followed the rules. A bit of information from the pub, fine. Serious digging around? At the very least, he would have put Becca Armitage on the list of registered police informers, and she wasn't there. Dinah had checked.

Someone had exposed her to danger without caring – getting her to ask questions and sleuth around. Andy, a trained and experienced DC, had been blown. Becca, with no training at all, would stand out like a neon light on a country lane.

Dinah was as certain as she could be. Andy would not have done that.

And now, no one knew where Becca was. She had a horrible feeling she could work out what had happened.

She was aware of a sudden surge in activity and went across to where Hammond was talking urgently to two men. She waited on the edge of the discussion, listening.

'The drugs were taken from here – this is the first storage place. We think the house was supposed to be empty, but there was some kind of cock-up at the estate agents and it got let accidentally. They'd got word of the pub raid, and they were moving the latest consignment to a safe place. Only it wasn't. We've got them. Most of them.'

'Sir,' she said.

Hammond turned to her. 'Dinah.'

'Becca Armitage. I think someone was using her as an unofficial informant in the pub. I don't know what was going on there, but she got in the way of something and they've taken her.'

'We're aware of that, Dinah. I've got people out—'

Before Hammond could finish, a man came running over, his face urgent. 'Sir! We've just had a report in. A car's been dumped in the estuary at Spragger Drain sluice.'

Dinah felt the hairs on her arms lift as she heard Hammond's '*Jesus*.' Becca had arrived here, and then she'd vanished. Now, Dinah knew where she was. There was no way a car would stay afloat in that water for more than a few minutes. Her whole body went cold.

Becca was the worst kind of evidence – a walking, talking witness. 'Sir!' she said urgently. Hammond's eyes met hers, and she saw the same understanding and the same horror.

Then a car pulled up, slewing half across the road, and Curwen jumped out. In the flashing blue lights, his face was white. He must have heard the news via his radio. 'Come on!' he shouted.

And she was scrambling into the front seat beside him as he pulled away and turned his car towards the estuary.

Becca rolled over and tried to kick the lid of the boot, to force it to open and release her. Her breath was coming in short gasps; her face was tingling and she was dizzy as if she didn't know up from down.

She was trapped, she was buried alive, and they were going to . . .

She couldn't get enough air!

Better to die now than trapped in the sinking car. She was going to drown and there was nothing she could do. Her face was wet with tears, and the skin on her face felt raw from where the tape had pulled it when she'd tried to scream.

Soon. Soon she'd feel the car slow down, stop, and then it would start moving again, roll forward and . . .

Becca.

Calm down.

It wasn't Matt. She knew it wasn't Matt. It was just words in her head, but it used Matt's voice because that meant she would listen.

If she wanted to escape, if she wanted to survive, if she wanted not to drown, trapped in the car . . .

Panic yammered in her head.

No. She had to think. She forced herself to breathe slowly.

No Becca here. No Becca here.

The hammering of her heart slowed and her thoughts began to come together. To escape, to get out, she needed her hands.

Then she realised she was breathing more easily. Her nose was blocked up, but she could still get air – because the tape round her mouth was loose, was coming free. She had no idea how, but she shook it off and breathed in deeply.

Then she remembered the tears running down her face, and suddenly she was back in the supermarket, opening boxes, ones that had been left out in the rain. She'd tried to lift one, and it burst open, sending tins across the floor. The wet tape hadn't held.

Her hands were behind her. The tape was tight, she knew that, she'd struggled against it.

But . . .

She worked her wrists against each other and gradually – yes – she felt the grip on her arms start to ease.

She pulled one hand out, and for a moment had to lie still as pain shot through her shoulders.

She'd wet herself in her panic. Now the tape round her wrists was wet, and now her arms were free.

Come on, Becca! No time!

The car was moving fast. Suddenly, it swerved, then straightened up again as the horn sounded. Then it lurched round a corner, and jolted, bouncing her back so that she hit her head against the metal sides. She crammed her hands against her mouth to stop herself from shouting out with the pain.

She heard Lewis cry out, and the same dead voice say, 'Shut up.'

She was working frantically on the tape round her legs. The car turned again and now they were off the main roads and bumping along a track. The estuary must be so close, and she was still trapped, locked in the boot.

Would they open it? Would they check that she was still in there? And if they did, what were her chances of getting out, even though her hands weren't tied any more?

Her breath was coming in sobs as she struggled to focus.

Stop it, Becca. If you want to live, stop it!

The catch. There had to be a way of operating the catch from the inside.

She made a kind of gasping noise and tried to focus on the lock that was holding the boot shut. Her hands groped along the base in the pitch black until she found it.

Her mind seemed to be working in a place that was far away, that was paying no attention to the darkness, the wet, the stink. Her brain was telling her that the catch operated from the front of the car. There was a button, or a lever, or something. And that meant a cable.

She had to find the cable, pull it, get the lock to open.

Frantically, she felt around the lock again. It was protected by the trim. The way out was just on the other side of this thin sheet of plastic, but she couldn't reach it and she didn't have any time left.

Wait! The trim was loose along the bottom of the hatch. She forced her fingers under it, feeling it pinch her hand against the metal edge of the door. Her hands felt slippery as she pushed them further behind the trim.

It wouldn't give.

The car lurched, and turned again down another bumpy track. She could feel tears of terror running down her face, but tears couldn't save her now. It was close. Any minute, the car was going to slow down, stop, the people in the front were going to get out. And then . . .

She was sitting on the floor of her bedroom and Matt was carefully putting a picture frame back together, one that Becca had smashed in a room-wrecking rage. He looked up and smiled at her. 'See?' he said. 'Take your time. Good as new.'

Her mind was playing tricks, taking her away from this place, trying to make her less scared, trying to take her to somewhere safe.

Take your time.

Her hands, that had been grabbing frantically, slowed down. She closed her fingers around the plastic and pulled as hard as she could. This time, it gave. It moved enough for her to slip her hands behind it. Now she could feel the lock mechanism.

She ran them carefully round, trying to feel her way. *Take your time.* A cable. There had to be a cable. There was nothing! Panic started to bubble up, and she forced it back down. *No Becca here!*

Again.

Try again. It was here, it had to be.

And she found it. A thick wire, running away from the lock. She got her hands round it and pulled.

Nothing.

She tried again, the panic rising up in a way she knew she wouldn't be able to control. Once it took her this time, she'd start screaming and screaming and she wouldn't be able to stop until—

Locks move two directions – one to lock, one to unlock. If she'd been pulling the cable the wrong way ... She gripped it with a hand that was now so slippery it was hard to get purchase, and pulled in the opposite direction hard as she could.

There was a popping noise and the boot lid unlatched.

Becca froze, then grabbed at it before it could fly fully open.

Now her breath was coming in short, sharp gasps and her heart was thumping.

She had to get out.

And then get away, that was the thing. Get away and get help.

It was dark. The driver wouldn't see what was happening. OK. *Now!* She shoved the boot open, swung her legs, still tied, over the edge. There was an old newspaper on the floor of the boot, and, acting almost on instinct, she grabbed it before she rolled out, landing on hard ground with an impact that knocked the air out of her lungs.

She raised her head. Just a few feet away in the moonlight, water flowed by, fast and silent.

The estuary. They were that close.

The car slowed to a halt on a hardstanding. In the headlights, she could see a low mesh fence with warning signs attached. The fence was broken and sagged away in front of the car.

The car doors opened, and two people got out. The moonlight caught Alicia's long, fair hair that gleamed as she stretched, like someone taking a short and welcome break after a long drive.

Becca ducked her head down so her face wouldn't catch the light. She was working frantically on the binding round her legs, tearing off her trainers and socks, and now the tape was loose enough, now the wet was making it less sticky and she was peeling it off as fast as she could.

She pulled the last of the tape away and spider-crawled backwards to keep herself in the shadow.

'Okaaay.' Alicia drew the word out. 'Let's get this done.'

As Becca watched, the man, just a silhouette against the car lights, opened the back door and dragged a small figure out by the arms. Lewis. Lewis was struggling and shouting. 'Get off me! Get off me!'

'You talk too much. Come on, Stoner, get him in the boot.'

Lewis's scream was cut off as the man clamped a hand over the child's mouth. Alicia moved to the back of the car then stopped. 'It's open. She's gone!' Her voice rose to a shout. 'Fuck it, Stoner, what did you do?'

'I didn't do anything. She's gone? She can't ... Look! She was bleeding. She can't be far away. We'll find her.'

Bleeding? Becca looked at her hands and saw they were covered in something that shone dark in the moonlight. She must have cut herself when she ...

But that didn't matter. She couldn't run away. They'd just dump the car into the water with Lewis, just a kid, trapped in the boot to drown. She would have to fight and she had nothing to fight with, except ... the newspaper. *Just hit him with a newspaper*. She was rolling it up in her hands almost as she thought of it, rolling it up tight, folding it over.

It seemed like nothing, it was nothing, but it was all she had.

She heard that laugh again, the same one she'd heard in the yard that night, and understood something about Alicia.

She wasn't doing this because she needed to. She *wanted* to watch the car sink slowly under the water, knowing that someone was trapped inside. The only thing she would regret was that she couldn't see them struggle. Two would have been good, but one would do.

Chapter 46

Spragger Drain sluice

Becca staggered to her feet. She had to stop this before Lewis was locked in the boot. 'Lewis!' Her voice barely made a sound. 'Lewis!' she tried again. 'Fight! Get away! Don't let them . . .!'

But the man had lifted the struggling Lewis up off the ground – Becca hadn't noticed before how small Lewis was – and flung him into the open boot. The lid slammed down.

The two figures turned towards her. She'd escaped, she'd got herself out, she'd done all of that, but she couldn't run away, couldn't leave an eleven-year-old kid in the car that was close to the edge, with just the handbrake and a broken fence protecting him from the deep, dark waters of the estuary.

She had to get there, get to the car, stop them somehow. But they were between her and Lewis.

Alicia.

And the man. Stoner.

Becca sidestepped, trying to get them to move away. If she had a clear run to the back of the car, she could pull the boot open, get Lewis out and try and get lost in the darkness, but her legs were numb from being tied so tightly and she stumbled as the man came towards her, cutting off her route.

In the harsh light from the headlamps, she saw his face, and knew why he'd sounded so familiar.

Toby.

Toby, who was her mate because they'd worked together behind the bar for months. Toby, who was always on the games machines so he could chat with anyone he wanted to and no one would pay much attention.

Toby who had listened to her, heard her identify Doc, and then vanished.

Toby who was going to watch while Alicia drowned her and a child.

He reached to grab her arms, and she jabbed upwards with the newspaper cudgel, catching him on the side of the jaw. He staggered back, clutching his face, and she spun round to face Alicia, face the crazy woman who was coming towards her with gleam in her eyes that told Becca Alicia wasn't scared, wasn't worried. She was enjoying this, and she knew she would win.

Becca kept her eyes focused on Alicia's arms, so missed Alicia kicking something on the ground. She felt something smack into her leg, and a sharp pain made her gasp and stagger sideways.

Her legs started cramping and she fell.

Then Alicia was there, grabbing her by the hair and hauling her to her feet. Becca jabbed backwards with the newspaper, and heard a grunt. 'Bitch!' The grip loosened and Becca rolled away, scrambling to her feet, but her legs still wouldn't hold her.

Alicia grabbed her hair again and swung her round. Her hand smacked across Becca's mouth, once, twice. 'You hurt me, you fucking bitch!' In the dazzling light of the headlamps, Becca could see her face, the teeth bared, the eyes narrowed in rage.

Becca jabbed again with the cudgel, but this time Alicia was ready, taking it on her arm with a grunt of pain, moving round smoothly and twisting Becca's arm up her back. 'Drop it, bitch! Drop it!' The weapon fell from her hand and she heard Alicia laugh again.

'Back in the car, baby!' She forced Becca onto the ground face-down and kneeled on her back. Becca could feel her arms being pulled behind her.

'Get the fucking tape,' Alicia shouted. Then she was speaking in Becca's ear in a low mutter. 'You know what I'd like to do? I'd like to pour petrol over you and set you alight. I set your cat alight. I didn't get to hear it scream – but I could hear *you* scream. Now. I could do that. *Becca.*' She spat the name out like a curse. 'Hear you burn then hear you sizzle when we chuck you in the water.'

Becca saw Toby's feet approaching. He couldn't do this. Not Toby. He couldn't.

'Come on! Tape her!' the woman said.

'Toby!' Becca tried to call to him but her face was pressed into the dirt.

Toby's voice sounded muffled. 'That fucking hurt. I can't . . . Jesus. My neck.'

'Shut the fuck up and do it!'

'Do you think I carry the fucking stuff around with me? Look, you're wasting time. Just shove her in the car and get it done with.'

'OK . . .' Becca heard the sound of Alicia breathing hard. 'Hold her while I—' She was dragging the belt out of her mac.

'Toby! You don't want to do this!' Becca struggled against his hands as they grabbed her, but she barely had any strength left. 'Toby!'

'Shut up.' He sounded uneasy, and a small glimmer of hope sparked. He'd been OK while she didn't know he was there, while he couldn't see her, but now she was in front of him – he didn't want to do this. But he held her as Alicia grabbed her arms and tied them with the belt. When Becca tried to kick her, she just sidestepped.

'Now . . .' Alicia pulled the back door of the car open, leaned in and pulled something out. Becca could hear Lewis in the boot, crying.

'Get her in,' she said.

Toby ignored her. 'Fuck's sake, Alicia. What are you doing?'

'What does it look like? I'm going to torch it. Burn it out.'

The smell of petrol was heavy in the air as Alicia opened the can she had taken from the back of the car and started throwing it over the roof, through the windows, in the boot.

'What the fuck? We're dumping them, that's what we agreed! You want half of Sunk Island here to see what's burning?'

'All six of them? Who cares?'

In her head, Becca was screaming, *You can't! You can't!* Toby's grasp had loosened as he argued, and she managed to pull herself free. Alicia chucked the empty can through the car window and turned as Becca threw herself forwards. Alicia staggered under the impact then steadied herself and kicked Becca's legs out from under her.

Becca hit the ground hard enough to wind her. She tried to get back onto her feet, gasping for breath that wasn't there. Alicia was scrabbling in her bag for something – a lighter. Becca had to stop her, had to—

Something shot past her, something big, moving at high speed. Alicia's mouth dropped open. She leaned forward into the car quickly, then leaped back as a huge dog knocked her to the ground.

But the car was rolling forward towards the broken fence. She'd released the handbrake.

Becca tried to scramble to her feet, and fell. The car was going to go over, go in the water.

Lewis!

The dog was snarling as the woman struggled, then it yelped, and she jumped free.

Someone was running past her, a big man, and he vaulted the fence and let himself down towards the water, hanging onto the mesh, reaching for the car door. The bonnet dropped down, then the car stopped, hanging almost vertically, caught on the fence.

Becca managed to free her arms from the belt and crawled forward. The car was slipping, she could hear the creak of metal as the remains of the fence started to give way. The water, deep and dark, flowed past below. She looked for something to grab, something to hold to stop it going over, but it was beyond her reach. There was nothing else to do.

'Where is he?' the man was shouting.

'The boot!' Becca yelled back, and he was swinging himself across, grabbing the lock, pulling it open. Then he was in the boot, pushing Lewis out ahead of him.

Becca reached forward to grab him, grab his clothes, anything.

The man in the car half threw Lewis onto the concrete, then as the fence gave way, he shouted and grabbed at the concrete edge.

The car fell, leaving him hanging there.

Lewis was half on, half off the concrete and she could see him start to slip. She grabbed his top as the man who had pulled him out hauled himself up on the remains of the fence.

Alicia was standing above them. She was holding a knife and there were dark stains on her hands as she kicked, and kicked, trying to make the man fall, make

Becca let go of Lewis, trying to force them into the water. Becca rolled, trying to keep hold of Lewis, trying to avoid the kicking feet. Alicia stamped on her arm, making her scream and curl up, then she saw the foot draw back to deliver a kick that would come straight to her face.

She had no way to protect herself. It was a death kick.

But it had given the man enough time to haul himself up onto the safety of the concrete. He was lying beside Becca on the ground and his hand closed round the ankle of Alicia's other leg, and pulled it away. She screamed and lost her balance, staggering towards the edge.

She grabbed at the broken fence, pitched sideways, and fell. Her hand briefly gripped the mesh then she dropped into the fast-flowing water. Becca heard her scream once, then there was nothing.

Out in the estuary, the car slid under the water. Becca lay there watching as its lights faded then went out. She didn't move. She was done. She had nothing more to give. Beside her, Lewis was moaning.

Now the car was gone, there should have been darkness, but there was a faint greyness in the sky that allowed her to see.

Dawn. The night was over.

The man pulled himself to his feet and looked down at her and Lewis. 'Take care of him,' he said abruptly. It was no surprise to her to see Russ, the homeless guy from the pub. She'd known it was Russ as soon as the dog raced past her.

Russ and Champ.

'Toby?' Becca said. He was around somewhere and still dangerous.

'He's going nowhere.' There was almost a chuckle in Russ's voice as he turned and walked away.

Lewis moaned again. Becca couldn't think about Toby now. Russ was dealing with him. Lewis was soaked and he was cold and he was probably in shock, whatever that meant. She couldn't get his wet clothes off. She pulled off her jacket and wrapped it around him, but she wasn't sure what good that would do.

Then she heard voices, and turned. Everything went cold and still. She wasn't strong enough to fight any more, and she had to. There was only her to protect Lewis.

Russ wasn't here to help her. Russ was here to help himself and his mates. He was one of them.

Standing there with Russ, looking down at her, was Johnny Dip.

Chapter 47

'Nice one,' Johnny Dip said to no one in particular. He came slowly across to where Becca was crouched over Lewis.

'Fuck off.' Becca only had her voice to threaten him with.

'Just checking,' he said.

Russ came back. He was pushing someone ahead of him – Toby, whose leg was dragging as if it would no longer work. Russ was holding him with his arm screwed so high up his back he must be in agony. Becca hoped he was in agony. His trousers were torn and bloody. Champ was following closely, his eyes fixed on the man. The dog was limping, but Becca heard a low growl.

Toby looked at Becca. 'I tried to stop her,' he said. 'You've got to tell them. I tried to stop her.'

She wanted to spit in his face but she didn't have the energy. She didn't say anything. There was nothing that was bad enough. She wanted him to be under the water with Alicia. No, under the mud. Drowned in the mud, that was where they both belonged.

For Andy.

She couldn't worry about that, not now. There was something seriously wrong with Lewis. He was soaked from the water but he'd stopped shivering. She was pretty sure that wasn't because of her jacket making him warm. In the dim light, his lips looked blue. She didn't know what to do for him.

Nothing seemed real. As she watched, Russ started dragging Toby towards the broken fence, the place where the car had gone over. Was he going to dump Toby in the estuary as punishment as well?

If Lewis died, if Toby went in the river, there'd only be her who could tell anyone. She scrambled to her feet. Her legs felt like pieces of wet string. She hated Toby, but she didn't want him drowned, not like that. 'Don't . . .' she began, then saw that Russ was cuffing Toby's arms to an unbroken part of the fence, securing him.

She looked up at him. 'What are you going to do?'

'I'm leaving them a present. They're sending a launch down – they'll take care of that piece of shit. Your lad there needs to go to hospital. You should go too.'

She didn't know what was happening with Russ, or with Johnny Dip either, but she was beginning to understand they were on her side.

'What about you?' His fingers were bruised and bleeding, but he shook his head.

'The bitch cut Champ. It's not much but he needs fixing. Once the launch is here, we're off.'

She could see Johnny Dip waiting by the side of the track, his bike beside him. She turned back to Russ. 'Who are you?' she said.

He shook his head. 'I told you before, love, only you didn't listen. Leave it alone.'

Then she heard the sound of a car as it pulled up by the hardstanding. Curwen's car. She recognised it. And she could see Dinah Mason with her fair hair and red glasses, pushing the door open almost before Curwen had stopped. A large four-wheel drive pulled up behind them and people piled out. Russ backed away, whistling gently, and Champ followed, limping slightly. In seconds, he was gone, and Johnny Dip had faded away as well.

Becca stood there, dizzy and confused, as Dinah came running over to her, Curwen close behind. 'Becca! What happened? Are you hurt?'

'A bit.' Her arm was throbbing where the woman had stamped on it. 'Lewis needs help.'

Curwen was kneeling down next to him. 'He's cold.' He was ripping off Lewis's wet clothes as he spoke and wrapping him in the jacket Becca had put over him. He pulled off his own jacket and wrapped that round Lewis as well. 'Fucking kids,' Becca heard him mutter. 'We need an ambulance.'

'They're sending a launch down with paramedics,' Dinah said. 'What happened to the people who brought you here?'

Becca looked across to where Toby was slumped against the fence. The water flowed past, fast and deep. She and Lewis could be under that, trapped in the boot of the car, dead by now.

It would all have been over.

Lights appeared on the water. 'The launch is here,' Curwen said, looking up from where he was checking Lewis's pulse.

Dinah put her jacket round Becca's shoulders. 'You need to go with them. You need to see a doctor.'

'No. I just want to go back to the house.'

'You should go to hospital, Becca. Really.'

'She'll be fine.' It was Curwen who had got to his feet as the paramedics came from the launch to take over.

Becca glared at him. 'You didn't do anything,' she said. 'I told you and you didn't—'

'Yeah. I fucked up. It worked out in the end. Come on. I'll take you back to the house.' He looked over his shoulder. 'You coming?' he said to Dinah.

'I'll stay here. Go up to the hospital with them.'

Curwen nodded and led the way to his car. As he held the door for her to get in, he said, 'You did OK.'

She hadn't. She'd messed up in every way. She'd left Lewis, hadn't made sure he was on the bus and safe, and he'd almost ended up in the river. Lewis would have been trapped, drowned, if Russ, whoever he was, whatever he might have done, hadn't gone into the water to get him.

It wasn't just Curwen who'd fucked up.

Chapter 48

Kay gave Becca a hug and refused to listen to anything until Becca had had a shower and a change of clothes. After Becca had vanished upstairs, she fixed DS Mark Curwen with a laser glare. 'Well?' she said. Becca had been hurt and she was in no mood for prevarications.

He gave her a brief account of what had happened to Becca, and what had nearly happened. She felt herself go cold.

'There were two of our guys here,' Curwen said. 'Working undercover. I didn't know. I think one of them tried to keep Becca safe, keep her here, but this woman, Traynor, Alicia Traynor . . .' He said *Aleesha*, and Kay realised suddenly who this woman was who had been in her house and attacked Becca. 'She was the one who decided to take Becca to the estuary. And the kid, apparently.'

'What about the child? How was he involved?'

'He's one of the kids who hangs around with the dealers – they use the kids to move the stuff around. It looks like they picked him up at Becca's flat.'

'You're saying she was involved?'

'There are some people getting their underpants in a twist about it. Don't worry. She'll be fine.'

His glib reply annoyed Kay. Becca was getting that lawyer, no matter what.

'I don't get what they were doing here,' she said. 'This house – they've been using it to store stuff, haven't they?'

'In that outhouse, that shed place you've got. The house is close to Stone Creek, where they were bringing the stuff in. There was a sick old woman living here, no one to stop them.'

The family who had cared for Hettie Laithwaite. Catherine Ford had spoken admiringly about the care the family had given her, but they weren't family. Had they been kind to the old lady? Had they looked after her at all? No one would ever know. And after she'd died, they must have been confident the house would be left empty, at least for a while. They'd probably paid someone off to make sure.

And then an estate agent had been off sick, Kay had come along willing to take a short rental on the first house the suited her needs and suddenly they had to find a new place to store their stuff. She remembered the signs of use in the kitchen, the bags of compost that had vanished overnight, the trapdoor in the floor that she couldn't open. What would she have found if she'd investigated a bit more?

Becca came back and they stopped talking. She was wearing a tracksuit that was too big for her and her hair was dripping round her shoulders. Kay tutted under her breath and made her sit in the huge armchair that was pulled up in front of the open fire. 'Get yourself warmed up.' She assessed Becca for damage. Physically, she didn't look too bad – a lot of cuts and abrasions, and a nasty, swelling bruise on her arm – but emotionally? Kay didn't know. Becca still had a lot of fighting to do, and if she was going to survive, she had to stay strong.

'Lewis,' Becca said urgently, looking at Curwen.

He checked his phone. 'Text from DC Mason,' he said. 'The paramedics think he's going to be OK. He'd cold, exhausted, but he'll be all right.'

'What's going to happen to him? Will they lock him up?'

'He's eleven. He's old enough to be in trouble. If he tells his story, tells them what he knows, they won't charge him. Probably. Depends if his mum can take care of him – she's not done a good job up until now.'

'She's doing her best,' Becca snapped.

'Yeah. And her lad's been running wild and nearly got drowned in the estuary. Get real, Becca.'

Becca glared at him and Kay decided they needed a change of subject. 'Tea,' she said. 'You need a hot drink.' She looked at Curwen. 'Sort that out for her, will you?'

'Yes, miss,' Curwen said, almost but not quite under his breath. Becca giggled and Kay felt relief flood through her.

Chapter 49

Bridlington

Dinah drove slowly back to Bridlington. She'd gone to the hospital in Hull with Lewis, and waited there until the medics gave him the OK, and Hammond's team arrived with his mother in tow. Jade Acklam was bristling with anger and hostility. She blamed the police for her son's problems and made it clear she wanted nothing to do with them.

Dinah didn't know what she thought. Lewis's mother clearly had a tough job with her son, but he'd been running out of control for weeks; at least, that was what Dinah had heard. They'd question him, and depending on what came out of that, he might well end up in detention, or in care. It couldn't be her problem.

The colours from the rising sun glowed in her mirror and it was full morning by the time she got back to the town. She seemed to be on the other side of tiredness. Everything had an odd, glassy clarity, and her head felt as if it was floating. It was like a hangover, only without the headache and the nausea.

She'd arrived at the house on Stone Creek Road last night to find the search in full swing. Her ex-boss, Gallagher, had been there, as well as Hammond. She'd found out more about what was going on when she talked to members of the team who were at the hospital, waiting to talk to Toby Sharman.

The drug smugglers were on the run, trying to empty their caches and dump what they couldn't dispose of. The full picture still wasn't clear, but one of the routes they had been using to bring drugs in was up the estuary, where bags of spice, disguised as garden compost, were picked up by a small boat, brought in via Stone Creek, and hidden in the house on Stone Creek Road.

When she finally got to Brid, the station was buzzing with the news of successful drug raids coordinated between Bridlington and Hull, with big hauls found in Sunk Island, and in several holiday lets. A Bridlington pub had been raided, and the landlord arrested – Curwen's nemesis, Carl Lavery. She saw Hammond in the middle of a back-slapping crowd. Curwen was there too, looking uncharacteristically cheerful. He saw her, and gestured her over.

Hammond looked at her. 'DC Mason. Well done. We're just going to get something to eat – the whole team, Come on. Breakfast's on me.'

There was a greasy spoon just across the road from the nick that was used to catering for large groups of cops, either celebrating or drowning their sorrows in cholesterol. Dinah sat at one of the tables, and people kept pulling up chairs until she was in the centre of a happy crowd.

Curwen looked at her and grinned. 'Did you hear, Mason? We got that fucker Lavery. He's facing money-laundering charges.'

'He's not part of the drugs?'

'No drugs. Just the money.'

She wanted to ask about Becca's role, but Hammond was talking, bringing those members of the team who hadn't been there up to date. Someone dumped a plate filled with sausage, bacon, eggs, tomatoes, fried bread and beans in front of her. She looked at it and felt her stomach turn over. 'You take this one.' She shoved it across to Curwen.

Hammond was explaining about the undercover operation. Dave Sykes frowned. 'You mean we've been wasting our time? I'm not happy if I've been taken for a mug.'

'Don't worry, Dave. You haven't. We knew who killed Yeatson, but we couldn't prove it. We've been collecting the evidence that will make the murder charges stick.'

Dave Sykes wasn't ready to be mollified. Dinah could see he felt as though he'd been made a fool of and wasn't prepared to let it go. 'Against who? Traynor? She's dead at the bottom of the estuary.'

'Toby Sharman and Carl Lavery. There may be others.'

Dinah spoke up. Something had been bothering her ever since she'd heard about the NCA operation. 'The undercover officers,' she said. 'They were there, weren't they, when Andy was killed?'

Hammond nodded. 'One of them was. Andy was set up by two members of the gang – the woman, Alicia Traynor, and the one they called Stoner, Toby Sharman. Carl Lavery is an accessory after the fact – he'll be charged under the law of common purpose. Killers, all of them. They're responsible for his death. No one else.'

'And the undercover guy?'

'He was there. That's how we know what happened.'

'And he just stood back and watched?' That made him as guilty as the other two, in her eyes. He'd let them kill Andy rather than put the operation in jeopardy.

Hammond held her gaze. 'Andy put himself in the way of an ongoing operation because he didn't follow orders. The undercover guy did his best to keep Andy out of it but Andy put himself in there anyway. The Traynor woman decided to get rid of him so the undercover guy went with them to get Andy out of there safely. But Andy had his own plans for getting away, and the first thing he did was kick our guy's knee in, left him helpless. After that, it was just the Traynor woman and Sharman. As it was, Andy almost got away.'

Dinah felt her stomach knot. Andy, fighting for his life and putting the one person who could protect him out of action. 'Do we know for sure what happened to her? To Traynor?'

'She fell into the water. No way she'll survive that. She'll probably wash up in a day or two, somewhere along the coast.'

'And the kid?'

'He's been hooked-in to the drugs gangs for a while, and now he's old enough to prosecute.'

'Will they?'

A huge plate of food arrived in front of Hammond. Dinah had managed to pass all the plates on and just had toast and coffee. Hammond looked across at Dinah as he picked up his knife and fork. 'Depends. He could get out of it if he talks to them. I don't know. To be honest, I don't care.'

'So we've got Sharman for the murder, and a kid for the drugs?' Dave Sykes sounded disgusted. Put that way, it didn't sound like much to weigh against Andy's death.

'Wrong, Dave. Traynor killed Andy. She's dead. The NCA have a load of people for the drugs. Traynor was the importer, but she had plenty of people working for her, and they're bringing them in – the people at the charity who cooperated, the people at the massage parlour, the people who worked for Lavery. Sharman's talking, so we've got the driver, the woman who drove the car down to Sunk Island, the night they killed Andy.'

'Who was that? One of Lavery's people?'

'No. One of the users. A young woman called Poppy Brooke.'

Chapter 50

Hull

Poppy was sitting in a chair by her hospital bed. Kay pulled her own chair close and listened as the two detectives began their questions. Her first reaction, when she heard that Poppy had been arrested for murder, was shocked disbelief, but as she heard the story, she realised it was all too credible. Poppy was still a bit slow in her responses, prone to get tired and querulous, but she had agreed to be interviewed, waiving her right to legal representation.

Kay had gone straight to Dev, who was suddenly revealing himself to be much better at his job than she had realised, and finally prepared to see that Kay, too, knew what she was doing. 'She can't be on her own. What about her parents?'

'Poppy doesn't want them there and she's old enough to be interviewed on her own. She's waived her right to legal representation. I've talked to the doctors. They insist she's well enough to be questioned. It's a serious

charge – accessory after the fact to murder. Joint enter-
prise. I've talked to the legal team. We can't force her
to have legal representation. What we can do is ask for
an appropriate adult.'

Appropriate adults existed to safeguard the rights
of children and vulnerable people in police custody. 'Is
Poppy eligible?'

'Given her mental health issues, and the effects of
her recent overdose, yes. The police want to question
her as soon as possible. I think they'll agree rather
than hold things up. Kay, can you do it?'

Kay had done the training – the kinds of kids she
and Matt fostered had their share of trouble with the
police, so she'd sat in on several interviews over the
years. 'Of course.'

Now, as she studied Poppy's pale face and listened
to her stumbling words, she wondered if they could
have fought harder to stop this from happening. 'Take
your time,' she said to Poppy now as she struggled to
respond to a question. 'Poppy's willing to talk to you,'
she reminded the detectives who were here to question her, 'but she's still recovering.'

The cocktail of drugs Alicia Traynor had given
Poppy could easily have been fatal. The woman had
tried to kill Becca and made a good attempt on Poppy's
life. Kay wasn't sure if she was glad or sorry that
Leesha had drowned in the estuary, rather than being
brought to account for what she had done. 'It was
Xanthe,' Poppy was trying to explain. 'She got me this
job. With Alicia.' She said it the same way the

detective had. Not Leesha, but Aleesha. Kay had misheard all along. 'It's like ... I didn't *know*,' she said suddenly, gripping Kay's arm.

'We understand, Poppy.' The woman leading the questioning radiated sympathy and understanding – but Kay knew that her aim was to get enough information to charge Poppy, and to get evidence to support charging other people. She probably was quite sympathetic to Poppy, but that wasn't what she was here for.

'Poppy, just try and tell us what happened. You can have a lawyer any time you want,' Kay reminded her.

'I don't! I want it to stop!'

Kay said, for the benefit of the tape, 'I'm not sure that Poppy's being fully rational here,' and saw the detectives share a quick glance, but Poppy said, 'I'm fine.'

Slowly, the story came out. Xanthe had found Poppy the job with Alicia Traynor. At first, Traynor had got Poppy working for the girls at the massage parlour, doing hair and make-up. She had been generous with the roll-ups and the pills – sweeties, she'd called them. 'Xanthe was OK with it,' Poppy protested. 'She said it wasn't like the hard stuff I'd been on, it was just, you know, party stuff, like everyone does.'

'And then what happened?'

It had started slowly, Traynor asking Poppy to be 'nice' to this guy or that guy, but it had escalated fast, going from one man, and then it had been two, and then it had been like a party, and when Poppy expressed reluctance, Traynor made her roll-ups, and somehow, it was all a laugh after that.

And very soon, Poppy needed the stuff that was in the roll-ups, but Traynor wouldn't hand it out for nothing, not any more. 'I made some videos,' Poppy said, her face flushing, not meeting anyone's eyes. 'Alicia said she'd send one of them to my dad if I didn't do what she said.' Her eyes filled with tears. 'I didn't know!'

'What didn't you know, Poppy?'

Kay felt herself tense. She wasn't sure she wanted to hear this, and as the story came out, she wanted to shake Poppy until her teeth rattled for her docile compliance in something she must have known was dangerous and illegal; for sitting there and letting murder happen.

Poppy had driven Traynor and a young man down the coast to Stone Creek. She had witnessed the early stages of an attack on the man, but he'd managed to escape. Traynor had gone after him, taking a motorbike across the rough ground. 'There was a fight,' Poppy told them, 'and he ran away. Alicia went after him. One of the guys tried to stop her, but he'd been hurt in the fight and he couldn't stand up. Then she came back and said it was OK. I drove her back. I didn't know they'd killed him.' *Just like that*, Kay thought. Poppy was crying as she talked. 'Am I going to prison?'

Kay wondered what Poppy had thought was happening that night. Her fear of Traynor might have kept her compliant at the time, but there was no justification for her continued silence, apart from the drugs that Traynor went on supplying. Becca had risked her life to save an eleven-year-old boy. Poppy had watched an attack that became fatal and had asked no questions at all, told no one what she knew, just retreated into the drugs haze, where she felt safe.

The cynic in Kay said that Poppy's grief now was more to do with the prospect of prison than about the death of the young man whose child had already lost her mother. But Poppy had agreed to talk to the police, and she seemed to be telling them everything she knew.

Maybe that was a start.

Curwen sat in on the questioning of the MLRO from the Bridlington Building Society, Gordon Fletcher. He was an ex-police officer, he wasn't short of cash, and he lawyered up at once. Curwen expected him to go 'no comment', but the woman from the financial crimes team, Angela Hayes, didn't think he would. 'He's on pretty safe ground,' she told Curwen. 'He went by the book. He just didn't follow any of it up – took it all at face value. His finances look clean – I'm sure he got something for doing soft reports, but where he's stashed it . . . If we can't find it, we can't charge him with anything.'

'I did the report,' the man kept saying in response to DS Hayes' questions. 'I looked at everything I needed to.'

'Did you check the source of the money Docklands Holdings was donating?'

'I did. It came from the sale of property, and from a range of legitimate businesses.'

'Did you look at the businesses themselves? Did you look at the original property sale?'

'There was no requirement to do so.'

And that became the refrain. *There was no requirement to do so.* He'd done the barest minimum, but his back was safely covered.

Angela Hayes moved on. 'I want to ask you about your relationship with Xanthe Adamos.'

'No comment.'

'Where did you meet Ms Adamos?'

'No comment.'

'Why did the relationship end?'

'No comment.'

'It was because Ms Adamos went to the US, wasn't it?'

'No comment.'

'Did you expect that? How did you see your future with Xanthe Adamos?'

'No comment.'

'And did you subsequently have a relationship with Poppy Brooke?'

'I did not.'

After the interview, Curwen took Angela Hayes for a coffee – not in the canteen at the police station, but in one of the coffee shops near the harbour. 'Are you going to go after him?' Curwen asked as they sat down at the table.

Hayes stirred sugar into her coffee. 'Probably not. The evidence isn't there. Oh, he won't work as a

MLRO again, but he did his job. Just very badly. He's not the only one like that.'

'You reckon he knew?'

'I reckon he didn't care. I'm pretty sure he wasn't getting paid – not in cash, so he could tell himself it was all OK.'

'So what did he get?'

'He got a girlfriend. Xanthe Adamos. I'm willing to bet he thought it was the real thing, or he told himself it was. He wasn't going to drop Adamos in it, but did you notice how pissed off he was when I asked him about Poppy Brooke?'

'So what was that about?'

'Well, it looks like Lavery and Traynor were working together. He looked after their cash for them, Traynor supplied the girls to keep our man Fletcher happy. But he wanted a proper girlfriend, not someone who was doing it for money. We've been investigating Adamos, and so has Hammond's team. She worked for Tania's House and probably persuaded Fletcher not to tie the donation up in too much red tape. But she did a runner a few months ago, got a place in a US university and left without letting anyone know. She got the money for the fees from somewhere. We're still looking into that. Adamos must have realised she was getting into big trouble, and I suspect she knew Traynor wouldn't let her go willingly, so she just dropped out and went without telling anyone. Hammond and my boss, they both want to question her, but whether we can get her back . . .' She shrugged. 'Who knows?'

Curwen leaned back in his chair and thought about it. Once Adamos had gone, Fletcher would have been less cooperative. He'd kept on the right side of the law, so they didn't have anything on him. Lavery would have been looking for another way to launder large sums. And suddenly Curwen organises the police raid on the pub, looking for drugs, using a warrant which he was prepared to admit, at least to himself, was obtained on pretty dodgy grounds. Soon after that, Andy Yeatson starts hanging round asking questions. Lavery spots Andy as a cop, thinks they're on to him, and panics. He tells Traynor they've got to cool it for a while, there's an undercover cop hanging around. Traynor can't sit on all this cash for weeks – she needs clean money to pay her people, so she decides to do something about it.

He'd organised the raid, and he'd sent Andy in there. How did he feel about that? He felt bad, as bad as he'd felt when he thought Becca the Bar – Becca Armitage had been drowned in the estuary. His own reaction had surprised him – but then it had never been personal. It was the job.

If he'd known what he knew now, would he have done it any different?

But he hadn't known, and it was too late to change anything. Curwen didn't go in for existential angst.

People had been arrested and charged, the CPS seemed happy with the cases, one or two people on the periphery had got away with it, but would presumably be more careful in future, and he, Curwen, was

back in the good books. He hadn't been near the pub
– as far as anyone knew – and given that there had
been successful outcomes, no one was going to blame
him for getting in the way of an operation he knew
nothing about. He'd get his promotion now.

Debits and credits. The operation had cost Andy's
life and that was a massive debit, but policing was
hazardous work.

He gave himself a mental 'Could do better', and
headed back to the office to write up his final reports.

Chapter 51

Bridlington

Andy Yeatson's funeral was held three days after the arrests of Carl Lavery, Toby Sharman and Poppy Brooke. Lavery and Sharman had already been charged with murder. The usual post-investigation celebrations had been low-key and muted. They'd made arrests, the evidence supporting the cases was strong enough for the CPS to approve charges. They'd done what they set out to do.

But Andy Yeatson, one of them, had died along the way, in the line of duty.

Dinah reflected on this as she pulled in to what looked like the last parking space in the crowded crematorium car park.

Andy. Her colleague who had given her help and advice in her first investigation as a DC; Andy, who had been almost, but not quite, a friend. His death just seemed like a terrible waste.

She joined the rest of the mourners, following the coffin that was draped in the constabulary flag into the crematorium, edging her way into the pew next to Curwen, who sat slightly bowed over, studying his hands, which were resting on his knees. His face was solemn.

Music was playing and she checked the order of service. It was a cello piece by Bach. It was very beautiful, but Andy would probably have chosen some hard rock to play him out of this world. Funerals weren't for the dead. They were gone. It was for family and friends. Dinah tried to focus as people stood to pay tribute to Andy: Gallagher, who read the eulogy, talking about his bravery and his sense of duty; a friend, who reminisced about his life before he joined the force; and then Andy's father spoke.

'We've heard some words of praise for my son, and I don't argue with any of them. He was a brave man, a devoted father, a good friend and the best son we could ever have wanted. But we've lost him and we will have to live with that. I'll use the words of Shakespeare to say, much better than I ever could, how we feel today:

"That time of year thou mayst in me behold
When yellow leaves, or none, or few, do hang
Upon those boughs which shake against the cold,
Bare ruin'd choirs, where late the sweet birds sang . . ."'

Dinah tuned the poem out. She was close to tears as it was. Without moving her head too much, she cast a glance round the chapel. Colleagues she knew,

Hammond sitting near the front, other members of the investigation team, Andy's boss, DCI Gallagher, other people who must be friends or family she had never met.

And in the back row she caught a glimpse of pale red hair. She turned her head a bit more. Becca Armitage was there, her jacket wrapped round her as if she was cold. Her features looked almost sketched-in – the light brows, the colourless lips, given a slight quirk by the scar that stood out, white against her pale face.

The sonnet came to its conclusion:

> " '... *which makes thy love more strong,*
> *To love that well which thou must leave ere long.*" '

The final music started, and Dinah hurried from the crematorium to try and catch up with Becca, but there was no sign of her. Dinah stood there, scanning the grounds, beside the sea of flowers that had been laid out in Andy's memory.

Some were already starting to wither.

Andy was dead, and that had to be the end of the story.

Chapter 52

Hull

Kay looked in the mirror Poppy was holding up. Her hair was cut close to her head, with slightly longer tendrils around her face. It was tapered neatly into the nape of her neck and shaped round her ears. *Earrings*, Kay thought. She needed to get her earrings out again. And the colour – it was much brighter than Kay had expected. She'd asked Poppy to get rid of the grey, but Poppy has used foils and colours, making Kay look as though she'd spent a long summer in glorious sunshine. And the red was back. There, among the gold and the brown, highlights reflected the redhead Kay had been most of her life. She gave Poppy her verdict. 'I love it.'

Poppy's pink and white face flushed with pleasure, but she tried to look nonchalant. 'Yeah, well, you've got nice hair.'

Kay went back to studying herself in the mirror. It was like finding herself again, the Kay she had been before Matt got so ill, the Kay who liked looking smart and who took pride in the fact she could still turn a head or two when she walked into a room; not a dowdy, defeated woman trudging into old age.

Not that her future – wherever she was going – was that certain. Tania's House was being investigated for assisting in money laundering, and a large part of its income had been confiscated. A couple of other drugs charities had stepped in to support some of the work, but Tania's House was broke and Kay's job ended in a fortnight. Once again, Poppy might be left without support. Kay was trying hard to get her into an NHS-funded rehab programme.

Poppy's arrest on a murder charge had been a major shock to everyone except Poppy. She'd seemed resigned, almost relieved, as if something she'd dreaded was finally here. Acting on the advice of the solicitor Tania's House had found for her, she had agreed to turn Queen's Evidence. The police had made no promises – Kay suspected they were keeping the pressure on Poppy to make sure she didn't renege – but so far, there had been no attempt to charge her.

It could be a new start for her. It could be a happy outcome, but the cynic in Kay said that Poppy still had too many lessons to learn. If Kay had remained Poppy's counsellor, she would have helped her learn to take responsibility for her own actions, to understand that she made her own decisions and would have to stand by them – or hang by her thumbs from them some day.

'I've been to see them at college,' Poppy said. 'They say I can go back, finish the course.'

'That's good. You're very skilled.' Kay turned her head again, pleased with what she saw in the mirror.

'Yeah. Thanks.' Poppy's cheeks flushed. 'My tutor, Mags, she's really cool. She says she'll look after me this time, make sure I don't, you know, get behind and let myself get all mixed up about it.'

'It's good you're getting support, but don't you think,' Kay suggested, 'that's something you can do for yourself a bit more now?'

Poppy looked panicky. 'But I don't know . . . I kind of think I can, you know, deal, and then . . . I get scared and I run away from it, and I might . . . I might get in trouble again.'

'You ran away last time. It didn't work, did it?'

'Only because Alicia—'

'No. It didn't work because you put yourself in a bad place and hid from the people who were supporting you. That gave Alicia her chance. Listen, your tutor can help you, but she can't do anything if you won't help yourself.'

'I don't know how to!' Poppy's voice was almost a wail.

'Poppy, you're doing it now – you're facing up to the things you did. You're helping the police. That's a start. It's like everything else. The more you do it, the better you'll be.'

Poppy turned away, as if she was rejecting what Kay had just said, but as she sorted out her brushes and combs, the vials of chemicals, the scissors and all the other tools of her trade, she seemed to stand a bit taller, as if here, at least, she knew what she was doing.

All Kay could do now was hope she kept that in her sights, and kept on trying to work it out.

Chapter 53

Bridlington

'Do you like it, then?' George was beaming with pride. It was two weeks after the events down by the estuary. Becca had stayed with Kay for the duration, coming back briefly for Andy's funeral which had been . . . She didn't know. All she knew was that Andy hadn't been there.

She'd contacted George, her landlord, the day after it had all kicked off down by the estuary, half expecting him to tell her she was evicted. Instead, he told her he was doing the flat up for her. Someone – Dinah Mason, she suspected – told him kids had trashed the place, and he blamed himself for what had happened. 'If I'd fixed that lock on the gate,' he'd said, 'they wouldn't have got in. Vandals.'

He was looking after Spice. 'She's a right one, that cat of yours,' he'd said cheerfully. 'Don't you worry, she's fine. And I'll sort the flat out for you.'

And he had done.

She stood in the middle of the room and turned slowly, looking round. The walls were freshly painted. The old window had been repaired so that it actually fitted and he'd replaced the worktop in the kitchen area. The bathroom had shiny new lino instead of the old, cracked stuff, and clean, white paint on the walls.

She had what was like a brand-new flat. He'd emptied the downstairs kitchen and cleaned it up, cleared up the backyard, put in a new gate that locked, and a new back door with a cat flap.

That was the best news. He'd found Spice shut in the bathroom upstairs and taken care of her. Now, he and Becca were sharing her. During the day, Spice was called Kitty and spent her time in the shop with George, sitting on the counter, getting fussed and stroked. At night, she was called Spice, and lived upstairs with Becca, chasing bits of paper, climbing up the curtains – Becca had new red curtains, a present from Kay – and curling up on the bed at night.

What Becca didn't have was a job. Bryan had sacked her when she hadn't gone in the day after all the trouble. But then Kay went and had a talk with him, and Becca got a letter saying she was being made redundant instead. The supermarket was letting staff go and Becca was one of them.

She got one week's pay, which was better than nothing.

The pub had closed down. Carl had been refused bail and was waiting for his case to come to court. His other businesses were being taken apart as the police followed the money trail. It looked as though Andy had been telling most of the truth all along. Carl had been on the fiddle, in a really big way.

Becca didn't understand it, and she didn't care.

She tried hard not to think about what had happened down at the estuary. Lewis had recovered, but he wasn't home. Jade admitted he was out of her control, so he was at a residential school during the week and temporarily in care. Becca didn't know how that was going, as Jade wouldn't talk to her. She seemed to think what had happened was partly Becca's fault. 'She needs someone to be angry with,' Kay had said. 'She'll come round.'

Becca had a talent for losing friends. She missed Jade.

And now she had some serious thinking to do. Winter was coming, work was scarce and she couldn't stand all the shit they put you through when you were on benefits. Kay had given her some money to live on, but Becca wasn't accepting any more. She could support herself.

Job hunting should have been a priority, but something was holding her back. She knew if she went back to a pub, or a café, or a supermarket, she'd end up in the same trap; work, work, work, always broke, no time to think about her life and no time to make changes. She needed that time, but without money, she couldn't have it.

Once again, she was at the bottom of the heap. It sometimes felt like she was climbing a mountain of sand – hard, hard work that never seemed to get her anywhere.

A great weariness engulfed her. She wanted to slump in her chair, switch on the telly and turn off the world for a while. Instead, she pulled on her trainers and a jacket, put her phone in her bag and set out for a walk. It was late November and a wintry chill was starting in the air, but today was fine and sunny. A walk would do her good.

She decided to head along the front and watch the sea, maybe go into some of the cafés to try and find some work. It was time to get real.

She hadn't got far when a car drew up beside her. 'Becca!'

It was Dinah Mason, her fair hair shining in the sun, her red glasses looking jaunty. Becca gave her a side-look. They weren't friends. 'Yeah?'

Dinah got out of the car and looked round. 'Lovely day,' she said.

Becca shrugged. It was one of those things people said when they didn't know what to say. 'It's OK,' she agreed, and waited to see what Dinah wanted.

'There's something I want to ask you, Becca. Do you mind if I walk with you, and we can talk?'

'Up to you.' Becca knew she sounded unwelcoming, but she didn't know what to make of Dinah.

'We could get some coffee if you'd rather,' Dinah said.

Becca would kill for a coffee, but she was broke.

'My treat,' Dinah added. For a moment, Becca wanted to say she didn't need anyone buying coffee for her, then nodded in abrupt agreement. After all the hassle the coppers had given her, they owed her a cup of coffee. Dinah led the way to a table outside one of the cafés. It was sheltered from the breeze, so it was warm enough to sit out. Dinah ordered coffee with doughnuts.

Becca lit a cigarette and stared out across the water, watching the dark waves hit the sea wall, throwing up clouds of spray. She had a sudden image of Alicia, leaping up over the sea wall, carried by the water. She was out there somewhere.

She shook her head to clear it.

'Are you OK?'

'Yeah. I'm fine.' She looked back at the sea, and Dinah Mason answered her unspoken question.

'We haven't found her yet. The tide was turning. She could have been carried out to sea. We might never find the body.'

Becca chewed her lip. Alicia Traynor, or Sal Capone, or whatever her name was, appeared in too many of her dreams – soaked, battered, barely human, but alive. She crept over sea walls and crawled in through windows and Becca just wanted it to stop.

'Have you thought what you're going to do?' Dinah said, changing the subject.

'Yeah. Get a job.' Becca was glad of any topic that took them away from her thoughts of Alicia.

'Just a job? What about college? Or training?'

Becca shrugged. 'What do I live on if I go to college?'

'You can get loans, you know.'

'Yeah, right.' Like she was going to put herself in hock for the rest of her life.

'There is another way.' Dinah's gaze was on the table, where she was drawing patterns in spilled coffee with her teaspoon. 'You gave us a lot of help, you know. The photos you got were important evidence in the money-laundering case, and if you hadn't been there, I don't think that kid would have survived.'

'What are you saying? That I could be a copper?' Becca said sharply.

'No! No, that wasn't what I meant. It's – look, if you'll register as someone who gave us information, they can pay you for what you did.'

Was that what Dinah thought of her? A snitch? 'I didn't do it to get paid.' She crammed the remainder of her doughnut into her mouth crossly. What Dinah had said made her feel anxious and uncertain, as though something she'd always believed in suddenly wasn't working. She told herself it was because she was angry, though it didn't feel like anger. 'I've got to go.'

'Becca . . .'

'I said, I'm off. I'm not a snitch.'

'So the next Alicia Traynor who comes along, you're OK with her sticking knives in people? Trying to drown a kid?'

Of course not. Who did Dinah think she was?

'If you'd known enough about her before it all kicked off, would you have told someone? Would that have been snitching?'

No. Of course it wouldn't. But the coppers – you tried to tell them, and they blamed you. *Becca. You know that's not true.* Like last year when they'd accused her of setting fire to Kay's cottage, and worse. You couldn't trust them. But Dinah wouldn't stop talking.

'And the other kids like Lewis? If you could stop what was happening to them, would that be snitching?'

No. It wouldn't. But . . .

In her head, she heard someone laughing. She heard the click of a lighter and the *whoof* of something igniting, the rags that Spice was wrapped in. People like Alicia didn't just need stopping, they needed getting rid of, chucking away like they'd never been born.

But it wasn't that simple. She felt confused.

'I didn't really do anything,' she said slowly.

'You nearly got killed, Becca. And you saved Lewis. You kept Traynor off him until help arrived. I didn't do half as much as you did, but I got paid. Why shouldn't you get something?'

'Because . . .' She couldn't explain. It just felt wrong.

'Sign up,' Dinah urged her. 'We seized a substantial cache of drugs worth – I don't know – over a million, easily. What you did has to be worth a few thousand pounds. More, in my books, but I don't make the final decision. Becca, you know the kinds of things that need stopping. All I'm asking is that you tip us off officially if you come across anything like that again.'

A few thousand pounds. That was a lot of money. It would buy her time to think about her future. It would be some money to get her started at college, or . . . lots of things. She needed to think about this. Hard. It looked too easy, and things that were easy often hid the teeth of a trap.

Snitch bitch.

Her mind played with the ideas as she walked back to the flat. She had rejected Dinah's idea out of hand when she first suggested it, but now . . . even if it was just the once, it would make a massive difference to her.

But you didn't snitch. Snitching felt dirty. But was it snitching when you came across someone like Alicia? Or Carl? Or was it just fighting back? She didn't know the answer.

And Dinah Mason. Dinah worried her. She was all *trust me*, and nicey-nicey. Well, she hadn't actually said that, but that's what she meant. And maybe Becca hadn't learned a lot, and maybe she still screwed things up, but one thing she did know: the nicey-nicey coppers were the ones who let you down.

Every time.

Becca wasn't making that mistake again.

Which left Curwen. Curwen was a shit. He'd played her, used her, then he'd dropped her right in it and left her there. OK, that meant she'd know what to expect. There would be no let downs with Curwen, no nasty surprises, because you didn't expect anything else from coppers like Curwen.

But he'd got Carl the perv banged up. Carl Lavery would have got away with it if Curwen hadn't been onto him.

That was OK by Becca.

A few thousand pounds. It would make all the difference. It would give her something to live on if she went to college, or if she wanted to train for something. Or she could do what Jared did; pack up and go where she wanted to, live how she liked – for a while, anyway.

It would give her something she hadn't had since her stepfather had moved into her mother's house.

It would give her freedom.

Chapter 54

Bridlington Harbour

'What?'

The incredulity on Becca's face made Kay want to laugh. 'I'm buying the house on Stone Creek Road,' she said again. 'The owner wants to sell, I've sold the cottage, what's the problem?'

They'd bought fish and chips and were sitting outside the café on the harbour, looking out across the bay. The waves washed up the slipway and fell back. 'Dunno,' Becca said. She was staring at the sea as if she half-expected to see something in the water. 'It's, you know, a bit ... There's nothing there!'

This time, Kay did laugh. 'There's walking, there's Spurn Point, there's quite a community once you start looking.' She almost said, *There's the estuary*, but she didn't want to remind Becca, not that Becca would have forgotten. Kay certainly hadn't.

'Spice is lovely,' she said, changing the subject.

Becca gave her a narrow look. 'Yeah. But the house. It's falling down, right?'

She'd interpreted Kay's subject change as a wish to avoid talking about the house – Kay was happy with that. Anything to get away from the events at Spragger Drain sluice. 'It's actually in better condition than it looks.' The structure was sound. They'd probably built houses to last in that inhospitable environment. 'But this time, I'm having central heating.' No more stoves or open fires, no matter how much Matt had loved them. 'It's fine, Becca. I'll be fine.'

Becca grunted, unconvinced.

'I like what your landlord has done with your flat.'

'Yeah.' Becca stuffed the last of her chips in her mouth and scattered the scraps for the gulls.

'You'll get in trouble,' Kay said as they watched the birds diving down and squabbling over the remains.

Becca smiled one of her rare smiles. 'So what's new?'

They walked slowly along the harbour wall, companionably arm-in-arm. Kay felt more relaxed about Becca now. She'd been seriously worried the more she heard about what had been happening over the past few weeks. The young detective, Dinah Mason, had told a lot more about the events leading up to Alicia Traynor's attempt on Becca's life, all stuff that Becca hadn't chosen to share with her. Her heart ached for her foster-daughter. She wished Becca would open up, talk about what she had gone through, but that had never been Becca's way. Kay would have to be patient. In time, if Kay didn't push it, Becca would tell her.

'So,' she said, looking up at the sky. It was one of those early winter days when the sun shone and the sky was an impossible blue. 'What are you going to do?'

'Dunno,' Becca said vaguely. 'I've got some plans.'

Kay opened her mouth, then closed it. Now was not the time to start a row. 'Good,' she said.

Becca sat with Kay on one of the stone seats built into the harbour wall. In summer, it was always busy along here, but now it was quiet, just a few people wandering around, and the shouts of the fishermen unloading the boats. The sea was calm, the movement of the water making the moored boats rock gently, bumping against each other and creaking.

The grey stone stood solid against the promise of winter storms. The waves could crash against it, but it wouldn't break. Nothing could creep out of the sea. Nothing could cross it. Bridlington was safe while the sea wall stood.

She smiled.

Acknowledgements

There are always more people to thank for their help and support in the writing and production of a book than it is possible to name.

I want to thank my agent, Teresa Chris, for her belief in me and her determination that the books will be the best they can be.

To my editor, Anne Perry, who understands the books so well, and who cares about Becca and Kay as much as I do, and who helped me with the finishing touches that make book what it is.

To Bethan Jones for helping me to shape the final version from the original manuscript.

To Janet and Jenny, the members of my writing group, who saw this book through from the first, terrifying blank page, to the final, completed version.

I would also like to thank the people of Sunk island who answered my questions on the Sunk Island Facebook page, including Richard Makey for the images, and Matt Wright and Kay Barker for information about Spragger Drain sluice.

And finally, but most importantly, to Ken; my husband, my support, the man who brought me coffee when I was banging my head on the desk, and red wine after a tough day. This is the last book you will help me with, but, as Kay still has Matt in her head to help her, so I know you will be there for me. In fact, I suspect you are reading this over my shoulder, your eyebrows lifting, and I can hear the ironic inflection in your voice as you say, 'Indeed.'

About the Author

Danuta Kot grew up with stories. Her Irish mother and her Polish father kept their own cultures alive with traditional tales they shared with their children. For many years, she worked with young people in Yorkshire who were growing up in the aftermath of sudden industrial decline. She uses this background in her books to explore some of the issues that confront modern, urban society: poverty, alienation and social breakdown, using the contexts of the modern crime novel. She now works as a senior education consultant, work that involves travel to establish education and training in other parts of the world. She is a regular academic speaker at conferences and literary festivals, and has appeared on radio and television.